THE WATERFRONT LASS

ANNEMARIE BREAR

Boldwood

First published in Great Britain in 2023 by Boldwood Books Ltd.

Cover Design by Colin Thomas

Cover Photography: Alamy and Colin Thomas

A CIP catalogue record for this book is available from the British Library.

Paperback ISBN 978-1-80162-775-7

Large Print ISBN 978-1-80162-776-4

Hardback ISBN 978-1-80162-774-0

Ebook ISBN 978-1-80162-777-1

Kindle ISBN 978-1-80162-778-8

Audio CD ISBN 978-1-80162-769-6

MP3 CD ISBN 978-1-80162-770-2

Digital audio download ISBN 978-1-80162-772-6

Boldwood Books Ltd
23 Bowerdean Street
London SW6 3TN
www.boldwoodbooks.com

Dedicated to my sister Margaret, born in Wakefield and who has always shared her love of books with me, especially historical family sagas.

1

WAKEFIELD WATERFRONT, YORKSHIRE, ENGLAND, 1870

With a muttered oath, Margaret May Taylor, named after her maternal grandmother, but shortened to Meg, plunged the dolly stick back into the grey soapy tub and twisted it numerous times. Arms aching, for she'd been hard at it since before five o'clock, she pulled out the wet, tangled clothes and dropped them into the next tub of clean water with Reckitt's Paris Blue added to keep the garments white. Sweat dripped off her forehead, despite the sun only just rising over the rooftops, and the morning was heralding another frigid January day.

In the corner of the small paved yard, her younger sister Mabel was, at fourteen, old enough to be trusted to use the dreaded mangle to squeeze the water out of the clothes and sheets.

'Meg, there's no more bread,' stated Susie, another sister, aged eleven, as she came out of the back door to collect more coal from the lean-to shed next to the lavatory. Having their own lavatory was something of a rarity in Wellington Street. Their neighbours had to share lavatories, usually one between two or more houses, but for some reason unknown to all of the street's inhabitants, number seven, the Taylors' home, had its own. Meg's mam liked to think it was because number seven was a special number, but Mr Pike from number eleven said it was because their house had originally been the last one in the street and didn't have a neighbour to share with. However, that changed some years ago when more terraces were built on to number seven to the railway at the end of Wellington Street.

Mabel tossed her head. 'There's never enough food in this house.'

'Who ate it all?' Meg puffed, using her wrist to wipe her dark brown hair back from her face. 'Mam's not had her breakfast yet.'

'Betsy and Nell. You know Betsy can't cut it thin enough.' Susie scooped up pieces of coal into a bucket.

'Then you should have been up earlier to cut it,' Meg fumed. 'I can't be out here and in the kitchen at the same time. You've to pull your weight.'

'I do!' Susie snapped.

'And go steady on the coal,' Meg warned. 'It's all we've got. Just use a few pieces.'

Susie heaved up the bucket full of coal and hobbled with the weight of it back inside, struggling to keep the filthy bucket away from her stockings and skirt.

Meg hoisted a basket of wet clothes over to Mabel, who was hanging out the clothes she'd just mangled. Three ropes stretched across the paved yard to cope with all the washing, but it was unlikely any of it would dry on such a winter's day.

Nicky, the youngest of Meg's siblings, leaned against the kitchen doorjamb. At six, he was too small for his age, the legacy of being ill most of his life and being born into the family when her father was struggling to make any money with his narrowboat.

'Get away inside and sit by the fire,' Meg said to Nicky, adding more clothes to the tub.

'Mam said I can go to school today.' His faint voice barely reached across the cramped space to Meg.

'I don't think so.' Meg gave a grim smile. 'It's too much for you.'

'Mam said.' He frowned, upset. His grey eyes, so like Meg's, were expressive of his hope.

'Aye, but Mam doesn't see how you suffer after a day at school, does she?' Meg twisted the dolly stick vigorously, half-annoyed that her mother, who was practically bedridden upstairs, had undermined her rule.

'I want to go!' Nicky stamped his foot.

Sighing, Meg shrugged. 'Then go with the girls, but don't cry to me when you can't leave your bed for a week afterwards.'

Thrilled, Nicky disappeared inside.

'That was harsh,' Mabel said, back at the mangle.

Meg gave her a stern and exhausted look. 'You know as well as I do how he gets after being at school.'

'Aye, but he wants to be like the other boys. Let him go.'

Meg straightened her aching back. 'Right, I will, and you can help look after him *and* Mam.'

'I already do, don't I? When you're at work.' Mabel pouted angrily. Not one for working was Mabel or doing anything that she didn't want to do. Mrs Fogarty, the neighbour next door, said Mabel had been born into the wrong family and should have been the daughter of a gentleman, not a narrowboat skipper.

In silence, the two sisters continued the arduous task of washing, mangling and hanging out as the sun rose and the back-to-back terraced houses came alive as men went to work and women began their housework and getting children sorted. Many neighbours were already washing as the Taylor sisters were. Mondays in this poor area of the waterfront were washing days for those women who had the strength to do it.

From the canal and the River Calder came the sounds of activity. Horns blasted from boats and barges, while the mills and factory steam whistles blew, summoning the workers into their gates. Trains shuttled and rattled along the viaduct that had been built over the end of not only Wellington Street, but all the streets running east to west from the river.

Meg's father, Frank, owned a narrowboat. He had been transporting goods along the canals since he was a boy helping his father and now his sons, Freddie and Arthur, helped him. For weeks they'd be gone from home, travelling the waterways from Wakefield to other parts of Yorkshire, leaving Meg to run the family, the house and take care of her ailing mam, as well as work her few shifts a week at the local pub, the Bay Horse.

When her father was home, it wasn't for long, a few days, and then he and the boys would be gone again. At times, Meg wished she could simply jump on a boat and leave behind her responsibilities for weeks, and she resented Freddie and Arthur's freedom. If she'd been born a boy, she'd be on the boat now, watching the countryside go by, jumping up to open the locks, to dock at the many wharves and meet different people, to sleep under the stars in summer, to have a bond with the others who traversed the waterways.

Instead, she broke her back, cleaning, cooking and skivvying after her family with no thanks, no kind word from her father. She was the eldest and a girl. She shouldn't expect thanks.

'I'm going to have to go soon,' Mabel said, hanging the last shirt on the line from her basket. 'I don't want to be late.'

'No, it's fine. You go.' Meg waved her away. Mabel's job at the woollen mill further up Thornes Lane Wharf was another income to help keep the family clothed and fed. In the summer, Susie would leave school and join Mabel in the mill and the extra pennies would come in handy. 'Make Mam a cup a tea before you leave.'

'Then I'll be late. I ain't having the gaffer telling me off and docking me wages.' Mabel flounced towards the door.

'Say *my* wages not *me* wages. Mam wants us to speak properly like she does.'

'Who cares?' Mabel declared.

Meg flung the clothes down, annoyed at being both the sister and the parent. 'Don't worry about anything, Mabel. I'll make Mam's tea. I've got to make sure the others are ready for school, anyway.' Meg sighed and left the clothes to soak and went inside.

The kitchen contained a range by the wall and a square table that wasn't large enough for the whole family to sit around, especially when her father and brothers were home. Stone flags covered the floor, and the whitewashed walls were past their best. Plaster, cracked and brittle, fell every day like blossom and Meg swept it up every morning and night. She'd told the rent man about it each week for over a year, but the landlord so far had done nothing about it.

Years ago, to accommodate the growing family, her father had knocked down the dividing wall between the kitchen and the poky front room, creating one larger room where a green horsehair sofa could fit under the front window. The girls had made a rag rug for the floor and rag-stuffed cushions for them to sit on by the fire.

Wellington Street was a series of two-up and two-down terraced houses, all in various states of dilapidation. The walls ran with moisture, the windows iced over each morning in winter, and the rats were constant visitors in the roof and walls. The chimneys smoked and the shared water pump often didn't work so she had to walk to the next pump at the end of the street and carry back full buckets of water, which didn't last long enough. The lavatories overflowed and some years the polluted river flooded, swamping them in foul, stinking water up to their knees. Mould grew as quickly as flowers in a hothouse, and in the warm summer weather the stench from the factories and dye houses made Meg gag.

How she longed to get away. The idea of leaving consumed her night and day, but how could she go away with no money? The little amount of money she made working behind the bar at the Bay Horse was barely enough to buy her new boots and a hat each year. She put most of it in the tin on the mantel to pay the bills.

Sighing, Meg stirred the porridge as Nell sat at the table, scratching her head. 'You'd better not have nits again,' Meg warned.

'I can't help it.' Nell scratched harder.

Meg ladled out bowls of porridge and passed them about the table. 'Betsy, you can go to Boyd's Bakery and buy a loaf of bread and bring it back here before you go to school, since you cut it too thick. How many times have I shown you how to slice it?'

'I try!' Betsy stomped over to the chair and picked up her spoon. 'Why can't Susie do it?'

Susie, standing in front of the small wall mirror, plaited her long brown hair. 'I do it every day. You need to learn! Soon I'll be at the mill and gone in the mornings like Mabel. You are next in line to do your share.'

'Come and eat, Nicky.' Meg mashed the tea and poured half a cup for each of them.

By the fire, Nicky sat drawing, the one thing he loved to do, and he was rather good at it, though he got enough practice for he spent most of his short life sitting by the fire, too ill to go out and play. They didn't know what was wrong with him. The doctors said it was because he'd been born too early, which resulted in a weak heart, undeveloped lungs, and predicted Nicky wouldn't make old bones. The thought sent shivers down Meg's back.

'Nicky. Eat,' she commanded, and waited until he came to the table and took a tiny nibble at a spoonful of porridge. 'I want it all gone or you don't go to school.'

Rolling his eyes, he dutifully ate more of the porridge.

'I ain't bringing him home when he gets too tired,' Susie snapped. 'I'm on blackboard duty today.'

'You'll do as you're told,' Meg warned.

She loved Nicky the best out of all her siblings. She'd been fourteen when he was born and the first to hold him when the midwife handed over the bundled little mite after he took his first weak breath. They'd nearly lost him and their mam in the birthing process. Nicky felt like her child, for she had fed and bathed him, cared for him like he was her own baby. Their mam had never regained full health. Again, the doctors said a weak heart, something passed down from mother to son.

Meg had never known her mam to be a strong woman, not like their neighbours, who lugged washing and shopping, buckets of coal, who scrubbed floors on their knees and cooked up huge pots of stew, and who brought babies into the world and continued to work straight after. The women of Wellington Street and all the streets and lanes of the waterfront were tough, fearless, big-hearted and looked out for each other.

But Lucy Taylor wasn't among their ranks. Delicate, pretty and sweet-natured, Lucy Mellor, as she was, didn't fit into the squalid waterfront area like the other women did. She'd met and fallen in love with narrowboat owner Frank Taylor and married him within six weeks, much to her parents' disgust.

The harsh reality of living in a slum knocked the stuffing out of Lucy more each year that passed and with each birth of a baby.

Besides the eight Taylor children living, another six had died before full term. So many pregnancies.

Meg hated the thought of her mam suffering so much. She wished her Mellor grandparents would help more, but they had moved away after Lucy married the unsuitable Frank Taylor and stopped visiting when Meg was three years old. She didn't remember them.

For a while they had her father's mother, Aggie, living with them until she died when Meg was ten. Meg had loved her Grandma Aggie. A big woman full of spirit and laughter. She'd shouldered the heavy burden of Mam's frail health and the never-ending babies and when she died suddenly, Meg felt a hole had opened in her life which would never be filled.

With the children gone to school, Meg poured a cup of tea, using the last of the milk and sugar, and climbed the steep narrow stairs to the bedrooms above. The largest bedroom was given to the girls and Nicky, her parents had the other bedroom, while Freddie and Arthur slept either on the narrowboat or on the floor and sofa downstairs.

Opening her parents' bedroom door, Meg sniffed at the staleness of the room and waited for her eyes to adjust to the dimness. 'Tea, Mam.'

A rustle came from the bed. Meg placed the teacup on the bedside table and then turned to draw back the threadbare curtains and let in the weak sunshine. The light did nothing to soften the dreariness of the room that only held a double bed and a chest of drawers and a narrow wardrobe.

Mam pulled herself up further on the pillows, her face as pale as the white pillowslip she rested against. 'Thank you, dearest.'

'Could you eat something?'

'Maybe later. This tea is enough.'

Meg doubted it, but her mam ate less than a sparrow. Her

bones protruded sharply, as though her skin was the only thing keeping her together.

'Milk?' Mam sighed happily, sipping from the cup. 'That's a treat.'

'And sugar.'

'Perfect.'

Sitting on the side of the bed, Meg wanted a chat before her mam went back to sleep. 'I think we should call for the doctor again. You seem weaker.'

'I'll be fine in a few days. I'm just having a bad week. Save our money for more important things than a doctor who will say the same thing he always says.'

Meg was tempted. Nicky needed new boots, and the girls were due dresses for the summer, for they'd all grown and last summer's dresses were too short now. Usually, Meg passed each dress down to the next one in age, but when she was sorting out the clothes yesterday, she'd realised the dresses were becoming so threadbare they were nearly indecent.

'The children need clothes,' Mam said, as though reading her mind.

'Aye. Nell's stockings are more darn than stocking now.'

'Yes, not aye. Speak properly.' Mam gave a wan smile.

Meg blushed at being caught out, especially as she'd just reprimanded Mabel for the same thing.

Mam cradled the cup in her thin hands. 'The children grow so fast. Perhaps go to the market and find some clothes on McHanley's stall? I can sit here and unravel what you find and knit some new socks or vests.' Mam brightened. 'Yes, I can do that, can't I?'

'Of course.' When would she find time to go to town and rummage through a clothing stall? Trying not to sigh with impatience, Meg stood. 'I'd best get back to the washing.'

'And you'll go to McHanley's?'

'If I get time after I've done the washing.'

'Oh, yes. Washing day. I forgot.' Mam grabbed a handful of the blankets. 'I'll get up and help you.'

At the door, Meg scowled. 'You're not well enough to get out of bed, never mind do washing! Go back to sleep.'

Plodding downstairs, she paused in the kitchen and poured herself a cup of black sugarless tea, the pot now lukewarm. Her tea was always cold when she managed to get a cup.

At the washing tub, she took out her frustrations on the wet clothes, pummelling them until her arms ached in protest.

'Hey, Meg, lass.' A head popped over the side fence on the left. Mrs Fogarty grinned, her grey hair covered in a scarf. 'You've not got any Blue spare, have you? I've run out.'

Grabbing her last block, Meg passed it over the fence to their neighbour who had been a constant in their lives for as long as Meg could remember.

'You're a blessing and no mistake.' Mrs Fogarty frowned. 'Did you hear Seth Percival died last night?'

'No, I didn't.' Meg felt it had been a long while since she'd seen their elderly neighbour two doors along. 'That is sad. He was a nice man.'

'Aye, decent.' Mrs Fogarty nodded. 'He's no family either, so it'll be a quiet funeral for him. A pauper's one at that.'

For that Meg was thankful, she didn't have the spare money to buy food to give to a grieving family, as was the custom in these parts. Then she instantly felt guilty for thinking it.

Mrs Fogarty peered at Meg. 'Ey, what's up, lass? You've a glum expression. Seth was an old man in ill health. I think he'd be pleased to have gone.'

'Oh, yes, I know.'

'You're not upset about Seth, are you? It's something else,' Mrs

Fogarty persevered. 'I've known you since you were born, lass. You can't hide anything from me.'

'It's nothing.'

'It seems to be everything by the look on your face.'

'I'm just sick of my life, Mrs Fogarty.' Meg blinked rapidly. She didn't often give in to tears. In fact, crying was something she rarely did.

'Course you are, lass. A lovely young girl like you trapped into being a mother and housewife before you've even got yourself a man. It's hard.'

'I know I shouldn't resent it, but I do. I'm the eldest and it's my duty, I know, but...'

'Aye, but how old are you now? Twenty?'

Meg nodded. 'I turned twenty last week. Not that anyone would know it.' The family had barely acknowledged her birthday. Mam hadn't even remembered.

'At twenty, you should have a lad of your own by now. Someone to take you to the theatre or go on walks with. Someone to spoil you a bit, make you feel special.'

'Huh,' Meg huffed. 'Someone to spoil me? That's a laugh.'

'You need to get out more, lass, and I don't mean just your shifts at the Bay Horse. Take some time to be on your own.'

'You know I can't, not with Mam and Nicky.'

'I saw your Nicky went to school today. That's a pleasing thing to see. He should be with kiddies his own age. For a few hours you've not got to worry about the others. Go for a walk to the shops. Even if you don't buy nowt, just look in the windows.'

'I can't leave Mam alone.'

'Nay, Lucy will be fine for an hour or two. Tell her to knock on my wall should she need anything. I'll hear her.'

'Thanks, but I've too much to do without spending an hour seeing to myself.'

'Well, you should, lass, before you go doolally! Ta-ra.' Mrs Fogarty disappeared behind the fence, leaving Meg feeling even more out of sorts.

By noon, she'd done all the washing and scrubbed the kitchen floor, black-leaded the range and made a potato and kidney pie for the evening meal. Warming up the last of the thin barley and pea soup she'd made the day before, Meg had a small cupful herself and then made a tray for her mam of soup with a bread crust and another cup of tea.

The front door opening made Meg turn in surprise. Her brothers, Freddie and Arthur, came in.

'How do, our Meg?' Arthur took off his flat cap and hooked it on a nail by the door.

'I wasn't expecting you home.' Meg smiled warmly, though her heart raced at the thought of stretching the pie to three more people. 'Where's Father?'

'Talking to old Mr Henderson.' Freddie sat at the table. 'Is there more tea?'

Meg shook her head. 'Let me take this tray up to Mam and I'll make some more.'

'I'll do it.' Freddie took the tray from her. 'It'll be a nice surprise for her.'

'Stay until she eats it all, Freddie.' Meg gave him a knowing nod. He was the one she spoke to the most about family life. He understood her frustrations, her worries and how she coped with it all by herself. Tall for eighteen, he already looked a man, with wide shoulders from moving cargo for years. His handsome, weathered face belied his years.

'Owt to eat?' Arthur asked.

'No. If you've any money, get yourself down the street to the bakers and buy some bread.'

'I've just sat down,' he whined.

Meg gave him a grim look. 'What time did you tie up this morning?'

He shrugged.

'I bet it was early, wasn't it?' Meg folded her arms, knowingly. 'So, you've been down by the wharf doing nothing for hours instead of coming home and seeing if I needed help.'

'I weren't doing nowt. I had to see to Blossom. She needed stabling and feeding.' He spoke of the shire horse they owned that pulled the narrowboat along the canals.

'Get away to the bakery. If you, Freddie and Father are home for a few days, I'll need more bread.' More of everything, and she didn't know how she'd provide it if her father didn't offer her some money, which he wasn't always forthcoming with. Many a time he'd told her to survive on her and Mabel's wages until he delivered his next load. She struggled to keep a roof over their heads and many times she went without food to make what she had stretch that bit further.

'We're going again in the morning, if you must know,' Arthur said, reclaiming his cap from the nail.

'So soon?' Meg frowned, but inside was secretly glad. She loved having Freddie home, and Arthur when he wasn't being cheeky, but not her father. Their relationship was taut with tension. Frank Taylor was a man who saw to himself first, the needs of his family were an afterthought.

'Father got a new load this morning. It was hard won, he had to drop his rates.'

'Why?'

'Because the railway is taking all our business, you know that. Companies can send their cargo by rail cheaper and quicker than we can take it on the canals.' Arthur shrugged and turned the handle on the door. 'Father's worried.'

Left alone, Meg pondered the situation. For years, the railways had been the competition to the canals. So far, her father had kept in business, loyal to several companies who were loyal to him. Yet, only last summer, two companies had dropped him from their books. Transporting by railway was faster and economical, as Arthur said. The boom of the canals as they were when her father was a boy had long gone.

Movement on the stairs stopped her mid-stride. Freddie, his arm around their mam, led her downstairs and over to the sofa, where he gently lowered her.

'Mam?' Meg couldn't believe her mam had managed the stairs, something she rarely did, and only in the summer when she wanted to sit for an hour once a week in the sunshine.

'I thought I'd make the effort,' Mam panted. 'Your father and the boys are only here for one night.' She smiled adoringly up at Freddie.

Anger gripped Meg's chest. Oh, it was fine for Mam to *make an effort* for Father and the boys, but when she asked her to come down and sit with Nicky when he was poorly or to give some attention to the girls, she was never well enough! Even if Mam could make it downstairs just once a day, it would help Meg and be one less trip up the steep staircase carrying a tray or coming down balancing the pot to empty into the lavatory.

'Shall I make some tea?' Freddie beamed.

The door opened and Frank Taylor entered, taking off his flat cap. His face, normally so severe, lit up in surprise on seeing his wife downstairs. 'Now, isn't this a lovely thing to see, lass?' He knelt before Lucy and kissed her gently. His hair, thinning and grey at the sides, didn't detract from the good-looking man who'd won their mam's heart as a girl. 'You seem better, my lass.'

'I feel well today.' Indeed, colour appeared on their mam's cheeks for the first time in weeks.

Meg turned away and busied herself in the kitchen making

tea, shoving Freddie out of the way as he searched for tea leaves and cups.

'Where's the sugar?' he whispered, not wanting to disturb their parents, who chatted quietly.

'There's none to be had,' Meg snapped. 'Like most things.'

Freddie frowned. 'What's wrong?'

'Nothing.' Meg added more pieces of coal to the range. She looked at Freddie. 'Arthur said Father is struggling for business, or is at least worried.'

'Aye. Arlington's have taken to transporting by railway now. One more company to turn their backs on the canals.'

'What will Father do?'

'He's been talking to old Mr Henderson, who is still keen to give us loads.'

'Then what's the worry?'

'Father has had to drop his rates to compete, and, well, Mr Henderson is an old man, isn't he? Who will run his brewery when he goes? His son, Barney, is a drunkard. A useless fool. How could he run the place? He'll sell at the first opportunity and then where will we be? Though even before that happens, who can say how long Henderson's Brewery will last? Old Mr Henderson is losing custom to other brewers, those who transport by rail further afield.'

'Let's hope that old Mr Henderson lasts a good few years yet.' Meg mashed more tea as the younger ones came home from school and made a great fuss of their father and older brothers being home.

Meg told the girls to gather the washing in and hang some of it on the airer in front of the fire and to put the rest on the airer that hung from the ceiling on pulleys.

The small house filled up quickly, and the noise and steam from the damp garments rose. Meg kept an eye on her mam, but she seemed to be coping with all the attention. Nicky, as predicted, came home tired and droopy. Meg quietly passed him a cup of tea and told him to sit by the fire.

'Did you have a good day?' Meg whispered to him.

'Aye, grand.' He yawned. 'I mean, yes, it was good.'

'Bed early tonight, my lad.' Meg gave him a stern look and ruffled his dark hair.

Putting the pie into the oven, Meg boiled a pan of carrots and cabbage to go with it, to make the meal stretch for more mouths. She needed to talk to her father and ask for housekeeping money, or at least get her mam to do it.

The little clock on the mantel chimed six times as Mabel walked in, a scarf wrapped about her hair as a safety precaution working at the mill. 'It's starting to rain,' she announced.

'That smells delicious,' Freddie said, coming to stand near the range. 'Are you working tonight?'

'Yes,' Meg answered. 'I'll leave in a few minutes. I start at half six tonight.' She'd start her shift early and that would be one less plate to fill.

'But you haven't eaten.'

'Oh, I'll get something in the kitchen there.' If she was lucky. She might get a cup of stew or whatever was left over from the evening rush at the Bay Horse. Don, the cook, was a miser when it came to the staff eating his food, unless they paid for it.

'I'll come with you, have a pint,' Freddie added. 'I'll eat there too.'

'You don't have to. Save your money.' Meg knew he was thinking the same as her. The pie wouldn't stretch for all of them.

'I've a few pence in my pocket.' Freddie turned to Mabel. 'I'm walking Meg to the pub. You'll have to dish out.'

Mabel rolled her eyes. 'I've just got in.'

'Aye, and Meg's been cleaning all day and now off to do her

shift. I think you can serve pie and veg.' Freddie stepped over to kiss his mam. 'I'll be back in a bit.'

Mam smiled and cupped his cheek.

Father frowned. 'Don't be drinking too much, our Freddie. We've an early start in the morning.'

'Aye, I know.' Freddie waited for Meg to wrap her brown shawl around her shoulders.

Meg glanced at Mam. 'You'll not be tiring yourself out too much, will you?'

'No, I'll be fine,' Mam answered. Her grey-streaked dark hair was coming free from the ribbon she'd tied it back with. Her grey eyes, which Meg had inherited, looked weary, but Mam smiled and held Frank's hand in both of hers.

Meg couldn't look at her father. She hoped to God he wouldn't inflict himself on Mam tonight, or any night. Another baby would kill Mam. She barely had the strength to keep herself alive, never mind grow a baby.

Leaving the house, Meg kept her head bowed against the drizzling rain. A mist curled over the cobbles from the black river, turning the gaslit street lamps into golden halos. The freezing night air would turn the rain to ice by morning.

'You're quiet,' Freddie murmured. 'You're usually shouting your head off at that lot.' He indicated with his head the household they'd just left.

'I'm tired. I've been up since dawn washing.'

'It's more than that.'

Before she had time to reply, there was a shout and scuffle ahead. A woman screamed and then a thin youth ran by before Meg could even react.

'Jesus!' Freddie sprinted ahead to the crumpled form on the cobbles.

'What's happened?' Meg asked, reaching them.

'He stole my purse.' The woman regained her feet with Freddie's help. The hood of her cloak slipped back, revealing a pretty face, with caramel-brown eyes. She was taller than Meg by a few inches, with black hair like a raven's wing tied back away from her face.

Meg knew that face. 'You're Mr Chambers' daughter, aren't you? The boatbuilder from across the river?'

'Yes. Lorrie Chambers.' The young woman still held on to Freddie's arm, looking pale.

'I've seen you and your father at church,' Meg said. Chambers' boatyard was just one of the many businesses that hugged the riverside. Father had taken his narrowboat to Chambers whenever it needed repairing.

'Come into the pub. You need to sit down for a minute,' Freddie suggested, leading her towards the Bay Horse.

'Oh, I shouldn't. My father will be wondering where I am.'

'You've had a shock,' Meg said. 'Sit for a minute and then Freddie will walk you home.'

'Do you want to go to the police?' Freddie asked as they entered the pub's smoke-filled, stuffy taproom.

The noise of many men talking and laughing drowned out Miss Chambers' reply.

'Hey there, Meg. Get us a pint, lass.' One old man thrust his tankard at Meg as she passed.

'In a minute, Reg. I need to help Miss Chambers. She's been robbed.'

'Robbed?' The word filtered about the men and the noise quietened.

'Right outside?' one man demanded to know as the men mumbled their grievances of thugs out robbing decent folk.

'Yes!' Meg took Miss Chambers from Freddie and guided her

into the small snug, which, thankfully, was empty. 'Sit here, and I'll get you a brandy.'

'What's all this?' A large, barrel-chested man stood in the doorway, his face florid and nose bulbous. Terry Atkins was the landlord, and most days was as snarly as a wet cat, but kind-hearted beneath his formidable exterior.

'Evening, Terry. Miss Chambers, here, was robbed outside. She's a bit shaken.'

'Chambers? Boatbuilder?' Terry frowned. 'He doesn't drink in here.'

'What has that got to do with it?' Meg shook her head at him.

'He doesn't drink anywhere,' Lorrie said with a rueful lift of her lips. 'My father has a tot of whisky at home before bed and that's it.'

Terry folded his arms across his wide chest. 'Are you going to report it to the police? If you do, go down to the station. I ain't having no trouble on my premises.'

'No,' Lorrie sighed. 'I shan't report it. I don't want to worry Father.'

'But you've been robbed,' Meg argued, annoyed on her behalf.

'A young lad.' Lorrie shrugged. 'I only had a few pence in my purse. I'll not see it again. Besides, I didn't even get a look at the lad. I'll not be much help to the police.'

'Slimy buggers,' Terry muttered. 'Excuse my language.' He raised his bushy eyebrows at Meg. 'Let her sit in here for a few minutes. I'll get Fliss to bring a brandy.' He peered at Miss Chambers. 'No charge this time.'

'Thank you. That's most kind.'

'Meg, your shift starts in five minutes. I want you behind the bar.' Terry shut the door on them.

'Thank you for your help, and your man, too.'

'Freddie?' Meg grinned. 'He's my brother.'

'Oh.'

'I'm Meg Taylor.'

'Lorrie Chambers, as you know.' Her caramel-brown eyes smiled with warmth. 'It really was good of you to stop and help.'

'It's funny how we've never met when you live only on the other side of the river. We must be close to the same age, too.'

'I'm busy at the boatyard most days. I work in the office to keep my father's account books in some kind of order. He's useless at it and we can't afford to hire a clerk.' Miss Chambers' eyes widened. 'Forgive me. I shouldn't have spoken so frankly.'

'I'll not be telling anyone. Having no money isn't something strange to me.'

'Taylor... Are you Frank Taylor's daughter? He has a narrowboat and he takes loads for Henderson's Brewery.'

'Among others, yes. Nothing escapes you, does it?' Meg laughed.

'I make it my business to know all the boats and their owners working the river and canal. I have to. At some point, we usually have their vessels in for repair. Our living rooms are above the office overlooking the boatyard and the river and weir. All my life I have watched boats and boatmen going about their business. Your father, Frank, has a black narrowboat named *Ness*.'

'Yes, it was named after one of my great-grandmothers.'

The door opened and Fliss Atkins, a tiny young woman with reddish-blonde curls, peeked in as though afraid of disturbing them. 'Sorry to interrupt.' She held out the small glass of brandy.

'Miss Chambers, this is Fliss Atkins, Terry's niece,' Meg introduced them.

'Thank you and nice to meet you.' Miss Chambers took the glass and sipped at it before screwing her face up with distaste.

Meg nodded to the glass. 'It's not nice, is it?'

'No.'

'But it'll help the shock.'

Fliss stepped a little closer to them. 'You were robbed, Uncle told me.'

'Freddie and me helped her,' Meg said.

'How shocking.' Fliss, her blue eyes wide, shook her head in dismay. 'We're not safe to walk the streets any more.'

'Hardly. It was just some young lad trying his luck.' Miss Chambers waved away her concern. 'I've walked these streets at night for years and never been bothered.' She suddenly gasped. 'Oh, that sounded dreadful. I didn't mean it like that, I meant on my way home from... from—'

Meg laughed. 'We know what you meant. We didn't think you were a woman of the night.'

Miss Chambers blushed.

'You're very brave, Miss Chambers,' Fliss added.

'Please, call me Lorrie. I get enough of being called Miss Chambers by the boat owners that come into the yard.' She took another sip of the brandy and grimaced. 'I really should be going.'

'I'll get Freddie to walk you home.' Meg went out and called for Freddie, who stood by the bar with a half-pint in his hand. 'You'll walk Lorrie home, won't you?'

'Aye, of course.' Freddie slapped his flat cap on his head.

'It was nice to meet you, Lorrie,' Meg said, meaning it.

Lorrie paused, as though hesitant to speak. 'In a way, I'm glad I got robbed. It meant I got to meet you both.' She cast her eyes down. 'I don't meet other young women my age much, only at church, but that's not the same. It's only Father and me at home.'

Meg took a moment to study Lorrie Chambers and realised the other woman was lonely. 'We'll be your friends, if you want? Won't we, Fliss?'

'We will?' Fliss' mouth gaped. 'I mean, yes, we will. I don't have any friends at all either.'

Meg nudged Fliss. 'I'm your friend.'

'We only talk when you're here working. You've never invited me to your house.'

Surprised by the sadness in Fliss' voice, Meg admitted that was the truth. She'd known Fliss for six months since she started working at the Bay Horse after leaving another pub she used to work at further away in town. 'I've never thought to invite you to my home,' Meg admitted. 'I'm always so busy, I don't have time to entertain.'

'How about this?' Lorrie said suddenly. 'You both come for afternoon tea at my home on Saturday. Say three o'clock?'

Both Meg and Fliss stared at their new friend. 'Afternoon tea?' they chorused.

'Yes...' Lorrie appeared flustered. 'If you want?'

'We'd like that.' Meg nodded, filled with a rush of happiness at being invited out to someone's house for afternoon tea. That never happened to her. 'We'd like that a lot.'

Lorrie beamed, her grave face transforming into something rather beautiful. 'I'm looking forward to Saturday now! Goodbye.'

When Lorrie had left with Freddie, Meg rushed behind the bar and tied a white pinny over her brown skirt. She quickly served two labourers, ignoring Terry's scowl as he changed a barrel under the bar.

Fliss also served a man, but she kept glancing at Meg, grinning.

'What's with you?' Meg whispered as she took the coins the men gave her and deposited them into the box on the shelf under the bar.

'I'm so happy,' Fliss murmured. 'Afternoon tea. It sounds very grand.'

'It's Chambers' boatyard, not Buckingham Palace,' Meg mocked, wiping a cloth over the sticky bar top.

'Aye, but don't pretend you're not excited, too? I can't believe I've made a new friend.' Fliss hopped about excitedly.

'Gracious, you're not going to burst into song next, are you?'

'I could, really I could.' Fliss twirled.

'What the hell are you two doing?' Terry shouted. 'Stop messing about and get serving.'

Fliss froze, a blush creeping up her neck, and a terrified look entered her eyes. 'Sorry, Uncle.'

Meg frowned at her and then at Terry. 'We're serving, keep your hair on!'

For the rest of the evening, Meg barely stopped. She served the men their drinks, she washed the empty glasses and tankards, swept the floor and threw sawdust down on spilled pints. She kept the fire going in the main taproom and carried dirty plates into the kitchen, where a young lad washed them up in the stone scullery sink.

Don, the surly cook, handed her a plate of roast chicken leg and potatoes swimming in gravy. 'Eat.'

'I've not got any money to pay you.'

'It's the end of the night. It'll not keep,' he said gruffly.

'Thank you.' Meg's stomach rumbled at the delicious smell. She stood by the door and ate fast, knowing Terry would close the bar soon and she'd be needed to help lock up and clear away.

The door leading to the yard out the back opened and Gerald Atkins sauntered in. Terry's son thought himself to be the cock of the walk and always wore a cravat as though it would make his shabby suit look more impressive. He was the son of a pub landlord, but he behaved like a squire's son, born to wealth and privilege. It didn't help that he hung about with some young men of the town who had money and status. It gave Gerald the idea that he was cut from the same cloth. His mother, Hilda, fully encouraged him, thinking her son would one day become a gentleman.

Meg hated him.

Gerald's smarmy smile grated on her nerves. He stepped towards her. 'Good evening, sweet Meg.'

'We could have done with your help tonight. The bar was busy.'

He chuckled. 'When do I ever work behind that bar now? It's been months. My time is taken up with other more important things.' He stretched out his arms and yawned. He was as tall as his father but not as wide. He had dark eyes that narrowed often in displeasure. Whereas Terry could often share a joke with the patrons if he was in the mood, Gerald felt it beneath him to mix with the working class in the bar.

Fliss came into the kitchen carrying a tray of dirty glasses. The glasses rattled as she saw Gerald.

'Ah, the foundling,' he sneered. 'Hurry up, girl!'

His bark made Fliss jerk forward, and the glasses toppled from the tray to smash over the stone floor.

'You bloody idiot!' Gerald surged forward, fist raised at Fliss.

Meg jumped between them, angry that he would dare raise a fist to Fliss, someone half his size and a girl. 'Back off, Gerald. It was an accident.'

'She's a waste of air, that one. God knows why my parents took her in. She should have stayed in the orphanage.' He marched from the room, slamming the door behind him.

'Thanks,' Fliss muttered, bending to collect the broken pieces of glass.

'Forget him. He's a nasty bully, that's all.' Meg knelt and helped her.

'I like that we are to be friends, Meg.' Fliss wiped a tear from her cheek.

'Course we are, and I'm sorry I didn't make an effort before now. I've been working here for six months and I should have invited you to my house for a cup of tea.'

'I should have done the same and invited you here, but well… my aunt can be funny about who comes up to our private quarters.'

'It's fine. Anyway, we're off to afternoon tea on Saturday, just think of that.'

That brought a weak smile back to Fliss' face.

As Meg walked home to the sound of the water lapping gently against the side of the wharf, she thought of Lorrie and Fliss and how having them as friends could be exactly what she needed. Time with others her age, away from her family and all the responsibility she shouldered. Like Lorrie and Fliss, friends were not something she had. At Sunday school she'd known lots of girls, but only a few remained in the streets nearby and most were married now and they'd drifted away. In the past, Meg had too little time to worry about spending hours with girls her age. Mam and Nicky's illnesses took all her energy.

However, now it might be different. Nicky wanted to go to school, to be a proper boy and play with the other lads, and perhaps he should. Was it time for her to stop protecting him, keeping him inside? Should she let him out and see what happened? He might thrive. And Mam showed she could come downstairs if she wanted to…

Yes, it was time for Meg to leave the house more for her own entertainment. Excited by the thought, she quietly let herself into the house. Saturday couldn't come quick enough.

2

'You can't go,' Mabel whined.

Meg paused before a vegetable stall in the market and asked for a bag of onions, a bunch of carrots, a cabbage and three large turnips. Her order taken, she whipped back to Mabel. 'You don't get to tell me what I can or can't do, Mabel Taylor,' she hissed.

'But why do I need to look after them all while you're out enjoying yourself?' Mabel took the vegetables and loaded them into her basket while Meg paid.

'Enjoy myself?' Meg snapped. 'You make it sound like I go out every day!' She marched between people strolling the market, frustrated at her sister.

'I was going to meet up with some girls from the mill. It's our day off.' Mabel hurried to keep up with her.

Meg paused by the stall selling reels of coloured cotton, skeins of wool and embroidery threads. 'You see the girls from the mill every day at work. I never have an afternoon to please myself and for once I'm doing it. I've made a new friend, Lorrie, and Fliss from the pub is coming, too.' She turned to the stallholder. 'Good morning, Mrs Kirton. Do you have my order?'

'I do, lass.' Mrs Kirton handed over a brown paper-wrapped parcel. 'Dark blue wool, enough to make your Nicky a nice vest, and the deep red wool you wanted as well.'

'Thank you. Mam will be pleased.' Meg took the parcel and gave her the correct change. Although Mam had gone straight back to bed the minute Father and the boys left, she had taken up her knitting again and seemed more alert to the goings-on in the house, even to the point of once more reading serials from the newspaper to the children at night before bed.

'Give your mam my regards.' Mrs Kirton waved them away.

'Why can't Susie look after Mam and Nicky for this afternoon?' Mabel asked, weaving between shoppers.

'Because you're the next eldest.' Meg bought two pig's trotters from the butcher to make a broth and then at the baker's paid for a loaf of yesterday's bread, which was cheaper than the freshly baked loaves.

Pausing by a bookstall, Meg ran her gloved fingers over some of the spines. She didn't have spare money to buy books, but if she was rich, she'd buy new books every week for Mam to read. Nicky loved listening to stories, it enthralled even Nell and Betsy enough to sit at the end of Mam's bed and listen. If only she had money, she would be so happy. She'd spoil her family, buy them anything they wanted...

'Meg, you're not listening to me,' Mabel moaned.

'No, I'm not.'

'You're being unfair.'

'Sweet heaven, will you stop your whining? I'm going out and that's the end of it.' Meg left the market, the small amount of money her father had left on the mantel spent. At least the rent was paid for another week and the food she bought would stretch a few days until she got paid. Next week's rent would be paid from Mabel's wage. They'd get by, they always did, as long as Meg was thrifty. She wondered if this would be her life forever. Was there a slim chance she could ever do anything else than work, shop and clean, and worry about money? Was it terrible to want something more?

At home, Mabel sulked as they put away the shopping. Susie, Betsy and Nell were out on the street talking to the other children who lived on Wellington Street. The bitter January day didn't deter them from being outside and Meg prayed it wouldn't snow or rain to bring them back inside and under her feet. Nicky sat by the small fire, drawing.

'How are you, pet?' Meg ruffled his hair.

'Fine. Just drawing. It's a dog, see?'

Meg studied the drawing. Nicky really was talented. 'That's the finest puppy I've seen.'

'I wish we could have one.'

'We can barely afford to eat ourselves, never mind feeding a dog.' She added a few lumps of coal to the glowing embers. Before Father and her brothers had left, a random sack of coal had found its way to the coal shed out the back, and Meg guessed Freddie had got it for them.

'You'll not be gone long, will you?' Nicky asked, head down, concentrating on his drawing. 'I don't like it when you're not home. At least when you're at work I'm in bed and fall asleep, but this is different. You're not going to be home for hours.'

A pang of guilt struck Meg's chest. 'You'll hardly know I'm not here. You're busy drawing and Mam is always pleased to see your drawings if you take them up to her. The time will pass by quick enough.'

'I like you being at home,' Nicky said in a small voice.

Guilt made her wince. 'You enjoy being out with your friends, don't you? Well, that's what I'm doing. Just an hour or two hours with friends.' Heating water, Meg leant against the kitchen table, wondering if all this had been worth the hassle. Mabel and Nicky didn't want her to go for different reasons, and what if Mam took ill? Or if one of the girls hurt themselves playing outside?

Half-heartedly, Meg took a jug of hot water upstairs to wash. She wanted to look her best for tea with Lorrie, to impress her new friend, though she was probably wasting her time and she'd only stay half an hour and return home. This Lorrie Chambers might not even be that nice, but instinct told her otherwise.

'Meg?' Mam called out as she passed the bedroom door.

'Yes?'

'Come in for a moment.'

Reluctantly, Meg placed the jug on the floor and stepped into her parents' bedroom, wondering if Mam would also say something to prevent her from going. 'Do you want something?'

'No. I want to give you this. You can wear it to your afternoon tea.' Mam pointed to the chair in the corner where a white silk bodice hung over it. 'I wore it when I first met your father, but I soon realised it wasn't the attire I needed for Wellington Street.'

Meg gently lifted the white bodice. It was delicately stitched with white lace on the collar and cuffs. 'It's beautiful. I've never seen you wear it.'

'No. I put it away after you were born. I sponged it last night, so it shouldn't smell too musty from being stored in the bottom of the wardrobe.'

'You did that for me?' Meg felt instantly guilty that her frail mam had used her limited energy and washing water to clean the bodice.

'You deserve to wear something nice. It's about time you had some excitement in your life. You spend all your time looking after me and the others. I'm sorry about that. Anyway, the sleeves are a little straight for the current fashion.'

'It'll not matter to me.' Meg smiled. The bodice would fit, she knew it would.

'Sadly, the skirt didn't survive. White is not a practical colour for the waterfront.'

'No.' Meg had never worn white in her life.

'Perhaps you could wear it with your blue skirt, the good one you keep for best.'

'Yes, I was planning to wear that and my pink bodice.' Meg had spent last evening sewing a tear under the arm of her best bodice that she wore to church each Sunday, but the garment was well worn and showing signs of age. 'Maybe I shouldn't go. Mabel is complaining and Nicky wants me to stay and then there's...'

'And then there's me,' Mam finished for her. 'No, Meg. You need an afternoon away from us all, and not at the pub working hard. It's time for you to venture outside this house and do something to please only you.'

Meg dithered, torn between her responsibilities and wanting to visit Lorrie.

'I'll put your hair up for you if you like?' Mam raised her eyebrows in question. 'I think I can still do a good enough job of it.'

'I'd like that.'

'Go and get ready then.' Mam lay back on the pillows tiredly.

In the larger bedroom that she shared with her sisters and Nicky, Meg stripped down to her corset and washed her face and neck thoroughly before donning a clean shift and then her midnight-blue skirt and, lastly, Mam's white lace bodice. She couldn't see herself fully in the small cracked mirror hanging on a nail near the window, but she felt instantly more mature and refined. If this was how she felt with a new bodice, imagine wearing a whole new outfit, or a ball gown like she'd seen in a shop window once. How wonderful must it feel to wear fashionable clothes?

Unable to stop smiling, Meg returned to Mam's bedroom with her brush and ribbons.

Sitting up straight, Mam shook her head. 'No, not those ribbons. Fetch me my box.'

Meg collected a wooden box that she and all her siblings had admired since they were little. The box was shiny mahogany, with a painted rural scene on the lid. Inside, purple velvet lined the two trays. One tray held a pearl necklace that her grandparents had given Mam on her eighteenth birthday and the other tray held two tortoiseshell combs, a white silk ribbon and a sapphire brooch.

'The combs and the white ribbon.' Mam took them from the box and began to brush Meg's long dark-brown hair. 'I'll make a loose plait and secure it with the ribbon and then twist it up gently at your nape. The combs will hold it in place.'

When she'd finished, Meg looked in the handheld mirror her mam kept on the tall drawers. Meg stared at herself. She wore her hair up every day in a tight bun at the back of her head to keep it from being in her eyes as she scrubbed and cleaned. But she'd never had it styled like this, with soft wispy bits hanging by her ears.

'You look like me at that age.' Mam sighed. 'How my parents would be shocked to see the resemblance.'

'Do you miss them?'

'Most days.' Mam picked at the top blanket. 'But I made my choice, and they made theirs. They have their opinions about the choices I made...'

'Do you regret marrying Father?'

'No... but I should have waited a bit longer as my father

wanted me to. If I'd kept in favour with them, our lives would have been so different.'

'In what way?' Meg replaced the mirror on the drawers, giving Mam her full attention, for the past was rarely spoken about.

'My parents would have stayed in Wakefield and let us live with them while your father plied the canals. My parents' house was on Horbury Road, one of those nice ones with a small garden out the front. Only, I was impatient. I didn't want to wait a year to marry Frank. A year felt like a lifetime to a seventeen-year-old. I ignored their wishes and got swept away by the excitement of love and adventure. We ran away and got married at a church along the river within six weeks of meeting each other. Frank had bribed a vicar to marry us. My father was furious, as he had a right to be.' Mam sighed again, longer this time, as though the memories were sad and difficult.

'They still spoke to you for a few years. I have a vague memory of them, I think.' She tried to imagine her grandparents in her mind but wasn't sure if she had the picture of them correct.

'Yes, but they never came to terms with my marriage to a man who owned a narrowboat and worked on the canals. My mother felt it was beneath our family. They moved away, down south for my mother's health, but I think they just wanted to leave so they didn't see me living here in poverty. I was too proud to take hand-outs from them, of course. My situation shamed them.' A wry smile appeared on Mam's face. She gently shook herself. 'Enough of that. Go. Enjoy your afternoon. I want to hear all about it later. Oh, and take my good cloak. You can't go for afternoon tea in an old shawl. That really would shame your grandmother.'

Meg kissed her mam's cheek. 'Thank you. I will.'

Downstairs, Meg found Mabel in the yard, coming out of the lav. 'I'm off now.'

'Don't you look fancy?' Mabel's eyes widened, adjusting her

skirts. 'It's only tea in a boatyard, you know. Why do you get to wear Mam's clothes and I never do?'

'Because I'm the eldest.' Meg gave her a pointed look. 'Make Mam a cup of tea.'

Leaving the house, Meg pulled up the hood of the black cloak and, head down against the nippy breeze, hurried along the cobbles. She waved to the girls but didn't stop and just told them to behave while she was gone.

At the end of Wellington Street, she turned left to walk along Thornes Lane Wharf to the ferryman. She hoped that since he was a good friend of her father's, he'd let her cross for free.

'Meg!' Fliss waved, coming from the opposite way. 'I was about to get on the ferry. Now we can go together.'

Meg was pleased to see that Fliss wore her Sunday best under her coat, so Meg didn't feel she'd overdressed. 'I'll see if Harry will let us cross for free.'

'Really?' Fliss grinned. 'Brilliant.'

'Hey, Harry,' Meg called to the old man coiling a rope on the deck of a boat below. His ferry took workers across the river to the mills and maltings on the island, which saved them walking further up the wharf and around past the weir to the bridge. 'Will you let me and Fliss cross? We haven't a penny between us.'

Harry, heavily whiskered, chuckled. 'Aye, since it's you. Come down then. I was heading across anyway to take this load of crates to Arlington's warehouse.'

Meg nudged Fliss happily.

They held each other's arms down the green slippery steps to the boat below. Once seated on the hard wooden bench, Harry cast off the ropes and the ferry began drifting across as he pulled on the winding wheel to cast in the thick, wet rope that dragged them across to the other side.

'You're dressed up, lass,' Harry said to Meg as he pushed a long pole into the water to keep the vessel straight. 'Going somewhere special?'

'Off for afternoon tea, Harry.'

'Now, isn't that nice?'

Fliss beamed. 'I've been so looking forward to this afternoon. Uncle Terry wanted me to work, but I begged him to let me go and he did.'

'It was a nightmare trying to get away from the house. Mabel was being a right madam about being left to take care of everyone.' It still annoyed Meg that she had to fight for a simple afternoon for herself.

'But surely you deserve an hour to have some fun, don't you?' Fliss murmured. 'I hardly ever leave the pub and at times... well... I feel like I'm drowning amongst all the people and noise and tasks I have to do. Aunt Hilda never leaves me alone and always has something for me to do.'

'I know how you feel.' Meg squeezed Fliss' hand. 'From now on, we'll watch out for each other more, yes? At the pub we'll share the jobs and try to visit each other when we can.'

'And I'll come to your house whenever I manage to escape my aunt and help you. Your family is larger than mine.' Fliss smiled her crooked smile which endeared her to Meg all the more.

Harry soon had them on the other side, pulling up the boat near the opening of the canal lock and nestling the stern between two barges. He helped the girls up onto the dock. 'I'm off home at five, lass,' he said to Meg. 'If you finish before then, I'll take you back across.'

'Thanks, Harry. If it's later, we'll walk across the bridge.' Meg gave him a wave and, with Fliss, they walked past the lock and across a patch of open ground to Bridge Street, which ran across the island from the canal up along to Wakefield Bridge.

The island, known as Fall Ings, was created when the canal

was cut through by the Calder and Hebble Navigation to bypass the weir that sliced across the River Calder further up the bend. The canal joined the river on the other side of the island.

Although not an extensive land area, mills, ironworks, maltings and breweries, boatyards, dry docks and wharves dominated the cramped space, creating a world of industry and unpleasant smells.

'Along here?' Fliss asked when they reached Tootal Street, branching off to the left.

'Yes. Chambers' boatyard is near the dry dock, isn't it? You can see it from the bridge.' Meg led the way, confident that they'd soon find it. All the boatyards were situated on the waterfront.

They passed some young boys wheeling hoops along the road and then went down through a small alley. At the end of it was a two-storey blue-painted wooden building with the words Chambers Boat Builder and Repairs written in white paint on the side wall.

The black gates were flung open, one of which hung drunkenly, broken. Meg noticed rust flaking from the gates and weeds growing around the posts. Boats on wooden blocks in various states of repair littered the large yard like huge toys. The water lapped against the boat ramp, green slime coated the wet, aged wood. A gull stepped lightly at the edge of the water, its beady eyes trained on the newcomers.

Numerous coils of rope, iron buckets, wooden barrels, blocks and winches, buoys and nets were scattered about the yard or spilled from sheds. A large grey stone building had its doors open and Meg spied the skeleton of a boat being constructed, but no sound came from within. Tall stacks of timber were kept under a large open structure by the house and tarpaulins covered more timber near the gates.

Meg expected to see a hive of activity, but it was deathly quiet, just the odd cry of a gull soaring on the chilly breeze above them.

'Up here!' Lorrie called from the top of the wooden stairs that ran up the outside of the blue building.

Fliss waved, but as Meg walked closer, she noticed the state of disrepair and neglect of the area. She had expected the place to be in better shape. The boatyard had been around for as long as she could remember. Surely Mr Chambers was successful at what he did? It was a shame the boatyard didn't reflect that.

Climbing the stairs, more paint peeled off the handrail, but the shabbiness ended outside. Inside, Lorrie invited them into a warm, spacious room.

'This is where we live. This room is the living area and there are two bedrooms.' She pointed to the two doors. 'The office is downstairs underneath us,' Lorrie explained, nervously twisting her hands. 'I'm so pleased you both came.'

'Thank you for inviting us,' Fliss gushed.

'It's a beautiful room,' Meg told her, looking around the well-furnished quarters. A cheery fire burned beneath a carved mantel that held ornaments and pictures in frames. In front of the fire, a red sofa was placed with two matching occasional tables at either end. The walls were papered in a soft green print, not painted or whitewashed, as Meg's home was. A small chandelier hung in the centre of the room over a round, polished table that was set beautifully for afternoon tea.

'Do hand me your cloaks and sit down.' Lorrie hung the garments on the tall stand by the door, then stood by the table. 'I'll mash the tea. Please, help yourselves.'

Meg's eyes widened at the display of food on the table. Plates of sandwiches of thinly sliced beef or egg and cress, jam-filled sponge cake, lemon curd tartlets and a small glass bowl of candied fruits. For the second time that day, Meg felt guilty, only this time for a different reason. She was sitting down to a table laden with food while at home, her family went hungry. 'You've gone to so much trouble, Lorrie.'

'No, not at all.' Lorrie brought a delicate green and white teapot to the table and it matched the rest of the tea service. She sat down and poured out three cups of tea and then handed out the sugar cube bowl. 'There's milk in the small jug.'

Meg's hand shook a little as she picked up the silver tongs and added a cube of sugar into her cup, then a dash of milk. The elegant teacup looked as though the tiny handle would break in her rough fingers. She wished she had lace gloves to cover her red and cracked hands.

'Your father isn't at home?' Fliss asked, selecting triangles of sandwiches to place on her plate.

'No, he's meeting with a client.' Lorrie smiled, a look of gratitude in her caramel eyes. 'He didn't want to be in my way. I've been busy all morning, and he was glad to go in the end.'

'You shouldn't have gone to so much trouble,' Meg repeated, taking a beef sandwich.

'I wanted to. I've not entertained much, well, not at all for myself, only the odd visitor of Father's, or when my cousin and his wife call at Christmas.' Lorrie's expression fell. 'Have I done too much?'

'No!' Fliss patted Lorrie's hand. 'It's wonderful.'

Meg nodded. 'I agree. It's a lovely spread, just don't expect the same at my house.' Shame flooded her as the words left her mouth.

Letting out a long breath, Lorrie relaxed her shoulders. 'I've been a little nervous. I want this afternoon to go well.'

'We all do, I think.' Meg nodded, adding a slice of sponge cake to her plate. She sipped her tea, savouring the taste. She couldn't remember the last time she had tea with milk *and* sugar in it and it tasted delicious.

'I bought the cake because the first one I made, I burnt it. I'm not a very good cook, but I try. I have my mother's cookbooks which I read all the time.' Lorrie looked self-conscious. 'My father was so pleased I had invited you. He's always saying I should make friends, but it's not as easy as that... I spend most of my time alone.' Lorrie nibbled at a sandwich.

'It sounds like all three of us struggle to make friends,' Meg said. 'I never have a minute to myself. Yet I still felt guilty coming here and leaving them.'

'Your mother is not in good health, is she?' Lorrie asked. 'I remember your father telling mine about her one time.'

'The doctors say she has a weak heart, something she has passed on to Nicky. Though the rest of us are fine.' Meg shrugged, not understanding the science of biology or medical theory.

'Well, I'm pleased the three of us are here today.' Fliss raised her teacup in a small salute. 'I've not had a good friend since I was in the orphanage.'

Lorrie stared at her. 'You were in an orphanage?'

'Yes, my parents died of fever and they, some strangers, took me to an orphanage when I was ten. I stayed there for about a year before my Uncle Terry found out that his brother had died and that I'd been taken away. They, my uncle and father, weren't close. Anyway, Uncle Terry found me and took me back to his public house. He said no niece of his would be brought up in an institution.'

'That was kind of him.' Lorrie ate more of her sandwich.

'It was,' Fliss agreed. 'Except I wish my Aunt Hilda had wanted me too. She didn't.'

'I remember seeing you at odd times when we were kids,' Meg said. 'You were always the little shy one standing in the street by yourself.'

'None of the girls would pick me to play with because I was

new to the waterfront. The orphan girl.' Fliss shrugged, but sadness had entered her eyes. 'My aunt didn't encourage me to have friends. She kept me by her side. I was forever running errands for her.'

'I feel bad now. I should have talked to you,' Meg admitted.

'You were always busy chasing after your brothers and sisters to get them inside or to behave, or you'd be scurrying past with baskets of shopping.'

'Nothing has changed there then,' Meg grunted. 'Even coming here felt like I was betraying them in some way.'

'I'm pleased that you did.' Lorrie poured out more tea. 'I hope you both can come again.'

'I'd like that.' Meg ate some of the sponge cake and made a silent promise that she'd devote some time to herself.

'Well, none of us shall be lonely any more.' Lorrie brightened. 'We have each other now, don't we?'

Meg nodded and smiled. 'The three of us will be best friends.'

'Forever,' Fliss added.

'Though don't expect to get afternoon tea like this at my house,' Meg warned. 'You'll be lucky to get bread and dripping and weak black tea in a wretched old house full of people.'

'And at mine, we'll have Aunt Hilda sitting in the room watching and listening to us but pretending not to.' Fliss rolled her eyes.

They laughed, feeling relaxed with each other.

'Then we should make a pact,' Lorrie declared. 'No matter where we are, or what we are doing, the three of us will be there for each other, no matter what. Amongst all the madness, we will remain the best of friends and have each other's backs until we die.'

The three of them tapped their teacups together and cheered.

3

Meg carried two jugs of ale to the table by the roaring fire. The pub was full tonight, wages were being spent, and the patrons were in a jovial mood. Smoke hung like a thick cloud above the men's heads while outside a blustery wind with sleet battered anyone foolish enough to be out in it. Wild weather for the beginning of March.

'Thank you, Meg.' Barney Henderson poured the jug straight into his pewter tankard. His friend did likewise from the other jug.

Back behind the bar, Meg nudged Fliss. 'Barney will be swaying tonight, you'd best tell Terry.'

'Tell me what?' Terry, as large as he was, had the ability to appear quietly when least expected.

Meg wiped down the counter, turning her shoulders a little so that no one else would hear her, which was doubtful in the noisy taproom. 'Barney Henderson. He's on to his second jug in less than an hour.'

'Has he paid?'

'Yes. He paid for the first two jugs and his friend has paid for the second two.' Meg placed the cloth in a bucket under the counter.

'He'll be drinking his sorrows, I imagine.' Terry, holding a bottle of whisky, took two glasses from the shelf behind the counter.

'Why?' Fliss asked, serving a customer.

'Old Henderson is doing it tough. The brewery is struggling. How that is possible, I don't know.' Terry shook his head in amazement. 'They used to brew the best porter in town, but old Mr Henderson is failing, health-wise, and Barney over there would rather drink the product than make it.'

'What will happen?' Meg asked, thinking of her father and the cargo he carried for Henderson.

'Not sure.' Terry stepped to the end of the bar. 'Henderson's will probably go under unless someone comes and bails them out. Shame, really. They were a good brewery once.' He left to take the whisky to the snug.

'Fill me up, Meg, lass.' Reg offered his tankard over for Meg to refill. He placed the right number of coins on the bar top. 'When's your father back?'

'Any day now.' Meg took the coins and gave him a full tankard back. Father and the boys had left for another trip four weeks ago, venturing further west for more cargo as bartering for loads became fierce amongst the narrowboats. Father now searched further afield for cargo, which meant they were away for longer periods. Meg found it a struggle to make ends meet without the regular, if lesser, amounts of money Father left on the mantel.

'Are we meeting up tomorrow?' Fliss asked her, refilling a man's tankard with cider.

Meg's teeth worried her bottom lip. 'I'd like to. But not if Father returns. He's been gone four weeks and we're desperate for money. I need to buy food and we're behind on the rent now.'

'Lorrie will be disappointed.' Fliss served another customer.

'I can't help it. If Father returns, I need to go shopping, and Nicky has been unwell all week. He's pale and listless, no strength.'

'Still?' Fliss took the coins on the counter and put them in the box underneath. 'Did you send for Dr Carter?'

'No. We can't afford the doctor. Mam's not well again. She's not been out of bed for a fortnight. It worries me.' Her eyes ached with tiredness. She'd lived with Nicky and her mam's illness for years, but it didn't make it any easier. She just hoped that they got through each bout of illness and carried on as she always did.

Fliss paused and stared at Meg. 'You look done in.'

'I am. I've been up for the last three nights with Nicky. His breathing is laboured and is so weak. When I'm not watching over him, I'm sitting beside Mam, but I've got everything else to see to as well.'

'Doesn't Mabel or Susie help you?'

'Yes, of a sort, but Mabel works, too. She can't be in the mill dead on her feet, she'll have an accident.'

Fliss tutted. 'Listen, I'll see how much money I have upstairs. You can have it for the doctor.'

'No, Fliss.' Shocked, Meg shook her head. 'You're saving up for new boots.'

'These will last me a few more weeks.' Fliss stuck out a dusty, scuffed boot. 'And if they don't, I'll ask Uncle Terry for some.' She grinned. 'At least, I'll ask him when Aunt Hilda isn't about. Though if I say people at church were commenting on my boots, Aunt will drag me to the cobblers straight away. We can't have Aunt's church friends thinking we are not up to standard.' Fliss snorted with laughter.

'I'm sick of being poor.' Meg sighed heavily. If she had money, she'd never go hungry again. Her family would eat well and wear better clothes. Her dreams of having a different life were nothing but silly wishful thinking. Women like her didn't have fancy lives. They worked and struggled and simply existed. She was foolish to want more.

'Aye,' Fliss agreed. 'Though I know I'm in a better situation than you,' she added quickly. 'Which is why I can give you my money. I have food on the table every day.'

'Thanks, but I'll manage as long as Father returns home soon. Twice now I've had to say no to Lorrie's suggestion we go for tea and cake in town. I can't afford the rent, never mind tea and cake in town.' Meg filled another jug from the barrel of ale behind her. Mam always instilled in her to not borrow money from others, as it was just one more person to repay with money they didn't have.

'It's nice that she asks but we aren't like her. We don't have any spare money for tea in town.' Fliss took an empty tankard from a regular and waved him goodnight. She knelt and washed the tankard in a bucket of cold water before drying it and placing it on a shelf where the regulars kept their own tankards.

'I'm not sure she has a lot herself,' Meg said, returning to the bar after taking a jug to a table. 'The boatyard is run down, you've seen the state of it, and I heard that Mr Chambers is struggling to keep the yard open.'

'Really?' Fliss' eyes widened. 'That's terrible. Poor Lorrie.'

'From what Lorrie mentioned last week when I saw her, she said she's worried her father might have to close the business.'

'Close? Oh my. What will he do instead? He's not a young man.'

'Work for another boat repair company, perhaps? He has contacts in Liverpool, apparently.'

'Lorrie will move to Liverpool?' Fliss moaned. 'We've only been friends for six weeks. We can't lose her now.'

'I know.' Meg wiped the counter again, taking another man's

empty tankard, and watched him stagger over to the door. It took him three attempts to open it before he finally got out of the pub.

'Jesus, man!' yelled Floyd, a docker, jumping up from his stool. 'Ye gods, Percy! You've pissed yersen again.'

Meg crossed her arms in annoyance. 'I'm not seeing to him again. I helped him last time.'

'Oh, no, I can't...' Fliss squeezed her hands together under her chin. 'I helped him one time he had an accident. He's a dead weight. I nearly fell with him on top of me.'

Meg snorted, remembering the sight of it. 'Stupid old man. He shouldn't come in here and drink for hours if he can't hold his water,' Meg fumed. Dealing with old men pissing themselves was a step too far tonight.

Terry came out of the snug and took in the situation. 'Percy?'

Meg nodded.

'Jesus wept.' Terry, quick to anger, strode over to the senseless old man and heaved him up. 'Out, Percy. Go home.'

Percy, his grey beard hanging down onto his chest, moaned insensibly.

'Floyd, help me get him outside in the freezing wind. He might sober up enough to walk home,' Terry urged, dragging the old man to the door.

'I doubt it.' Floyd knocked back the last of his drink. 'I'll see him home. Me missus will have me bed warm by now.'

'Is it time to ring the bell for last orders?' Meg was tired, her feet ached, and she hadn't had a decent night's sleep for days.

'Not yet.' Fliss checked the clock on the shelf. 'Ten more minutes.'

Meg watched Barney Henderson grab the two jugs from his table and walked to the bar. 'They drank those fast,' Meg whispered to Fliss.

'Two more jugs, or just the one, Barney? We'll be closing soon,' Meg told him.

Although Barney was only in his early thirties, he'd lived a life of privilege and it showed in his bloodshot eyes and excess weight on his face. 'Two jugs, please, Meg.'

'You've a thirst on you tonight.' She took the jugs and Fliss helped her fill them from the barrel.

'Drowning our sorrows,' he replied, looking glum.

'I'm sorry to hear it.'

'You will be because it affects your family, too.'

Meg stiffened. 'How so?'

'My father's business is failing.' Barney scoffed. 'He must be the only brewery in the country who can't make a profit.'

'Why is that?' She tried to keep the panic from her voice. Father needed that company's cargo. She dreaded to think what would happen without it. Her father complained already about the lack of cargo loads he was getting.

'Who knows? I stay out of it. Father's ways are as old as him. He's not in good health and his suppliers know that and take advantage.'

'You're his son. Can't you help him?'

Barney frowned. 'Help him?'

'Take over running the business?'

Barney took the jugs from her and paid. 'Why would I want to do that? Father has never looked at me favourably. Why should I save him?'

'Because he's your father, and it's your family business.'

An unhappy laugh erupted from Barney. 'You know nothing, Meg Taylor, but I'd tell your father to look elsewhere for cargo from now on.'

When he'd gone back to his table, Meg felt Fliss' hand on her arm.

'He's drunk,' Fliss murmured.

'But what if he's right? If Henderson's go down, that's another business Father won't be working for. He's finding it harder and harder to get loads.'

'Something will turn up, be positive.' Fliss squeezed her arm, then left the bar to start cleaning up.

Meg went about her tasks with half a mind, worrying about what the future would bring. She wasn't close to her father and couldn't confide in him about her concerns. Susie would be in work soon and perhaps if she found Betsy a job now she was ten they might cope, but Mam was adamant about the children not working until they were eleven or twelve. It was easy for Mam to say, a woman who'd never worked in her life, but Mam wasn't the one struggling to pay for food and rent.

Patrons leaving the pub stepped aside to allow a man inside. Wearing a long black coat, holding a smart top hat in his hand and his legs encased in shiny black calf-length boots, he stood out from the working-class men lingering in the room.

Sweeping up the sawdust in front of the counter, Meg paused and gazed at the man as he scanned the room. Taller than most of the men, he had a proud bearing, straight-backed, but it was the expression of suppressed anger on his handsome face that held Meg's attention. The man stared at Barney.

Not wanting a fight to start so near to closing, Meg rested the broom against the counter and took two steps towards the man, but when he turned and looked at her, she faltered.

Light blue eyes pierced straight at her.

She swallowed, breath suspended, unable to take another step. His presence silenced the room. A gentleman in a working man's pub. There was something about him, some force which captivated her.

'Christian?' Barney said in surprise, slowly standing.

'You are needed at home. Immediately.' The man stood as still as a post, his tone deep and unforgiving.

'I'm nearly finished.'

'Now.'

One word. It sent a shiver down Meg's back. She didn't know whether to be alarmed or intrigued by the stranger.

Terry entered the pub, bringing with him a blast of chilly wind and cursing Percy's weak bladder. He paused, taking in the situation. 'Are we going to have any trouble here, gentlemen?'

The man, Christian, lifted his chin in defiance. Terry, a big man, would scare most people, but the newcomer was just as tall and far more imposing.

'Christian. Sit down, have a jug with us,' Barney cajoled, his smile strained.

Christian's icy stare was full of contempt. 'If you have any decency, you will come with me.'

Sighing deeply, Barney grabbed his hat off the table and he and his friend joined Christian by the door. Without another word spoken, they left.

As the door closed, Meg let out a breath.

'Gracious, who was that?' Fliss asked no one in particular.

'I think he's a Henderson, the old man's nephew if I'm not mistaken,' Terry said, placing stools and chairs on tables. 'I heard earlier that old Mr Henderson is very ill. Seizure of some sort. Happened yesterday, but it's been kept hush-hush because the brewery is in dire straits. His creditors will come swooping in like a flock of birds on a worm when word gets out.'

'Father can't lose another regular cargo.' They couldn't afford such a loss, yet that wasn't the only thing she thought about. As Meg swept the sawdust, her mind was full of a tall, handsome man called Christian Henderson.

* * *

In his uncle's overheated drawing room in Meadow View House, Christian Henderson paced, waiting for the doctor's report. Upstairs, his uncle, Royce Henderson, lay dying. Everyone knew it, though no one wanted to acknowledge it.

Wiping a tired hand over his face, he listened to the longcase clock in the entrance hall chime once in the silent house. Apart from the butler, Titmus, all the servants were in bed. He wondered if his uncle would see a new dawn.

A sniffle from his Aunt Gertrude joined the soft shift of the applewood logs in the fireplace as the only sound in the room.

Christian stepped to the drinks trolley and poured himself a small brandy.

'I'll have one,' Barney said from the red silk sofa by the fire.

'I would have thought you'd had enough tonight,' Christian replied, but poured his cousin a small measure and handed it to him. 'Aunt?'

'Nothing for me, thank you.' Aunt Gertrude's birdlike face was pinched in utter despair. She sat on a chair in a gown of burgundy taffeta, diamonds shining from her throat and her grey hair immaculately styled on top of her head. 'Royce cannot die on me, Christian. We have been married thirty-five years...'

'The doctor will do everything he can, and Uncle is tenacious.' He didn't know what else to say. He and his uncle wrote regularly and, with him, his uncle was honest about his business and his life. Did his aunt know of the stress his uncle had been under for so many years trying to keep the brewery afloat? The brewery was something his uncle had inherited from his wife's family when they first married, and it had come with thousands of pounds of debt. Debt that his uncle had been paying off his whole married life, as well as trying to keep his wife in the lavish lifestyle into which she was born.

More than once, Christian had given his uncle money to stem the tide of debtors from knocking on the front door of Meadow View House. He genuinely liked and respected his Uncle Royce, but he also knew he was no businessman. Henderson's Brewery languished while other breweries grew in dominance. The reason had to be down to his uncle's mismanagement of the debts.

Titmus entered with a basket of short logs and placed it by the fire, taking the empty basket out with him when he left. The door opened again and Dr Maynard, apparently the best doctor in Wakefield, or so his aunt told him, walked in carrying his black bag.

Barney stood and moved next to his mother. 'Well?'

Dr Maynard took off his glasses and rubbed his eyes. 'It is not good news, I am afraid to say. Mr Henderson is terribly weak. The stroke has rendered his body useless. We do not yet know of his mind. Should he make it through the night, we might have some hope, but my advice is to prepare for the worst. I am awfully sorry.'

Aunt Gertrude cried into her handkerchief while Barney patted her shoulder. 'I shall go and sit with him,' she murmured, stemming her tears.

'I am willing to stay the night, if you wish it?' Dr Maynard replaced his glasses in a tired gesture.

Instantly, Aunt Gertrude became the diligent mistress. 'Indeed, of course. I insist you must, Doctor. It is so late and, well... my husband might need you...' Her chin wobbled. 'Barney, please show the doctor up to the rose bedroom. It is all prepared.'

'Certainly, Mama.' Barney indicated for the doctor to follow him out of the room.

Aunt Gertrude rose unsteadily from the chair and Christian quickly put his hand under her elbow. 'You must rest, Aunt.'

'I shall, later. But now I want to sit with Royce. Just the two of us.' She smiled sadly at him. 'Your luggage is in the green bedroom, your usual room.'

'Thank you.'

'No, thank you for coming north so quickly on receiving my telegram. You must have forgone all that you were doing and boarded the first train out of London?'

'Yes, I had just returned from Oxford where I had been visiting a friend. Mother told me the telegram had arrived only minutes before I did.'

'I shall ask about your mother and sister tomorrow, but before we go up, I just want to say that your uncle admired you very much.' She gripped Christian's hand. 'You were the son he wished he'd had. Barney failed him in so many ways.'

'The respect goes both ways, Aunt. My uncle is all I have of my father's family. His stories of my father have sustained my image of him.'

'I hope you get to hear those stories again.' Her voice wobbled.

'I shall stay with you for as long as you need me.'

'The brewery,' she glanced at the door, 'it is not doing well.'

'No.'

'That is my father's fault. Papa left the business to me with so much debt, I am ashamed to say. I believe Papa thought I would sell it, but Royce insisted he could make a go of it, keep it in the family.' She shrugged helplessly. 'He changed the name to Henderson's and believed it would be the start of a brewing empire. Royce has done his best, but he was never a true business-man, not like his brother and you. Barney is even worse.' A look of sadness came into her eyes.

'Leave the problems of the brewery to me.' Christian was

loath to see her upset. She was the nearest person to a mother he knew. She was kind and gentle, the exact opposite to his own mother. His times spent here at Meadow View House in his school holidays were the best of his life. With his uncle and aunt, he'd been shown love, something his own mother had failed at.

'I would hate to sell the brewery. Papa began the business when I was a child. However, I do understand that it is only a business, a business that caused my darling Royce nothing but concern and anguish.'

'Aunt, it may be beyond salvaging.' He was worried the blow might be too much for her on top of his uncle's ill health.

'Indeed, but you will study the books and see what can be done?'

'Of course, but it may be too late.'

'Another potential loss.' Tears ran down her lined face. 'How will I bear any of this?'

'With strength and I shall be by your side.' He held her hands in his.

She reached up and kissed his cheek. 'You are dear to me. Like a son. Better than that because you *chose* to be here, to give me, us, your time and devotion. I can ask for no more than that. Thank you, my dear boy.'

Left alone, Christian poured another brandy. Despite his tiredness, his brain started working furiously. The brewery needed to be saved for his aunt, but he also needed the challenge to prove that he could do it. Christian's late stepfather Geoffrey Burton's moderate wealth was now his own. Yet he had to show everyone that he could be an excellent financier, unlike his uncle, but definitely like his father, Jonathan, had been before his premature death, when Christian was only a baby. Since university he'd been investing in deals, buying shares, learning all he could about how to be successful in business, just as his father had been.

He knew his friends thought him to be well set up now his stepfather had died and left him his modest fortune, but Christian wanted to demonstrate his own abilities in not only making his own income, but in pitting his intelligence against a problem that needed solving, such as the brewery haemorrhaging money. He wanted to show his mother, especially, that he was the replica of his father, the man she quickly forgot about after his death, for within five weeks of his burial she had married Geoffrey.

Besides, he had no wish to return to London just yet. Waiting for him down south were his uncaring mother's suffocating ways, Susan, his sharp-tongued half-sister, and Ruth Crawford, who expected his constant attendance and for him to propose imminently.

Time in the north was exactly what he needed.

4

Dipping the cloth into the warm soapy water, Meg squeezed it out and then wiped her mam's arms. Outside, rain lashed the windows, preventing Meg from meeting Lorrie and Fliss for a walk into town.

'Enough, Meg, please.' Mam winced.

Gently, Meg helped her mam to don her nightgown and then wrapped her cream knitted shawl about her shoulders. She plumped the flat pillows behind Mam's back, making a mental note that she needed to buy a bag of feathers to fill them more, and then straightened the blankets. 'Comfy?'

Mam nodded slightly, as though even that movement was too much. 'Go see to the others. I'll sleep for a bit.'

'I'll bring you up a cup of tea soon.'

'I'm not thirsty.'

Taking the soiled nightgown and sheets, Meg left the bedroom and took them straight to the washing tub in the kitchen.

Susie had poured hot water into the tub ready for the sheets to soak. 'Is our mam all right?'

'Yes,' Meg lied. How could she tell her that Mam was not able to manage climbing from the bed to get to the pot? That she was so weak she soiled herself and her shame sent her mood spiralling downwards? 'Put another kettle on to boil.'

'For tea this time?' Susie asked hopefully.

'No. I need to get these sheets washed and dry as quick as I can.' Meg sat on a chair by the table and bowed her head, exhausted. Mam's health had deteriorated over the last week. A cold on her chest had quickly turned to pneumonia. They had banned Nicky from going into their parents' bedroom and seeing Mam. Meg couldn't risk him catching it. He wasn't strong enough to fight such an infection.

'Where are the others?' Meg asked Susie.

'Mabel is at work. Doing an extra shift, she told me, to cover for someone who is ill. Betsy and Nell are next door. Mrs Fogarty asked them to help her unravel some old woollen clothes she got off the market. Nicky is still in bed drawing, though he says he's nearly out of charcoal and paper.'

'I've no money to buy him more.' Meg listened to the little clock on the mantel chime eight times. The rent man would be here by ten o'clock. She had two hours to find the rent money. How was she to do it?

Susie moaned loudly and held the empty tea caddy upside down. 'There's none left.'

Meg stood. 'I forgot to ask Betsy to run to the grocer's and buy some more.' She went to the tin on the mantel and opened the lid. The few halfpenny coins in the bottom wouldn't buy them much and she wasn't getting paid for another three days. They had nothing left to pawn, either, except the clock and she was loath to part with it.

'When is Father home?' Susie asked.

'Who knows?' Meg snapped, angry that her father had not

been home for a month. How did he think they were surviving on her and Mabel's meagre wages?

She threw her shawl around her shoulders and put the last few coins in a small leather drawstring pouch. 'I'll go and buy us a twist of tea. Look after Mam and Nicky.'

In the pouring rain, head down, Meg ran down the street, the cobbles slippery beneath her feet. Along Thornes Lane Wharf, boats plied the river or were moored at the docks offloading cargo. The rain hitting the buildings drowned out the shouts of men and whistles. Dock cranes were silhouetted against the grey sky and horses pulling wagons, their coats drenched, passed by, looking as dejected as Meg felt.

She slowed to a walk, not having the energy to run for long. She'd not eaten breakfast, giving what food they had to the others. The thought of food made her stomach rumble at its emptiness. She knew she wasn't the only person on the waterfront to be hungry, to be miserable and anxious about money, but that didn't give her any comfort. She had to find a way to lift her family out of the despair of poverty. But how?

At the front of the Bay Horse, she suddenly had an idea and went around to the back entrance, crossed the muddy yard and went into the kitchen. Don was cooking a stew and the tasty smell made Meg reel with hunger.

'What you doing here?' Don asked, tossing handfuls of barley into the large pot.

'Is Fliss here?'

'Nay, she's gone shopping with her aunt.'

'Terry?'

'He's gone to a meeting with one of the breweries. Why?'

'I just needed to speak to them.' She averted her gaze from the food.

'Are you wanting more time off? Terry won't like it. You had three days off last week.'

'Mam's sick.'

'Aye, and you've other family who can look after her. You need to work to earn.' He waved his wooden spoon at her.

Meg glared at him. 'I don't need you telling me what I need to do or not do, Don!'

'Please yourself, but you'll lose your position here if you don't turn up. There's plenty looking for work, you know.'

'Oh, shut up!' Meg stomped from the kitchen back out into the rain. Don was right, of course he was, but she didn't need reminding she could lose her job. She hurried down the wharf towards the ferry. Luckily, Harry was on her side of the river.

'Harry, have you heard if my father is returning soon? Has anyone seen him further along the river?'

'Nay, lass, not to my knowledge. He's been gone a good long time, hasn't he?'

'Yes.' A spark of worry that something might have happened to the boat or one of her brothers wormed into her head. 'If you see him, tell him to come home straight away, will you?' She held her skirts up and sprinted along to Mark Lane, hoping to stop in at Peters' grocery shop, which took credit.

Inside the shop, she shivered with cold while waiting to be served. The two women in front took their time in buying their goods, filling their baskets with an assortment of food that Meg wished she was taking home.

Finally, it was her turn and Mr Peters gave her a smile. 'Now, Meg, how are you?'

'Wet and cold, Mr Peters.'

'Indeed. Nasty out there. It is meant to be spring. What can I get for you?'

Thankful that the shop was empty, Meg lowered her voice in shame. 'I need a twist of tea, Mr Peters. On credit?'

'Let me see what's against your name.' He took out his little book from under the counters and flipped a few pages. 'You've one and six against your name, lass.'

'I know, and I'll pay as soon as my father returns. All I've got to my name are three halfpennies and I need to give those to the rent man, even though I'm still short. It might be enough for him to give me another week's grace.'

'Aye, giving the rent man something is better than nothing. Your father not home?' the older man inquired, taking a piece of paper and laying it on the scales.

'No. I'm beginning to worry.'

'Let's hope he is soon, lass.' Mr Peters scooped up a small amount of tea leaves and placed it gently on the paper. He checked the weight and, with a shrug, he tipped the rest of the scoop into the paper and then expertly twisted the paper to hold the tea leaves inside.

'How is your mam?' he asked, handing the twist of paper to Meg.

'Not good.' She watched him write the sum in the book. 'Thank you for your kindness, Mr Peters.' Hunger and cold and despair crowded in on her. Tears burned hot behind her eyes.

'Pay me when your father is home.' His kind smile nearly brought her undone.

'I'll come straight away. Father gets annoyed with me when I tell him we've got credit. I try not to do it, but he's been away so long...' Humiliation at having credit and knowing how angry her father would be when he found out made her tremble.

'Go home and dry off, lass.'

She gave him a watery smile and dashed out of the shop. The

rain had eased to a drizzle, not that it mattered, for she was soaked, her wet shawl heavy on her shoulders.

A boat's horn sounded and, with the rain lifting, dock men worked quicker to get their work done before the next downpour. The cobbles glistened, and the swollen, polluted river was a muted grey colour reflecting the low clouds above.

Walking along the crowded wharf, the smell of damp added to that of fresh horse dung. Wagons rolled by and cranes swung cargo nets from boats onto the docks for the scurrying men to unhook and offload.

Normally, Meg enjoyed walking along past the warehouses, peeking in to see what assortment of goods they piled inside, but not today.

The worries of not having the rent money and food weighed heavy on her mind and she took no notice of the crates of tea and tobacco, the chests stamped with names of foreign countries. Cargo came from the canals which began in the London docks, bringing north exotic liquors such as French brandy and red wine from France or imported tobacco from the West Indies and bolts of silk from China. Normally, she was intrigued by the strange smells of spices and the cheeky shouts of the dockers working, but not today.

She walked past the large iron gates of the mill where Mabel worked and hesitated. Could she ask the gaffer for Mabel's wages in advance? Would they allow that?

Before she had a chance to go inside the gates, a party of men came out of a maltings building next door. Meg's heart raced at seeing the tall man from the pub the other night. Christian Henderson.

He stood with three other men and shook their hands in turn. Farewells were said then he turned and strode towards where Meg stood.

For a moment he paused, then his eyes widened in what seemed to be fear. Suddenly, he shouted at her.

Shocked, Meg had no time to react before he lunged for her and pulled her with him to the side. They fell to the ground as crates crashed and smashed only a yard from where they lay. Shouts and yells filled the air. Men ran towards them. Horses neighed and jibbed in their harnesses. A whistle blew loud, several times.

'Are you hurt?' Christian Henderson asked her, his head close, his body half covering hers. His blue eyes gazed into hers. His face only inches away.

Shaken by the near miss or by his closeness, Meg didn't know which, she tried to gather her thoughts. Men gathered around them, offering help, to fetch a doctor, to take her into the warehouse office.

'Meg, are you all right, lass?' one man, a regular at the pub, asked.

She nodded, unable to speak from the shock.

Christian Henderson slowly stood and helped her to her feet, keeping his hand under her elbow. 'Are you sure you are not hurt?'

Meg stared into his blue eyes, her heart thumping in her chest. 'I'm all right.'

'You saved her life, sir.' Another man pumped Mr Henderson's hand. Another slapped him on the back.

'The net broke.'

'I heard it crack.'

'She'd have been squashed like a fly, for sure.'

'He's a hero.'

'What luck!'

'That net should have been checked.'

'Was it carrying too much weight?'

The voices whirled around Meg's head, making her dizzy. The filthy tang of the contaminated river was suddenly unexpectedly overpowering.

'Miss?' Christian Henderson's face swam before hers. 'She needs to sit down,' he said to the men hovering about them.

'Take her into the office. Mr Carstairs won't mind,' someone said. 'Make her a cup of tea.'

Tea.

Meg jerked forward. She no longer had her twist of tea, or her leather pouch. Panic filled her. Three single halfpennies was all she had to her name. She was going to offer it to the rent man.

'Where is it?' She searched amongst the broken crates.

'What are you looking for?' Mr Henderson took her elbow again.

She shrugged her arm from him. 'My money. The tea.' Then she saw it. The twist of tea lying on the wet cobbles, trodden on and soaking. Ruined.

Misery made Meg cry out. She picked it up, knowing the tea was wet, but maybe she could still use it. She searched again for the little leather pouch.

'Miss, can I help you?' Mr Henderson came to her side.

'I've lost my money.' She felt sick to the stomach.

'I'll help you search for it, but we are in the men's way. They want to clean up the mess.'

'I don't care. I need those coins!' Head pounding in anguish, she tossed aside pieces of crates, their broken contents of tins of molasses creating a pool of sticky black mess over the cobbles. The sweet stench of it made Meg gag. Her skirt swished over the molasses, coating the hem.

'Meg, lass, you need to move out of the way,' Simon, another pub regular, told her.

'My money, Simon.' She kept seeking beneath the crates for the pouch.

'If we find it, I'll have it taken to your house, lass. Go and get cleaned up.' As he spoke, the rain fell hard once more.

Defeated, Meg stood on the wharf, molasses sticking to her skirt, her wet shawl slipping off her shoulders, her hair soaked and dripping from the plait. Why of all people did this have to happen to her? Didn't she have enough to concern her?

'May I walk you home?' Christian Henderson asked. 'You seem a little shaken.'

Ashamed of the state she was in, Meg shook her head. 'Thank you for pulling me out of harm's way. You probably saved my life.' The thought hit her with a shock. Her hands shook and she didn't know if it was from the near miss or the man standing in front of her looking concerned.

'You are welcome.' His light blue eyes, the colour of cornflowers in the summer fields, were warm when he smiled. He held out his hand. 'Christian Henderson.'

She took his hand, feeling the strength from his hold, then quickly dropped it. 'Meg Taylor.' Her chest tightened at his smile.

'I have seen you before.'

'Yes. I work at the Bay Horse.' Despite the rain pounding their heads, Meg didn't want to be the first one to walk away. It wasn't every day a handsome gentleman saved her life.

'Ah, the other night.' Rain dripped off his top hat which he'd retrieved from the cobbles.

'I heard your uncle is unwell.' She was anxious to hear if the old man had recovered.

'Yes. He lingers. We are waiting for the inevitable.'

'I'm sorry.' Her hopes dashed, and feeling sorry for this charming gentleman, Meg wanted to take his hand again just to feel some comfort and to give it in return.

His gaze roamed her face for a long moment, then he bowed his head. 'Good day, Miss Taylor.'

'Thank you again, Mr Henderson.' Meg stepped past him, wanting to look back, but didn't. Christian Henderson had been on her mind too much since first seeing him in the pub, and now this. He'd held her, his body had been against hers and the sensation of his closeness still tingled.

The church bells struck. She counted them. Ten. Sweet Jesus. She needed to get home. The rent man would be knocking.

* * *

'How handsome is he, then?' Lorrie asked quietly, sitting in Meg's kitchen the following morning.

'Blooming gorgeous,' Fliss answered. 'No one is talking about anything else. The pub was full of talk about the accident last night.'

'I'm glad I wasn't there then,' Meg said. The unexpected visit of both Fliss and Lorrie arriving after Sunday church service put her on the back foot. She had no tea or food to offer them and the shame of it was mortifying.

Just as the conversation with the demanding rent man had been yesterday, until Mrs Fogarty heard them and came out to tell the man to bugger off and that if he didn't start fixing the state of the terraces, they'd all not pay another penny. The man had made a run for it when more neighbours came out to shout at him.

All that on top of Mr Henderson's heroic act had given her much to think about as she lay in bed that night. She'd replayed the accident in her head repeatedly. Remembering every word and every look that passed between them. Christian Henderson consumed her thoughts and she had to stop it.

Now, though, she smiled at Lorrie and Fliss and wondered

why they were still her friends when she had nothing to offer them but woes. Mabel had taken the children to Sunday school and Mam was asleep upstairs, so Meg could sit and pretend that she wasn't in the worst circumstances of her life.

'How's your mam doing?' Fliss asked.

'Not well.' Meg rose as a knock sounded on the door. She opened it to find a young lad standing on the doorstep holding a large hamper basket. 'Yes?'

'Miss Meg Taylor?'

She frowned. 'Yes. Are you lost?'

'No. This is for you.' He thrust the hamper at her and with a cocky salute strolled away, whistling.

'What is it?' Lorrie asked, coming to help Meg carry it to the table.

'Who sent it?' Fliss clasped her hands together in excitement.

Carefully, Meg untied the leather straps and opened the lid. Inside lay an array of food parcels. 'Goodness. That lad has come to the wrong house.' She made to go to the door to call him back when Lorrie lifted out a piece of paper.

'A note.'

'Read it,' Meg commanded. 'It's the wrong house, I'm telling you.'

Lorrie scanned the note, then grinned. 'It's from Mr Christian Henderson.'

'No!' Meg couldn't believe it.

'It says, "Dear Miss Taylor. I trust you have recovered from your ordeal yesterday. This hamper is a token of my best wishes. Christian Henderson. P.S. I hope they returned your purse to you."'

'Oh, now, that is kind of him.' Fliss gazed at the assortment of items in the hamper.

'What a true gentleman,' Lorrie commented, passing the note to Meg.

'Such a gift...' Amazed, Meg took out a fruit cake, a loaf of white bread, *white*, not the days-old coarse-grained hard loaf that was all she could afford, a hock of cooked ham, a jar of pickles, a bag of apples, a *two-pound* weight bag of tea, the same of sugar and, lastly, a box of miniature sugared fruits.

'This is too much.' Meg couldn't believe what she was looking at. Never had such wonders been on her kitchen table. The sweetest treat she'd ever had was sugar mice at Christmas, but a box of sugared fruits? It was something she and her siblings looked at through shop windows.

The present was overwhelming. True, a basket of vegetables and meat would have been more useful than sugar fruits, she could live without those; even so, the thought was deeply endearing and she was immensely grateful. She could make this food stretch for days. They'd have the ham and pickles tonight and an apple each for breakfast in the morning.

'You will have to send a thank you note in return,' Lorrie said.

Meg rubbed a hand over her face. 'I don't own nice paper, or a proper pen. I've a stub of a pencil and Nicky's charcoal sticks.'

'I have plenty,' Lorrie assured her. 'I'll go home and get it for you.'

'I can't let you do that.'

'Go and thank him in person then,' Fliss suggested.

'No!' Meg barked. 'That would be too embarrassing for us both.'

'I'll be back with paper and pen.' Lorrie grabbed her reticule and coat and left the house.

'She is a good person,' Fliss said, helping Meg put away the bounty.

Meg put the kettle on to boil. 'At least now I can offer you a cup of tea.'

Fliss put her hand over Meg's. 'I didn't realise it was so terribly bad for you.'

'We're behind on the rent. I went to the pub yesterday to look for you, to ask to borrow some money until Father returns.'

'You know I'd give you whatever I had. I've a few shillings. They're yours.'

Meg smiled miserably. 'A few shillings aren't enough, but thanks. If Father isn't home by the time rent day comes around again, I'll take you up on it.' Though it shamed her to do so. The kindness of Fliss, Lorrie and now Mr Henderson overwhelmed her. She wasn't used to such compassion. She wished she'd had friends years ago, just to help shed some of the loneliness of struggling to do it all by herself, but she'd been too busy to have friends. Caring for her mother and looking after her family didn't afford her time to spend with friends.

'Save your tea. I'd best go, Aunt insists on me being home on Sunday afternoons, as if I'm off gallivanting every day. I never leave the pub unless I'm here or at Lorrie's,' tutted Fliss, donning her cloak. 'See you tomorrow night for your shift.'

When Fliss had gone, Meg made the tea and carried it upstairs to her mam with a slice of fruit cake.

'Where did you get that?' Mam asked, struggling to sit up against the pillows.

'Mr Christian Henderson, old Mr Henderson's nephew, sent it.'

'Why?'

'Because he saved me from being squashed by falling cargo on the wharf yesterday.'

'Why didn't you tell me?' Mam coughed weakly.

'I didn't want to worry you. I'm fine.'

'That's kind of him to send a cake.'

'He sent a whole hamper of things. The hamper itself is worth a bit. It'll come in useful.' She thought she could perhaps pawn it for the rent money.

'Mr Henderson's nephew,' Mam mused, sipping her tea. 'I didn't know old Mr Henderson even had a nephew.'

'Old Mr Henderson is on his deathbed, apparently.'

'That's sad.' Mam closed her eyes. 'Sugar in tea. Such a treat, and cake. It's been so long since I had fruit cake.'

'Enjoy it. I'd best go back down. Lorrie is coming with some nice paper, so I can write a thank you note to Mr Henderson.' Meg pulled a face. 'Though my writing is awful.'

'Take your time with it.' Mam smiled. 'You want to make a good impression.'

'Why?'

'Because he's obviously an agreeable gentleman to save you and then send a hamper. Having friends—'

'We aren't friends, Mam,' Meg cut in. 'Don't think it's more than it is. A kind gesture.'

'He's gone to some trouble, Meg, don't dismiss that.'

'I'll never see him again, Mam,' Meg chuckled. 'He's a stranger.'

'Then maybe you should find a way to make him less of a stranger.' Something in Mam's voice made Meg frown.

'What do you mean?'

'Think of the future, Meg. If you could marry a man from a good family, get away from Wellington Street, away from the whole waterfront, then you should grab the chance with both hands.'

Meg laughed. 'Me marry a gentleman?' Yet inside, for a tantalising moment, her heart somersaulted as Mr Henderson came to mind, before common sense reverted her thoughts back to her real life.

'He doesn't have to be a gentleman, just someone with excellent prospects. Please don't marry a man who can't pay his rent. Don't repeat my mistakes.' Her earnest tone made her cough again.

'You know about the rent?'

'Nothing is a secret in this house. One of the girls told me you had to beg the rent man to let us pay next week all that we owe.' Mam picked at the fruit cake. 'Your father has been gone a long time. He's obviously struggling for loads.' The worried expression her mam wore upset Meg.

'He'll be home soon, Mam.'

'I hope so.' But her mam's tone held little faith.

Downstairs, Meg let Lorrie back in and they sat at the table to compose the brief note.

'Heavens, my writing is like a child's scrawl,' Meg complained, peering at the uneven lines of writing. 'I can't send that.'

'Do you want me to write it?' Lorrie took a clean piece of paper. 'He'll never know.'

'No, he won't. Yes, you write it.' Meg watched Lorrie copy what she'd written.

'There, what do you think?'

Taking the paper from Lorrie, Meg read:

Dear Mr Henderson,

Thank you for your generous gift. It was very kind of you to send it.

You have my gratitude for your brave actions in saving me from a serious accident.

Best regards,

Meg Taylor

'Heavens, I sound like a toff.' Meg laughed.

'You sound respectable and respectful.'

'Should I put my full name?' she asked Lorrie. 'Margaret May Taylor.'

'That's a pretty name.' Lorrie smiled.

'Too pretty for Wellington Street, which is why I've always been called Meg.' She snorted.

The door opened and Meg stared in surprise as her father and brothers walked in. 'You're home!'

The dejected faces and slumped shoulders and barely a smile between them caused Meg to leave the table, heart thumping. 'What's happened?'

'Old Mr Henderson has died. We just heard the announcement as we docked,' Freddie told her.

'That's terrible news.' Meg's shoulders slumped.

'The brewery is closed for a week for mourning,' Arthur added.

'How's your mam?' Father asked.

'She's been ill, very ill for weeks, but she's a little better today.' Meg swallowed the panic their news brought. Surely her father had a plan to better their situation? It couldn't be down to only her. He needed to find more cargo.

'And who is this?' Father indicated to Lorrie.

'Lorrie Chambers, my friend.'

'From Chambers' boatyard?' Father asked. 'Ernie Chambers' daughter?'

'Yes. I'm pleased to meet you, Mr Taylor.' Lorrie gathered her things. 'I'll leave you to your family, Meg.'

'Thank you for the paper and everything.' Meg smiled.

When Lorrie had left, Meg made more tea while her father went upstairs to sit with Mam. Freddie cut two slices of fruit cake, one each for Arthur and himself.

'Where did you get this from?' he asked as Arthur went upstairs to see their mam.

'It's a long story,' Meg replied. 'I'll tell you later.'

'I thought Miss Chambers might have brought it.'

'No.' She thought of Christian Henderson as she cleared away the paper and pen, placing the note quickly in the envelope Lorrie had brought. He'd be grieving for his uncle. Should she still send the note? She bit her bottom lip. She didn't have the money to post the note. She'd have to walk to the Henderson house and deliver it in person. The Hendersons' home, Meadow View House, was on Barnsley Road, near Sandal Common, a mile away. She'd often walk past the house in the summer when taking the children to the ruins of Sandal Castle.

'Meg?'

Startled, she turned to Freddie. 'Sorry?'

'I asked how has it been here? We've been gone so long on this trip. I was worried about you all.' His direct stare over the rim of his cup spoke more than his words.

'It's been terrible, if you want the truth. We're behind on the rent for starters.'

'Hell's fire,' Freddie muttered angrily and shook his head. 'We've had to travel as far as Sowerby Bridge to get loads. Now with old man Henderson's passing, we won't have his cargo.'

'You don't know that for sure.'

'With Barney in charge? He'll sell the brewery and likely the house as soon as he can. He has a worse head for business than his father did.' From his pocket, Freddie pulled out several coins. 'There's about ten shillings there. Use it for the rent.'

'How did you get that much?'

'While we were docked and waiting for loads, I'd work in the warehouses whenever I could.'

'Father has money, too?' Meg hated taking money from Freddie.

'He'll have some, but not much. He's just paid for Blossom's stall and feed. She needs reshoeing as well. Then there are the mooring costs while we are home.' He shrugged and wouldn't meet her eyes.

'Mabel and I don't earn enough to pay for the rent and food, clothes and fuel,' she complained. 'Father has to help.'

'Is that so?' Father snapped from the bottom of the stairs. 'Do you not think I don't know my own responsibilities, girl?'

Meg stiffened at his furious tone. She was also angry and scared. 'It's been difficult, Father.'

'Life is, girl.'

She hated it when he called her *girl* as though she didn't deserve a name. Meg raised her chin, a burning fury boiling inside. 'I have done my best.'

'And it's not been good enough, has it?'

'That's unfair, Father,' Freddie cut in.

'Then it's probably wise that we move to the boat,' Father declared. 'I've been thinking about it for a while.'

'Move to the boat?' She couldn't believe what he'd just said. 'There are ten of us. How can we fit?'

'I'll reduce the cargo space. Summer is coming. We'll moor up each night and the children can sleep outside on the bank under an awning.'

'But Mam and Nicky are not well enough to live on a boat. It's cramped and... and...' The more she thought of it, the more terrible it sounded. All ten of them living on the confined narrow-boat, which was dirty from years of carrying cargo, was ridiculous. Words escaped her.

'We'll give this place up, then we can save on rent,' Father said. 'Pour me some tea.'

'But Mabel has a job at the mill. Susie, too, in a few months. Betsy and Nell and Nicky need to go to school,' she argued. 'I have my shifts at the pub...'

'We can't afford to live here, so we'll live on the boat. We'll travel to Castleford and find work there.'

'Mam is too ill.' She couldn't put her mam through that. Besides, Meg knew she couldn't live with her father in such a confined space. They didn't get on.

He gave her a dismissive wave. 'She'll manage.'

'She won't. It'll kill her. Mam has never wanted to be on the boat. We've always lived in this house.'

'And now I'm saying we will be on the boat. It's the only way. That's my final word.'

'But if—'

'Will you shut up, girl! I said it's my *final* word!' Father shouted, silencing her.

A deep rage fuelled her movements as she grabbed the note she'd written and her mam's cloak from the nail by the door and stormed from the house.

Under a blue sky with pockets of flat grey clouds, Meg strode along the wharf, noticing her father's narrowboat where it was moored near Harry's ferry. She paused for a minute to stare at it. So many times, growing up, she'd clambered over the boat with Freddie. As a child, it had been a wonder, something that had taken her father away down the mystic canals she'd only ever heard tales of. The boat was her father's home, really, not the house in Wellington Street. Yet it could never be hers and the rest of the family's. It was too cramped. How would they live being so confined in such a small space? And the children sleeping on the bank under an awning? They'd catch their deaths in bad weather and Nicky would never survive it. She'd have more people to care for and no room to do it in. What was her father thinking? How long would Mam last living in such conditions?

No, the idea was impossible. She'd have to think of something else and convince her father that there had to be another way.

Harry gave her a salute, and she waved back, but she continued on, for she had no money to cross. Instead, she walked further along the wharf to where the river curved and was cut by a weir that sent water cascading down under the bridge.

Crossing the bridge, she noticed Lorrie's father working on a boat in his yard. From all that Lorrie had mentioned to her, Ernie Chambers was a considerate father, if a little remote, but at least he cared for his daughter, unlike Meg's father. Frank Taylor didn't care about any of them.

She kept walking, her steps slower now as her anger dissipated a little and was replaced by despair.

The road forked as she headed south, and Meg took the road to the right, Bridge Street. The clangs and bangs from the many mills, forges and malthouses competed with the cries of the gulls soaring above her head. An omnibus full of passengers trundled past, heading for the centre of town, and she watched it go by wistfully. She'd only been on the omnibus once, as a treat when she was younger with Mam. Since then, she'd walked into town and walked back again, lugging heavy baskets of shopping. How must it feel to have money to waste on an omnibus?

Crossing a smaller bridge over the canal, she continued on to Barnsley Road and the open fields, leaving the noise of industry behind. Dotted along the road were farms surrounded by fields, either ploughed or grassed with small herds of cows on them. Grander houses also dominated; Belle Vue House was a luxurious residence in the distance.

But it was the red-brick Meadow View House hidden amongst large trees that Meg aimed for, with its dozen chimneys and big sash windows on both floors. She knew it had a circular drive and black iron gates. Many times, when walking with the children, she'd peered through the trees at the manor.

Nearing the house, her steps faltered, as did her courage. What was she doing coming here when old Mr Henderson had just died? It was disrespectful to disturb them.

Still, she kept walking as though tied to a rope that was pulling her along. The large trees blocked out her view of the house, but suddenly a carriage came out of the gates and Meg jumped to the side of the road to get out of its way.

Before she lost all courage, she hurried through the gates and down the drive. In front of the stone portico, an older male servant was sweeping the steps. Black ribbon hung on the double doors.

He glanced up as Meg approached and frowned. 'Trades entrance is around the back.'

'I'm not here for a position.' She drew the envelope out of her sleeve.

'What do you want then?'

'To give this to Mr Henderson.'

The man tapped the black armband on his sleeve. 'Mr Henderson died this morning. Come back another time.'

'No, this is for Mr Christian Henderson. Can you give it to him for me, please?'

The man, obviously a butler or someone in a high-ranking position considering his neat and expensive-looking suit, scowled, his grey eyebrows meeting. 'Now is not the time to disturb the family. Show some respect.'

Meg closed her eyes for a moment and strove for patience. 'I am very respectful, sir. That is why I am asking you to deliver it to him at a convenient time.'

'Give it here then!' the butler snapped.

Meg took a step back. 'I trust you won't throw it in the fire?'

Suddenly, the old fellow grinned. 'I'm not a monster. Mr Christian is a kind gentleman. I'll see he gets it.'

'Thank you.' She gave him the envelope and headed back down the drive. She'd reached the gates before she heard her name called.

'Miss Taylor!' Christian jogged along the drive towards her, wearing a black suit and no coat or hat.

For some silly reason, Meg's chest tightened at the sight of him and a flicker of happiness that he wanted to speak to her fluttered in her stomach.

'I saw you from the window,' he said, stopping a few feet from her. 'This is a surprise.'

'I wanted to deliver a note. To thank you for the hamper.' She nodded to the envelope he held.

'There was no need.'

'There was. It was very kind of you. Most generous.' She could have added shocking and surprising and all the other words to describe her disbelief.

His cornflower-blue eyes softened. 'The accident has played on my mind. You could have been seriously injured or worse.'

She stared at him, wanting to really look at him. His eyes were incredible, such a vivid light blue, and his lips curved naturally, as though he smiled a lot. His dark hair needed a trim, and he had a strong, clean-shaven jaw. Christian Henderson made her skin tingle in awareness of his maleness and his good looks. It was a most bizarre feeling.

He returned her stare with a small smile playing around his mouth. 'You have no ill effects from the incident?'

She thought about the question. She'd slept well with no bad dreams of being crashed by falling cargo. 'No. I'm stronger than I look, Mr Henderson.'

He grinned, a rakish grin that sent a shiver of perception over her. 'I have no doubt about that, Miss Taylor.'

'I'm sorry about your uncle.' She was, in many ways. Mr Henderson's death had affected more than just the Henderson family.

His expression saddened. 'It is a blow. He was a good man.'

'What will happen to the brewery now?' Was she being rude to ask that question now?

'That is to be decided. There is much to be decided after the funeral.'

'Will you return to your home?' She didn't even know where that was, or if he had a wife and family waiting for him there. For some reason, she didn't want him to have a wife and family. That would mean he would be untouchable, which was silly, really, for she could never have such a man as him.

'I'll not be returning south for some time. My aunt needs me. Then there is the reading of the will. As I say, much to sort out.'

'I hope the brewery continues operating.'

'We shall have to wait and see.' He tilted his head at her. 'Why are you so interested?'

'My father has taken many loads of Henderson's ale over the years. He's been a loyal transporter for Mr Henderson. We'd hate to see that no longer happen.'

'Your father works on the railway?'

Her shoulders slumped. 'No, he has a narrowboat. Father and my brothers work the canals.'

'Ah...' His tone changed. 'I should have guessed the canals. My uncle transported very little by railway.'

Meg needed to fight for her father's business. 'That's why I'm interested. Father would like to continue working for Henderson's.'

'I cannot swear that things will remain the same.'

Meg's heart sank. 'The brewery might be sold?'

'It's a possibility, but even if we keep it in the family, many things need modernising. My uncle was not inclined to think of the future, or consider the new, modern ways and inventions.'

'But you will?' Hope flared.

'I will try to steer my cousin that way if I'm able, and one of those modern ways is to use railway transport.'

A wave of dread washed over her, dissolving the hope. 'But the canals are still useful.'

'Not really. They are slower, that is the first fact.'

'But to deny narrowboat men work by using the railways, you are creating hardship for their families.'

'Then those families need to reflect on their choices, their way of earning a living. I am not responsible for those men who work the canals, or for their families.' He had the grace to look apologetic. 'It is simply business, Miss Taylor.'

'No, Mr Henderson, it's not simply business. It's my life, my family's life. We survive or we don't by the work my father gets on the canal.' She fought her tears. She wasn't a crier, for that solved nothing, but right now, emotion clogged her throat. 'So, to me, it's very important that my father is able to fit into this new, modern world of yours. But I can see it is no concern of yours. Good day.' She turned and strode away, incredibly hurt by his words, which surprised her even more.

5

'Are you sure you're warm enough, Mam?' Meg fussed over her as she sat on a chair by the fire.

'I am.' Mam, pale but determined to be dressed and downstairs, sat straighter, chin up. 'If changes are happening in this family, then I want to be a part of it, not shut away upstairs, unable to have a say in what is decided.'

Meg glanced at her father. Having him and the boys home for a week was wearing thin on her patience, especially when Freddie was hardly ever at home to help her. She spoke to her father only when he asked a question. The fractured relationship caused the others to be silent and on their best behaviour.

She added a piece of coal to the small fire. 'When you get tired, Mam, I'll help you back upstairs.'

'Your father can do that,' Mam told her with a smile.

Again, Meg looked at her father where he sat on the sofa reading yesterday's newspaper. Frank Taylor, frustrated at the decline in work, stomped about the house, snapping at anyone who dared speak out of turn. He and Freddie had argued more in the last five days than she'd ever seen before. The children were glad to go to school each morning and Mabel worked extra shifts at the mill. Freddie was out every day and Arthur spent all his time at the stable with Blossom. That left Meg to face their father's bad moods.

'Make some tea, girl,' Father demanded without looking up.

'I need to buy some tea leaves.' And so much more, but Meg quailed at the thought of asking him for money. She'd fed them meals made from scraps of the cheapest meat from the butcher's and bought poor-quality vegetables that Mr Peters, the greengrocer, was about to throw out because they were turning bad just to make what little money she had from Freddie and her wage stretch to feed such a large family.

'She'll need money, Frank,' Mam suggested.

'Again?' He scowled.

'Food and fuel costs a lot, Father,' Meg tried to explain.

'Don't talk to me as though I'm stupid, girl.'

'I'm not.' Anger built again, the anger she'd fought to control all week. 'All I'm saying is that mine and Mabel's wages don't go far with this many people.'

Father threw the newspaper down and jerked to his feet. 'I give you money!'

'But not enough,' Meg snapped back, exhausted from the stress of keeping the family fed.

'I gave you money last week and what did you do?' Father fumed. 'You paid rent with it instead of buying food!'

'Yes, so we could have a roof over our heads,' she yelled back.

'Don't you dare raise your voice to me, girl!'

'Meg! My name is Meg or Margaret May but not girl!'

He slapped her cheek hard. The force of it made her head snap back. She stumbled a step.

'Frank! No!' Mam cried in shock.

'She's got to learn she can't speak to me like that. I'm her father. She'll show respect.'

'Respect has to be earned,' Mam replied sadly. 'Meg sees to us all, keeps this family together. Hitting her isn't right, Frank.'

'And what do *I* do?' he sneered. 'I work bloody hard, too, going from one end of the county to the other, begging for any load I can get.'

Ignoring the burning sensation on her cheek, Meg grabbed her shawl. She had to get out of this house. Away from *him*. 'I'll see if there are more shifts at the pub.'

The door opened and Freddie walked in, grinning. 'I've got work.' His expression fell as he noticed the serious faces. 'What's happened?'

'What do you mean, you've got work?' Father glared. 'We could have a load to take in the morning. I'm off to the docks now to see what I can contract.'

'Aye, and every day for a week, there's not been any loads.' Freddie shrugged, not looking at his father. 'I got work at Henderson's Brewery. I just happen to walk in there this morning and was speaking to Mr Pepper, and he mentioned that one of the warehouse lads broke his leg yesterday, messing about near a mineshaft. I said I'd do a few shifts to fill in until we get a load or I might stay working there. I'll see how it goes.'

'*See how it goes*?' Father's hands balled into fists.

'Who is Mr Pepper?' Mam asked, her face worried.

'Henderson's foreman.'

'Well, you can tell Pepper you can't take the shifts.' Father reached for his cap. 'I need you to be ready to go at a moment's notice. I'm off down the docks.'

'I'll not tell Pepper that at all,' Freddie said, his grey eyes hard like granite. 'He was decent enough to hire me and I'll not let him down.'

'What about letting *me* down?' Father barked, jamming his cap on his head.

'You're not even sure you'll get a load today or tomorrow or next week,' Freddie argued. 'And if you do, Arthur can go with you. I'm done working on the boat.'

'You're done?' Father looked ready to explode. 'You're done, boy, when I say you're done.'

Freddie squared his shoulders. His expression was one of loathing. 'I'm a man, nineteen next week. I'll do as I please.'

'Will you now?' Father advanced on him.

'You're going to take me on?' Freddie taunted.

'Stop! Stop!' Mam cried, then coughed before crying great, chest-heaving sobs. 'No more.'

Meg rushed to her and knelt by her side. 'Shush. Take a breath.'

The look on Father's face was scathing. 'See what you've done. You've upset your mam. Now, listen to me. We work on the *canal*, not in a *warehouse*.'

'Work is work and money is money. This family needs money.' Freddie, taller than his father, stood his ground. 'I'll earn it for them.'

Red in the face, Father's nostrils flared. 'You'll not last a day being ordered about by others.'

Freddie's lips curled in contempt. 'I'm ordered about by you, so there's not much difference, except this way I'll get paid properly. So, we'll see, shall we?'

'Don't come whining to me when it all goes sour and you crave the canal life again,' their father spat and left the house, slamming the door behind him.

'Don't be angry at him,' Mam soothed, wiping her eyes. 'He's finding it difficult not being in constant work. He's not used to it, and he's worried.'

Meg stood with her shawl gripped in her hands. She would never forgive her father for hitting her. His condemnation of Freddie getting work just showed his own selfishness. Whatever feelings she had for the man who sired her disintegrated into dust. 'I will not live on the boat. I'll tell you that now, Mam.'

'I'm hoping it won't come to that,' Mam said quietly.

'That's why I've been looking for work.' Freddie flung himself down on the old sofa and it squeaked in protest. 'We all can't live on the boat. There's not enough room. But happen with my wage to add to Meg's and Mabel's we can afford to stay here.'

'Your father needs you to help him,' Mam murmured. 'You're a canal boatman.'

'I'm whatever I need to be, Mam, and right now I need to be here. *He'll* cope without me.' Freddie picked up the newspaper and opened it, but Meg noticed his hands shook a little and the confrontation with Father had affected him.

'Susie will be at the mill soon,' Mam said. 'That will help.'

'Her wage will be small, Mam. She's a young girl with no experience.' Meg wrapped her shawl about her shoulders. 'If Terry won't give me more shifts, I'll ask at other pubs, or get another position during the day somewhere.'

Mam sighed heavily, her back bowed. 'Don't feel too badly against your father, Meg. He's upset.'

Meg knotted the ends of her shawl at her chest. She couldn't look at her mam, for she might say something she later regretted. 'Freddie, there's a fish pie in the oven for when the others get in. Bread and dripping for supper.'

'Your shift doesn't start yet,' Mam protested weakly.

Without replying, Meg opened the door and walked out.

Mrs Fogarty was opening her front door, only a yard away from Meg. 'You all right, Meg? I heard shouting.'

'Fine, Mrs Fogarty.' She swallowed back any emotion.

'Your father still home?'

Meg nodded, feeling wretched. 'I wish he was gone. Life is hard when he's on the canal but it's so much worse when he's home. I'm nothing but a slave in his eyes...'

'Bless your heart, lass. You're a dutiful daughter and sister. Everyone knows it.' Mrs Fogarty put her arm about Meg's shoulders. 'How's your mam?'

'She's downstairs, only because *he's* home and she's trying to be strong for *him*.'

'Well, that's an improvement, isn't it? Lucy likes to be downstairs when your father's home. She might have a spell of good health.'

Meg couldn't trust herself to comment on that. *Mam was at death's door two weeks ago yet as soon as Father turns up, she's forcing herself downstairs and pretending everything is fine.* Meg would have to deal with her once again when he'd got a load and was off once more. 'I'd best get on.'

'Aye, lass. I'll pop in and have a cup of tea with Lucy, shall I? Take her mind off things.'

With a wave, Meg hurried up the cobbled street, passing young children playing in the gutter despite the chill.

A sharp, stiff wind blew across the river as Meg walked up Thornes Lane Wharf, bringing with it the harsh smells of industry and pollution.

In her head, she replayed the scene of the slap she had received, felt the sting all over again. She'd stood up to her father, not that it had done any good. He didn't care about her. His precious narrowboat was all that concerned him. Let him stay on his boat. He could rot on it for all she cared. It was time she started to live for herself. She needed a better job, more money. Now Mam was getting out of bed more, Meg didn't have to fetch and carry for her as much. Perhaps Mam would begin doing a few things about the house, cook the odd meal? It would free up Meg's time, which she could use in a position elsewhere, working every day, unlike the three or four shifts she got now.

At the Bay Horse, she let herself in through the kitchen and was relieved to see Terry sitting at the table eating.

He glanced at the clock on the wall. 'You're early. I didn't agree with you starting at this time.'

'I'm not here to work. I wanted to talk to you.'

Dipping his thick chunk of bread into the big bowl of stew before him, he grunted. 'What now?'

'I'd like more shifts, or longer shifts? I can come in earlier every day. Please.'

Terry snorted. 'Your father has no work, has he?'

'Not at the moment.'

'I heard. It's tough times for boatmen.' He chewed thoughtfully. 'And what of your mam? She's bedridden. Won't she need you like she's always done?'

'My sisters will have to do more.'

'Sorry, lass, there's no more work for you here, only the nights you already do.'

Meg kept the disappointment from her face. 'I thought to ask, that was all.'

'And you've the answer.' Terry ate a spoonful of stew.

'I'll be back at six.' She closed the door behind her and walked across the yard to the alleyway.

Fliss was coming through the gate with her aunt, both carrying baskets of shopping. 'Meg.'

'I'll be back at six.' Meg nodded to them both and kept going, not wanting to stop and chat.

'Meg!' Fliss caught up with her out the front of the pub. 'Is something the matter?'

Although desperate to confide in Fliss, Meg knew that

complaining about her family or her father slapping her wouldn't do any good. Dwelling on her misfortunes wouldn't change the fact she had to find a better-paying job and the sooner she did, the better. 'I'm in a hurry, Fliss. I'll talk to you tonight.'

'I'm not in the bar tonight. My aunt wants me to accompany her to a church meeting to begin the Easter preparations.' Fliss rolled her eyes. 'I'd rather be behind the bar.'

'Maybe we can go and see Lorrie tomorrow?' Meg suggested. The less time she spent in the house with her father, the better.

'Yes, let's do that. I'll knock for you at ten?'

Meg squeezed Fliss' hand. 'See you then.'

Meg walked for an hour along the roads and lanes surrounding the waterfront. At times she stopped at different shops and asked if there were any positions available, only to be told no each time.

She passed the busy wharves, the cranes moving cargo, passed the corn mills and malthouses, all who used the railway to carry their goods. Her father was fighting a losing battle. Should he sell the boat and get work elsewhere? As soon as the thought came into her head, she knew he never would give up working the canals. It was his life, the only one he'd ever known. But it wasn't hers.

Hearing the factory whistles, she turned and hurried back to the Bay Horse, finding it already full and Terry red-faced from serving thirsty customers.

'Where have you been?' he demanded, passing frothing tankards of ale to two men.

She looked at the clock. 'I've got another half an hour before I start.'

'Not any more you don't. I'm run off me feet.'

'Where is everyone?'

'Hilda and Fliss are at a church meeting and Gerald is God knows where, but never here!'

'And Kel?' She spoke of the older man who had a club foot and did odd jobs around the pub.

'He's in the cellar sorting out the barrels.'

'I've not seen it this busy in ages,' Meg commented, pouring jugs of ale from the tapped barrel behind the counter.

'There's been a meeting of sorts at one of the warehouses.' Terry wiped a cloth over his red, sweaty forehead. 'The foundry workers are wanting to go on strike for better conditions and wages. They've come in here afterwards looking to garner support from the other industries.'

'A strike?'

'I hope it doesn't happen 'cos striking men don't drink much, but they drink a lot while they are talking about it.' He grinned. 'They've eaten everything Don's made. So, there's no food for the rest of the night if anyone asks. Don's gone home. He refused to make any more food. Useless man. I don't know why I keep him on.'

The first couple of hours passed quickly. Meg didn't stop serving or cleaning up and was grateful when Fliss gave a hand after returning from the church meeting.

'How did it go?' Meg asked.

'Boring as usual.' Fliss filled a tray of dirty tankards to take into the kitchen to wash. 'Aunt has me volunteering for all sorts of task. I've got to make twenty paper angels and help set up the refreshment stall for the Easter parade. Oh, and she's trying to matchmake me with one of the churchwardens, Herbert Greene.'

'Herbert Greene? I know him. We went to Sunday school together. He used to sneeze a lot.' Meg laughed, which surprised her, as earlier she'd felt like never laughing again.

'He still does!' Fliss snickered, picking up another tray. 'He sneezes a lot the more nervous he gets. This evening, Aunt pushed us together to collect the prayer books and he could barely finish a sentence without erupting into a fit of sneezing.'

Meg chuckled, but noticed the door opening, and Freddie dashed in, his face pale. 'Freddie!'

'It's Mam. She's had a bad turn. You've got to come,' he panted.

Meg turned to Terry, who was wheeling in another barrel. 'Mam's had a bad turn.' Fear clutched her chest.

'I'll stay behind the bar,' Fliss quickly added.

Terry sighed. 'Go on then.'

Freddie grasped her hand, and they raced from the pub without waiting for Meg to get her shawl.

'How bad is it?' Meg held her skirts up with one hand as they raced over the slippery cobbles.

'Mabel is with her. I've been for the doctor. He's on his way,' Freddie told her as they turned the corner on to Wellington Street.

'Where's Father?'

Freddie pushed open their front door. 'Gone. He got a load this afternoon and sent Arthur back to tell us.'

'Is that what gave Mam the turn?' Meg asked, taking the stairs in a rush.

At the bedroom door, Freddie held Meg back. 'It was that and also Mam got a letter in the last post.'

'A letter? Mam never gets letters.' Shock widened her eyes. A letter?

'I didn't get a chance to see who it's from. Mam read it and then collapsed. I carried her upstairs, then went for the doctor and you.'

Quietly, Meg entered the bedroom. A candle stub flickered on the drawers, casting dancing shadows. Mabel sat on the chair beside the bed, holding Mam's hand.

Going closer, Meg steeled herself. 'Is she...'

Mabel shook her head, tears slipping down her cheeks. 'She's alive, but so weak.'

'Where are the others?'

'In bed.' Mabel made way for Meg to sit on the chair.

For a long moment, Meg gazed at the waxy-skinned appearance of her mam's beautiful face. Shadows bruised under her closed eyes. Her thin chest hardly moved. Gently, Meg brushed her hair from her forehead. She was cool to the touch. 'Rest, Mam. Everything is going to be all right.'

Freddie left the room and returned with the letter. He gave it to Meg to read.

In the dim light, she quickly scanned the text. 'It's from a Mr Moffatt, a solicitor. He writes that Winston Mellor and Margaret May Mellor passed away from fever on 15 March.'

'Who are they?' Mabel asked.

'Our grandparents,' Meg whispered, glancing at Mam, who hadn't moved. 'Mam must have been so upset to read that.'

'She was.' Freddie nodded sadly. 'She cried out and then collapsed.'

Meg continued to read. 'Our grandparents have been buried and their wills and personal effects are to be divided at the reading of the will, the date of which will be decided upon when the reply to this letter from the deceased's daughter Lucy May Taylor, née Mellor, is received by Mr Moffatt.'

Mam moaned softly.

Meg thrust the letter aside and gripped Mam's hand. 'Lie still. Just rest. The doctor is on his way.' For a second, Meg worried how she was to pay the doctor, but pushed that to the back of her mind.

Mam's eyes opened and stared at the ceiling before lowering them to Meg. 'The letter...'

'Yes, I know. I've read it.'

'It's true?' Tears slipped out of the corner of Mam's eyes to run into her hair.

'I'm sorry, Mam.'

'Bury me with them.'

'What?' Meg reared back. 'No!' The hand she held went limp. 'Mam!' She jumped up and pulled her mam up off the pillows and shook her. 'Mam!'

Mabel screamed.

'Jesus, no,' Freddie swore and buried his head in his hands.

'No, Mam. Hold on, please!' Meg cradled her against her chest. 'Oh, Mam, no, don't leave me.'

Mind blank with shock, Meg tried to make sense of it. How could this be happening? Her mam had survived so much, multiple pregnancies, a weak heart, poverty, an absent husband, constant sickness and yet it was a letter that killed her. A letter bearing the awful news of her parents dying before she had made it up with them. That had been the blow to finish her. Meg couldn't accept it.

The other children crowded into the bedroom and soon were crying as Mabel hugged them.

Nicky climbed onto the bed and rested his head on Meg's back. 'Mam's not hurting no more, Meg.'

'No, darling, she isn't.' But they would hurt for years to come. Meg was ashamed of all the times she'd moaned about her mam not coming downstairs, or all the times she ached from carrying trays of food up the stairs to her, or buckets of water up to wash her. She'd do it all again if only her mam was back with them.

Dazed, Meg slowly laid her mam on the pillows and arranged her hair neatly. A knock on the door downstairs had her straightening her spine. She kissed the top of Nicky's head, gazed at her distraught siblings, and then went downstairs to let the doctor in.

6

Christian tapped his fingers on his knees, trying to stem his impatience. He sat in the Henderson's Brewery office, his uncle's old office, which overlooked the River Calder. Beyond the room, the brewery workers continued operations of making Henderson's ale, not knowing the future of the business.

Barney flipped through one of the ten ledgers on the desk. 'Clearly I am unfamiliar with all this.' He closed the ledger.

'Did you not discuss the business with your father at all?' Christian asked, finding it difficult to accept that his cousin showed no signs of interest.

'Not really. Father liked to keep things close to his chest. Certainly, he wouldn't discuss anything financial with me.'

'The bank is looking to foreclose on the mortgage, Barney,' Christian stated. 'Uncle was behind in payments, not only to the banks but to suppliers as well.'

'Do we have nothing with which to pay them?' Barney stepped to the window and the drinks trolley placed under it and poured himself a glass of whisky.

'Not in the bank, no.'

'Assets?' Barney stared out of the window at the river below.

'You could sell the house.' Unable to contain his energy, Christian paced the carpeted floor. He'd been cooped up in the office here or the study at the house for days trying to sort out his uncle's affairs. 'Do you wish to do that?'

'Where will we live?'

Christian strove to keep calm. 'More importantly, what will you do for an income? What will you and Aunt live on? You must think of the future, Barney. It is up to you to provide for your mother. Your father has left her nothing, and he has left you a debt-ridden business.'

'I shall never forgive him for doing that to me.' Barney threw back the contents of his glass.

Fighting the anger he felt towards his useless cousin, Christian strove for patience. 'Then perhaps you should have helped him while he was alive. Insisted on learning the business. Who knows? You might have actually done some good if you had tried.'

'I doubt I could have helped. Business bores me.' Barney shrugged. 'Mother must have some capital somewhere, from her parents. They were wealthy.'

'All her money has gone into the brewery over the years.' Christian was amazed his cousin didn't know that fact already. He stared at Barney, noticing his paunch, his flabby jowls, the thinning hair. He had few prospects to entice a wealthy man's daughter into marriage to save himself from bankruptcy.

'What do you suggest?'

Christian strode back to the desk and held up a sheet of figures. 'Sell the brewery to pay off your debts.'

'My father's debts.'

'Which are now yours.'

'That is so unfair.' Barney swore.

Christian clenched his jaw in irritation. 'You have inherited a fine house and a business. That is more than most can claim.'

'A house I cannot afford to run because the business is in debt. This brewery is a noose around my neck. Who will want to buy it?'

'Selling it will pay off most of the debts. You will have to find a position that pays enough to keep you and Aunt.'

Barney's small eyes widened in horror. 'Work for a living?'

Christian glared at him. 'Yes!'

'How can I possibly do that?' Barney poured more whisky.

'You are an educated man. Think of what you are good at. Where do your talents lie?'

'I do not know. I assumed I would take over this place once Father passed.'

'Then do that. Work at changing the fortunes of the brewery around, so it becomes a success,' he encouraged, smothering his frustration.

'I do not have the first idea of how to do that. I never expected Father to leave me in this mess.'

'No, you wanted it all handed to you on a silver platter, a profitable business and a pleasant house and for you to do nothing but idle your days away drinking and socialising.' Anger made his voice sharp.

Stung, Barney's top lip curled. 'It was what I was brought up to expect. That is hardly my fault.'

'But it has not turned out that way. So, now you have to actually work.'

'Not here,' Barney scorned, his hand sweeping down towards the yard. 'I hate this place. I shall sell it and the house.'

'And what of your mother?'

'She will have to realise that Father failed her, and I am all she has and what I decide to do is my business.'

'How will you afford to live?' Christian was tempted to punch some sense into him but held back.

'The sale of the house will keep us for a while. We can buy something smaller in town or even move away. Mother's family, on her mother's side, is in Manchester. We could go there.' Warming to his ideas, Barney nodded enthusiastically. 'Yes, that is what I shall do. Go to Manchester. Start again.'

'You are going to sell everything?'

'The whole lot,' Barney beamed, excitement in his eyes.

'Then I shall make an offer on the business and the house.' Christian had been thinking about such a decision for days.

'You?' Barney stared. 'Why in God's name would you want either of them?'

'Because I know Uncle would want me to.'

Barney huffed and swallowed a mouthful of whisky. 'Huh, he always did favour you over me.'

'That is not true,' Christian lied, knowing full well his uncle had been terribly disappointed in Barney.

'As long as I do not have to worry about it all, I do not care.'

'I will have my solicitor draw up an offer for both properties. I shall pay market value.'

'Good.' Barney poured more whisky. 'Why you would want to lumber yourself with this anchor I cannot imagine, but it is your choice. I will sell it to you at a fair price since we are family.'

'Thank you.' Christian tried not to think of the burden he'd just put upon himself. A failing business and a house he didn't need. Still, his father had a reputation for taking businesses on at the point of bankruptcy and making them into successful ventures. Could he do the same? Did he have the same intelligence, the same strength of character as his father had to achieve it?

All he knew was that he had to give it a try, for his uncle's sake and maybe his own. Returning south wasn't something he was keen to do at the moment.

The image of Meg Taylor rose in his mind. There was something about her that sparked his interest. He exhaled deeply. That was a complication he didn't want. He had enough problems with the women in his life, his mother and sister, and especially Ruth. All three of whom wrote to him incessantly, begging for his return.

* * *

Meg sat cradling a cup of black tea in her hands, the room dark. The only light came from the fire's flickering flames. The children were in bed, but she couldn't sleep even though her eyes were gritty with tiredness.

The stairs squeaked. Meg glanced up to see Freddie creeping down, wincing with every creak.

'I thought you might be awake.' He sat opposite her, his expression as exhausted as hers.

'I'll go up in a minute.' Meg took a sip of tea. They'd been taking it in turns to sit with Mam since she'd died the night before.

'There's no hurry, stay a bit longer,' Freddie murmured into the fire.

In silence they stared into the flames, each lost to their own thoughts. They'd spent the day dealing with the issues of death. Old Mrs Flannigan came and laid Mam out properly. The proprietor of Dobbs Funeral called and discussed a simple funeral, none of which they could afford, but they were loath to give Mam a pauper's funeral. Neighbours came in and out, paying their respects as word spread through the street. In their sorrow they brought bits of food to help ease the burden of grief, a dish of oxtail soup, loaves of bread, jars of jam, pickles, pots of stew, pasties, anything that they could spare, despite being just as poor as the Taylors. It was what the people of this area did. They took care of each other when times were hard.

At one point, Meg vaguely registered that all the food would feed them for a week and the ease of that worry was great. However, to have that food meant a death in the family. The idea of *her mam* being dead didn't seem real. Even when she was sitting beside her, staring at her pale, cold face, none of it seemed real. On top of that she dealt with her brothers and sisters crying, sobbing, wailing for their mam.

Mrs Fogarty, bless her, had come in this morning and stayed all day and saw to the feeding of the children, made tea for those who called while Meg helped Mrs Flannigan lay out Mam. Meg felt it was the last thing she would do for her mam.

Fliss called and then went and brought Lorrie over to stay for an hour. Lorrie sat beside Nicky and drew little birds as he drew angels.

'I'll have to go into work tomorrow,' Freddie mentioned, breaking into her thoughts. 'They've just given me this job and already I've not turned up for a day.'

'They'd understand. Jimmy went and told them.' She spoke of Jimmy, a young lad three doors down who was quite happy to run errands for anyone in the street. Jimmy's mother, Dora, encouraged him for it meant she got all the gossip first-hand and the odd farthing tip.

'When I went out earlier, it was to send a telegram to a public house in Sowerby Bridge,' Freddie murmured.

'A telegram?' Meg lowered her cup and stared at him as though he had lost his mind. They didn't send telegrams.

'Mr Waltham would have paid to receive it.'

She continued to stare at him. 'Who is Mr Waltham and why were you sending him a telegram?'

'He's a publican of the Red Lion where Father and I drank sometimes when we'd finished offloading cargo. I thought if Father goes there for a pint, he'll be told the news about Mam and come straight back.'

'Did you put that she had died in the telegram?' Meg dreaded the thought of her father returning but knew he must.

'No, just that she was dangerously ill.' Freddie took the iron poker and jabbed at the glowing coals. 'We can't bury Mam without Father. She wouldn't want that. No matter what we think of him, Mam would want him there.'

Meg wiped a hand over her eyes. She feared the day of the funeral. Would she be strong enough to see it through, especially when her brothers and sisters needed her? 'Let's hope that Father calls in at the Red Lion then.'

'I think he will. We go there every time we are in Sowerby Bridge, because it's a canal terminus.' Freddie flushed red and looked away.

Meg saw it. 'Why do you go to the Red Lion? Do you have a girl there? Someone you're sweet on?'

'No. Father likes it.'

This surprised her, for she'd never known her father to frequent any of the pubs around here. 'He goes to a public house?'

Freddie hung his head with a small groan.

'Freddie?'

'Don't ask me anything more, Meg. I beg you,' he whispered, staring at the floor.

Her blood ran cold. 'What are you hiding?'

'Meg...'

She grasped his chin and lifted his face to look into his eyes. 'You *will* tell me, and I mean tell me everything.'

'I can't...'

'You're scaring me, Freddie.'

His face had lost all colour when he finally turned away. 'Father doesn't know that I know.'

'Know what?'

'His secret.'

Meg frowned. 'Go on.'

'He'd leave me and Arthur on the boat for hours, tell us to oversee the unloading of the cargo, check the numbers, count each crate or sack. At the time, I thought it was because he was securing more loads to take back with us or seeing to paperwork in the warehouse office.' He ran a hand through his dark hair. 'I felt proud that he trusted me to be in control of the cargo.'

'And that wasn't the case?'

'I worked so damn hard to please him. To make him proud of me, his eldest son, taking care of our family business, of the boat and Blossom, and Arthur. I enjoyed having the responsibility. I was good at it.'

'What was Father doing while you were in dock, doing *his* job?'

Freddie's grey eyes dulled to the colour of pewter. 'He was seeing his fancy woman.'

It took several seconds for Meg to register his words. 'Fancy woman?'

'Aye.'

Meg stared, mouth open, shock rendering her speechless.

'I saw them together on our last trip.'

'But he can't have!' The words sounded stupid to her own ears, but the blow of such a thing being true was mind-numbing.

'I didn't want to tell you, or anyone. I was hoping I was wrong.'

'Are you sure you aren't? I mean, could you have been mistaken? Father might have been helping some woman...'

'I saw them kissing.' Freddie jabbed the poker at the glowing coals.

'But he loves Mam...'

'That's what I thought. And he does love her, but he has this woman, too.'

'A mistress?' A knot of anger twisted in her gut. She wasn't that naïve that she didn't know men had urges more basic than women, that's what Mam had told her. And she'd seen many a couple kissing in the alley behind the pub, even in Wellington Street. She knew that docker George Sutherland was married, but that didn't stop him kissing and groping Mrs Flagstaff when her husband worked nights. She'd seen them at it on her way home from the pub one night. 'So, Father has been caught kissing another woman.' Meg tried to think rationally, though it was difficult.

'That's not the worst of it.' He gently placed the poker down and his expression twisted in agony.

'I don't think I want to know,' Meg murmured, afraid.

'When I saw them, the woman had two kids with her. Father picked one of them up as they went inside a shop.'

A cold weight landed in her stomach. Meg felt sick, then suddenly full of rage. 'Are you telling me he has another family in Sowerby Bridge?'

'It seems that way,' Freddie answered grimly.

Unable to sit still, Meg paced the room. She couldn't take it in. It couldn't be true. It was absurd to even think it. Father? *Her father?* Another family? He couldn't afford to keep this one! He didn't even really like this family. He had no time for them, showed no interest in any of them.

Then it dawned on her. That was why they were always poor and why over the years her father gave her only a few shillings despite him working non-stop. He was paying for two families.

She wanted to cry and scream at the injustice of it, but her mam lay dead upstairs. Oh, Mam. Meg wrapped her arms about herself, feeling the most wretched she'd ever felt.

'What do we do?' Freddie asked.

'I'm not sure, not yet.' Questions filled Meg's head. 'First, I think...' God, what did she think? 'Um... well, first we should find out if he really does have another family.'

Freddie stood and went over to the range and added coal to the dying embers. 'I need a cuppa.' He poured water from the bucket into the kettle. 'I'm glad Mam never found out.'

Meg clenched her fists. 'She didn't deserve such lies. To be made a fool of, to suffer because of his selfish needs. So many times, I had to go without food to make what we had stretch because he wouldn't give us enough money. I bet his fancy piece and her children never went hungry.' She closed her eyes, striving to keep calm. 'I can't believe it, Freddie.'

'I know. I couldn't believe it either. I waited for Father to come out of the shop. Then I followed them to this house. I sat hidden hours, waiting for Father to come out of the house, and it was very late when he did. He kissed the woman on the steps and then headed back to the canal. I had to run as fast as I could to beat him back to the boat.'

'And you've said nothing to him?'

'How could I?' Freddie shrugged. 'But as the days went by, I found it harder to look at him. I got angry.'

'That's why you and Father have been arguing ever since you got back? And why you were hardly home when Father was here?'

'Aye. I didn't want to be in his company. To see him making a fuss over Mam made me sick to my stomach, it did.'

'How could he have done that to Mam, to us?' Hatred tore deep in her heart. 'After Mam's funeral, we'll go to Sowerby Bridge and see this woman,' Meg decided.

'And what about Father?'

'If he really does have another family, then... then we have nothing more to do with him.' Her anger burned as hot as the coals in the fire.

'Arthur thinks the sun shines out of his arse,' Freddie scorned.

'I don't care. Besides, that sun won't shine so brightly once Arthur knows his father has another woman and children to care for.' Meg drew in a shuddering breath. If all this was true, then in the space of two days, she'd have lost both her parents.

7

Meg watched the gulls fly overhead, preferring that to the scene of the cheap coffin being lowered into the ground. Trees were bright with new leaf and blossom scattered on the warm breeze.

Sobbing and sniffling sounded from all her siblings, but her eyes were dry. The whirring sound of the machines in the sawmill near the cemetery provided a fitting note to the occasion, reminding Meg that life went on, that people still were working, eating, talking, living.

Only she felt held suspended in time.

Since Freddie's revelation, she couldn't function properly if she spent a moment thinking of her father's betrayal. Instead, she had pushed it from her mind and concentrated on preparing for the funeral and comforting her brothers and sisters.

Her father hadn't made the funeral. They'd heard nothing from him. If he had received the telegram from the Red Lion, he'd not moored the narrowboat and taken the train home. Was he in blissful ignorance drifting down one of the canals or the River Calder? Or did he have his feet up in front of another woman's fire? And what of Arthur? Her brother had missed his own mam's funeral too.

'Miss Taylor.' Mr Rendale, the vicar, took her hand in a soft hold. 'My sincere condolences.'

'Thank you, and thank you for the service.'

'It's all in the name of God's work, my child.' He moved away to chat with other mourners. Mrs Fogarty now shook his hand, and then Terry and Hilda Atkins. Meg turned and smiled at Lorrie and Fliss. Both had been her rock during the last few days.

'We'll head back to the Bay Horse,' Fliss said. 'Uncle has put on a little spread.'

'That's kind of him.' Meg ushered Nicky and Nell before her, while Mabel, Susie and Betsy walked behind with Freddie.

'My father sends his regards,' Lorrie said as they left the cemetery and walked along Doncaster Road to the open ground which cut across to the river. Here, Harry waited for them to ferry them across, refusing to charge for the crossing.

'Uncle Terry has kept the snug free for you all.' Fliss unclasped her cloak as they entered the pub's main room. 'I'll fetch the food platters.'

'That's really good of you all to do this for us.' Meg felt the tears rise at such kindness.

'It's nothing much.' Fliss waved away her thanks. 'A bit of ham and bread and butter, cheese. Aunt made a sponge cake with jam and cream.'

'I'll help.' Lorrie made herself useful as the neighbours entered the taproom.

The snug wasn't very big, and the roaring fire made it too warm, but Meg was grateful to sit down and have her brothers and sisters fussed over in their grief. Fliss encouraged the children to eat, and Lorrie poured them glasses of small beer as a special treat.

Soon the mourners were spilling out from the snug into the bar and, as the afternoon drew on and workers came in for their pints, Meg was inundated with well-wishers. Those she'd served behind the bar were keen to say how sorry they were for her loss. Many spoke of her father, mentioning how he must be devastated at not being home for the funeral. Meg simply nodded, not trusting herself to speak. They all thought Frank Taylor to be a decent, solid man. One who worked hard for his family. Meg wanted to ask them which family would that be?

'I have to get home and make Father's supper,' Lorrie told Meg, holding her in a tight embrace. 'I'll call in tomorrow and maybe we can go for a walk if the weather is nice?' Lorrie turned to Fliss, who was serving behind the bar. 'A walk tomorrow, the three of us?'

'Sounds lovely. It'll get me away from Easter preparations.' Fliss passed a frothing ale to an older man. 'That's your lot, George. Your Elspeth will be wanting you home for your supper.'

Strangely, Fliss' words had Meg's head spinning. Was her father with his woman having supper right now? Was that why he wasn't here with them, mourning their mam?

'I'm going to Sowerby Bridge tomorrow,' Meg suddenly blurted to Lorrie as she put on her coat. 'I'm getting the train.' She'd never been on a train in her life and still hadn't worked out how she'd find the fare, but she was determined to go and find this other woman and see for herself what was the situation.

Both Lorrie and Fliss stared at her.

'It's important,' she added, lowering her voice.

'Are you going on your own?' Lorrie asked, fastening the buttons.

'Yes, Freddie is at work, as is Mabel, and the younger ones are at school.'

'You can't go by yourself,' Fliss said, horrified.

'I have no choice. I must go for my peace of mind.'

'Then I'll come with you,' Lorrie said.

'Me, too,' added Fliss.

Meg rubbed her forehead. 'I would like that, of course I would, but I was hoping to borrow the fare from you, Fliss.'

'I've enough money for both our fares.' Fliss smiled. 'If I tell Uncle that I'm travelling with you to see a relative to tell them about the loss of your mam, Uncle will probably give me the money. He's kind like that.'

'I'll pay you back,' Meg promised. Filled with love for these two women who'd come to mean so much to her, Meg took their hands in hers. 'Thank you.' She didn't want to admit that making the journey on her own frightened her. She'd never been out of Wakefield.

'What time?' Lorrie asked, checking her hat was on straight.

'The earliest train we can get. I don't know the times, but I'll leave the house as soon as the others have gone to school and meet you at the station.'

'What are you three talking about?' Freddie suddenly asked, coming up behind them.

'Train times,' Fliss admitted, then realised she might have made a mistake. Her eyes widened at Meg, and she mouthed, 'Sorry.'

Lorrie pulled on her black gloves. 'I might go to Leeds,' she quickly told him.

Freddie stared at Meg. 'We must have the truth between us. We only have each other now.'

Meg nodded. 'You're right. I'm going to Halifax tomorrow by train, then I'll catch a coach to Sowerby Bridge.'

'Then I should go with you.'

'No. You've missed enough work days already. I can go with Lorrie and Fliss.'

'You've never been to Sowerby Bridge before. How will you know where to go?'

'Can you draw your sister a map?' Lorrie asked with a small smile. 'She'll be fine with Fliss and me to help her.'

'All right, but I'll go to the train station now and get a timetable.'

'Good,' Lorrie said. 'I'll walk with you, so I'll know what time to meet Meg and Fliss in the morning.'

'Freddie, come back and tell Fliss the time. I'm taking the others home now.' Meg gathered Nicky and Nell from where they sat playing marbles by the fire in the snug. 'Come on, everyone, it's time to go.' Meg ordered the children out the door.

'Can I stay?' Mabel asked cheekily, her face flushed from too much beer.

Meg gave her a stern look. She'd noticed how Mabel had enjoyed the young men chatting to her in the bar, despite being told to stay in the snug. 'You'll not see the inside of a pub again, miss, unless you get a job in one, which you won't be doing. Now go.'

The following morning, Meg dressed carefully. For the funeral she'd dyed her mam's white bodice black, for white wasn't a colour she'd be wearing again for a while and black would be more useful for the weeks of mourning to come. From Mam's wardrobe, she found her Sunday best black skirt and a pair of boots that were still good from lack of use. She also wore her mam's cloak. She wanted to look her best while facing the enemy, which the other woman was, at least to Meg.

Lastly, she grabbed her mam's small reticule from the top drawer. It was dark blue with black beads around the edges. Meg had never seen her mam use it.

Carefully opening the clasp, Meg gasped on seeing two ten-shilling notes folded inside and a note. She took it out.

Dearest Meg,

If you are reading this, it means I'm in God's hands.

Use this money for something worthwhile. I've saved it for such a purpose. My father sent it to me some years ago, but it felt wrong to use it.

It's yours, with love,

Your mother,

Lucy Taylor

Amazed, Meg read the note twice more. Twenty shillings wasn't a fortune, but that Mam had it in a drawer and didn't tell her, especially when so many times they struggled to pay the rent or buy food, confused her. What had she been thinking?

Disturbed by the note and the money, Meg went downstairs. Would Mam agree that spending this money to travel to Sowerby Bridge was wise? Nevertheless, now she wouldn't have to borrow money from Fliss. Having enough funeral food to last them a week, she'd taken a chance on dodging the rent man until she could do more shifts at the pub and Freddie got paid.

Taking a deep breath, Meg let herself out of the house.

Mrs Fogarty was donkey stoning her front step. 'You all right there, lass?'

'Morning, Mrs Fogarty. Yes, I'm fine.'

'You're out early.' The older woman leaned back on her knees.

'I'm off to look for work. I can get a daytime position now.' She didn't enjoy lying to her, but she could hardly tell her the truth.

'Good luck then, lass. Your father didn't come home during the night then?'

'No. Still no sign of him.'

Mrs Fogarty shook her head. 'What a business. A man missing his own wife's funeral.'

'I'd best go.' She hesitated a step. 'If I'm not back before Nicky and the girls come home from school, will you keep an eye for them?'

'Aye, lass. I will.' Mrs Fogarty resumed her scrubbing.

A cry of the rag-and-bone man echoed down the street, his holler bouncing off the terrace walls. Meg gave him a nod as she passed and turned the corner on to Thornes Lane Wharf. Thankfully, the sun shone from a clear blue sky. Spring warmed the air.

Fliss was waiting outside the Bay Horse. 'It's a lovely day.' She linked her arm through Meg's. 'Are you nervous to be going on a train for the first time?'

'Yes.' Actually, it had only fleetingly crossed her mind. She was more concerned to be meeting her father's mistress.

'Are you going to tell me why we are travelling to Sowerby Bridge?'

'Not yet.' Meg remained silent as they passed the weir and under the railway bridge.

Turning right, they walked towards the railway station. Horse-drawn vehicles crammed the road, carriages, gigs, hansom cabs, flat-topped wagons, and huge drays carrying many types of cargo. Porters were loading or unloading wooden chests and large baskets from a train in the station while passengers assembled on the platform. First-class ladies wearing silks and taffeta grimaced at the bustle of people, their white gloves in danger of being blemished with coal-fuelled smoke bellowing from the steam engine.

The station manager blew a whistle while the harried porters dashed about with baggage trolleys. A small white dog on a lead barked furiously. The boy handler kept yanking at the lead, only to be told off by an older girl.

'There's Lorrie!' Fliss waved, having spotted her amongst the crowd.

'Isn't it busy?' Lorrie said, giving them both a kiss on the cheek. 'We need to buy our tickets. The next train is ours. It'll be here in twenty minutes, the porter told me.'

On the platform, Meg had to squeeze between a large man puffing a cigar and another man reading a newspaper. A queue formed at the ticket office window, and she waited in line, trying not to be anxious about her first journey at speed.

'Miss Taylor?'

Meg spun around at her name being spoken. She stared at Christian Henderson as though he were an apparition. 'Mr Henderson.'

'How are you? I was sorry to hear of your mother's passing. Mr Pepper, the brewery's foreman, told me yesterday.'

'I'm sorry my brother had time off when he has only just started working there.'

'Gracious, I believe a man should have the day off work to attend his own mother's funeral, do you not think? We Hendersons might be many things, but we are not that cold-hearted.'

'Yes, of course, forgive me.' Meg couldn't drag her gaze from his lovely eyes, which today were soft and the colour of cornflowers that grew in the barley fields.

'Which train are you catching?' he asked.

'The one to Halifax.' She prayed he wouldn't ask her why.

'The same as me.' He inclined his head with a smile. 'And who are you with?' He smiled at Fliss and Lorrie.

Feeling far from sophisticated, Meg realised she'd made an error in good manners by not introducing them. 'My friends, Miss Lorrie Chambers and Miss Fliss Atkins.'

Mr Henderson shook hands with them both. 'Ah, Miss Atkins from the Bay Horse.'

'Yes, sir.' Fliss nodded, flustered.

For a moment, Meg thought Fliss was going to curtsy to him.

The noise of the train's whistle and the belching of steam

drowned all chances of talking. The clank of the wheels pulling the enormous beast out of the station added to the commotion.

Meg stared in wonder. She'd seen many trains rattling over the viaduct at the end of Wellington Street and had taken the younger children to watch the trains puff along the tracks in the summer, but today she would be actually travelling on one. She felt slightly giddy and wished Nicky was with her to share the experience, as he'd have enjoyed it.

'Ladies, this line is long. Please allow me to get all our tickets while you find a seat inside the waiting room.' He indicated the doorway next to the ticket office.

'Oh, we couldn't do that,' Lorrie murmured, blushing.

'I insist. It looks like a full train. Shall I get us four first-class tickets?' Mr Henderson stepped away, eyeing the line.

'First class?' Meg squeaked. 'We are travelling third class, Mr Henderson.'

He turned and gave her the most dazzling smile that had her stomach swooping like a bird in flight. 'My treat, Miss Taylor. Please allow me to do it. After all, you've just suffered a tragic loss.' Without waiting for an answer, he stepped further into the crowd.

'Gosh.' Lorrie brought her hands together. 'First class.'

'How kind of him,' Fliss sighed happily.

'He shouldn't have done that. It'll cost a small fortune.' Meg didn't know what else to say. Gentlemen didn't buy first-class tickets for three working-class women. Why had he done such a thing?

Lorrie gave her a side-eye. 'I do believe Mr Henderson is rather smitten with you, Meg.'

Fliss gasped and clapped her hands. 'Do you think so?'

'Don't talk rubbish,' Meg scorned, feeling hot. She couldn't deny that the man had an effect on her, but she doubted he felt the same, not a gentleman such as him.

'First he saves you from falling cargo, then sends you a hamper and now this?' Lorrie raised her eyebrows. 'It's all very interesting.'

'You're making something out of nothing.' Meg looked away, not wanting to discuss any of it. Her head was too full of what she had to do today without her fancies running away with her. Though the little voice inside her head plagued her with possible and completely ridiculous ideas of having Mr Henderson's admiration. None of it made sense to her. She was not a lady. Why would he look twice at her?

They went into the waiting room and found it full of women and children and the small white barking dog.

'Goodness,' Lorrie murmured, looking around. 'Shall we stay out on the platform?'

Meg felt light-headed at the noise and crowd. She'd been too nervous to eat breakfast and now regretted not having something.

Mr Henderson weaved his way back to them, tickets in hand. 'That was a close call. We got the last remaining seats.'

'We can't thank you enough, Mr Henderson, and we will pay our share,' Lorrie said.

'It is my gift, Miss Chambers. Please accept it. I couldn't rest being seated in first class knowing you ladies were crushed in third.'

'You're very kind. Isn't he, Meg?' Lorrie nudged her.

'Yes, it's generous. Thank you.' She flicked a smile his way, but suddenly felt conscious of his nearness. Such a tall, good-looking man drew the stares of the other women on the platform. She expected some of the first-class women were wondering why he was standing with them. The cut of his fine black suit fitted him perfectly. His black boots shone and the leather satchel he carried had his initials on it embossed in gold.

With relief, Meg heard the next train coming into the station.

'I've never been first class, so it'll be an experience for us all,' Lorrie whispered as Mr Henderson handed Fliss up the step into the carriage.

Meg waited until the other two were inside before giving her hand to Mr Henderson. She shivered at his touch and their eyes locked, nearly causing her to trip up the first step.

In the carriage, Meg sat next to Lorrie, leaving Fliss to sit beside Mr Henderson, as she didn't want to spend the next two hours trying not to accidentally touch him. Only she realised now that he sat opposite her, and she didn't know where to look without looking at him. She groaned inwardly.

'Are you travelling to Halifax for business or pleasure, Mr Henderson?' Lorrie asked him.

'Business.'

The train lurched and Meg gripped Lorrie's arm, although she was not frightened – how could she be when people did this every day? Yet the sensation of moving at speed was alien to her and thrilling at the same time. The train picked up momentum once in the countryside and Meg gazed out of the window in awe at the passing scenery.

'Your first time, Miss Taylor?' Mr Henderson asked with a grin.

'Yes.' She grinned, for an instant forgetting all her other problems and just savouring the experience.

'You're not frightened?'

'No.' And she wasn't. It was thrilling. The hissing sound of the steam engine, the rattle of the wheels on the tracks, the rocking of the carriages and the scenery flashing by were all exciting.

He kept his gaze on her. 'My sister Susan fainted the first time she went on a train. She was only a child, and I had been teasing her, saying a monster was breathing fire in the engine. My stepfather wasn't amused.' He chuckled, showing a playful side.

'I have a sister called Susan, or Susie, as we call her,' Meg shared, and wasn't sure why. Mr Henderson wouldn't be interested in her family.

'My sister Susan would never tolerate being called Susie.' He shook his head with a mocking laugh. 'So, you have a sister and brother, Freddie, who started at the brewery?'

'I have three brothers and four sisters.'

His eyes widened. 'Indeed.'

'And you?'

'Just my sister. Believe me, that is more than enough.' He turned to Lorrie. 'Do you live close to the river, too, Miss Chambers?'

'Yes. My father owns a boat repair yard near the weir.'

'Ah, yes, Chambers' Boat Repairs, it's not far from the brewery.'

'My father and I were very sorry to hear about Mr Henderson's passing. Father attended the funeral. He'd known him for many years,' Lorrie said sadly. 'He was a kind gentleman.'

'Thank you. Many people respected my uncle. I am proud to be his nephew.' He looked sad for a moment.

'And the brewery will continue?' Meg asked.

Mr Henderson sighed. 'Yes. I have bought it.'

'So, you'll be staying in Wakefield?' Fliss asked.

'Yes. I have also bought my uncle's house. My cousin has no wish to continue living there.' He looked a little uncomfortable.

Lorrie glanced out of the window. 'We are stopping.'

'It is the next station,' Mr Henderson told them.

'We are in another town already,' Meg said in wonder, unable to hide her excitement. 'Isn't that wonderful?'

'I agree. A magnificent way to travel. Easy and fast,' he replied, his lips curling in a warm smile.

She couldn't deny it was a superior way to travel and now understood why the mills and factories were sending cargo by train and turning their backs on the canals. As sad as it was, the modern way of transporting goods was the death knell for people like her father and the waterfront.

Father.

She slumped into the seat, remembering the real reason she was on this train. With Mr Henderson present, she couldn't even discuss it with Lorrie and Fliss.

'Refreshments, ladies?' Mr Henderson asked, standing. 'I will return directly.'

'Good heavens, Mr Henderson is a fine gentleman,' Lorrie gushed.

'Easy on the eye, too,' Fliss teased.

'He's barely taken his gaze off Meg,' Lorrie commented.

'Stop it.' Meg's pulse raced at the idea. Yet she wasn't a fool, or blind. There was an attraction between her and Mr Henderson, something that sizzled between them like water drops on hot coals. She didn't understand it, but nor could she ignore it. However, they were very different people from different worlds.

Christian brought back with him a waiter who held a tray of tea with cakes for four. A small table folded down between the seats and the tray was placed upon it. The waiter served them in smart green livery, and after he had asked if they had everything they needed, he then left them.

Meg felt like a queen. The fine bone china service, being served by a waiter, the plush seats and Mr Henderson's attentive courtesy, all while watching the countryside flash by, was overwhelming.

She never wanted the journey to end.

They spent the next hour chatting about things in general, the spring weather, which was on form today, sunny and bright, the constant reporting in the newspapers about the nation's lack of confidence in Queen Victoria and her prolonged mourning period.

'But she loved Prince Albert very much,' Fliss defended their monarch.

'It has been nine years since he died,' Mr Henderson said. 'She has her duty to this country and the British Empire.'

'I read in the newspaper only last week that there are calls for us to become a republic,' Lorrie added, frowning.

'A republic?' Meg didn't have time to read the newspaper, even if they had the money to buy a copy. She felt self-conscious that she couldn't talk to Mr Henderson on his level.

'No monarchy is what the republican clubs are demanding,' he told her.

That surprised Meg. To not have their royal family on the throne? She'd never heard of anything so daft.

'Do you agree, Mr Henderson?' Fliss asked.

'No, I do not agree. This country needs the royal family. The Queen's voice is a wise one, but she does need to be involved more. Prince Albert would not have wanted her to continue to mourn like this, still wallowing after all this time.'

'I agree.' Lorrie nodded. 'She must think of her people.'

Meg didn't comment as the train slowed as they reached Halifax. There was a great deal of gathering things and disembarking at the station. Steam from the engine swirled across the platform, adding to the overall mayhem of passengers crowding the platform and porters pushing trolleys of luggage and goods. Elegant women walked past in dresses with large bustles and larger hats. A nanny ushered three children away from the platform edge.

'I need the pot,' Fliss whispered to Meg.

'Oh, Fliss. There's nowhere to go.' She pointed to a sign above them of two men wearing bowler hats. 'Only the men have restrooms. You'll have to wait.'

Fliss looked concerned. 'Wait for where?'

'Ladies, I shall bid you good day.' Mr Henderson tipped his top hat and bowed. 'It has been a pleasure to share the journey with you when I expected to spend the time alone.'

'Thank you for your kindness, Mr Henderson.' Lorrie shook his hand and then gave Meg a small elbow nudge as she and Fliss moved away.

'Thank you, Mr Henderson,' Meg said, shaking his hand and again feeling that tension of being aware of him. Their gazes locked. Her stomach fluttered like a moth trapped against a lamp.

'Can I be of any assistance to you while you are in Halifax, Miss Taylor?'

'Oh, no, no. Thank you.' She stepped back. Being in his company made her fantasise about being someone else, a woman of his own class. How she wished she was the same as him, that she was only here for a simple shopping trip. But that wasn't her life. He'd be horrified if he knew the real reason for her visit. 'Goodbye, Mr Henderson.'

'Enjoy your day, Miss Taylor. It has been a pleasure to spend the last two hours with you.'

She knew he meant it and her silly heart melted.

Reluctantly, Meg turned away, burying her desire to stay in his presence longer. She admired him for not asking her business as to why a working-class young woman had travelled so far so soon after her mam's funeral. Surely he must be curious?

Outside the large sandstone building, Meg found Lorrie and Fliss waiting for her. She noticed a line of hansom cabs for people to hire, but she'd rather keep her money and walk.

'So, what is this trip all about?' Lorrie asked as she joined them.

'We need to get to Sowerby Bridge.'

'Goodness, why?' Fliss asked, adjusting her gloves.

'Fliss, how did you get those bruises on your wrists?' Lorrie asked suddenly.

'Oh, them. It's just me being clumsy.' Fliss pulled down her sleeves. 'So why are we here, Meg?'

'Let me ask for directions and then I'll explain on the way.' Meg hurried over to a hansom cab driver, feeling more herself now Mr Henderson was no longer around. The driver told her they could walk to Sowerby Bridge if they wanted to. It would take them an hour and he gave her the directions.

'Are you going to tell us now?' Lorrie asked as they negotiated the unfamiliar streets.

Meg took a deep breath. 'I'm going to find my father's mistress,' she said, crossing the street.

—————

8

'Good God!' Lorrie's gasp was drowned out by a passing cart. The horse pulling it emptied its bowels onto the road and the stench of it had them wrinkling their noses.

'Did I hear you right?' Fliss said, catching up to her.

'You did. Freddie found out, saw them.' Meg read the road sign and kept going, trying to remember the directions the cabbie told her.

'And you are going to confront her?' Lorrie asked in amazement.

'I must.' Meg shrugged, striding ahead, eager to get the ordeal over and done with.

'Do you think you should confront this woman?' Lorrie asked as they crossed another road.

'Yes, I do. I need answers.'

'It's so shocking.' Fliss dodged a man walking with a cane. 'You're very brave.'

Meg didn't reply and kept walking. She didn't feel brave. She felt angry and became angrier with every step she took. She had to know the truth of it all before she faced her father and told him she knew it all. What would happen after that, she couldn't think about.

They left behind the streets busy with shoppers and workers and moved through a long road edged with terraced houses on either side. She stopped at a corner, confused for a moment about which way to go.

A woman was washing her front window and paused to study them.

'Excuse me, is this the right way to Sowerby Bridge?' Meg asked.

'Aye, keep going down this street and at the end, you'll see a sign at the edge of the fields,' the woman answered.

'Ta very much.'

Without talking, they continued on. Meg glanced at the open fields spreading out past the last row of houses. A dirt road parted the fields. Sowerby Bridge was denoted on a tall wooden sign pointing to the south-west.

'I need the pot so bad, I might have an accident,' Fliss moaned halfway along the road.

Lorrie pointed to the strand of trees at the edge of the fields. 'Over there is your only choice.'

Fliss groaned. 'I'll take it.'

Lorrie laughed. 'We should all go, while we can, and we can watch out for each other. Meg?'

Meg nodded. The sun held a good deal of heat, and with every step she was getting warmer wearing all black. Her bonnet when she touched it was hot. She welcomed the cool shade of the trees. Hawthorn bushes grew in clumps near the grove, but they went further into the woodland until they found a spot that dipped sharply near a small beck. A large rock jutted out between two silver birches.

'Go behind there,' Lorrie instructed Fliss. 'We'll keep watch.'

When all three of them had relieved themselves and washed their hands and faces in the beck, Meg led them out of the trees just as two young lads came scampering over the fields, long sticks used as fishing rods in hand.

'That was close.' Lorrie grinned.

'I feel so much better,' Fliss replied. 'I should never had had that cup of tea Mr Henderson got for us.'

'Nothing more to drink for me, either,' Lorrie agreed. 'We are too far from home to hold our bladders. Why they don't build ladies' public restrooms is ridiculous.'

'It was making me feel ill, truly,' Fliss added. 'Men are so lucky. There are places for them to have comfort breaks, but not us females.'

While Fliss and Lorrie talked, Meg kept her gaze on the road ahead as it headed downwards into a valley. Eventually, at the bottom of a hill, they reached a wider road which ran alongside the canal, and beyond that was the River Calder.

Meg opened the rough map drawing Freddie had done for her. She took the towpath along the canal, wondering if her father was still here or if he had already started the journey home. Did he still not know that Mam was dead and buried? Had he received the telegram at the Red Lion? And if he had, was he worried as he drifted down the canal right now somewhere, him and Arthur, eager to see Mam? Did he care? Or would he simply think it was just another period of Mam being ill and there wasn't a need to rush home?

'Do you know where she lives?' Lorrie asked, breaking into her thoughts.

'Freddie said it's the end terrace two rows behind the Red Lion.' She looked around. In parts, the valley's slopes were steep, with houses perched on top, but down near the water large mills were crowded along the riverbanks. A great many narrowboats were moored by the locks.

'Freddie told me that this terminus is for the boats that can't fit into the narrower Rochford Canal, so they have to unload their cargo into warehouses along here.' Meg paused beside a large brick wall. Above them was a sign with a prancing red lion on it. Her chest tightened. 'We need to get up there.' She pointed up the hill past the pub.

'Look.' Fliss pointed ahead. 'I see a staircase further along to get us up to the road above.'

Meg searched the numerous narrowboats below, trying to pick out her father's boat, but there were too many vessels, and the canal curved away, hiding the rest from view.

The Red Lion public house faced the river, but also had a side entrance on the steps and another entrance from the road behind it. The white paint was stark in the sunshine and the black wood-work seemed freshly decorated. This was where her father came to drink.

Ignoring the pub, Meg crossed the road and headed up the hill until she reached the next street and the end house of the grey-stoned terraces.

'Is this it?' Fliss asked, face flushed from the uphill hike.

'I think so.' Nervous, yet also fighting her resentment, Meg stood on the stone step and knocked on the raw wooden door.

The door opened within seconds, and a harassed-looking woman scowled at Meg. 'I thought you were the doctor.'

'Doctor?' Meg wondered if her father was ill. Was she even at the right house?

'Yes, for my little boy, Tommy. Can I help you?' The thin woman was dressed in a filthy grey skirt and a bodice that once might have been cream but was now a dirty beige colour.

Meg's mouth went dry. 'I... I... I am looking for my... for Frank Taylor.'

'Frank? He's down at the docks. I've sent someone to fetch him. I need a hand with Tommy and the others. What do you want him for? I've no money if that's what you're after. If Frank has a debt to pay, then take it up with him.' A child's cry came from behind the woman.

Meg swayed.

Lorrie and Fliss stood either side of her and took her elbows.

'Who are you, anyway?' the woman asked, half turning away.

'I'm Frank Taylor's daughter.'

It was the woman's turn to be shocked. Her mouth gaped, the crying baby ignored. 'What?'

'Frank Taylor is my father.' A cold weight landed on Meg's chest as she spoke.

'Not my Frank?' The woman stepped backwards into the dim house. A little girl came to stand at her mother's skirts.

Meg stared at the girl, for she was the image of Nell and Betsy.

The woman rallied. 'I've got to see to my son.' She hesitated, her expression unsure on her unclean face. 'You'd best come in.'

Meg followed her inside with Fliss and Lorrie at her back. The room they stood in was not only dark but grim and bare of any comforts. No fire burned in the grate that was full of dead ashes. No curtains hung at the only window. Mould and damp coated the walls. Dirty pots and plates were stacked on the table. The stone-flagged floor, not swept, didn't even have a rag rug to offer respite from the coldness of it. An unmade bed took up one corner, but it was through another door that Meg stepped, unable to help herself.

In a double bed, a small boy of about four years lay crying, sweat beading his flushed face. Against the wall were a set of drawers. The top drawer was pulled out and inside lay a newborn baby. The little girl came in and sat on the floor. She looked no more than two years old and wore a plain grubby shift, her hair in tangles about her shoulders, her skin thick with grime.

Meg continued to stare. Did all three children belong to her father?

The woman sponged the boy's face, crying herself. The blankets on the bed were tatty and worn. Meg would have been ashamed to have sold them as rags. They were good for nothing but scrubbing the floor with.

'Where do you come from?' The woman turned weeping eyes to Meg.

'Wakefield.'

'That's where Frank is from,' she whispered.

'Yes.'

Noise behind her heralded the doctor, a large man who bustled his way into the small room with an air of importance, yet stank of alcohol. 'Ah, what do we have here, Mrs Taylor?'

Meg jerked at the woman being called Mrs Taylor. *They were married?*

'It's Tommy, Doctor. He's had a fever since last night.'

'Right, let me have a look at him.' The doctor glared at Meg. 'And you are?'

'She's a visitor,' the woman explained.

'Then out, if you please. I need room to see to my patient.' The doctor waved Meg away.

Back in the other room, Meg couldn't stop shaking. Lorrie and Fliss fussed around her, but she couldn't answer their whispered questions.

Suddenly, the door opened, and her father walked in. It took him a moment to recognise that his eldest daughter was in the room. 'You!'

So, it was all true. A veil of hatred cloaked her like a second skin. This man, her father, had another family. Her knees buckled, but she fought to stay upright. She gathered her courage to face him.

'What are you doing here?' he managed to say, looking pale as death.

'I came to find you.' She spoke without emotion. It was as though he was a stranger, which she realised he was. He wasn't the man she had thought he was. He was a walking lie. She stood straight, shoulders back. 'Did you get the telegram from the Red Lion?'

'No.' Father frowned. 'I only arrived here this morning. I've been doing loads between Brighouse and Dewsbury.'

'Frank?' The woman came out of the room. Her expression was one of exhaustion and something else – wounded.

'Josie.' Father paled even further.

'Is this your daughter?' She indicated Meg with a tilt of her head.

Father nodded just once.

The woman, Josie, slumped. A flash of pain entered her eyes. 'We'll talk about that later. The doctor is here. Tommy's sick. He's been calling for you.'

Her father gave Meg a defiant glare. 'Go home!' He strode into the other room.

Meg rushed out of the house, desperate for air.

'Oh, my lord.' Fliss puffed out her chest. '*I* can't believe it, so I can't imagine what *you're* feeling.'

Lorrie rubbed Meg's back. 'What do you want to do?'

'I honestly don't know.' Meg shrugged. 'Scream. Shout. Wake up from this nightmare.'

'We can go back to the station.'

Meg glanced around at the unkept street. A mangy cat sat atop a stone wall, and below it piles of rubbish spilled into the road.

The house next door had boarded-up windows and further along weeds grew amongst more rubbish piles.

Wellington Street might be poor, but it was tidy. The neighbours didn't allow people to tip their waste wherever they fancied. Mrs Fogarty kept everyone in order to help keep vermin and disease down. All the tenants got their share at the communal water tap and some standards of cleanliness were upheld or they shunned you, called you a dirty trollop. Woe betide anyone who had a dirty front window or front step.

But here... Meg shuddered. The place was filthy, inside and out. Why would her father prefer here? The house on Wellington Street wasn't a palace by any stretch of the imagination, but she spent hours cleaning it. They had a fire in the range and, once a year, all the children helped her to whitewash the walls. She scrubbed and washed and did her best to fight the ravages of time and the landlord's neglect to keep a pleasant home on a limited budget.

And what of Mam?

Whatever her personal feelings for her father had been over the years as she became an adult, never once did she think he didn't love his wife. Each time he returned home, all he wanted to do was spend time with Mam. He didn't go to the pub for hours, as some men did. Instead, he would sit beside the bed, or lie down beside Mam and they'd just talk and hold each other. Her parents' love was something Meg had been proud of. Unlike her friends growing up, she didn't have a father who knocked her mam about, giving her a black eye, or who would rather spend all his money on ale or gambling.

Their love had been uplifting and dependable.

Until now.

Meg knew it all to be a lie, at least on her father's side.

A small part of her was glad Mam was dead to save her the

pain and anguish of finding out the truth. Frank Taylor was a bigamist.

'Meg,' Lorrie whispered.

Meg turned to see her father standing on the doorstep.

'We'll go for a walk,' Fliss said.

'No, stay, for a minute more.' Meg didn't want to be without her friends.

'I suppose you've got questions?' her father asked, running a shaky hand through his sparse hair.

'How could I not?' she scorned, hating him. 'You have a whole other family we knew nothing about.'

'You were never meant to know. I was careful. I never thought you'd find out. How did you?'

'You weren't careful enough. Freddie saw you kissing her.'

'Ahh.' Father leant against the doorjamb. 'That's why he was so testy with me.'

'Wouldn't you be?' Meg spat. Then a thought struck her. 'Where's Arthur?'

'On the boat.'

'Does he know?'

'Of course not.'

'Where does he think you are?'

'Meeting gaffers to get the next load.'

'For all this time?'

'He has Blossom to take care of. I give him enough jobs to keep him busy for hours.'

'While you come here and see your secret family?' she sneered in contempt. Poor Arthur.

'No one was meant to know.'

'Especially Mam.' Meg's voice cracked, and that irritated her. She didn't want to cry in front of him.

'Definitely not your mam.' The look he gave her was full of contempt.

Rage filled her. 'It doesn't matter any more. You can *flaunt* your hussy in front of everyone now. *Mam's dead!*'

'No!' Her father stumbled, grabbed the wall, and fell to his knees.

'We buried her yesterday without you.' Meg stood over him. 'Not that you'd care. You've got another wife already lined up.'

'My sweet Lucy.'

'*Your Lucy?*' Meg shouted, her temper ready to explode. '*Your Lucy?* The woman you betrayed! For years!' A sob broke from her. 'How dare you pretend to care!'

'I care!' He lurched to his feet. 'You know nothing, girl!'

He'd called her girl, again. Incensed, Meg squared up to him. 'If you *cared*, you'd not have another wife and three children in this filthy pit.'

'Quiet!' The woman, Josie, stormed out of the house, the doctor right behind her. 'My son is ill.'

'Mr Taylor,' the doctor soothed. 'Perhaps this altercation can be postponed for the moment? Your son needs you.'

Meg glared at the three of them. 'Yes, Father, go see to your son. Give him the love and attention you never give to Nicky when he's ill.'

'Nicky?' the woman asked, confused.

'You wouldn't know, would you?' Meg taunted. 'There's *eight* of us. And we buried my *mother* only yesterday.'

The woman fainted.

Meg watched the scene of her father and the doctor attending to Josie as though from a distance without emotion or thought.

'We should go,' Lorrie murmured.

'Yes, we should. I need to find Arthur.'

'No, Meg!' Father shouted as she walked away. 'Leave Arthur alone.'

Meg ignored him and strode down the hill to the steps. She kept up the fast pace until she was at the docks. There, she searched along the wharves, looking for her father's narrowboat.

'We'll stay here,' Lorrie told Meg. 'Remember, the train we need to be on leaves Halifax at three. We can't risk staying here much longer or we'll miss it.'

'Give me five minutes then we'll start back.' Meg hurried away, her eyes picking out her brother where he stood on the boat's deck coiling a rope. 'Arthur!'

Surprised, he sprang from the deck up onto the dock. 'Meg? What are you doing here?' He jogged to her, his smile wide and his hair overlong. He'd begun shaving and looked so much older than when she last saw him only a couple of months ago.

Meg embraced him. 'It's a long story, but I need you to come with me and I'll tell you on the way.'

'Come with you? Leave the boat?'

'Yes. We'll get the train back to Wakefield.'

'The train?'

'Go and get your things!'

'What about Father? He's around somewhere.' Arthur searched the docks.

'Don't worry about Father. I've seen him.'

'He wants me to leave?' Arthur screwed up his face, not convinced.

'Yes, come along. We have to hurry.'

'Arthur!' Their father ran down the wharf, passing Lorrie and Fliss.

Furious, Meg faced him. 'Arthur's coming home with me.'

'No, he's not,' Father panted, stopping a yard from them to suck in a deep breath.

'What's going on?' Arthur asked, confused.

Meg took his hand. 'Father has another family.'

'Shut your mouth,' Father warned.

'Another family?' Arthur scowled at her as though she was mad.

'Yes. He has a woman living up there.' She pointed to the hill. 'Behind the Red Lion. They have three children.'

Arthur stared at his father. 'Is that true?'

'Aye, lad, but I can explain. Get back onboard and we'll talk.'

'No.' Meg grasped Arthur's hand tighter. 'You need to come home with me.'

'He's *my* son!' Father scorned, grabbing Arthur by the shoulder. 'He will do as *I* say.'

Meg turned to Arthur, blocking out her parent. 'Mam... Mam has died,' she said as gently as her anger would allow. 'You need to come home. Leave Father. He doesn't deserve you. Freddie and me will help you get work.'

Abruptly, Father ripped Arthur's hand from Meg. 'Get away from him. You've done your damage, now go.' His anger matched her own.

'Arthur?' Meg beseeched. 'You need to come home with me.'

'Get on the boat, son.' Father pushed him towards the edge, forcing him to jump onto the deck.

Arthur, tears in his eyes, looked at Meg. 'Mam?'

'We buried her yesterday. We couldn't wait any longer for you to come home.' Seeing her brother so upset brought a lump to her throat. 'I'm sorry I had to tell you like this. You've got to come back with me, please.'

Father jumped onto the boat and wrapped his arms around Arthur's shoulders, before glaring up at Meg. 'Go!'

Arthur pushed him away. 'Don't touch me. Get back to your

fancy woman!' He sprang from the deck and raced along the wharf.

'Arthur!' Meg shouted, but he was as fast as a whippet and soon was lost amongst the cranes and cargo. She turned back to her father and looked down at him standing on the deck. Once she had been proud of her hard-working father. As a child, in her eyes he'd been something of a hero, travelling the waterways across the county, suntanned in the summer and with tales of the locks and canals, the river wildlife he saw, the people he met and their ways.

In the last few years his controlling ways, his rudeness to her, his lack of love towards her, had smudged that image. Now she saw him just as a man, a flawed, lying, selfish man.

Pain shifted in her heart. She'd lost her mam, and she realised she'd never really had her father. 'You are dead to me, to us all.' She had no emotion left to feel for him. 'Never come to Wellington Street again. You're not welcome. If you have any decency left in you, you'll send Arthur home, but we are no longer your family, understand?'

'You'll not tell me what to do, girl.'

Meg clenched her fists. 'If you come near any of us again, I'll go to the police. You'll be jailed for being a bigamist.'

His eyes widened. 'You wouldn't.'

'Try me.' Her stare was full of disgust before she walked back to Lorrie and Fliss, who threaded their arms through hers, and the three of them began the long walk back to Halifax train station.

9

Meg dropped a stitch and tutted with impatience. She was finishing the vest her mam had been knitting for Nicky. The candle flickered in the draft. She'd only lit one out of habit, to economise, but in some ways they were doing better than ever before.

In the months since her mam's death and the truth about her father was revealed, Freddie's steady income had helped enormously. Susie had started at the mill, working alongside Mabel, another small income to add to the pot, and Meg had picked up more shifts at the Bay Horse because of Terry working less due to painful gout in his foot.

Without the constant worry of Mam's illness, the fetching and carrying up and down stairs all day and night, Meg gained more time in her day to do other tasks. Her parents' room and been whitewashed and from the second-hand stall in the market she'd bought green curtains for that bedroom and red ones for the downstairs front room. Her parents' bed was now shared between Mabel and Susie while she'd squeezed an old camping cot that Freddie got off some docker beside the double bed for herself.

Betsy, Nell and Nicky shared a double bed in the other bedroom and Freddie now slept in there as well on the single bed.

No longer having to rush home to check on Mam, Meg could shop further afield, go into town properly and search out decent prices even if it took her hours.

The back door opened, and Freddie came in carrying a bucket of coal. 'It's still warm out.'

She smiled. 'We might have a pleasant summer.'

'We might if this good weather we've been having for May continues.'

'May. It'd have been Mam's birthday next week.'

'Aye.' Freddie fed the fire a few pieces of coal and then added more to the range fire. 'Fancy a late cuppa?'

'Go on then.' She glanced at the small clock on the mantel. 'It's just gone nine. We should be off to bed.'

'Aye, but the nights are drawing out. It wasn't dark until after supper tonight. I enjoy walking home in the daylight.' He stoked the range to build the fire up.

'Are you still happy working at the brewery?'

'It's a good job. Mr Pepper told me today I could have a permanent position. The lad I was filling in for isn't coming back.'

Meg put down her knitting. 'That's great news. Why isn't the fellow coming back?'

'His broken leg turned bad. He's had it cut off.'

'Gracious. That's terrible.'

'Aye, poor sod.'

'Why didn't you mention all this earlier?'

He grinned as he filled the kettle from the water bucket. 'You know what it's like when everyone is home. You can't get a word in. Nicky was excited because his drawing won first place in class.'

She smiled fondly, thinking of his happiness at winning. 'Bless, he was so thrilled.'

'He could go far with his drawing if he keeps at it. He's clever. Artistic.'

'He can't make a living from it when he's older, Freddie. You shouldn't put ideas into his head. I heard you when we were eating. Telling him he could be an artist. He'll end up in a factory or warehouse, too.' She felt sad at the thought, but had to be realistic.

'Who says he can't be an artist?' Freddie defended, adding spoonfuls of tea leaves into the brown earthenware teapot.

'What call is there for an artist around here?'

'Plenty. Every shop has painted signs and there's the portrait painter in town and those who design cards. Why can't Nicky do that? Why should he have to work in a factory or mill?'

Meg gave it some thought. 'You could be right.'

'We need to help him achieve it, Meg.' Freddie set out two cups. 'He's clever. And have you seen the way Betsy adds all those ribbons and things on hers and Nell's bonnet? She's clever, too.'

Meg frowned. Betsy had always enjoyed finding leaves and feathers while playing outside and using them to sew on bits of rag. She had an entire collection of such pieces upstairs under the bed.

'That feather she put on Nell's bonnet looked nice.' Freddie mashed the tea. 'She could be apprenticed to a milliner. She's handy with a needle and thread. She sewed my button back on my trousers in no time at all.'

'You should have sewn your own button on,' she chided.

He laughed. 'Why should I when I have five sisters?'

'You cheeky beggar!' She couldn't help but laugh, too. It was so nice to have him living at home. She felt as though her worries had been halved just by his presence in the house. For the first time, she didn't feel as though she was drowning in worries, but had her head above the water, with Freddie swimming alongside her. The future didn't seem so bleak.

Freddie sank onto the sofa, which was past its best. 'Seriously, though, Betsy should become apprenticed to a milliner or dressmaker.'

'Heavens, you've thought this through,' Meg chuckled.

'I think of a lot of things while working. Loading barrels of ale takes my strength, not my mind. Thinking about things passes the time more quickly. Though the brewery has become busy in the last few weeks since Mr Henderson has taken over. Orders have been coming in at a fast rate. Mr Henderson has been travelling all over Yorkshire and beyond getting orders. We hardly see him.'

A small thrill came over her when she thought of Christian Henderson. He was showing the town what a fine businessman he could be, that he could undo the damage his uncle had done and make the brewery a success. 'I'm happy for him.'

'His cousin isn't.' Freddie snorted. 'He reckons he's been swindled.'

'How so?'

'Well, old Mr Henderson had run the business into the ground, and Barney never took an interest. He sold it to his cousin and his cousin is making a good go of it.' Freddie gave Meg her cup of tea with a teaspoon of sugar in it as a treat.

'Barney Henderson didn't have it in him to make the brewery a success, or he'd have helped his poor father before he died.'

'We all know that, but Barney reckons his cousin has bought the brewery cheap, knowing that it could become a triumph.'

'If the brewery is doing well, that's through Mr Henderson's hard work.' Meg felt slighted on his behalf.

'Of course it is. Still, it didn't stop Barney shouting his head off in the office at Mr Henderson today. We all heard him. Anyway,

Barney is off to live in Manchester or somewhere with his mother or so the rumours have it.'

Suddenly, the front door opened. Arthur stood there looking gaunt and dirty.

'Arthur!' Meg jerked to her feet, spilling her tea.

Freddie went to him. 'You all right, brother?'

'Father's dead,' Arthur stated, eyes dull.

'What?' Freddie stared at Meg, his surprised expression mirroring her own.

Meg took Arthur's hand and led him into the room and shut the door. 'What happened?'

'Fever.' Arthur's tone echoed the exhaustion in his face. His hair was overgrown down to his shoulders, his clothes stained. Grime coated the back of his neck and under his fingernails.

'When?'

'Last week. The doctor said fever was sweeping through Sowerby Bridge and Halifax. They buried him quickly.' Arthur's voice broke. 'He's in a pauper's grave near Tommy and the baby.'

Meg stared at him. 'Tommy and the baby?'

Arthur gazed at her with dead eyes. 'Father and me have been living with Josie.'

'Why didn't you come home?' Meg demanded, hating the fact Arthur had been with that other woman.

Shrugging, Arthur sank back against the sofa, exhausted. 'Father needed me.'

Although she wanted to rant and rave, she did neither of these things. For one, she would wake up the others and, two, looking at Arthur, she realised none of this was his fault.

'I can't believe he's gone,' Arthur muttered and, as though that admission burst the dam wall of his emotions, he erupted into tears.

Freddie clasped him tightly. 'That's it, lad, let it out. You'll feel better.'

Meg turned from them, tears hot behind her eyes at seeing her brother so upset. Her father's death barely registered. She'd mourned the loss of him the day she confronted him in Sowerby Bridge. Since then, she had hardly thought of him, and if she did, it was with loathing. Besides, she didn't have the time to grieve. The family needed her.

She quickly put a pan of water onto the range to heat. Arthur stank and needed a good wash. 'Freddie, go up and fetch him a clean shirt and trousers. His Sunday clothes will do. I put them in a box under your bed.'

Arthur wiped his eyes with his forearm. 'You saying I stink, our Meg?'

'I do. No brother of mine will walk about in such a state. Come over here and start washing.' She found a cake of soap and a clean towel from a cupboard and put them on the table.

Stripping off his shirt, Arthur let out a long sigh. 'I'm sorry I ran away from you, Meg.'

'I understand. You were upset. So was I.' She poured warm water into a tin bowl.

Lathering up the soap in his hands, he washed his face and neck. 'I felt I couldn't leave Father, especially when he took me to see Josie and the kiddies. Tommy was at death's door and died the next day after you were there.'

Meg recalled seeing the ill little boy in the bed and it saddened her that he'd died. 'You've stayed there ever since?'

'Aye.' Arthur rinsed his face. 'Father and me did a few short runs with loads to Dewsbury, but Josie needed Father. She didn't handle Tommy's death well, and then the baby died the following week. A couple of weeks later, Father became ill. He rallied after a few days, but then he became really sick and died three days later.'

'How did you get home?' Freddie asked, returning from upstairs.

'I brought a load back on the boat.' Arthur allowed Meg to tip water over his hair and then scrub it with the soap.

'By yourself?' Freddie poured him a cup of tea.

'No, I had a lad with me who walked with Blossom while I steered,' Arthur replied, his head bent over the bowl as Meg used cold water to rinse it. 'Jesus!' Arthur shivered.

'Use the rest of the warm water to wash your body.' Meg turned from him. 'I'll go up and grab a blanket for you. You'll have to sleep on the sofa tonight.'

'That's fine. I'll be back on the boat tomorrow.'

Later, with Arthur sitting on a chair, Meg lit another candle and began cutting his long hair.

'We'll have to sell the boat,' Freddie said, spreading beef dripping on a piece of bread for Arthur.

'Sell it!' Arthur jolted in the chair.

'Whist! Stay still or I'll cut your ear off, silly,' Meg tutted.

'We can't sell it!' Arthur glowered at him. 'I've a load to take in the morning. I've been working down the docks all evening unloading and talking to some of the gaffers for another load. Stevenson's have said they'll load me up in the morning.'

'You're sixteen,' Freddie pointed out. 'You can't run the boat.'

'The businessmen along the canal know me, they knew Father. I can keep doing it, especially if you come back onboard.'

Freddie shook his head. 'No. I'm not spending my life chasing loads. The canal is finished.'

'*You* might think so, but I don't,' Arthur snapped. 'I'll do it by myself then.'

'Don't be ridiculous. You're a lad,' Freddie dismissed him.

'I got a load here, didn't I? Mr Stevenson trusts me to take another load in the morning!'

Meg slapped his shoulder. 'Keep your voice down before you wake the entire street!' she hissed. 'Both of you. Enough.'

Freddie stood and yawned. 'I'm away to bed. I'll talk to Mr Pepper tomorrow and see if I can get you a job at the brewery.'

'I don't want a bloody job at the brewery!' Arthur whispered harshly. 'I have a boat. I work the canals! We can do it together, Freddie,' he pleaded.

Freddie spread his hands wide. 'I don't want to spend my life chasing loads, Arthur, or worrying about repairs to the boat and mooring fees, or if Blossom goes lame. I want a future where I get paid every week.'

'And be told what to do by others?' Arthur scorned. 'Never to be your own man again?'

'Maybe I *am* told what to do, but that doesn't bother me. Father told me what to do, didn't he? So, what's different? I do my work and I get paid for it with none of the hassle of owning a narrowboat.'

Arthur grunted. 'Another man's skivvy.'

'I'm also free of worry, Arthur, and that's a mighty thing.'

Meg was proud of Freddie's maturity.

Freddie glanced at Meg with a smile. 'Besides, I get to come home to the family every night. I'm not freezing sleeping on a cold boat.'

A fierce look altered Arthur's face. 'I want to work the canals.'

'Not any more you aren't,' Meg told him. 'You're sixteen. None of the gaffers will take you seriously. Without Father, they'll rob you blind.' Meg tidied everything away. 'I'm the eldest, I decide.' She gave them both a stern stare. 'I have the paperwork for the boat upstairs in Mam's old box.'

'We aren't selling it. It's been in our family for generations.' Tears welled in Arthur's eyes. 'And what about Blossom?'

Meg knew he loved that horse more than anything in the world. 'She will have to go, too. We have no use for her. I'm sorry, but the money from the sale of the boat and Blossom will benefit us greatly. I can buy us all new clothes and have rent money for months.'

Arthur shook his head, his chin trembled. 'I should never have come back.'

Freddie yawned again. 'I know it's tough, but this is the only option we have.'

'Come on,' Meg encouraged, giving Arthur a quick embrace. 'Let us all get some sleep. The morning arrives soon enough.'

When Meg came downstairs at dawn the following morning, Arthur wasn't sleeping on the sofa. Her chest tightened in alarm.

Freddie glanced at her as he came in from the backyard. 'Don't panic, Arthur's in the lav.'

Meg relaxed. 'I thought he'd run off.' She took the bowl of soaked oats and tipped it into the pan to warm up and added water. Freddie had already stirred up the embers and got the fire going ready to heat the kettle for tea.

'No. He was fast asleep when I came down.' Freddie added more coal to the fire. 'He was exhausted, poor lad.'

'I know he'll take this hard, but we have no other choice.'

'I agree with you.'

'I'll see to the others, then I'll go to the docks.' Meg stirred the porridge. 'I thought to speak to Mr Chambers, Lorrie's father. He might know of someone looking to buy a boat.'

Arthur caught the conversation as he came in. 'I don't see why I can't do loads.'

'Not on your own.' Freddie set out the bowls. 'You'd be robbed blind.'

'Not only that,' Meg interrupted, 'but you can't see to the boat and Blossom single-handedly.'

'One of the girls can come with me. I'm sure Betsy could handle Blossom.'

'No, they won't. Mam wanted all of us educated like she was so we can better our lives.' Meg walked to the bottom of the stairs. 'Mabel, Susie, you're going to be late!'

Standing back at the range, she stirred the porridge as it bubbled. 'I know you're disappointed, Arthur, but that's life, I'm afraid. We all have to make the best of what we're dealt.'

Mabel came downstairs, yawning, only to stop with her mouth open as she saw Arthur at the table. 'You've come home then?'

'Nothing escapes you, does it?' Arthur took a bowl and spoon as Meg ladled the porridge into bowls.

Susie hurried down the stairs, still plaiting her hair. 'Arthur!'

Mabel sat and took a bowl. 'Aye, he's home along with his smart mouth.'

'And Father?' Susie asked.

'No. He's dead,' Arthur said bluntly, staring into his bowl.

'Arthur!' Meg glared at him. 'I was going to tell them tonight.'

'Father's dead?' Nicky asked from the bottom of the stairs, Betsy and Nell standing behind him.

Meg went to him and cradled him close. 'Yes, dearest.'

Mabel and Susie started crying, breakfast forgotten. Betsy and Nell took their stools at the table subdued, but still wanted their porridge. They'd had less to do with their father; being young girls, he had no time for them.

'I ain't going to the mill today,' Mabel cried.

'Yes, you will, or you'll lose your place,' Meg said, knowing Mabel would do anything to get time off work. 'Eat up.'

'They can't sack us for having a death in the family,' Mabel cried.

'They can and they will.' Meg urged Nicky to sit and eat, which he did, not overly dismayed about the news. But then, their father had very little to do with Nicky since his birth. A sick child was something their father had no wish to concern himself with.

Her mind ran in another direction. The other children he had begot with that woman. Tommy had looked about four years old. Nicky was six. Mam had been ill ever since Nicky was born. Was that why her father went with another woman? Had Mam told him not to touch her and so he got his pleasure elsewhere?

'Meg?' Nicky tugged on her skirt. 'I want to go to school.'

'You can, sweetling.' She ruffled his hair.

'We should all stay home today,' Mabel said, her expression mutinous. 'Out of respect.'

Meg flinched. Respect. Her father deserved no respect.

Freddie stood and placed his empty bowl in the bucket. 'Everyone is going to work or school and that's the end of it. I'm away, Meg.' He grabbed his hat and coat from the nail behind the door. 'Mabel, you best hurry, too. Susie, are you ready?'

Grateful for his help in getting the others into line, Meg poured hot water from the kettle into the bucket. 'I'll have a look in Mam's box for the boat papers.'

Arthur pushed his bowl away. 'I'm off to see to Blossom.'

'Ask around for a buyer for her today,' Freddie told him, opening the front door. 'The sooner we don't have to pay her stabling and feed bills, the better.'

'You're a heartless arse,' Arthur snapped. 'She's been a good horse.'

'Aye, I know it.' Freddie grabbed his arm. 'And I know you're upset, but call me that again and I'll wipe the floor with you.'

Meg breathed a sigh of relief when the house emptied. She washed the dirty dishes and tidied the kitchen. She had a stack of ironing to do, but instead she went upstairs. From the wardrobe, she took the small box from the bottom of it and placed it on the bed. Before she could open the lid, knocking sounded on the front door.

She heard voices talking outside, and opening the door she saw Mrs Fogarty talking to a well-dressed gentleman, who turned to Meg with a look of enquiry.

'Is this the Taylor residence?' he asked.

'I told you it was.' Mrs Fogarty raised her eyebrows. 'I ain't one for lying.'

The man ignored her and gave Meg a tight smile that was more of a grimace. 'Are you Mrs Lucy Taylor?'

Meg frowned. 'No, that was my mam. She died recently.'

'Oh, I see. That explains it then.'

'You are?'

'Mr Moffatt, solicitor.' He doffed his hat.

Meg's mind worked quickly. 'Mr Moffatt. You sent my mam a letter.'

'I did.'

'She died after reading it.'

'My condolences.' He bowed his head, concern in his eyes. 'Is your father home?'

She flicked a glance to Mrs Fogarty. 'Father died last week in Sowerby Bridge. Arthur came home late last night and told us. I was going to tell you this morning.'

'No!' Mrs Fogarty gasped. 'Oh, Meg. Lass, I'm that sorry to hear it.'

'I'll come over for a chat later, Mrs Fogarty.' Meg pushed the door open wider. 'Would you like to come inside, Mr Moffatt?'

Thankful that the house was clean and tidy, Meg clasped her hands before her. 'Would you like to sit down?'

'No, thank you.' Mr Moffatt peered around the front room and adjoining kitchen, his expression unreadable. 'I won't take up too much of your time, Miss Taylor.'

She noticed that he'd wrinkled his nose. Did the house smell? She'd scrubbed the floor only yesterday. Was it the damp? Meg sniffed. She could definitely smell damp, but it wasn't too bad, not like in the winter. Was it the lavatory? That usually stank in hot weather, but she didn't think it was overly smelly today. 'Tea?'

'Thank you, but no. I've not long eaten. I arrived yesterday, you see, and stayed overnight in a hotel.' Mr Moffatt took off his top hat and placed it and his bag on the table. 'It was your mother I wished to see since I hadn't received word from her. Now I understand why.'

'I'm sorry for not having written myself, but there's been a lot to deal with since Mam died. I simply forgot.' How could she explain all that had happened since Mam's death to a stranger?

'Of course.' He looked uncomfortable. 'And now your father has passed, too.' He pulled out sheets of paper and read a few lines. 'Are you Margaret May Taylor? The firstborn child of Lucy?'

'I am, yes. Meg.' It was rare for her to hear her full name. Only her mam sometimes used to call her Margaret May.

'And you have a brother, Frederick Francis,' he read from the sheet. 'You and he were all the children listed in my clients' will.' He looked at her. 'My clients were your grandparents, Mr and Mrs Mellor.'

'They listed us in their will?' It sounded incredible. Had they been prosperous enough to make a will?

'Yes, in the event of your mother being deceased, you and your brother were listed as the next beneficiaries.'

'But I have four sisters and another two more brothers.'

He frowned. 'Your grandparents did not know of them. They told me they had two grandchildren. The last letter they received from your mother stated the birth of Frederick.'

'Mam did write to them, many times. I know she did. Only a few years ago, she wrote to them again. My grandfather sent her two ten-shilling notes. I don't think she heard from them after that. So, she stopped writing.'

'Your grandparents moved several times, from what I know. Your grandfather had employment in several places before he retired from teaching. He then worked solely as an artist. He painted miniature portraits.'

'He did?' Meg said in wonder. That's where Nicky got his talent from then. 'My brother Nicky is brilliant at drawing. He won a prize at Sunday school.'

'The artistic gift must run in the family.' Mr Moffatt shuffled his papers. 'Your grandparents left everything in their will to your mother, Miss Taylor.'

'They did?' Surprise made her voice crack. Her mother had disappointed them so much, especially by marrying Frank Taylor, a simple narrowboat skipper. Little did her grandparents know that they had been right. He was the wrong man for her lovely mam.

'Which is why I have made the journey north to meet with your mother.'

'I should have written to you when she died. I'm sorry you've wasted your time.'

'Not at all. Besides, it's agreeable to have time away from the office and see something of our great country. I've never been to Wakefield before.' He gave a glimmer of a smile. 'Now, you and your brother will receive an equal share in the inheritance.'

'We will?' Nearly everything he said shocked her.

'Your grandparents had put aside some money. From what I know, your grandmother had inherited some assets from her father, which have been sold over the years. However, there was a tidy sum of sixty-three pounds, three shillings and eight pence in their bank account when they died. That money is now to be divided between you and your brother, Frederick.'

'Goodness.' Meg had to sit down. She and Freddie had some money. All she could think of was she'd not have to worry about the rent money for a while. Oh, and she could buy herself a summer dress and new boots. She glanced down at her old scruffy boots with their broken laces and quickly tucked them under her brown skirt.

'I need you to sign a few papers, Miss Taylor...' He flushed bright red. 'Or make your mark.'

'All of us can read and write, Mr Moffatt. Mam insisted we learn.'

'The daughter of a teacher, I would expect nothing less.' He nodded, giving her a pen, a small inkpot and the official papers to sign. 'And your brother?'

'Freddie is at work. He'll not be home until six.'

'Indeed. Perhaps I can go to his place of work and see him there? I would like to catch the two o'clock train.'

'I can take you there now.' Meg carefully and slowly signed her name with the fancy gold pen, which she greatly admired.

'I would appreciate that.' Mr Moffatt packed away his things while Meg quickly pinned on her black felt hat. With money she could buy herself a new hat, too, and the others. She felt heady at the thought, like the time she drank too much gin at Christmas last year with Mrs Fogarty.

Along Wellington Street she nodded to her neighbours. All were staring at Meg and the unknown gentleman she walked beside. She hid a smile, knowing it'd be the talk of the street for a day or two, that and Frank Taylor's demise. She could rely on Mrs Fogarty spreading the news about her father's death. It still seemed surreal. Both her parents were gone.

'You have lived here all your life, Miss Taylor?' Mr Moffatt asked as they walked along Thornes Lane Wharf.

'Yes. I was born in that house on Wellington Street.'

'Yet your father was a narrowboat man. I'm surprised you don't live on the boat.'

'My mam wouldn't have it. She wanted us to be brought up decently, to go to school and church. To live a normal life as she did.' She paused by the steps leading down to the ferry. 'We need to cross the river.'

'Oh, I see.' Mr Moffatt didn't look comfortable to descend the green slippery steps.

'We could walk around the bridge, but it'll take longer.'

He took a deep breath. 'The ferry it is, then.'

Meg carefully trod down each step, the mucky water lapping at the sides. A slick of some kind of chemical run-off spread across the river's dark water. The odour wasn't pleasant, but not bad enough to warrant a handkerchief over his nose as Mr Moffatt had. He moaned a little, stepping onto the swaying walkway, and hurried across it to join Meg on the small ferry.

'Mind as you go,' Harry called out, releasing the ropes.

'After we've seen Freddie, you can walk straight across the bridge to the train station, Mr Moffatt. No need for you to use the ferry again.'

'Thank the Lord for small mercies.' He grimaced, peering around at the water sitting only a foot below the side. 'I'm not a man who enjoys being on the water.'

'It only takes a short time.' She pointed to the buildings. 'The brewery is on the other side of those mills.'

Harry got them safely to the other side and held out his hand for the fee to Mr Moffatt, who also kindly paid for Meg.

'Thank you,' she said when they were walking up the steps.

'It's the least I can do, for you have saved me a longer walk and the chance of missing my train. Now, where can I locate your brother?'

'This way.' She led him through the busy mill yards. The noise of steam machinery drowned out further conversation. A white cloud drifted on the air coming from the flour mill and the sweet hop smell from the brewery greeted them before they entered the large iron gates.

They passed a long dray piled high with beer barrels being pulled by a team of eight shire horses. The wording 'Henderson's Brewery' was written on the side of the dray in black and gold. Fresh horse dung stung Meg's nose.

She headed for the huge red-brick warehouse with its tall, wide doors and behind that the three storeys of storerooms and offices with a tower at the top. A large black and gold sign denoting Henderson's Brewery was also on the tower for everyone to see for some distance. Other outbuildings were joined to this main building, including a steam engine house, the noise of which was loud and constant.

Inside the warehouse, the sweeter smell of malt and the ale itself took away the acid aroma of dung. Men worked at various jobs, some unloading barrels of malt, others pulling trolleys filled with casks.

'Meg!' Freddie, looking concerned, ran over to her from where he'd been stacking kegs. 'What's happened?'

'Nothing. At least, nothing bad,' she quickly assured him. 'This is Mr Moffatt. He was our grandparents' solicitor. He came looking for Mam.'

Mr Moffatt shook Freddie's hand. 'My condolences, Mr Taylor. As I explained to your sister, I bring news of your grandparents' will.'

'A will?' Freddie repeated, stunned.

'Can we go somewhere more private, perhaps?' Mr Moffatt glowered at the noise and bustle around him.

'What is all this, Taylor?' An older man in a plain suit and cap came through a door and behind him Christian Henderson glanced up from the papers he was reading in his hand.

Meg's stomach clenched as he stared at her. She'd not seen him for weeks, not since the train journey. Although she hadn't been in his company since then, he'd been constantly on her mind.

He immediately walked towards her with a smile on his face that made her heart thud.

'Miss Taylor?' Christian's voice was full of astonishment, but his cornflower-blue eyes were soft with interest and warmth.

'Do forgive us for interrupting.' Mr Moffatt held out his hand to Christian. 'Charles Moffatt, solicitor.'

Mr Henderson shook his hand. 'Is there a problem?'

Meg stepped forward. 'I'm sorry for coming to Freddie's place of work. I wouldn't have come if it wasn't important.'

'Taylor?' The older man in the plain suit raised his eyebrows at Freddie.

'Mr Pepper, my sister has brought a solicitor to see me.' Freddie spoke politely but with none of the fear most working men have towards those in authority. Meg was proud that he'd mixed with so many kinds of people on the canals and docks that he felt assured of his worth.

'Mr Moffatt has papers for Freddie to sign regarding our grandparents' will,' Meg added.

'Then you must use one of the offices.' Mr Henderson waved them towards the door he'd just come through. 'It is quieter in Pepper's office.'

They followed him up a flight of stairs into a square, plain office where Mr Moffatt quickly sorted out his pen and ink and papers for Freddie to sign while Mr Pepper and Mr Henderson waited on the landing near another staircase which led up to the next floor.

'We have money, Freddie.' Meg grinned, still unable to believe it. 'You and me.'

'How much?' Freddie signed his signature.

'We share sixty-three pounds, three shillings and eight pence.'

Freddie whistled low.

'Isn't it grand?' she gushed.

'I will transfer the money into your bank account,' Mr Moffatt said, tidying away his belongings.

'Bank account?' Meg blinked rapidly. 'We don't have a bank account.'

'Ah, right. Well, now...' Mr Moffatt's bushy eyebrows pulled together. 'I shall return with the money, say... a week on Friday? Does that suit?'

'It does, very much.' Freddie shook his hand vigorously.

'Thank you, Mr Moffatt.' Meg also shook his hand.

'Excellent. I shall be on my way. A train to catch and all that.' He bustled from the room with a dip of his hat.

Meg stared at Freddie, unable to stop grinning. 'Sixty-three pounds, Freddie!'

'Three shillings and eight pence!' He laughed. 'We can buy things. New boots.'

'And food!'

'Taylor!' Mr Pepper stood at the doorway. 'I'd like my office returned and you've work to do.'

'Aye, Mr Pepper.' Freddie followed Meg out onto the wide landing where Mr Henderson stood at the bottom of the next flight of stairs. 'I appreciate you letting me do that, sir.'

'I am glad I could help.' Mr Henderson looked at Meg. 'Have you ever seen inside a working brewery before?'

'No...'

'Perhaps you would care to? If you are not in a rush to leave?' A small smile played about his lips.

Meg swallowed, her chest heaving in her corset at the anticipation of spending time with him. 'No, I'm not. In a rush, I mean. I would like that.' Her cheeks felt hot.

'Then I shall escort you and you can learn more about where your brother works.' Henderson nodded to Freddie, dismissing him.

'I'll see you tonight, Meg.' Freddie gave her a queer look before going downstairs.

Surprised to be alone with Christian Henderson, Meg seemed rooted to the spot.

'Shall we?' he asked, indicating the stairs. 'We should start at the top.'

Meg walked beside him up the staircase to another landing. Her stomach fluttered. He had singled her out. Why? He could have easily let her go on her way, but he'd asked her to take a tour, just the two of them. She snuck a side look at him. He was so handsome and well-attired. A gentleman in every way.

'On the right are more offices, mine included, but if we take this corridor to the left, we'll be in the tower where the fermentation takes place.' He gently took her elbow and guided her along to a wooden door.

Meg shivered at his touch, his nearness. Her head swam with the unexpectedness of being with him. Yet she liked it, liked him. His dark good looks did something to her not only physically but mentally. In his presence she wanted to be prettier, cleverer, more of everything that would make him keep looking at her.

'Here we are.' Mr Henderson led her to a viewing platform. 'This is the fermentation room. Here we have the hot wort mixture which is cooling down. See the vented slats around us?'

Meg glanced around at the vented tower, but in truth she didn't give a fig about the workings of the tower. Standing so close to Christian Henderson made her head spin. She simply wanted to stare at him.

'We use the air flow through the slats to control the cooling of the mixture. The wort is cooling in large open tanks, can you see how shallow they are?'

'I can, yes.' Meg nodded, trying to focus on what he was showing her, yet the sound of his voice, cultured and smooth, entered her heart and lodged there. 'They are shallow to allow them to cool quicker?'

'Yes.' His admiring look made her inwardly preen.

'The wort, once cooled, is run into fermenting vessels below. Gravity is doing our work for us. In the vessels the yeast is added,' Henderson explained.

'How long does all that take?' She was proud to ask a sensible question when her thoughts were so jumbled.

'About three days. After twenty-four hours, the yeast forms a thick skin on the surface which needs to be skimmed off.' He opened the door for her. 'If we go down to the next level, we can see the mashing and boiling room.'

Meg didn't care where they went just as long as she could listen to him, talk to him. For a short time, she could daydream that she was someone important, someone equal to him.

In the mashing room, he explained the process of the malt being ground to a grist which was then mixed with water, called liquor in this instance, which was all mixed in a cylindrical vessel called the masher. From there it ran into the tun. She asked more questions, genuinely interested. Some of the workers gave her odd glances, obviously wondering why a working-class lass was being given a tour of the building by the master.

As he took her into the sweet-smelling boiling room where a

large copper vat dominated the space, Meg asked a few more questions about this process, which seemed to delight him. She wanted him to think her clever. She thanked the fates that her mam had insisted she learn to read and write, to read the newspapers to broaden her knowledge.

'Sacks of hops are over there.' Christian pointed to the two men who were dragging heavy sacks across the floor. 'The hops are boiled with the wort.' He took her over to another large vessel. 'This has a perforated base for the spent hops to drop through.'

He led her through to another large room beside the warehouse, taking every opportunity to lightly touch her elbow. Meg's stomach swooped each time he did it. She didn't want the tour to end or for him to stop looking at her, talking to her. Was this feeling normal? She felt out of control and wasn't sure if she liked it.

Standing close to her, he pointed to the far wall. 'This is where the racking is done. After the ale is sent to the final checking and tasting station in the next room, we can then cask it and send the orders to our clients.'

'It's all very interesting, more than I thought it would be.' She smiled up at him, a little breathless at having him so close. It frightened her, this emotion, this sense of sadness that she had to part with his company.

'I am pleased you enjoyed the tour.' His warm gaze seemed to say more than his words.

She hated that the tour was over, and she'd have to leave him. In his presence, she felt like a woman, not a sister full of responsibilities, but a woman with her own thoughts and desires. 'Thank you for showing the workings of the brewery to me.'

'It was my pleasure, Miss Taylor.' His gaze locked with hers until a worker walked by and they took a step back from each other. 'Pepper told me that your brother mentioned your father's passing. You have been struck with such tragedy in a brief space of time.'

'I wasn't expecting to lose both parents so quickly, but nothing is for certain, is it?' It pleased her that he took an interest. He didn't have to, not a busy gentleman such as him.

'So, do you take the full responsibility of caring for your siblings?'

'Freddie helps me.'

'Such an enormous obligation,' he said with admiration.

'Yes, but it is the hand that has been dealt to me.' She couldn't stop looking at him. She didn't believe in fairy stories, but this felt like a spell had been woven over her and she couldn't think about anything else but Christian Henderson. Did he feel the same?

'I admire your generous spirit. To take care of your younger siblings will be difficult.'

'We'll manage. We always do.'

He took a step closer. 'Please remember that you are not without friends.'

Meg's breath hitched as she gazed at him. 'Oh, I know that. Lorrie and Fliss are wonderful, and I have Mrs Fogarty next door.'

He laughed gently. 'I was meaning me.'

'You?' Her eyes nearly popped from her head. Her heart somersaulted.

'Would that be such a bad thing?' His eyebrows rose. 'For us to be friends?'

She frowned, not understanding. 'People like us don't become friends, Mr Henderson. We are from very different lives.' Her thoughts flew suddenly in another direction, and she became breathless. 'Unless you are asking to become a *special* friend, sir?' She was both hot and bothered and insulted.

'Pardon?' He frowned and then sudden awareness dawned of her meaning and he held up his hands as if at gunpoint. 'Gracious! No! No, Miss Taylor, I assure you that is not my intention. Never would I be so crude and ungentlemanly. Not to you. I respect you.'

She sagged in relief and yet was a little disappointed. Wasn't she pretty enough for him? Of course she wasn't.

Mr Pepper appeared behind Meg. 'Sir, you have an appointment in ten minutes.'

Henderson straightened, instantly becoming a businessman again. 'I do, yes. Thank you, Pepper.'

'Good day, Mr Henderson.' Awkwardly, Meg shook his hand. 'Thank you for showing me around.'

He held her hand longer than necessary. 'I have enjoyed your company, Miss Taylor. Perhaps you would like to bring your brothers and sisters to my home one day? We have strawberries ripening in the gardens which they might like to pick soon? But there are also some early crops in the glasshouses that are nearly ready. They are the June crop, but in the hothouse they ripen a few weeks early.' He stopped abruptly, as though he'd caught himself rambling.

Once again, he'd rendered her mute. Had he just asked *her* to visit his *home*? Why was he acting this way? Did he feel sorry for her? An invitation didn't mean he would be there. It was for the children to pick strawberries, that was all. She shouldn't read into it more than it was.

Behind her, Mr Pepper coughed, snapping her out of her trance-like state. 'Thank you. The children would think that a wonderful treat.'

'Come any time. Next Sunday afternoon, perhaps? After church? If the weather is fine?'

Meg nodded, joy curling through her body. Yes, she wanted to see his home, and hopefully he would come out to the hothouse and greet them. 'Next Sunday.'

Unable to believe what had just happened, Meg strolled from the brewery, feeling light and unbelievably happy. The handsome Christian Henderson had invited her to his home, and she had received an inheritance. Could this day be any more glorious?

She felt for the first time in a long while that she could breathe easily, feel the sun on her face and take lighter steps. The burden of caring for her mam had lifted and her father's death removed any chance of him curtailing her life with his demands and rules or threats of living on the narrowboat.

No, the future looked so much brighter now. She had money to make her family a little more comfortable, and if she was careful with it, it could last her a year or two. For once, she'd have less worry and hopefully she could find some joy, to have small pleasures such as buying new clothes. Then she would appear more suitable for those times she was ever in Mr Henderson's company. Not that she expected to see him much, he was, after all, a busy man, but if they happened to meet, and she was dressed in new clothes, she would feel more comfortable, have more confidence to speak to him.

She thought of her grandmother, Margaret May, the daughter of a barrister, and held her head higher. She would do her grandparents proud and find a way to lift the family out of this wretched life they lived. She just had to find a way to do it. Perhaps she could find more suitable employment? Maybe work in a shop?

She turned into Wellington Street, stepped sideways around a boy wheeling a hoop along the cobbles, and thought to knock on Mrs Fogarty's door and tell her the news. Only a woman and a child were sitting on Meg's front doorstep.

A trickle of alarm pimpled over Meg's skin as she walked closer. Her father's mistress and daughter stood and stared at her.

10

'What do you want?' Meg barked, hating the sight of the dirty, ragged woman who reminded her of her father's treachery and years of deceit.

'I need to talk to you,' the woman, Josie, pleaded, her tattered shawl falling back off her greasy. lank hair.

'We've nothing to say to each other.' Meg pushed past her and turned the key in the lock.

'I'm not leaving until we've talked.' The hand Josie reached out was dirty with filth under her torn fingernails.

Furious, Meg spun back to her. 'How dare you come to my home and make demands? Get away from here!'

The door opened next door and Mrs Fogarty stuck her head out. 'Ah, Meg. You're home then. This one has been waiting for you for over an hour.'

'And now she's leaving,' Meg snapped. She went inside and slammed the door shut.

The woman banged on the door. 'Hear me out, will you?'

Meg ignored her and stoked the fire to boil the kettle. She was hungry and thirsty and also needed the lav. Going out to the backyard, she saw Mrs Fogarty coming in through the gate from the alley that ran behind the terraces.

'What's all this then?' Mrs Fogarty's expression was full of interest. 'That woman is fit to bang the ruddy door down.'

'I'll throw a bucket of water over her first,' Meg huffed, heading to the lavatory.

'Nay, don't waste good water on her, though she looks like she could do with a hard scrub. She's as dirty as I've ever seen a tramp to be. What does she want with you?'

'I'm ashamed to tell you,' Meg spoke through the door as she relieved herself.

'You can tell me owt, you know that. Nowt will pass my lips.'

Coming out of the lav, Meg sighed. 'She's Father's other wife.'

'Nay...' Mrs Fogarty's mouth gaped open. 'How can he have another wife? He had your lovely mam.'

'He had a whole other family.' Even saying the words out loud still brought out the rage and hurt enough to knock her sideways.

'Oh, lass. I'm sorry to hear it.' Mrs Fogarty patted Meg's arm.

'How he could live two lives with two families, I don't know. I'll never know.' Meg rubbed her forehead. Just half an hour ago she'd been floating in happiness. Now she was deep in the filth of the real world again.

'What are you going to do?' Mrs Fogarty's expression was full of concern.

'Ignore that woman. I want nothing to do with her, Mrs Fogarty. She's a stranger.'

'But that little girl...' Mrs Fogarty frowned. 'She's your sister then?'

'Half-sister,' Meg reluctantly admitted.

'Still... She's your blood.'

'We share a father, a lying, cheating man who deserved no loyalty from me and nor will his mistress.'

'I can't blame you, lass, really I can't.' Mrs Fogarty nodded in agreement, arms folded over her pinny. 'But I have a feeling that woman isn't going anywhere. She's desperate, lass. A desperate mother will do anything for her child.'

Meg sighed. Why did she have to deal with it? Didn't she have enough to worry about? 'Then she can sit on the front doorstep for hours for all I care,' Meg said defiantly.

And she did. With each passing hour, Meg's anger grew as the woman refused to leave and just sat on the step with the little girl. Meg did the ironing, then she made a large pork pie and cut up carrots and cabbage for the boiling pot and all the while she knew that woman was on the other side of the front door. The woman's presence also stopped her from leaving the house to go to the docks to talk to Mr Chambers about selling the narrowboat.

By the time the others came home from school, she was ready to burst.

'Who is that outside?' Nell asked first.

'Is she going to be living in the end terrace next to the malting house?' Betsy wondered. 'Mrs Browning said she was going to rent her back room.'

Meg poured them all a cup of tea. She'd been wanting to tell them about her and Freddie receiving some money and chat to them about going strawberry picking at Mr Henderson's house, but instead, she had to deal with the unpleasant issue outside the door.

'The little girl was asleep on the cobbles.' Nicky's upset expression mirrored his unbelieving tone. 'Why would anyone let their baby sleep on the cobbles?'

'Drink your tea.' Meg stirred the vegetables, irate at the woman for putting her in this position.

The door opened and Arthur walked in carrying the small

girl. Behind him stood the woman. 'Meg, Josie and Dolly are here.'

Meg gritted her teeth. She'd forgotten that Arthur had lived with the woman for a short time.

'They need a place to stay,' Arthur said, hitching Dolly in his arms.

'They can't stay here!' Meg stared at him.

'Why not?' Arthur, just as stubborn as Meg, glared back.

'She's not our friend or family. She's a stranger.'

'Josie is family.'

'No, she isn't!' Meg wanted to slap him. 'She's Father's whore!'

Arthur turned puce while the younger ones sat quietly at the table.

'I wasn't his whore,' Josie murmured. 'I married him. I was pure until my wedding night.'

'A wedding that was a lie!' Meg shouted at her. 'Get out of my house.'

'It's my house too, and I say she stays,' Arthur yelled.

Meg rounded on him. 'The day you start paying the rent is the day you can make any decisions!'

'Are you really going to make her and Dolly live on the streets?' Arthur looked at Meg as though he despised her.

Meg's stomach churned. She didn't want to fight with Arthur or be cruel, it wasn't her nature. Why did she have to be in this position? 'They aren't my responsibility.'

'Then just take Dolly,' Josie pleaded. 'I'll go, but please let Dolly stay. She's weak and another night in the open might make her even worse. I've had to beg for food along the way.'

A quick glance at the listless little girl in Arthur's arms weakened Meg's stance. Dolly, although filthy, was pale and terribly thin, wearing only a dirty, torn smock over her bare limbs.

'Why didn't you stay at your own home?' Meg asked Josie.

'I couldn't make the rent... Not without Frank.' Josie swayed, then the next moment she collapsed onto the floor, her head just missing the hearthstone.

Arthur thrust Dolly at Betsy to hold, and he and Meg fell to their knees beside Josie.

'Josie!' Arthur patted her arm. 'Meg, do something!'

Concerned but also frustrated at the task of taking care of more people, Meg lifted Josie's head up and patted her cheeks hard to bring her around. A moment later, Josie's eyes fluttered open.

'Nell, get her a cup of tea,' Meg ordered as she and Arthur dragged Josie to the sofa and helped her onto it. Josie's hair ran with lice, but Meg could also feel her bones poking through her ratty clothes. She closed her eyes in dismay. She felt she was being tested.

When the door opened and Mabel and Susie walked in, Meg wanted to disappear to somewhere pleasant, peaceful, anywhere but this house. Mabel and Susie wanted to know what was going on, and who were the strangers in their home.

While Arthur told them, Josie looked at Meg. 'I'm sorry. I had nowhere to go. Please take Dolly. She's your sister.'

Meg watched Nell, Betsy and Susie make a fuss of the little girl. Nicky gave her a sip of tea from his own cup. The gesture melted Meg's heart.

Mabel folded her arms. 'So, our father had a whole other family?' Spots of anger dotted her cheeks.

'Yes,' Meg answered.

'And you've known for how long?' Tears brimmed Mabel's eyes.

'Since Mam died.'

'And *you've* stayed with *her*?' Mabel turned her anger on Arthur. 'You betrayed this family to be with her?'

'Josie needed my help,' Arthur defended. 'Father became ill.'

'Father.' Mabel brushed away her tears furiously. 'I thought him such a decent man.'

'We all did,' Meg replied, bleakly.

Mabel glared at Josie. 'Why did *she* have to come here?'

'I'll go and I won't come back,' Josie murmured, bruising under her eyes from exhaustion. 'I promise. I know you'll give Dolly a good life, as best you can. I'll stay away.' A tear dripped over Josie's lashes and made a track through the dirt on her face.

Meg shied away from the distraught woman, not wanting to feel compassion for her. 'You can stay a few days until you can sort yourself out. That's all I can give you.'

'It's enough.' Josie sagged. 'Thank you.'

Meg stepped away and dragged Arthur with her. 'You brought her inside so *you* can help look after them.'

He jutted his chin out boldly. 'I know my duty.'

'Duty, is it?' She clenched her fist. 'Father had a *duty* to us *first*. Don't talk to me about duty. I know of it all too well.'

His shoulders sagged slightly. 'I will help.'

'Oh, I know you will, starting with going to the shops for more bread and oats for porridge. Then, when you get back, you'll go and fill another bucket of water from the tap. Ask Mrs Fogarty to lend us her spare bucket, too.'

His face altered. 'I don't have any money for the shops.'

She scowled at him. 'Didn't you get paid for the load you brought back?'

'Aye, but I needed to pay for Blossom's stabling and feed and the mooring fee.' He looked sheepish.

'You've nothing left?'

'I bought a meat pie today 'cos I was hungry.'

'You still should have something left over.' Meg couldn't make sense of it.

He lowered his head. 'I wasn't paid right.'

She took a deep breath to control her rising resentment. 'What do you mean?'

'The gaffer said I damaged some of the goods. They cut the fee they paid me.'

'Had you damaged the cargo?'

'No!' he flared. 'Father taught me how to look after the loads. I didn't damage a thing.'

Meg shook her head. 'No. No, they saw a sixteen-year-old standing before them trying to do a man's job and robbed you blind as Freddie and me said they would.'

Arthur hung his head.

She wanted to slap him silly but knew she didn't need to. He was learning lessons the hard way. 'Tomorrow we will ask around about selling Blossom and the boat. Then you'll find a position somewhere and start earning properly. Understood?'

He nodded.

A shift at the Bay Horse gave Meg the excuse to leave the house as soon as Freddie came home, and introductions were made. She left him and Arthur to dish out the pie and thoughtfully walked to the pub.

How had her life changed so rapidly? She missed the wise counsel of her mam. Mam would have known what to do about Josie and Dolly, or would she? Mam might have been educated but she failed at surviving in the harsh conditions of Wellington Street. She groaned softly. Mam would have been heartbroken to know of Father's deceit. Hatred for him rose again. It was impossible for Meg to forgive him or to grieve for him. Frank Taylor wasn't the man she had loved growing up. He was a liar, and she'd not waste her tears on him.

'What's wrong?' Fliss asked as soon as she took off her shawl and hung it up in the kitchen.

While they served the men in the bar, Meg told her about the eventful day she'd had.

'For that woman to just turn up...' Fliss scowled at the ale she was pouring. 'How is that fair to you?'

'I don't think Josie was thinking about what was fair. She just wanted Dolly to have a roof over her head. She said she'd go in the morning but wanted me to have Dolly.'

'As if you don't have enough mouths to feed?' Outraged, Fliss thumped a jug on the counter.

'I know, but how can I turn them out when they are skin and bones? I'll be sending them to their deaths, and I can't have that playing on my mind.' Meg took the coins from a customer and gave him his tankard of ale. 'I don't mourn my father and I don't miss him, but I wish he was here now to take Josie and Dolly off my hands.'

'You shouldn't have to deal with all that. Not so soon after your mam's passing.'

'I keep imagining how this would be if Mam lived. Would we ever have found out about Father's other life?' Meg served the next man. 'But I'm pleased Mam never knew.'

Fliss reached over for another jug and Meg noticed the bruising on her neck. 'What have you done to yourself?'

Immediately, Fliss pulled up her lace collar. 'Oh, being careless as always.'

Freddie walked up to the bar, distracting Meg from serving. 'Is anything wrong at home?' she asked, worried.

He shook his head. 'No. The girls wanted to put Dolly in bed with them and Arthur was talking with Josie, so I thought to come here for a pint and to talk to you.'

'Dolly in bed with the girls,' Meg moaned. 'They'll all have lice again by morning.' It was a daily fight to keep the lice from infesting the house and them.

'I couldn't say no.' Freddie scratched his forehead, looking tired.

Meg poured him a pint. 'Have I done the right thing?'

'About Josie staying? What else could you have done?' He sat on a stool and folded his arms on the counter. 'Dolly is our sister.'

'They can't stay more than a few days, Freddie,' Meg warned. 'We don't have enough room.'

'We could find a bigger place.' He leaned closer. 'We have the money to rent a bigger place with more bedrooms.'

'Leave Wellington Street?' Surprised at the idea, Meg stared at him.

'Aye. Find somewhere nicer.'

'We only have sixty-three pounds, Freddie. A bigger place will mean more rent. That money won't last long.'

'But if we are all working, Josie too, we could do it.'

'Are you mad? You want her to live *with* us?' Meg couldn't accept that idea. 'I can't live with Father's other woman. You're mad to even suggest it.'

'Do you want Dolly on the streets?' he whispered, looking about the bar.

'They aren't our family.'

'They are, Meg, whether you like it or not. We have a little sister we need to take care of now.'

'But Josie isn't our family.'

'She married Father in good faith, and she's buried two children within weeks and her husband, and now is homeless.'

Meg turned away and continued serving with sharp, unhappy movements. Why was this her predicament? Didn't she have enough to be burdened with?

'Where's me smile, Meggie May?' Reg taunted, nudging the man standing beside him.

'It's in the grave with both my parents, Reg.' Meg slammed his tankard down.

The surprising news filtered around the bar that Frank Taylor had passed. They gave condolences to both Meg and Freddie. More pints bought for Freddie, too.

Meg kept busy, not wanting to talk about her father, who everyone still thought was a good man. She wanted to shout to them he was a bigamist, a liar, a man with two families. But she didn't. She kept working, ignoring Freddie's efforts to talk about Josie until he gave up.

The evening became busier, more men dropped by for their nightly pint. Terry rubbed his hands together as the money box overflowed. Meg was rushed off her feet, but she froze when Christian Henderson walked in. His height and looks made every other man in the bar insignificant. She couldn't take her eyes off him as he walked towards her, a smile playing on his lips.

'We meet again, Miss Taylor.' He nodded to Freddie. 'Taylor.'

'Sir.' Freddie frowned. 'I didn't know you drank in here, sir.'

'I don't. I sell the ale, I do not drink it.' He waited for a man to leave the crowded bar and took his place. 'However, I was late leaving the brewery and tonight I did not care to return to an empty home.'

Meg felt his gaze on her. Happiness flooded her that he'd come into the pub when she was on shift. 'What would you like to drink, Mr Henderson?'

'A whisky, please. Irish if you have it.'

She nodded and turned to the shelves behind her and poured a measure into a small glass. When she handed it to him, their fingers touched. His gaze held hers. Heat flooded her face. She forced herself to let go of the glass, but his slow smile acknowledged she wasn't the only one to feel this madness between them.

Terry's son Gerald edged himself behind the bar. His smarmy face and bloodshot eyes turned Meg's stomach.

'You not married yet, Meg?' Gerald asked with a laugh, eyeing up Christian Henderson. 'It's not your fault, though. You've looks enough, but you're saddled with such a large family, no man would want to take all that on.'

'No man is good enough for my sister, Atkins,' Freddie sneered.

Gerald laughed. 'You Taylors think you're so much better than everyone else just because your grandfather was a teacher and your mother spoke well.' He poured himself a whisky. 'Yet you were all born on Wellington Street.' He chuckled. 'You'll all die in Wellington Street, too.'

'And what makes you the voice of authority and reason?' Mr Henderson asked Gerald. 'As I see it, you are the son of a publican. A man who, from what I can gather, does neither labour nor business. So, who are you to speak to Miss Taylor in such a way? Certainly not a gentleman as you seem to think yourself to be.'

Meg cheered inside at the rebuke.

Gerald glowered at Henderson. 'This business will be mine one day. You own a brewery. I'd be careful if I were you, Henderson. Us publicans tend to stick together, and we could prohibit your ale from our cellars.'

A calculating look entered Henderson's sharp blue eyes. He straightened languidly. 'Is that a threat, Atkins?'

Meg held her breath. This was a different side to Christian Henderson, and it awakened something in her, something primal. Before her stood a man of gentle strength and quiet intelligence. A man who forged his own destiny and stood up to those who got in his way. He would protect those he loved.

Taking a step back, Gerald waved a dismissive hand. 'All I'm saying is that you are new around here and need our business.'

'No, I do not.' Henderson drank the last of his whisky and turned his back on Gerald to face Freddie.

Flushing beetroot, Gerald's lips thinned into an angry line. 'Fliss, stop gawping and serve that docker, you useless wench!'

Fliss jumped and did as she was bid.

When Gerald had gone through to the back, Meg gave Fliss a tight smile. She knew Gerald disliked Fliss and made her life difficult at the pub. 'I'll go and wipe some tables.'

'No, let me.' Downcast, Fliss grabbed a cloth and left the bar.

'He always was a nasty piece of work,' Freddie grunted about Gerald.

Christian Henderson gazed at Meg. 'If he ever gives you trouble, you let me know.'

Freddie frowned, his eyes half closing. 'I can look after my sister, sir.'

'You need to be home to bed,' Meg warned. 'You've drunk more tonight than I've ever seen you.'

'People kept buying me drinks, because of Father.'

'You can refuse, you know?' Meg grinned. 'Go on. Go home.'

'Aye, I will in a bit, or I'll wait until you're finished, and I'll walk with you.' Freddie yawned.

'Taylor, go to your bed.' Christian Henderson patted his shoulder. 'I shall see your sister safely home.'

Meg's stomach flipped at the mention of him doing such a thing.

Freddie looked suspiciously at her. 'Meg walks home alone all the time, sir. She doesn't need you to escort her.'

'Of course I don't.' Meg laughed it off. 'Get off with you, Freddie, or you'll not get up in the morning.'

'May I have another whisky, please?' Christian Henderson asked.

Meg nodded, feeling the heat rise to her cheeks.

She served him and then five other men before she could get back to where he leaned against the bar. She wiped the bar down with a damp cloth, her feet aching, but she wanted to drag out the time while Mr Henderson was there, just a couple of feet from where she stood.

His gaze met hers and they both studied the other. He had a small scar under his jaw, near his ear, and she wondered how he got it. She dragged her eyes up from his jaw to his mouth, which now curved at the ends. Meg's breath caught in her throat. She itched to touch his face, to feel his skin under her hand.

Terry rang the bell for last orders, making Meg jump. As though a spell had been broken, she stepped back. A few workers ordered their last drinks, but most of the customers collected hats and coats and headed home to bed.

Surprised that Mr Henderson still stood at the bar and didn't seem in a rush to leave, Meg hurried to tidy up the area and pack away the tankards. Most of the regulars didn't like for their tankards to be washed, so Meg and Fliss put them in crates in a special order, knowing which tankard belonged to which customer from the initials or markings on them.

While she worked, Christian Henderson chatted with Terry, who was placing stools on top of the tables.

'Why is he still here?' Fliss whispered to Meg, implying Henderson.

'I think he wants to walk me home,' Meg whispered back, giddy inside despite her tiredness.

'Why?' Fliss looked stunned.

'No idea, really.' Her stomach flipped at the idea of Christian walking her home, but she also knew her reputation would be in ruins if anyone saw them.

'Does he want...' Fliss reddened. 'You know...'

'No, at least he told me today that he respects me.'

'None of it makes sense.' Fliss swept the sawdust-covered floor behind the bar. 'He does have an interest in you. We could see that on the train, and he's given Freddie a job and took you on a tour of the brewery, oh, and saved your life in that cargo accident.' Fliss stopped sweeping. 'Perhaps he wants you as his mistress.'

'Lower your voice,' Meg demanded, chancing a glance at the man in question.

'Why else would he be spending his time with you? You're not his class.'

Annoyed and a little upset, Meg flung the cloth into the bucket and grabbed her shawl. 'I'll be no man's mistress, not even to someone as handsome as Henderson.'

'I know that.' Fliss rubbed Meg's arm. 'Just make sure *he* knows it. See you tomorrow?'

Meg nodded and left the bar.

Henderson said goodnight to Fliss and Terry and joined Meg at the door. 'May I walk you home?'

'There is no need. I only live a few streets away.'

'Indulge me.' He opened the door for her and followed her out.

'Why do you want to?' she asked as they stepped into the hazy golden light of a street lamp.

'I like your company.' He pulled his coat collar up.

'You don't know me.'

Several moments went by, with the only noise being the soft slap of the river against the wharves.

'Can I get to know you?' he asked, reducing his long strides to match her shorter ones.

'I don't understand why, though? I'm a working-class girl. Daughter of a narrowboat skipper. You live in a mansion, and I live in a terrace on Wellington Street.'

'If you strip all that away, we are just two people.'

'You can't strip it away. It's what makes us who we are.'

'And I like who you are. Very much.' He stopped and faced her in the darkness. 'I do not know how it happened, or when or why, but all I know is that you are constantly in my thoughts.'

Her heart soared at his admission.

'Do you feel the same?' A thread of hope was in his tone.

Meg stared at him, barely able to see his face, only the outline. 'Even if I did, nothing can come of it.'

'Really? Is that what you believe?'

'It's what I know.' Was she losing her mind speaking to him like this?

'I disagree.'

'Mr Henderson, I am not a lady, not the kind you associate with, which means the only course is for me to become your mistress, and I won't do that. I might be poor, but I'm from a respectable family.' Her words faltered slightly as she thought of her father's bigamy. 'You don't need me in your life.'

'I think I do.' His fingers touched her face in the gentlest of movements. 'I need you more than I could ever have thought possible.'

She leaned into his hand, savouring the feel of a man's tenderness for the first time. His words moved her deeply. He lowered his head, and she raised her mouth to meet his. The touch of his lips sent shivers across her skin. She gripped his arms and his lips lifted slightly to move gently against hers.

A baby's cry shattered the silence of the night. A sudden light from a window filtered away the darkness. Meg took a step back.

'Don't,' he whispered. 'Do not walk away.'

'I must go.' She didn't want to, of course, but her mind reeled at what had just happened. She had kissed Christian Henderson, and she'd just told him she wasn't that kind of woman!

'Miss Taylor, I—'

'I must go!' Meg took several steps back. The situation was surreal. She felt out of control. She didn't kiss men. She'd never had the time to even look twice at a man and to fall for a gentleman so far out of her league was not only stupid, but dangerous to her mind and heart.

She fled along the cobbles. He called for her to stop, but she ignored him.

Inside the house, she leaned against the door. The embers in the fire winked. On the sofa slept Josie. Meg closed her eyes. This was her life. A house full of people she was responsible for, including her father's second family. How could she entertain any thought of Christian Henderson when her life was so ridiculous compared to his?

11

Christian finished writing his letter of thanks to a publican from Huddersfield, who had placed an order. The long hours of travelling and meeting publicans from around the shire was proving a useful marketing strategy. Orders were trickling in at a decent rate per week, and the brewery was starting to recover from the decades of neglect and mismanagement. It would take a good many years yet to be back on the right track for healthier profit margins, but Christian knew he needed time and patience and focus. The latter being difficult since he accepted that Miss Taylor was the woman he wanted.

For weeks he'd been struggling to think of anything but her. Sitting opposite her on the train had been a pleasant kind of torture. Her pretty face in front of him, her small smiles as she chatted to the other two women, and the delight he experienced when she turned her large grey eyes in his direction was the stuff of dreams.

Then, the tour of the brewery he gave her reinforced his opinion that Miss Taylor was intelligent, not highly educated, he understood that, but she had common sense and asked him clever questions. By the end of the tour, he knew he wanted to see more of her.

And then last night, the kiss...

His groin tightened at the thought of her lips, but it was more than that. He wanted her body, yes, but he wanted the whole of her in his life, in his bed. He wanted to wake up to Meg's smile and go to sleep holding her body against his. He wanted her as a friend, his partner, the mother of his children. This craving was something he'd never known, and it scared him witless.

Marriage had never been high on his list. Business was his primary concern. Yes, a wife would come in due course, at a time in his life when he felt it was right. Probably that person might have been Ruth, the daughter of his mother's friend. Though, in truth, Ruth irritated him more than she excited him. He had no high expectations of finding someone who delighted him enough to make his heart thud like a steam engine. Certainly no one in his class he'd met had done that. No. It had taken a working-class barmaid to snap him into life.

Christian couldn't understand it at all. He scratched his sexual itch with a certain woman in London who was discreet and had a string of lovers. So, he knew it wasn't frustration that made him ache for Meg Taylor. How much easier it would be if it were only physical.

His heart led him down a merry path of having Meg as his wife, but his head fought hard to make him see sense. Meg came from a different world to him. She had a large family that was her responsibility. Could he take all that on? He knew he could, but did he want her enough to become embroiled in all her other concerns? He believed he did.

What would his family and friends say to him, wanting a woman from the lower classes? His mother would have a great deal to say about it. He groaned at the thought of his mother's opinion and his sister, Susan, would parrot his mother's harsh words.

A knock interrupted his thoughts. His clerk, Jones, came in quietly. 'Sir, sorry to disturb you, but well... your mother and family are downstairs and insist on seeing you.' Jones' eyes widened as though the thought of his employer having a mother was rather mad.

Christian jerked to his feet. 'My mother?'

'Yes, and your sisters, I think.'

'I only have one sister.' Cursing, Christian rubbed his eyes. Blast. The last thing he needed was his mother meddling in his affairs. He wasn't ready for any of that yet.

He hurried down the staircase, weaved through the men busy working and out into the large yard where a black carriage stood, one he instantly recognised by the gold coat of arms on the side. His late stepfather's carriage.

The sun went behind a cloud, casting the area into gloom, which matched Christian's mood perfectly.

'Ah, finally,' his mother barked from the carriage where she sat as regal as a queen in a dress of dark grey silk edged in black trim, the colour she'd worn since shedding her black mourning a few days ago, or so she told him in a letter – the same letter which implored him to return south.

'Mother. This is a surprise,' he muttered, leaning in to kiss her powdered cheek. He never expected her to travel north.

'And by the look on your face, not a pleasant one,' she huffed. Her light blue eyes were the same as his, but hers were never warm.

He gave a wan smile to his sister and a kiss on the cheek. 'It's lovely to see you, Susan.'

'And you, brother, but why you had to come and live in this backwater, I will never know.' She pouted, ruining any claim to good looks. She had the darker eyes of her father and his square face and none of their mother's beauty. Sadly, Susan knew it and her personality matched the sourness of what she believed was the unfairness of not being beautiful.

He turned to Ruth, hiding his surprise at seeing her with the party. 'And you have made the journey to the untamed land of the north, Miss Crawford?' He tried to make a joke of it.

'For you, anything, sweet Christian,' she murmured sensually, squeezing his hand. Although stunning in appearance, Ruth believed every living thing should bend to her will, be it person or animal. She could be funny and witty, but also aloof and selfish and sometimes surprisingly childlike in manner and at other times display a sensuous side that as a man Christian could hardly fail to notice.

He nodded to Brodie, his mother's maid, and stepped back from the carriage. 'Do you wish to come inside and take a tour?'

'Gracious, no. Are you insane?' his mother sneered. 'You have bought a house, have you not, from your unreliable cousin? Take us there.'

Christian took a sharp breath. 'Certainly. I shall order for my horse to be saddled.'

'No, no. That will take you too long and we have been on the road since dawn after spending a dreadful night in some flea-infested staging inn somewhere remote and disgusting.'

'Sheffield, Mama,' Susan supplied.

'If I wanted your input, Susan, I would have asked for it.' His mother glared at his sister.

'Why did you not come by train?' he asked.

'Don't be ridiculous, Christian. Train? All the way from London?' His mother puffed her chest like a bantam hen. 'I do not want to travel the length of the country on the whims of a railway. *I* want to stop when *I* choose to, not be reliant on a station in the middle of nowhere without proper facilities. *And* I want to sleep in a proper bed and to eat food without being shaken like wheat in a threshing machine!'

'It takes much less time by train, Mother,' he argued.

'What, sitting with strangers for hours? I'd rather make my journey leisurely than in a rush with my own comforts about me. I shall not argue with you, Christian. Get in the carriage before we die of thirst.' She clicked her fingers at her daughter. 'Susan, sit by me to allow your brother next to Ruth. Brodie, get out and go and sit up with the driver.'

Squashing into the cramped carriage, Christian gave a nod to Pepper, who stood in the yard, and which he knew would be enough for the sensible man to take over running the brewery for the day.

As they exited the gates, Christian glanced out of the window and jolted. Meg Taylor walked along the side of the road. Was she coming to him? He wanted to stop the carriage, to shout to her to wait for him that he'd come back, but his mother tapped his hand, demanding his attention.

'Your house had better have good heating, Christian. Your uncle was not a clever man and likely lived as a miser due to his poor management. Do all the rooms have fires? Have all the chimneys been swept?'

'It's nearly June, Mama. We don't need fires in every room,' Susan tutted.

'Tell that to my arthritis, girl!'

Christian sighed. How ever long they were staying would be a moment too long. He wanted to see Miss Taylor, to talk to her and spend time in her company. He remembered their kiss and knew he wanted to repeat that experience over and over. He couldn't get her out of his mind. The sensible part of his brain begged him to forget her, but it did no good. She haunted his dreams at night and during the day, he couldn't concentrate from thinking about her.

The brief journey to his home took them along Barnsley Road and under a railway bridge.

'At least you don't live in the middle of town,' his mother muttered, as though that was something to be grateful for. 'The little I have seen of Wakefield is dirty and unspectacular.'

'When did you last come to Wakefield, Mother?' he chuckled, knowing she'd not been in this town for years.

'When your father and I were first married. We came to visit Royce and Gertrude.'

'So, thirty... thirty-three years ago? A year before I was born?' He raised his eyebrows. 'A lot would have changed since then.'

'The cathedral seems impressive from what I've read in a book,' Miss Crawford commented.

'You read a book, Ruth?' Susan scorned. 'About Wakefield?'

'I wanted to know a little about where I would be visiting.' Miss Crawford looked superior.

His mother nodded in approval. 'That shows intelligence, Ruth. Does it not, Christian?'

He groaned inwardly and let the remark pass by. 'To the right is a rather nice parkland associated with Sandal Castle,' Christian told them. 'A little further south are the ruins of Sandal Castle and the fields where the Battle of Wakefield was fought. The Duke of York's grave is around here too, I think.'

'Can you see the ruins of the castle from your house?' Miss Crawford asked.

'Was that not written in your little book?' Susan sniped.

Christian ignored his sister. 'Yes, from the top-floor bedrooms. There's a gap between the trees and you can see the mound and ruins quite well.'

Miss Crawford gave him a seductive smile. 'Perhaps you can show me to the ruins?'

'I am sure everyone would like to see them.' Christian looked at Susan to show he wouldn't be cornered into being alone with Ruth. He quickly leaned out of the window and informed the driver to turn into the black gates coming up.

Alighting from the carriage, he aided the ladies down the step. 'You can take the horses around the back to the stables, driver. There's a groom who will show you your quarters above the tack room,' Christian told the coach driver. He turned to the others. 'Welcome to Meadow View House.'

His mother sniffed and stared up at the house with pursed lips. 'Indeed, it is exactly what I expected. Royce Henderson was no man of taste.'

Christian offered his arm and kept silent. There was no point in trying to change her mind about his uncle or that the house was suitably appointed. His mother's second marriage had raised her higher than her first marriage. Geoffrey Burton had more wealth than Christian's father, giving his mother more power within her new social circle. She soon forgot all about her first husband's family, and even forgot about Christian when he was away at boarding school. Geoffrey Burton gave her all that Christian's father was unable to do with his early and untimely death.

'It's smaller than I thought it would be,' Susan commented as they went inside. 'How disappointing.'

'Extensions can remedy that,' Miss Crawford said, taking off her cloak.

'Or simply sell it and buy something nicer,' Susan added, looking around. 'It is very dark, Christian. Your aunt had a terrible sense of style.'

Christian frowned but said nothing as the butler, Titmus, came to take their outdoor clothes. 'Ah, Titmus, my mother, Mrs

Patrice Burton, my sister, Miss Susan Burton, and a family friend, Miss Ruth Crawford. Brodie is my mother's maid. They are staying with me for a time. I apologise we have sprung this upon you.'

'I shall see to the rooms immediately, sir, and have refreshments brought in. Your mother's maid can come with me.' He bowed and disappeared down the hallway past the staircase with Brodie hurrying to catch up with him.

'Well, Titmus seems to know his stuff,' Susan said, gliding into the drawing room on her right. 'Poor servants reflect on an establishment severely. You need to be in control of them at all times, brother.'

'Titmus is an excellent butler. My uncle employed very good servants that I have kept on,' Christian said before his mother could comment.

Sitting on the red sofa, his mother studied the room. 'This red wallpaper is in need of replacing. Green would work better in this room. How on earth did they entertain in here with all this furniture?'

Christian did agree that his aunt and uncle's taste ran to heavy dark wood pieces and plenty of them in every room. 'I shall make improvements.'

'Of course, it needs a woman's touch,' she muttered. 'Do you not agree, Ruth?'

Miss Crawford smoothed out her pale lemon skirt and lifted her gaze straight to Christian. 'A woman can work wonders in such a room when it is her own.'

Christian's heart sank. Ruth hadn't changed her mind about him. He took a deep breath. 'Changes can be made in time. I have a business to run.'

'Which is why you need to be married and allow your wife free rein to make this place worthy of you.' His mother scowled at the unlit fire. 'It is obvious you need help in running this house until you decide about your future.'

'My future?' Christian tilted his head at her. 'What do you mean?'

'I mean whether you are to remain in the north or return home to London.'

'I am staying in Wakefield for some years, Mother. I told you that in my letters. The brewery needs my attention. My life is here in Wakefield.'

And so was Miss Taylor.

She tutted harshly, her eyes sharp over her thin nose. 'I thought so. Well, you leave me no choice. Susan and I will move here to keep you company and fix up your house until you take a wife.'

'Move here?' He could barely take it in, such was the shock of her announcement. He stared at his mother's triumphant face and felt doomed.

* * *

Meg walked up the outside staircase to Lorrie's door and knocked, still thinking about Christian Henderson and seeing him just now in a carriage full of women. The look of surprise on his face when he saw her matched her own. Who were those women? What was he doing with them?

Did he think of her as much as she thought of him? Had what he told her been all true?

The door opened and Lorrie's smiling face welcomed her in. 'Fliss is already here.'

Lorrie took Meg's shawl and hung it up near the door. 'Fliss told me about Josie. I hope you don't mind?'

'No, I don't mind.' Meg sat at the table. 'I was going to tell you myself today. I didn't get a chance yesterday, it all happened so suddenly.'

Pouring out the tea, Lorrie handed around the teacups. 'Fliss said you had other news?'

'Yes, an inheritance of sixty-three pounds, to share with Freddie.'

'How fabulous!' Lorrie passed the plate of scones to Meg. 'I made these this morning, but I think they are a bit hard.'

'They'll be just fine,' Meg answered, taking one.

'So, what will you do with the money?' Fliss asked, adding milk to her tea.

'Freddie wants to move to a bigger house.'

'Leave Wellington Street?' Fliss gasped.

'Yes.' Meg sighed. 'It's a huge thing to do and I'm worried that paying a higher rent somewhere will gobble up the money faster than we expect.'

'But you must consider it, surely?' Lorrie said. 'Just one extra bedroom would make such a difference to your lives.'

'I agree,' Meg admitted with a sigh.

'What's wrong?' Fliss asked. 'Is it Josie?'

Meg didn't know how to answer. 'It's many things.'

'Such as?' Lorrie spread strawberry jam on her scone. 'We might be able to help.'

'I doubt it.' Meg suddenly felt close to tears and that alarmed her. She wasn't one for tearful emotion.

'Meg?' Lorrie grasped Meg's hand on the table. 'What is it?'

'Last night I kissed Christian Henderson,' she blurted, not meaning to.

Both Fliss and Lorrie stared at her.

'Don't think too badly of me.'

Fliss grinned. 'I knew it!' She clapped her hands. 'I knew it. I told you, didn't I, that he liked you? Too many times he's been involved in your life, the accident with the crane, the train journey, turning up at the pub, the tour of the brewery... It all makes sense!'

'And you like him,' Lorrie stated solemnly. 'Why wouldn't you? He's handsome and nice. A gentleman of business.'

'And I'm working class,' Meg said bleakly, thinking of the finely dressed women in the carriage.

'What does that matter?' Lorrie went back to spreading the jam. 'It's been known to happen that men and women marry out of their class. Your own grandparents stopped talking to your mam because she married a narrowboat skipper, someone they believed wasn't good enough for her.'

Meg sipped her tea, deep in thought. 'Yes, and my grandmother, Margaret May, married a lowly teacher when *her* father was a wealthy barrister or some such, Mam told me.'

'So, you see? You're following tradition,' Fliss teased.

'It's hardly the same,' Meg muttered. 'This would be marrying up. Lord, I'm talking marriage just from a kiss. Lots of lads have tried to kiss me since I was a young girl. It's a bit of a laugh, isn't it? Kissing a lad was silly nonsense. I shouldn't be making something out of nothing.'

'This isn't some lad messing about,' Lorrie said, seriously. 'This is a gentleman. And you're both adults.'

'And I'm not a gentlewoman.'

'You're good and honest and hard-working and loyal to your family and friends,' Fliss said in a rush. 'Mr Henderson should be lucky to have you.'

'What worries you the most?' Lorrie asked. 'That perhaps Mr Henderson isn't sincere?'

A mild headache pulsed behind Meg's eyes. 'Yes, of course. Not only that but where will it all lead?'

'Was the kiss nice?' Fliss asked dreamily.

Meg couldn't help but smile. 'Wonderful.'

'I think you need to talk to Mr Henderson,' Lorrie said practically. 'Find out what he expects from you.'

'How is it possible to have that kind of talk?' Meg rubbed her head.

'If he asked you to marry him, would you?'

Meg chuckled without humour. 'Such a thing isn't possible, Lorrie. Look at me. Look at him! He can have anyone he wants.'

'He clearly wants you.' Lorrie smiled tenderly.

'Does he though?' Meg jerked from the chair and paced the floor. 'How can he want me? I have seven brothers and sisters to care for, plus an extra half-sister that's been thrust upon me! He should want some wealthy man's daughter who is educated and can play a musical instrument or can paint or sing. Someone with grace and poise and sensible conversation.'

'I'm sure he could have a pick of any of those kind of women, but clearly he's picked you.' Lorrie sipped her tea. 'That says it all really, doesn't it?'

Meg slumped onto the chair. 'He doesn't know me or my life. How shocked would he be that this morning I was shouting at Arthur for taking too long in the privy, or that I was separating Nell and Betsy from fighting over a sock, and I snapped at Susie because she couldn't find her headscarf for work, and Mabel refuses to acknowledge Josie and Dolly in any way, so Arthur yelled at her, and then Freddie shouted at Arthur...' She bowed her head. 'Mr Henderson sees none of that.'

'Drink your tea before it's cold,' Lorrie encouraged. 'So, what will you do?'

'Nothing at all. Mr Henderson is a dream. I can't live in a dream.' How lovely it would be if she could escape into Christian's arms and forget her problems, and at night in bed, she thought only of him, of what it would be like to be his wife, but when morning came she knew it was only ever going to be wishful thinking.

'And what will you do about Josie and Dolly?' Fliss asked.

'The only thing I can do. Let them stay until Josie is well enough to find work.' She bit into a scone and found it harder than she expected. 'Lord, I nearly had a tooth out there!'

'You cheeky monkey!' Lorrie chuckled. 'I warned you.'

Fliss dropped her scone. 'I'm glad you mentioned it because I think I could skip my scone across the canal better than a stone!'

Lorrie gasped, then laughed. 'You could not!'

'No, it would sink like a rock!' Fliss giggled.

Snorting with suppressed laughter, Lorrie took the plate of scones over to the bin and threw them in. 'I'll never make them again.'

'Not unless we need them as weapons.' Fliss was bent over in fits of giggles.

Meg grinned, needing her friends to make her laugh. They enriched her life.

'Come on, it's a lovely day. Let's go for a walk,' Lorrie declared.

'No, I can't. I must get back.' Meg embraced Fliss, then Lorrie. 'I've food to prepare for supper and clothes to soak for washing on Monday. I've not cleaned my front step for two days and the women in the street will comment for sure.'

At the door, Lorrie touched Meg's arm and lowered her voice. 'About Mr Henderson. If you have feelings for him, don't be scared to act on them. I mean, if he comes calling, don't push him away. He could change your life.'

'Mr Henderson won't come calling, Lorrie. Why would he?'

Deep in thought, Meg walked home the long way instead of crossing on the ferry. Lorrie's words rattled in her mind. What if Christian did come calling? The very idea made her knees weak. Yet she also felt a burning desire to change her life, to alter her future in some way. Could Christian be the answer to that? Could he actually want her enough to one day offer marriage?

On the bridge, she paused and leaned over the side to watch the water flowing underneath, which today had a slimy oil slick on top. Factory whistles blew, adding to the hammering chorus of industry on the river.

Passing St Mary's Church, which was attached to the bridge and sat on its own little island, Meg left the bridge and turned left to stroll along the narrow path cut along the riverbank behind the buildings facing the road.

A waterfowl flapped at being disturbed and glided into the water. Meg nodded to an old man fishing. She'd banned her brothers from fishing in the polluted river years ago after a catch of eels had made them all sick.

Once back up on Thornes Lane Wharf, she weaved between the men coming in and out of mills and malthouses, those who worked on the wharves and boatyards. Carts and wagons plied the cobbles, and she waved to Terry as he stood by the cellar entrance as barrels were being loaded down into it from a long wagon, which had the Henderson's Brewery sign on the side. Reading the name gave her a little jolt.

So, Christian had done a deal with Terry to sell his ale, something his uncle hadn't managed to do, which was strange when the brewery was just across the river. It showed Christian's business sense and aptitude.

On the corner of Wellington Street, Meg paused. She didn't want to go home. Since Josie's arrival and her father's betrayal, the house no longer seemed the home it was. She was being fanciful, she knew, but without her mam and with all the changes that had happened, Meg felt unsettled. Perhaps Freddie was right, and they should move.

12

Meg entered the hat shop on Westgate. Above her head was the sign, Sharp's Fine Quality Milliners. It was the third business she'd visited that morning looking for an apprenticeship for Betsy. The other two shops had turned her away.

The bell tinkled above her head. Inside, two ladies turned and stared at her, but Meg ignored their curious glares and headed towards the back of the shop. A serving girl, her arms stacked with hat boxes, passed Meg, but it was the older, plump woman behind the counter that Meg went to.

'Good morning. I am Mrs Sharp. May I help you?' The woman's voice sounded calm, welcoming even, as she looked up from the fabric she was inspecting, her glasses perched on the end of her nose.

'Good morning.' Meg swallowed, wanting this to be a successful meeting. She adopted her mam's voice and straight-ened her shoulders. 'May I have a moment of your time? It's in regards to my sister, Betsy, who wishes to be apprenticed to a milliner.'

'And you are?'

'Meg Taylor.'

'Does your sister have any experience?'

'No. She's ten years old, but very clever at decorating bonnets. I thought an apprenticeship would be a wise choice for her to learn that trade. I understand you are the best in Wakefield.' She'd heard that from Mrs Fogarty and the other women in the street, not that buying hats from a milliner was something they did, of course. Everyone on Wellington Street only had enough money to buy second-hand from the market.

'My girls are older than ten.' Mrs Sharp frowned. 'I don't want the authorities ruining my reputation by saying I employ underage apprentices. They have to be in school until ten years old now.' Mrs Sharp eyed Meg closely. 'You look decent enough.'

Meg stiffened. She'd worn her Sunday best, polished her boots and had Susie neatly plait and twist her hair up under her black felt hat. 'My sister, Betsy, can read and write.'

This information surprised Mrs Sharp. 'Indeed. That is an advantage.'

'And my hat. Betsy sewed the flowers on it.' Meg tilted her head so the woman could see the small cluster of pink material flowers on the brim.

'And you are certain she is ten, not younger? I won't have anyone younger,' Mrs Sharp warned.

'I promise you.'

'Very well. Bring her to me tomorrow morning at seven o'clock. I will give her a week's trial and see how we get on. If I'm satisfied, she will start her apprenticeship. She will need to live in. My girls sleep in the attics above.'

'Live in?' Meg hadn't been expecting that.

'To be the best you must put in the hours, Miss Taylor. I treat my girls well, for a healthy worker is a good worker. They are fed and housed on the premises. So, I know they are getting decent food and proper sleep. We work long hours and I need my girls to be at their best. This arrangement, naturally, affects the wages because of expenses. However, the girls still earn a suitable amount. I will discuss that with you tomorrow. Understand?'

'I do, yes.' Meg had a moment of hesitation, but ultimately this apprenticeship would give Betsy a trade, a future where perhaps one day she might have her own shop. 'Thank you, Mrs Sharp. We shall be here at seven o'clock.'

'Use the back entrance down the side alley.' Mrs Sharp nodded and dismissed Meg as the two ladies came to the counter.

Meg, feeling excited by the prospect that Betsy would have a position, left the shop lighter in spirit.

She walked along the streets, thinking to head to the market, but as she waited on the corner to cross the street, she saw Christian walking the other way. His warm smile made her heart thump.

'This is a delightful surprise,' he said when closer.

'Good morning.' Why did she feel so much brighter just by seeing him?

'Are you on an errand? Do you have some time to stop and have something to eat? I must admit I am extremely hungry.'

She nodded eagerly. 'I do have time.' For him she'd make time.

They crossed the road, and he opened the door for her into a shop that sold pies and chops and baked potatoes. She had never been inside this place before, why would she?

Christian pulled out a chair for her and then sat on his own. 'What a stroke of luck to have met you.'

'I had been to Sharp's milliners.' Sitting opposite him, she could gaze at him all she liked.

'A new hat?' he asked cheekily.

'No, to get Betsy, my sister, an apprenticeship.'

'She wants to be a milliner?'

'When I spoke to her about it, she was excited by the idea, yes, maybe not the work involved or the long hours, but she'll adjust. Fiddling with bits of ribbon and flowers is the thing she likes to do the most.' She felt at ease with him, comfortable. He didn't seem to judge her.

'Then I hope she enjoys it immensely,' he said sincerely.

'She is to live in...' Meg still was unsure about that. Arthur was never home and now for Betsy to be gone, it was another change to adjust to.

'You will miss her,' he stated, his tone soft, kind.

'Yes. Betsy is the one who laughs a lot and is a jolly soul. Nell will feel it especially.'

'Then you must bring them to my house one Sunday, like we mentioned before.' His gaze held hers. 'Will you?'

She nodded just as a young man came to the table.

'Are you hungry?' Christian asked her.

'Yes.' She was always hungry. 'But a cup of tea is fine. If you have it?' she asked the waiter.

'We don't serve that here, miss. Just small beer,' the waiter said apologetically.

Christian gave her a half-grin and looked up at the fellow. 'We'll have two small beers and two baked potatoes with butter, if you please?'

'Certainly, sir.' The waiter left them, and Meg took a quick glance at the rest of the tables filled with a mixture of working men, clerks and such and the odd woman, all busy eating and chatting.

As though taking advantage of their lack of interest, Christian leaned forward. 'You do not mind being seen with me?'

'No.' She shrugged. 'We are simply having a baked potato. Nothing scandalous in that, surely?'

He chuckled. 'Unfortunately.'

Meg blushed, remembering their kiss.

'It is ungentlemanly for me to say this,' he lowered his voice, 'but I want to kiss you again.'

Her whole body shivered. She wanted him to kiss her and never stop.

He leaned back in his chair with an expression of disappointment. 'But I shall behave.'

She laughed. 'We are in public.'

'I shall walk you home after our meal, and perhaps we might find a shadowy corner somewhere and maybe we can stop and—'

'Your small beer, sir, miss.' The serving fellow put their glasses down.

Meg stifled another laugh at Christian's abrupt change in manner as he thanked the waiter. He sipped his beer, but his eyes held Meg's and they shared a hidden message.

'Tell me all about yourself,' Meg asked, wanting to know everything about him.

'My father died when I was a baby. My mother remarried a good and kind man. They had my sister, Susan,' he told her as the waiter returned with another tray of their baked potatoes.

'And where do you live?'

'You know where my house is,' he joked.

'I mean before you came here.'

'Oxford and London, mainly.'

'And do you wish to return there?' She scooped up a forkful of fluffy white potato dripping with melted butter, her mouth watering. She looked at Christian when he didn't answer straight away.

'I have no plans to leave Wakefield. Everything I want is right here.' The direct stare and earnest way he spoke sent a shiver along Meg's skin.

She knew he included her in that statement.

For an hour they talked and laughed. She told him funny

stories about her family, making him laugh, but kept her father and Josie out of the conversation. Christian told her about his travelling, of staying in Paris and visiting Rome.

She could have sat and listened to him all day, but regretfully, he took his fob watch out of his waistcoat pocket and checked the time.

'I must go. I have a meeting in fifteen minutes.' He sighed.

'Of course.'

'I do not want to leave this table, or you,' he whispered. 'I wanted to walk you home, but we have talked for so long I am in fear of being late.'

'I can walk with you instead, to your meeting,' she said boldly, rising from her chair.

'I would like that.' Christian paid the bill and followed her outside.

They fell into step, heading towards the end of the street. Meg didn't want him to go. The last hour or so had been so enjoyable, so natural. Yet it had given her more to think about, more to yearn for, when in fact she knew she could never have the very thing she wanted most. Christian.

They were quiet as they walked, as though each of them were deep in their own thoughts.

At the corner of Northgate, Christian paused. His tender gaze roamed her face. 'I have enjoyed this, very much.'

'Me, too.' She wanted to say more, but people were going past, and the noise of the busy street traffic wasn't easy to talk above.

A newspaper boy nearly knocked into Meg as he ran, and Christian put his hands out to steady her. 'Are you all right?'

'A near collision there, miss,' a man in a bowler hat said, passing them.

She nodded to him and turned back to Christian. He still held her arms.

'I shall find you a hansom cab to take you home.' Christian searched the street for a hansom waiting for a fare.

'No, I'm fine. I have a bit of shopping to do, anyway.' His kindness melted her heart. Whenever she was with him, life seemed sharper, more in focus. What did that tell her? What did that mean?

'When can I see you again?'

She smiled, wanting so badly to kiss him. 'I don't know. Soon.'

'I need to go to Halifax in the morning and shall be gone a few days, but when I return, I shall come to the Bay Horse and see you.'

'I'd like that.' She lingered a moment more, then forced herself to walk away from him.

* * *

Two days later, Meg, carrying her heavy shopping basket back from the market, made her way down Thorne's Lane Wharf. She'd also called in at the milliners to see how Betsy was getting on. The day before, Meg had taken Betsy to Mrs Sharp. Although excited, Betsy was nervous to be in a strange environment and away from home. However, Mrs Sharp plied her with tea and a piece of jam sponge and Betsy was won over. So far, Betsy was enjoying learning her new trade.

Clouds scudded the sky and threatened rain as Meg turned into Wellington Street, but it didn't deter the neighbours from standing on doorsteps to chat. The coal man served old Mrs Bains at number four and coming out of Meg's own door was Mrs Fogarty.

'Is everything all right, Mrs Fogarty?' Meg hurried to reach her.

'Aye, mostly, lass. They sent your Nicky home from school. Not feeling well. He'd been running about a lot, Nell said. She came and got me when she brought him home and found no one here. I've sent her and Nell back to school now.' Mrs Fogarty's voice dropped to a whisper. 'I see that woman's gone.'

'Gone?' Meg opened the door and rushed in, and Mrs Fogarty followed. Nicky lay on the sofa with a blanket over him. His face was as pale as a bed sheet.

He gave her a wan smile as she knelt beside him and touched his forehead. He wasn't hot. 'Do you feel feverish?'

'No. Tired.' His eyes closed.

'Then you're not to move off that sofa, understand?' Meg took off her shawl. 'Are you cold?'

'No.'

Mrs Fogarty turned for the door. 'I'll be back later, lass. I've to post a letter to my cousin in Canada. Do you want anything from the shops?'

'I'll send Nell if I do. Thank you, Mrs Fogarty, for looking after him.'

Mrs Fogarty paused by the door, her look unreadable. 'He's not a good colour again, lass. I don't like it.'

Fear gripped Meg. 'I'll send for the doctor.'

'I'll do it. You stay with the lad.' She closed the door behind her.

Meg knelt beside Nicky. 'I'll make you some tea.'

His thin little hand reached for hers. 'I'm so tired, Meg.'

'Just rest, darling.' She kissed his forehead.

Meg busied herself raking up the small fire in the range and putting the kettle on to boil. By the time she brought him the tea, he was asleep. She gazed down at him, her heart beating a little faster at his paleness, the blue edging his lips. She blamed herself for his latest decline. She'd been so busy with everything else she'd taken her eyes off him. She'd let him go to school, which clearly was too much for him. He'd lost weight, too, something she'd only just realised.

The door opened and Josie walked in with Dolly.

'I thought you'd gone,' Meg said, harsher than she intended. They were part of the problem.

'I went out looking for work.' Josie stepped closer to the sofa. 'What's wrong with Nicky?'

'He has a weak heart.' Meg brushed his hair back from his face. He needed a haircut.

'Like your mam?'

Meg glared at her. 'Yes, like my mam. How do you know about it?'

'Frank told me when he confessed to me about you all. The day you came to my home, well, after you'd left, Frank told me everything.'

'Everything?' she hissed.

'About your mam's illness. How she couldn't be a true wife to Frank.'

'A true wife?' Meg's anger rose. '*A true wife?* The same wife who bore him eight surviving children and several dead ones?'

'Don't be angry at me. I'm only telling you what he told me.' Josie sank onto a chair at the table. 'He lied to me too, for the whole time I knew him.' Tears rolled down her cheeks. 'I can't forgive him.'

'We have that in common at least,' Meg snapped.

'I lived in terrible conditions, as poor as I've ever been, but Frank said he would make things better. The next load would be enough to buy food and clothes, always the next load...' Josie drew Dolly close to her. 'I didn't know that any money he made had to be shared between two families. He robbed me of my children. His dishonesty starved them of food...' A dead look came into her eyes. 'Frank killed my babies, not the fever. I wish I'd never met him. I've been driven out of my home, away from the place where I grew up and had friends. The gossip was terrible and harsh. They hurled stones at me when they found out I wasn't truly married. My father disowned me. I didn't know Frank was married! *I didn't!*' She sobbed harder. 'I wish I had died, too.'

'Don't say that.' Meg moved to the range. Despite her feelings on the whole matter, she understood that Josie had been hurt just as much as she had. 'What's done is done.'

'Is it?' Josie shook her head and wiped her tears. 'You have every reason to hate me. I don't blame you for it.'

Meg's shoulders slumped. 'I'm not a nasty person.'

'No, I gathered that. Your brothers and sisters love you and you have allowed me to stay when you could have thrown me out on the street.'

Meg made two cups of tea and passed one to Josie. 'Did you find work?'

'No. I couldn't walk far with Dolly. Not that she complains, but she's not strong enough to walk far.'

'Tomorrow, leave her with me.' Meg heated some water in pans on the range. 'And I think you both need to wash. A proper wash in the tin bath. I keep a clean house, as much as I can with all of us here and limited water, and you've brought lice and filth with you. I'll not have the neighbours talking that our standards have dropped since Mam died.'

'I can't remember when I last had a bath. Frank never bought me one. We washed from a bucket.' Josie picked at her filthy clothes. 'I'm so ashamed. My father said I should have known. He was tired of giving me money to get by...' Tears flowed again. 'I have nothing to my name.'

'I have a spare dress you can have.' Meg glanced at Nicky, who slept soundly. 'We'll carry the bath upstairs, so you won't be disturbed. The doctor will be here soon, I hope.'

For the next hour, Meg helped Josie carry jugs of hot water up to the bedroom to fill the tin bath. She gave Josie fresh clothes to wear and a dress that Nell had grown out of for Dolly. 'It's too big, but we can turn up the hem,' Meg said, holding up the little grey smock.

'Thank you.' Josie stripped off, uncaring of Meg being in the room. Meg stared at the other woman's emaciated body. She could count each of Josie's ribs.

'I'll leave you to it.' Meg collected the clothes. 'I'll soak these.'

'No, burn them.' Josie stepped into the bath and lifted Dolly in with her. Dolly gave a little squeal of surprise. 'They remind me of the past. I don't want to see them again.'

Meg hurried from the room, disturbed by the sight of Josie and Dolly's undernourished bodies. After checking on Nicky, she threw the filthy, lice-infested clothes into the range and watched them burn.

She was peeling potatoes and turnips for the family meal when Nell came home from school.

'Is Nicky any better?' Nell asked.

'He's slept for the last hour. I'm waiting for the doctor,' Meg told her. 'Don't wake him.'

'Where's Dolly?' Nell looked worried.

'Upstairs having a bath, though they've been up there for a long time.' Meg hadn't wanted to go back up and disturb them. 'The water has to be freezing by now.'

'I'll go up and see.' Nell raced up the stairs.

After a few moments, Meg heard laughter and smiled.

'Meg?' Nicky's weak voice brought her immediately to his side. 'How are you feeling, poppet?'

'I don't know.' His eyes were sunk into his head with blue bruising underneath.

A knock preceded Dr Carter, a wiry man with a sharp nose

and round spectacles who walked straight into the house. 'Miss Taylor. I got here as soon as I could. It's been a busy day.'

'Thank you for coming. Nicky's not well again.'

'As I've mentioned before, your brother never will be well. But let us see what's what, shall we?' He bent over Nicky and began his examination, which was quick and thorough.

Meg clasped her arms about her chest and waited.

'It is the normal problem,' Dr Carter concluded. 'His heart. His pulse is weak, his breathing shallow. He must have complete rest for a few days.' Carter looked over his spectacles at her. 'Beef broth, egg custard, that sort of thing is best for him. No school and keep anyone who has any illness away from him. He's weak enough to catch any contagion.'

Meg nodded and took some coins from the rent box on the mantel and paid him.

'Call for me should he worsen, but we've been here before, haven't we, Miss Taylor?'

'Yes, Doctor.' She had wasted money by sending for him. He gave her the same response each time.

'Keep him rested. He cannot do what other boys can. Clearly, he has worn himself out. The boy is an invalid and mustn't forget that.' With those last parting words, the doctor left.

'I'm not an invalid,' squeaked Nicky from the sofa.

She kissed his forehead. 'No, darling. You'll grow big and strong and show him differently. Won't you?'

'I'll be as strong as Freddie.'

Meg turned away, fighting back the emotion that clogged her throat. Would Nicky make old bones? Dr Carter seemed not to think so and he'd been right about their mam.

The door opened and Mabel and Susie entered, chatting about someone they worked with at the mill. Behind them, Arthur appeared.

'Where have you been?' Meg asked him. 'You were meant to come with me this morning to see about Blossom and the boat. You wanted to be involved. I waited for you.'

'I went looking for work like you said to do,' he snapped back. 'And I got some, too.'

She put her hands on her hips. 'Oh?'

'I've been taken on Charlie Smith's boat. His son has got married and has got a job at the gasworks on the other side of town where his new wife's family live.'

'I'm pleased for you.' Meg relented slightly. 'But we need to sort out Blossom and the boat. We can't afford mooring fees or for the stable and feed.'

'Mr Smith said he'll buy Blossom.'

'And the boat?'

'Nah, he doesn't need two. Mr Smith went and saw Freddie today and gave him the money for Blossom. It was a good deal.'

Meg smarted. 'Why did he go to Freddie and not me? He shouldn't have disturbed Freddie at work and I'm the eldest.'

'And Freddie's the man of the house,' Arthur replied cheekily. 'Anyway, we leave in an hour, so I just came back to say goodbye to you all.'

'You on your way, then?' Freddie asked, coming in behind Arthur.

'Aye.' Arthur looked up the stairs as Nell and Betsy came down. 'Where's Josie and Dolly?'

'They'll be down in a minute, and you'll be surprised!' Betsy told him with a grin.

Freddie knelt next to Nicky. 'What's wrong with you, young fellow?'

'The doctor's been,' Meg said quietly. 'He collapsed at school. His heart.'

'Right.' Freddie ruffled Nicky's hair. 'It's a bit noisy down here.

Do you want me to carry you up to bed? You can draw for a bit, maybe?'

Nicky nodded, his eyelids heavy. 'I don't want to draw, though.'

'That's fine, matey.' Freddie scooped him up into his muscular arms just as Josie and Dolly came down the stairs.

Everybody stared at them. Meg gaped. The transformation of Josie was astonishing. She wore Meg's oldest dress of dark blue, which was too big for her in the bodice, and with her hair washed, its natural colour of light brown shone even in the room's dimness. Scrubbed free of dirt, Josie's face revealed her prettiness surrounded by her hair, which was no longer ratty and lank.

Dolly also had lighter-coloured hair now the dirt was washed from it and her little face was rosy, resembling Nell even more.

'May I help with getting supper ready?' Josie asked Meg, blushing at the admiring glances everyone gave her.

'Yes, that would be good.' Meg watched her brothers and sisters continue to stare as Josie began cutting slices of bread from the loaf.

'Does she think she's going to be our new mam?' Mabel quipped.

Josie turned. 'I would never want to replace your mam, Mabel. I just want to pull my weight while I'm here.'

Mabel folded her arms. 'And how long will that be, then?'

'Your sister has kindly let me stay until I find work.'

Meg marched forward. 'Enough, Mabel. Go out the back and bring in the washcloths I've hung up. They'll be dry now. Susie, we need more water. You and Nell go and fill the buckets.'

Arthur made for the door. 'I'm off. See you all in a few weeks.'

As each person left the room, Meg felt the tense atmosphere lift a little. 'I need to go to the Bay Horse and tell Terry that I can't do my shift, as Nicky is ill,' she told Josie.

'You don't need to. I can take care of Nicky with Freddie and the others. That's if you want me to?' A look of doubt crossed her face.

Meg didn't want to be in this woman's debt. 'I'm not sure.' She hated leaving Nicky when he was ill, but Josie was a mother and would know what to do. Meg had seen how good she was with Nicky.

Josie continued cutting the bread. 'It's the least I can do after all you've done for me. If Nicky needs you, Freddie will come and get you.'

'Thank you.' Meg relented. 'Nicky usually sleeps a lot when he's bad like this.'

'I'll sit with him. If you have any spare wool and needles, I'll do some knitting while he sleeps.' Josie buttered the bread thinly.

'You can finish my piece, if you want? It's a vest for Nicky.' Meg waved towards her sewing basket by the sofa. 'Or start another. I don't mind. I have little patience for knitting, really. Mam despaired I'd never be good enough to do more than a simple scarf.'

Josie gave a rare smile. 'I'll have a look at it later.'

At the Bay Horse, Meg stood in the kitchen and ate some of Don's stew. It was his birthday, and he was feeling generous enough to allow her a small bowl of it from the large pot he'd made for the pub's customers. Although he didn't talk to her, Meg was used to Don's quiet and terse ways with everyone.

Fliss came through from the bar, her eyes wide with excitement. 'Meg, you're wanted out the front.'

Meg nearly dropped the bowl. 'Is it Nicky?'

'What? Oh, no. Sorry, it's nothing like that.' Fliss took her hand and dragged her into the corridor separating the kitchen from the bar. 'It's Mr Henderson.'

'He's here?' Excitement filled her.

'Yes, and he's asked to see you.' Fliss picked a piece of fluff from Meg's shoulder. 'Go on.'

Meg walked through to the bar on legs that shook a little.

Christian Henderson was talking with Terry, their heads close together. Meg watched him for a moment, absorbing the way he stood, so self-assured, and the proud lift of his handsome head. She knew she could watch him for the rest of her life.

As if sensing her there, he turned and smiled at her. 'Miss Taylor.'

'Mr Henderson.' His name came out breathy and high. 'You wanted to see me?'

'Yes.' He walked closer to the bar. 'Would you care to accompany me on an evening walk?'

'A walk? But I have to work.' Regret filled her.

'I have asked Mr Atkins if he would allow you to miss your shift tonight, if you would care to, that is?'

Her gaze flew to Terry, who nodded like an indulgent father, before staring at Mr Henderson. 'A walk?' She wanted nothing more than to walk with him, to always be with him.

He smiled, a handsome smile that warmed his cornflower-blue eyes. 'Would you?'

Silently, she fetched her shawl and joined him on the other side of the bar. So what if she didn't get tonight's wage? Some things were worth the sacrifice. 'I'd like that very much.'

13

Outside the pub, Meg stopped, shocked that he had done this, spoken to Terry about taking her out for a walk. What would Terry make of it? She prayed he wouldn't think she was now a person of loose morals. However, she was thrilled to see Christian. 'Why did you speak to Terry about me? He will think the worst.'

'Will he? I doubt it.'

'How can you be so sure? My reputation is important to me.'

'Of course it is, and to me, too. But I desperately wanted to spend time with you.' His tender tone spoke to her more than his words. 'I have missed you while I was away.'

Her chest constricted. His honesty took her breath away.

'Do you deny there is something between us? An attraction?' he asked.

'No, I don't.' If he was being honest, then so would she. 'But what can come of it?'

His blue eyes softened. 'That is up to us.'

'You make it all sound so easy.' She walked along the river, away from the busy wharves. At the corner of Wellington Street, she paused and looked down past the malthouses to the terraced houses lining the street. 'This is where I live, Mr Henderson.'

'I know.' He stood beside her but stared at her, not the street.

'Look at it. *Really* look at it. It is a world away from your house, your life.'

'Do you think where you come from makes a difference to me?'

'It should. It will do.'

'Grant me the wisdom of knowing my own mind.' He took her elbow, and they kept walking along the riverbank, passing more mills, malthouses and sheds of industry until they were all left behind and fields opened up on either side of the river.

The sun was setting low, casting a golden light through a break in the clouds. Birds chirped their last chorus before night descended.

'You are all I think about, Meg. You have become important to me,' he said quietly, staring ahead. 'I have tried not to, I will be honest, but it is no use. I cannot fight it and nor do I want to. I accept my fate.' He glanced down at her with a smile.

'I know how that feels,' she admitted.

He stopped and faced her. The golden light washed their faces and shimmered on the river. Gently, he reached up and cupped her cheek. 'Everyone will say this is wrong.'

'And they would be right,' she breathed.

'It does not feel wrong to me,' he murmured, lowering his mouth to softly move over hers. 'Is it wrong, my lovely Meg?'

She melted against him, and he gathered her into his arms tightly, deepening the kiss. His touch awoke in her a fierce longing for more. She never wanted him to let her go.

'How can this be wrong? I beg you to tell me,' he murmured against her lips.

A whistle blew from a passing narrowboat and a young man

whooped at them, waving his hat in the air, before a woman yelled at him to shut his gob.

They broke apart and continued walking.

Meg felt dazed, like what she imagined walking through a cloud would feel like. Everything was out of focus. Her thoughts muddled, her breathing shallow. An immense joy filled her, and she put her fingertips to her lips, still feeling the imprint of his mouth's searing touch.

'Will you marry me, Miss Taylor?' He spoke as though they were talking about the weather.

Surprised, she stared at him. 'You want marriage? To me?'

'I do indeed. Very much so.'

'We haven't known each other long.'

'Does that matter? Is time the guide people use to make such decisions?'

'You know it is.'

'All I know is that you are never from my mind. Day and night you are all I think about. I do not need any more time to know my feelings for you. However, I will wait for you to decide, or if you need more time. A month, a year. Whatever you want.'

He was being sincere and honest with her. She had to be the same to him. 'I'm frightened.'

'Of me?' His eyes widened in shock.

'Not of you, but of everything else. Our lives are so different.'

'I feel that is an advantage.' He gripped her hand tightly. 'We can learn from each other, Meg. We can shape our future to however we want it to be.' He rested his forehead against hers. 'Are you bold enough to take a risk? To marry a man you have only known for months?'

'Is this a dare?' she whispered, a spark of fight igniting in her breast.

'It can be anything you wish it to be.'

She smiled; she couldn't help it. 'It's not the romantic proposal I have dreamt of, that's for sure.'

'Is it not? I thought I did it quite eloquently!' He grinned. 'You have dreamt of me asking you to marry me?'

She laughed. 'No, not you, just, you know, in general, of how it would be.'

'And how was it in your dreams?'

She looked over the water. 'A man on his knee, flowers, a vow of undying love.' She snorted at her own silliness. 'Blame my mam. She read us stories of high adventure and chivalrous men.'

He stopped and took her hand, his handsome face serious. 'I will give you everything you want, including my love, especially my love.'

She believed him, totally and unwaveringly. 'As you will have mine.'

'Truly? I did not expect that.'

Meg frowned. 'Why? What do you mean? That I would marry you without love?'

'Many people do. Some marriages are built on security, companionship, business, even. For you, it would alter not only your life but that of your family. I understand if that was the only reason you would marry me, and I would take it simply because I want you.'

Impulsively, Meg reached up and kissed him on the lips. 'I want love, Mr Henderson. Without it, there is nothing but friendship, and I have plenty of friends.'

He gathered her once more in his arms, smiling, a look of awe on his face. 'You have all of me, Meg Taylor, heart and soul.'

Tears filled her eyes. 'Good, as I think I'll need it.'

He grinned and kissed her hard as if to stamp his ownership on her. 'So, are you sure this is what you want?'

'I think so. I want you. I know that.'

'That is a brilliant start, then.'

'And everything else?'

He raised his dark eyebrows in question. 'Everything else?'

'My family. They come with me.'

'I will happily accept your family, but you will also have to accept mine.'

'There will be gossip.' She shied away from the thought of how much. 'And disapproval from both sides.'

'Yes, unfortunately. But I am willing to face that. Can you?'

She gave it a moment's thought. 'I have the courage to face it.' She sounded more confident than she felt.

He bowed his head against hers and sighed. 'You have made me very happy.'

'I hope I always do.'

As one they turned and walked back along the riverbank with the sunlight fading into a warm, dusky night.

'When do you want to tell everyone?' he asked.

'Not yet.' The closer she came to Wellington Street, the more unsettled she became. Christian Henderson had asked her to marry him. The unbounded joy she'd felt moments ago shifted and withered slightly. At home, she'd have to tell her family. This marriage would alter all their lives. Was she ready for more upheaval?

He took both her hands. 'My mother and sister have arrived unannounced. I want you to meet them, but they have brought with them a young woman who believes herself first in line to be my wife.'

Meg jerked back, a spark of jealousy igniting. 'She does?'

'I have no feelings towards her or anyone else.' He took a deep breath. 'I have to let my mother know about you. Prepare them all.'

'You mean let them know I'm not of their class,' she stated.

'Yes, that, too. This will come as a shock to them because I have never mentioned you in my letters. How could I when I was sorting this out in my head?'

She nodded. This news would shock everyone. 'Tell your family and break it to the young woman. I can, and will, wait for you.' But her thoughts ran away with her. They would think she wasn't good enough for him, and she wasn't. What did she have to offer but burdens?

His smile was full of love. 'I shall call on you tomorrow if I may?'

'Yes. If we are going to do this, then you need to know my family, too.'

'We *are* going to do this. It shan't be easy, but it shall be worth it.'

'Will it?'

Christian frowned. 'I would like to think that being married to me will make you happy.'

'But at what cost?'

'Please, do not look for problems before they arise.' He kissed her gently but briefly as two men were walking down the lane.

'You must know my full name to tell your mother. It's Margaret May.'

He smiled. 'Margaret May. I like that.'

Reluctantly, they let each other go and Meg took a few steps along Wellington Street, but she didn't want to leave him. Somehow it felt that if she did, it would all be a dream, and she'd wake with Nicky's knee in her back and Nell talking in her sleep.

'Tomorrow.' He dipped his hat to her and strode away.

She leant against the wall of the malthouse, deep in thought, but also smiling. Christian Henderson had asked her to marry him. He had kissed her passionately and promised to make her happy.

Was any of this real?

Her heart thudded in her chest. She could be the wife of a gentleman. She dared not imagine it. But if she did, just for a moment, the wonder of it made her breathless. No more poverty, of watching every penny and making it stretch. No more buying the cheap cuts of meat, of day-old bread, or standing for hours at a tub washing, or serving drunk men behind the bar…

She could help all her brothers and sisters. Her marriage would give them a wonderful future, the girls would meet other gentlemen, specialist doctors could see Nicky.

Tears welled in her eyes. She could do this for her family. For herself.

Pushing away from the wall, she straightened her back and lifted her chin in determination. She would marry Christian, for many reasons, but also because she loved him. The challenges ahead would be great, she knew, but she'd face them.

At home, they plied her with questions why she wasn't at work.

'I had a headache.' The lie fell from her lips easily. 'Besides, I couldn't rest knowing Nicky is unwell.'

'He's been asleep the whole time,' Freddie said, reading the newspaper at the table by lamplight.

'Tea?' Josie asked her, getting up and putting her knitting to one side. 'Nicky didn't eat anything.'

'He often doesn't when he's like this. I'll make some beef broth in the morning for him.' Meg stood by the fire, still not used to the transformation of Josie. She seemed to have changed, not only by a good wash and different clothes, but it was as though she'd found some inner strength and confidence.

'I'm away to my bed.' Freddie yawned, folding the newspaper. 'Everyone else has gone up. I'm glad tomorrow is Saturday and a half-day.'

Meg dithered. She needed to tell him about Christian.

'If the weather is fine, I'll take the girls to Thorpe Park, as Betsy will have her first half-day, too,' Freddie said. 'A band might be playing.'

'They'd like that.' Meg took his chair at the table. 'Though it'll upset Nicky to be left behind.' Meg swallowed. She had to tell him Christian was coming tomorrow.

'I'll treat him when he's well.' Freddie headed for the stairs. 'Next week we'll see Mr Moffatt again and I'll buy Nicky some new drawing pencils. We need to decide what we are going to do about everything else.'

The moment was gone. She'd have to tell him and them all in the morning. Meg accepted the cup from Josie. 'Thank you.'

'Mr Moffatt?' Josie asked.

'Our grandparents' solicitor,' Meg informed her, but didn't want to mention the money. She didn't know her well enough to divulge such information. Besides, sharing sixty-three pounds with Freddie seemed insignificant when she was going to be marrying a man who owned a brewery. She still couldn't believe it. How could a gentleman like Christian Henderson love her?

She stared into her black tea. Soon she would be able to have milk in it all the time...

The following day, Meg was on edge all morning. She wanted the family together when she told them about Christian coming to call. She'd slept badly, unable to stop thinking about Christian's proposal and also kept a worried eye on Nicky, who she slept beside in case he needed her.

The sun shone from a clear blue sky, not that Meg had time to enjoy the fine weather. While the girls went out and played in the street, Meg waited for Freddie, Mabel and Susie to return home from their half-days at work.

When a knock sounded on the door just after midday, Meg's

heart hammered and she couldn't move from where she stood by the range. Josie opened the door and Lorrie came in, full of curious smiles.

'I know you weren't expecting me today,' Lorrie said, placing her shopping basket on the floor. 'But I just saw Fliss in town.' Lorrie glanced at Josie.

Josie, taking the hint, picked up her knitting. 'I'll go up and check on Nicky.'

Meg waited for Josie to climb the stairs before dragging Lorrie closer. 'Christian asked me to marry him,' she blurted in a whisper.

'Oh!' Lorrie gasped, then hugged Meg to her. 'I'm so thrilled for you. So happy. Fliss said he came to the pub last night and whisked you away. That's why I came here to see if everything was all right.'

'We went for a walk, and he proposed.' Meg wrung her hands. 'I'm excited, but still think it's all a dream. He might change his mind. I've told nobody but you. I need to tell the others. Oh, God above, Lorrie, my head is just mad with thoughts.'

'Calm down.' Lorrie took both of Meg's hands and squeezed them gently. 'Do you want to marry Mr Henderson?'

'Yes. Yes, I do, but there's so much to consider. We are not the same class. He says it won't matter but it will. Of course it will.'

Lorrie pulled Meg onto a chair. 'Are you strong enough to overcome the obstacles you might face?' she asked honestly. 'Do you want him enough to fight for your happiness?'

'Yes, but—'

'There can be no buts, Meg.' Lorrie's smile was kind, sympathetic. 'Taking such an enormous step will mean many changes for you all. So, only do it if it's what you really desire.'

'I do want him. Christian is all I think about.'

'And he obviously feels the same.'

'He says so.'

'Then trust in that. Trust him to know his own mind. He's an intelligent man, Meg. He wouldn't go into such a marriage without weighing it all up.'

Meg took a deep, calming breath. 'It scares me.'

Movement on the stairs made them both turn. Josie stood at the bottom. 'Nicky is asking for you, Meg.'

Lorrie rose and picked up her basket. 'I'll go and we'll speak tomorrow.'

Upstairs, Meg sat on the bed beside Nicky. 'Are you feeling worse?'

'No.' As if to demonstrate, he pushed himself up against the wall. 'See? I'm much better.'

'I'm delighted to see it.' She kissed his forehead.

'Can I come downstairs?'

'Can you manage the stairs, or do we wait until Freddie is home and he can carry you? He won't be long.'

'I can manage the stairs.' Throwing the blankets back, Nicky put his feet to the floorboards and stood up.

Meg kept an arm around him as they carefully went downstairs. 'You're to stay on the sofa. No arguments,' she told him, placing a blanket over his legs as he lay back panting on the sofa.

'Tea?' Josie put the kettle on the boil.

It irritated Meg that Josie was quick to offer tea when she wasn't the one paying for it. 'I thought you'd have been out looking for work. Especially since Dolly is playing with Nell in the street.'

Josie blushed. 'I could do, but it's a half-day, most places will be nearly closed now.'

Annoyance filled Meg. Was Josie trying to pull a fast one over her? As far as Meg was concerned, she'd done her bit by letting her stay here. She had put a roof over her head and food in her belly and even the clothes on her back. Surely Josie could repay that by at least attempting to look for work.

'Can I draw, Meg?' Nicky asked.

'Yes, pet.' She fetched his pieces of paper and charcoals just as the door opened and Freddie, Mabel and Susie walked in.

Freddie's face was like thunder. 'What's this I hear about you and Mr Henderson?'

The blood seeped from Meg's face. 'What have you heard?'

'That the two of you went on a sweet little walk last night?' Freddie was as angry as Meg had ever seen him.

'We did, yes.'

'Why?' Freddie demanded, hands on hips. 'He's a gentleman. Why would he want to go walking with you? I actually liked the man until I heard that, but not now. My opinion of him is in the gutter. No gentleman goes walking with a working-class girl unless he wants something more.'

Mabel, her expression of eager interest, nudged Susie. 'Are you courting, our Meg?'

'Courting?' Freddie fumed. 'He's a gentleman and they don't court girls from Wellington Street or anyone from the waterfront.'

'That's enough, Freddie,' Meg warned, her own temper rising.

'What have you done with him?'

'Nothing!' Her cheeks flamed.

'Have you fallen for his charms? Is he promising you trinkets?'

In a flash, Meg slapped Freddie's cheek. 'How dare you! You've basically called me a whore!' she shouted.

'If the name fits?' Freddie snapped, eyes bright with fury and his cheek red.

Incensed, Meg ran from the house and along Wellington Street, ignoring Nell and Betsy's calls as she passed them.

Dashing tears from her face, she marched along Thornes Lane Wharf until she reached the ferry. She had no money on her but after one look at her face, Harry helped her on to the boat and took her across the river. She thanked him weakly with another onset of fresh tears.

'Nay, lass, don't take on so hard,' he said kindly. 'It'll all be right in the end.'

She couldn't answer him, but with a nod she turned away from the mills and the canal lock and walked south on Barnsley Road.

Twenty minutes later, she stood at the black iron gates of Meadow View House. Christian's house. This could be her home. Despite all of Freddie's harsh words, the pleasure of becoming Christian's wife could be a possibility. She, Meg Taylor, from Wellington Street, could one day be the mistress of this wonderful property. Could she do it? Was she clever enough to cope? Did she have skin thick enough to overcome all the gossip, rumours that would say exactly what Freddie had said and worse?

Without knowing why, she opened the smaller side gate and went into the parkland surrounding the drive. By a tree she stopped and studied the red-brick house with its large windows and wide steps, the gravel drive and the paths leading to around the side through ornate gardens. She even spied a white stone statue of a woman holding a pot in the middle of a rose bed.

Her courage failed her. All this was another world that she'd only ever looked upon from afar, never once believing she could be a part of it. How could she? But since meeting Christian, she had begun to dream, still not thinking any of it could be real.

'May I help you, miss?' a voice spoke from a grove to the left.

Meg spun around, not seeing the gardener until he came out from the deep shade. 'Forgive me.' Her cheeks went hot as though she'd been caught stealing.

'Are you lost?' the old man asked.

'Maybe my mind,' she joked half-heartedly.

He leaned on his rake and brought a pipe from the pocket of his ancient-looking coat. 'You wouldn't be the first, lass.'

'I *do* know Mr Henderson, I'm not a stranger.' She wanted to reassure him.

'Have you come to pick the strawberries? Mr Henderson did say a lovely young woman would be doing so.' He frowned. 'I thought he mentioned there'd be some kiddies, too, but that was weeks ago.'

Meg had forgotten all about bringing the children to pick strawberries. 'I didn't bring my brothers and sisters.'

'Perhaps you'd like to take some back to them?'

She hesitated.

'Or just have some for yourself.' The old man smiled. 'Follow me.'

Without a word spoken, Meg followed him through the grove and around to the back of the house and beyond the service buildings to a large walled garden.

Through a cream-painted gate in the wall, Meg stepped into a neat, ordered space of long, rectangular vegetable beds with gravel paths between. At the end of the walled garden was a glasshouse, the vents of which were open in the warm weather.

'What a wonderful place,' Meg murmured, impressed.

'A haven, miss,' the old man replied. 'I wouldn't want to be anywhere else.' He led her along the paths, and she gazed at the healthy vegetables growing in rich soil in some beds while in other beds young lads were turning over manure into the dirt. They'd trained fruit trees on wire along the red-brick walls and chickens roamed freely, picking at the insects in the sunshine.

At the glasshouse, Meg's eyes widened at the heat but also the lushness of the dark green tropical plants and their exotic flowers of the kind she'd never seen before.

'Mr Henderson's aunt, Mrs Gertrude Henderson, was a keen

gardener and collector,' he told her, leading her further along until they were in a section that grew tomato vines, young lettuce and smaller strawberry plants. 'This crop of strawberries is about to go outside, but early season strawberries are a favourite of Mr Henderson.' He pointed to larger plants in a raised bed. The plump strawberries hung over the wood, ready to be picked. 'These are the first of the June season.' He smiled proudly.

'I dare not pick them if they are his favourite,' Meg laughed, eyeing up the shiny red fruit.

'We'll have plenty more growing outside for a later harvest.'

Meg reached out to pluck one.

'Miss Taylor!'

She spun around guiltily to stare at Christian. 'Mr Henderson.'

His eyes were wide with surprise, and a slow smile followed. 'You came to my house.'

'I was out walking...' She'd come without a hat on, such had been her mad dash from the house.

Christian walked closer. 'Perhaps I could show you the grounds?'

'Yes.' Nodding her thanks to the old gardener, she walked back the way she came, with Christian beside her. 'It's a beautiful garden.'

'My aunt spent all her time outside if she could. My uncle left her alone all day and I think she was lonely. The garden and talking to the gardeners like old Seth back there gave her a sense of purpose.' He paused once they were in the walled vegetable garden and turned to her. 'I am so pleased you came.'

'I walked here without knowing I was doing it until I reached the gates.'

'Where are the others?'

'At home.' She stared down at the path and sighed.

'What is wrong, my darling?' He cupped her face.

She leaned into his hand for a moment. 'Freddie knows we went walking. He accused me of... well... He thinks you and me...'

'I can imagine.' Christian inhaled sharply.

'Freddie said gentlemen do not go for walks with girls from the waterfront unless they want something.'

'No, they do not. He is correct.' Christian looked up at the windows of the house. A muscle clenched in his jaw as he took her arm. 'However, this is different.'

'Not in his eyes, or anyone who lives in my street.'

'They will think differently once we are married.'

She sagged in relief. 'So, you mean that? You want to marry me? I thought I might have it all wrong or that you would change your mind.'

He gave a wry smile. 'I do not say things I do not mean.' He touched her cheek. 'Do not worry. I will never change my mind about you.'

'Of course I worry. How can I not when something like this is happening? I never expected any of this.'

'Nor did I, but we will be happy, Meg. I promise.' He took her hand, and they walked towards the outbuildings. 'Come, I shall take you home and speak to your family. They need to hear from me that my intentions are honourable.'

'How will this work, our marriage? I cannot leave the children behind.'

'Then they will live here with us.'

'You want that?'

'Do you not?'

'There are eight of us. Though Betsy and Arthur live out now, and Freddie won't come here.' She knew that for a fact. 'That leaves Mabel, Susie, Nell and Nicky.'

'I have five bedrooms. I am sure we can manage it.'

Meg pulled him to a stop, her heart and mind at war. 'You don't want us all living here with you. How can you? An instant family under your feet!'

'I want you, Meg, and if to have you means I have to live with your siblings, then I will.'

'Why? Why do you want me when you can have any woman?'

He grinned. 'I do not want just *any* woman. I do not know what it is about you, what draws me to you, but I will not deny it, or try to fight it. When I think of you, my heart twists inside my chest. When I see you, my body responds. I want to see your smile, hear your laughter. Yes, we are not from the same class. What of it? You will adapt because you are clever and have strength of character. You will face the challenges ahead because you, Miss Taylor...' He squeezed her hands. 'You are smart and beautiful, and strong. You have kept your family together despite losing both parents. We are so fortunate to have found one another. Together we shall be happy. I shall work every day to make sure you never regret marrying me.'

Her mind whirled at his speech. His declaration meant the world to her. If he was willing to try so hard to make it all work, then so would she.

Thoughts of the future buzzed in her head as they waited for the horses to be harnessed to the carriage.

Once on the road, Meg couldn't relax. Freddie's words had wounded her, and she'd slapped him. Would he forgive her? Would she forgive him?

Christian cupped her face. 'Stop worrying. Everything will be just fine, I promise you.' He lowered his lips to hers.

Desire ignited between them, and the kiss deepened. Was this what being married to him would be like, this all-consuming passion that enveloped her whole being? She couldn't think straight when he was touching her.

At the entrance to Wellington Street, the carriage stopped as the street was a dead end and there was nowhere for the horses to turn. Christian handed her down and, tucking her arm through his, they walked past the malthouses on either side and then one by one the terraced doors.

Children played on the cobbles, including her sisters, who were holding ends of an old rope for another girl to skip in the middle. Several boys were fighting with sticks as swords and a couple of housewives, Mrs Green and Mrs Hatchett, were gossiping on their doorsteps, and both nodded to Meg but stared at Christian.

Mrs Green nudged her neighbour. 'He held her arm. Did you see, Dilys?' Mrs Green said in astonishment.

'Aye, I did see, Sal. What do you make of that, then?' Mrs Hatchett replied. 'A gentleman with Meg Taylor?'

Meg cringed inwardly, knowing that by morning the entire street would know she was being familiar with Mr Henderson.

At the front door, she paused and took a deep, steadying breath.

Christian looked at her. 'I only want you to be happy. I know this is a momentous decision and change in your life, but you are not alone. You have me, always.'

Love for him swamped her.

Inside the house, Meg wrung her hands as Christian stood beside her. Josie was stirring something in a pot at the range. Freddie was mending someone's boot while Mabel was sewing a dropped hem in her skirt and Susie and Nicky were looking through some drawings Nicky had done previously. They all looked at Meg and the man she was with, their frozen expressions not hiding their surprise.

Freddie reacted first. He dropped the boot and stood, his face a mixture of anger and confusion as he glared at Meg.

Meg hated the tension between them. 'Mr Henderson has asked me to marry him.'

'Aye, Josie told me,' Freddie huffed.

She turned to Josie, irritated again by the woman. 'You had no right. You were listening to my conversation with Lorrie!'

'I thought it would ease his mind,' Josie defended. 'I overheard you, before, with your friend, and I'm sorry I did. I only thought it would help if Freddie knew this was a genuine thing and not a...' Josie flushed.

Freddie smirked. 'Genuine? You've only known each other five minutes.'

Christian stepped forward. 'I can see how it would look, but I can assure you that my intentions are honourable towards your sister.'

'Really? You could have anyone, yet you've chosen a lass from Wellington Street. I find it hard to believe myself,' Freddie mocked, and stared at Meg.

'Why is it hard to believe?' Christian's voice was low and full of meaning. 'Why would a man not find your sister attractive and interesting?'

'A man of our class would, yes, but not you.' Freddie was scathing.

'Am I not a man?' Christian asked, his eyes as blue as ice beneath the sea. 'Your sister captivates me. In my eyes, she is everything I want. Someone real and true, honest and hard-working, loving, loyal and kind. The type of woman any man would be honoured to call his wife.'

'Until you become bored with her simple ways.' Freddie snorted with contempt. 'Meg is all those things, but she isn't sophisticated or cultured compared to the women of your class. She'll be an embarrassment to you.'

'Freddie!' Like a stab wound, his hurtful words plunged into her heart.

Christian tensed. 'On the contrary, Miss Taylor will be the making of me. She is the breath of fresh air I need.' He took Meg's hand. 'Her happiness is important to me and if she has to choose between me and her family, I will take any decision she makes bravely as a man and support her. Can you say the same?'

Freddie reddened. He glared at Meg. 'You're a fool to think this marriage would work. You'll not be accepted by his lot.'

'That's for me to find out, Freddie.' Emotion heightened Meg's voice. 'But I'd like my own family to support me.'

'How do the rest of us fit into your plans?' he asked.

'You'll all come and live with us at Meadow View House.'

Freddie burst out laughing. 'Us lot? Go and live in the big house?'

'You would be very welcome,' Christian added, a strain to his voice, and he moved closer to Meg.

'Oh, aye, course we would,' Freddie mocked. 'With our arses hanging out of our trousers and holes in our boots and our fancy way of speaking! Your family and friends will love us.'

'That's enough, Freddie!' Meg barked, stung to tears by his behaviour. This wasn't the Freddie she knew.

'I can tell you right now.' Freddie scowled at her. 'We'll not be moving to Meadow View House.'

Her heart dropped like a stone. 'The children need me.'

He shook his head. 'You've made your choice. We are staying here, where we belong. You run along and play the madam of the house and we'll stay here.'

'You are upsetting your sister,' Christian said, anger in his voice. 'We can sort this out to a solution everyone is happy with.'

'Nah.' Freddie folded his arms. 'As I said, this is where we belong. I work for you and there is no way in hell I'd ever live with you.'

'The others can come,' Meg murmured, distraught.

'No. Them living in a gentleman's house will confuse them. We are working class, Meg. It's like putting an old nag in a thoroughbred's stall. They won't fit in amongst the toffs. Do you want them to be a laughing stock?'

'They can learn to fit in!'

'What? Like you are going to?' he scorned.

'We can give them a better life than living here. Don't you want that for them?' she pleaded, wishing they didn't have to fight about this.

'You fail to understand, Meg. Go and live your dream, but leave us out of it. I'm the man of the house now. What I say goes. They all stay with me. That's my final word on it.'

Christian touched Meg's elbow. 'Shall I leave you to talk about it? My presence here is making things worse for you.'

Upset, she didn't want him to go, but she knew that she needed to talk to Freddie without Christian.

Freddie raised his chin. 'There is nowt to discuss, Mr Henderson. My decision won't change. This is my family and what I say goes. My brothers and sisters will live with me.'

'You sound just like Father used to!' Meg snarled, torn between rage and tears of hurt.

Freddie stalked past them, grabbed his coat from the nail behind the door, and stormed out.

Christian put both hands on Meg's shoulders and leaned in close. 'He will come around to the idea. He just needs time. Leave it for now.'

She nodded, though not convinced.

'I will meet you at church tomorrow. We can speak to the vicar after service and talk to him about the banns. I shall also introduce you to my mother and sister.' He kissed her on both cheeks, knowing they had an audience, and left.

Silence held for a moment or two after he'd gone, then Mabel flung her sewing onto the table. 'I'll not stay here if there's a chance I can live in a mansion and become a lady.'

Meg closed her eyes. This was what she'd been dreading. 'I haven't discussed with Mr Henderson the details, Mabel, and you heard what Freddie said.'

Her sister's eyes widened in alarm. 'To hell with Freddie. I want to live with you.'

'Yes, I know...' Meg didn't have the answers and thought quickly. 'But we can't be a burden on Christian. We are a large family. You still need to earn, to buy yourself things. Mr Henderson shouldn't have to feed and house you all while you do nothing but laze about all day.' Just saying such things out loud reaffirmed the difficulties ahead.

'Isn't that what you'll be doing?' Mabel argued.

Josie turned from the range. 'No, Mabel, Meg will be Mr Henderson's wife. She will have her own responsibilities. She'll need to run his house efficiently, be the mistress of his servants, be his hostess for social events, become involved in good works and charities as the wife of a successful businessman should do.' Josie shrugged. 'Meg will be busy every single day.'

'I could help?' Mabel suggested.

Meg's mind had whirled at Josie's description. It sounded so much and so involved. She sat at the table, head in hands. Tomorrow, Christian would introduce her to his mother and sister. She dreaded meeting them. They would not be welcoming to her, a girl who lived on the waterfront.

'I don't want to live in a big house, though, with strangers,' Nicky's soft voice came from the sofa.

Her chest seemed to cave in. She looked over at him, seeing

his worried expression. 'You don't have to do anything you don't want to do.'

'I'll miss you, Meg, but can I stay here with Freddie?'

'Of course you can, and I'll miss you, too, sweetness.' She nodded, fighting tears. She was losing her family. 'Freddie wants you to stay here with him, but I'll visit all the time.'

'Will you stay here, Josie?' Nicky swiftly asked Josie.

'If your brother lets me, I will.' Josie smiled at him like a mother and Meg's shoulders bowed even more. Josie had become a mother figure to them, and Meg's place was redundant now.

She thought of Christian. She loved him. Meg knew she needed this man in her life, but what would the cost be?

14

Christian stepped down from the carriage as Titmus opened the front door.

'Sir, your mother has been asking for you.' Titmus stood straight, chin up and an air of tight disapproval about him. 'Did Miss Taylor get home safely, sir?'

At the top of the steps, Christian paused. Nothing got past Titmus, not even a visitor in the walled garden. 'She did, Titmus.'

In the drawing room he found his mother, sister and Miss Crawford seated about the room. His mother was reading a letter at the small satinwood writing desk, Susan was embroidering on the window seat and Miss Crawford was pouring tea for them. He had a task ahead of him that he knew would be unpleasant.

'You have returned,' Susan stated.

His mother turned in her chair. 'There you are. Gracious me, Christian, you do not leave your guests without telling someone where you are going.'

'Forgive me, Mother. I had to attend to something.' He was still concerned about Meg's situation. It worried him that she would listen to her brother and give up the chance to marry him and get away from Wellington Street. He hated that the woman he loved, and he knew he loved her without question, lived in such dire circumstances. He could look beyond the poverty because he saw only Meg, who was bright and beautiful and who had the strength of character he admired. He wanted to save her from that harsh life and give her everything she deserved. But to do that he had to speak to the women in his life and make them see what he wanted.

He smiled at Miss Crawford. 'May I have a moment of your time?'

'Of course.' A triumphant spark lit her eyes.

He ignored his mother and sister's look of interest and led Miss Crawford across the hall and into his uncle's study, which was now his, but still felt as though his uncle would walk in at any minute. He needed to redecorate. Perhaps Meg would help him with that? His chest tightened at the thought of Meg, of the confrontation with her brother. How he had wanted to punch the young pup for hurting his lovely girl.

Standing in her home, he'd realised just how different their lives were. However, the diversity wasn't insurmountable. The home was clean and tidy, difficult, he knew, in such circumstances with limited water and old buildings built on the cheap. Meg's family seemed sensible, cared for. He admired Meg's tender nature towards her siblings, another reason that drew him to her. He had no doubts that she would be a wonderful mistress of this house and a loving mother to their children, that alone made him love her. No child of his would have the cold upbringing he had had, not with Meg for a mother. He heard the love she had for her brothers and sisters. He knew she would love her own child.

'What did you wish to speak to me about?' Miss Crawford asked, hands folded neatly before her.

He sighed, not looking forward to the coming conversation.

Ruth looked demure, but Christian had seen another side of her when she thought he wasn't looking. The side that spoke harshly to servants, the side that whispered nasty gossip about acquaintances. He knew she ran rings around her father and demanded whatever she wanted. He could never live with someone like that.

'Dear me, Mr Henderson, you are making me nervous.' She laughed, but it was a high false laugh that he'd heard too many times before and that grated on him.

'Miss Crawford, we have known each other for some time through our mothers' friendship,' he started.

'Yes, we have.' She wore a winning smile.

'And in the last six months, I have become aware that there may be certain expectations harboured by our mothers and possibly you, too, regarding our friendship.' He faltered, knowing he had to tread carefully to not sound egotistical or unfeeling.

'Well, that is true. We have become friends, you and I, and naturally I would hope for something more between us.' Her eyes narrowed slightly, as though suddenly on edge. 'My wish is that you would also hope for the same.'

He felt terrible. 'I am very sorry, Miss Crawford, but I do not feel as you do. I wanted to tell you that any expectations you may have—'

'What are you saying?' she snapped.

He clenched his fists. Ruth Crawford might be the daughter of a gentleman and they widely spoke of her beauty in their social circle, if you liked the appeal of haughtiness and conceit, but he did not. Women who lacked empathy and charm left him cold. 'I simply felt the need to explain myself before you expected more from me than I am willing to give. Your arrival here suggests that you have come to spend more time with me. I did not want you to hope for something that will not happen.'

'So, I have left London and come to the middle of nowhere for nothing? You do not want our *friendship* to develop into something more?' Loathing filled her cat-like eyes.

'You are a welcomed guest at my home, but there will be nothing further from me.'

Her lips curled back in disgust. 'I am wasting my time here. My father said I could do better than you, and he was right. You might be handsome, Christian Henderson, but you are no gentleman.' She flung herself from the room in a blur of mauve skirts.

Tired, Christian rubbed his hands over his eyes. On his desk was a pile of correspondence and business matters to attend to, but he didn't have the mind to deal with it all.

His mother appeared in the doorway, furious. 'What is all this? Ruth has decided to return home to London. Why?'

'I told her I do not see a future with her.'

'You did what?' Her mouth gaped open in surprise. 'Why would you say that? We all believed that you would offer her marriage this summer. You danced twice with her at the Langham Hotel's Christmas Ball. She is often at my house.'

'At your invitation, not mine.' Christian studied his mother, a woman he had no feelings for. 'You made certain that every time I was visiting you, Miss Crawford arrived. You and her mother concocted this fantasy, not me.'

'You encouraged Ruth. You gave people reason to speculate.'

'A man should be able to dance with his mother's friend's daughter more than once without judgement as to whether that classifies as a betrothal.' He exhaled deeply. London society was full of traps for the unsuspecting singleton.

She took a step further into the study and closed the door behind her. 'We all believed you had marriage intentions towards Ruth.'

'How so? When have I given anyone reason to think so? Have I sought her out in public? Do I monopolise her attention at functions? Not once have I called on Ruth at her home. Nor have I written to her, sent her presents or invited her on an outing.'

'You said she could come here.' His mother paced the room. 'That has spread all over London.'

'Yes, as a favour to you and Susan. I did not want her here. Why would I?' he defended. He hadn't wanted his mother and sister here either, but he left that unsaid.

'Please, think reasonably about this. Ruth is an only child, Christian. She will inherit all of her father's wealth.'

'I do not want Crawford's money, Mother. I have my own.'

'I doubt that will be for much longer if you keep spending it on a worthless brewery!'

'The brewery is not worthless.'

'No, it's deep in debt and you are throwing good money after bad. At this rate, you'll be penniless before long.'

He frowned. 'What do you know about my finances?'

'Nothing, nothing at all. Only that your stepfather left you a considerable amount and you've wasted it on buying a ridiculous brewery and this ugly house when you could have stayed in London.'

'That is your opinion.'

'It is my opinion, and another opinion is you have ruined your future by throwing Ruth aside.'

'I do not agree.' He walked behind his desk and picked up a letter from the morning's post. 'My future is in excellent hands.'

'What do you mean by that?'

'I mean I am getting married, Mother.' There, he'd said it out loud.

'Who? Who is the lady?' Her tone wavered as though she was not only shocked but nervous.

'A local woman. So, no one you know. I will invite Miss Taylor for dinner one evening next week so you and Susan can meet her properly, but I will introduce you to her tomorrow after church.'

'This is all rather sudden. You have not mentioned that you are courting any young lady. And her family?'

'Mother, I shall not discuss this right now.'

'Not discuss it!' she flared. 'You drop this sudden announcement and say you will not *discuss* it!'

'No, I shall not. I am certain Miss Crawford needs you.'

'How long will it be until the engagement announcement is made?'

He sat down heavily in the soft leather chair, knowing she would not be satisfied until she knew everything. 'We told her family today.'

'Before telling me?' Her nostrils flared. 'Will there be a long engagement? A year is suitable.'

'It shan't be that long. We are speaking to the vicar tomorrow about the banns.' He needed a drink. Was it late enough in the afternoon for a whisky?

'So soon?' His mother paled.

'Is that a problem?'

She went to the window and stared out of it. 'I have just written a letter of instruction to my solicitor to close down my townhouse and ready it for sale.'

Surprised, he dropped the envelope he held. 'Why?'

'So Susan and I can come and live here with you. To make this house a comfortable home for when you marry Ruth.'

'You presumed a great deal, Mother.' He clenched his jaw in frustration. 'Surely my future wife would wish to make this house her own without interference from you?'

'Nonsense. Every young wife needs guidance from a mature lady within the family.' She fiddled with the rings on her fingers, not meeting his gaze.

Instinct told Christian that she wasn't telling him the full story. 'What were you planning to do after I married?'

'Well, if we all got along, I was intending to stay.'

'Permanently?' He couldn't keep the shock from his voice. In no way did he ever want to live with his mother again. They did not get along well enough for that. He'd spent most of his life at boarding school and found the holidays spent with her painful enough to make him rent a flat in Oxford and attend university there without returning home. On leaving university, he toured Europe for six months and then rented a set of rooms in a hotel in West London until his stepfather died and he received his inheritance. Then he came to Wakefield. Never in his wildest imagination did he think his mother would leave London and come to live with him. She had a busy life in the capital, full of friends and social activities. Why would she come to the hated north?

'It is a son's duty to take care of his family,' she spoke without looking at him.

'But you have been well taken care of in Geoffrey's will. You and Susan. My stepfather made sure of that.'

'A lot can happen in a year.' She continued to stare out of the window.

'Meaning?' A sense of dread tingled along his spine.

'I need to sell the townhouse.' His mother took a deep breath and stared straight at him. 'All the money is gone.'

'What?' Christian lurched to his feet. 'How can that be?'

'Do not judge me,' she said fiercely.

'Judge you?' He scowled, not understanding.

'I made some rash decisions while grieving...'

'What did you do?'

'I invested heavily. I did it for the right reasons, believing I could make more money for Susan and I to live well.'

'You *do* live well,' he said, with frustration.

'Yes, but with Geoffrey dying, it means the money he left us was all we had. Without him investing and growing his wealth, then we would be...' She faltered. 'I would have to live on the allowance Geoffrey left me.'

'Which was eight hundred pounds a year, Mother, plus a townhouse in London and a carriage and horses and five servants. How could that not be enough? Susan's dowry is safe in the bank. My stepfather thought of everything.'

'No, he did not think of everything. He did not think of me and what I would do without him,' she yelled, then quickly brought herself under control.

'He did not die on purpose, Mother.' Christian bowed his head, thinking of the kind and good man Geoffrey Burton had been. A man who took on another man's son and raised him with the love his own mother never gave him.

'Be that as it may, I have found myself in an unsuitable position.' His mother returned to the desk and held his gaze. 'I placed my money into an investment a friend's husband told me about. It failed.'

He felt uneasy about where this conversation was heading. 'How much did you lose?'

'A large proportion of what Geoffrey left me.'

Christian closed his eyes in dismay. 'What possessed you to do such a thing? You have no head for business.'

'I thought to try, to be independent. I convinced Geoffrey's solicitor to release the money. It was a sure thing, I was told.'

'No investment is a sure thing, Mother. There is nothing left?'

'Very little. Bills have gone unpaid, and the refurbishment of the house has created a rather large dent in the remaining capital.'

'The house did not need refurbishment. You only had it done

four years ago.' What had his mother been thinking to spend so much?

She banged her hands on the desk. 'You do not understand! Redecorating helped me in my time of grief. It gave me something else to think about, to focus on.'

'How much do you owe?' He took a notebook from a drawer and a pen from the inkstand.

'You will not have enough to cover it.'

Christian jerked back. 'What are you saying?'

'I need to sell the townhouse and everything in it to cover the debts.' She looked ready to faint. 'I need to sit down.'

He hurriedly helped her to a chair by the small fireplace and then poured her a brandy from the drinks trolley by the window. He knelt beside her, wondering how to fix the mess she'd made. He studied her, this unfeeling woman who had borne him, and then found no use for him when she remarried. Despite their distant relationship, he had to help her.

She raised her eyes from the glass, her blue eyes as hard as steel. 'I had no choice but to come here. You are my son, and it is your duty to care for me and your sister. You have done as you pleased all your adult life and now it is time to be the man of the family.'

'I will not shirk my responsibilities.' He hated that she thought he needed reminding of his duty, yet she had never said a kind word to him in years.

'Then Susan and I have a home here?' She scowled and sniffed and looked about the room as though it were offensive.

'You do,' he replied, though he felt like a condemned man. His mother living here with him, and with Meg? He'd been able to adjust his thinking to living with Meg's siblings, for they were children, but his mother as well? The very idea poleaxed him.

'And what of your intended?'

Christian could not picture Meg and his mother together in the same room. His mind refused to make that an image. 'Miss Taylor will welcome you, too.'

She sat like a queen, her chin tilted high, a disparaging expression on her face. 'I look forward to meeting her.'

'Let us make a start on sorting out your affairs.' He stood and went back to his desk. He'd focus on his mother's finances. Working out complex situations aided his mind to deal with complications, and this was a complication he had never expected.

Throughout the service, Meg kept looking across the aisle to the pews on the opposite side of the church. Christian sat further down from Meg, with three women. She'd been late getting to the church, Nicky had felt unwell again and Josie had offered to stay with him.

Of Freddie, there had been no sight of him since their argument the day before. After a mad dash to the church, Meg had urged her sisters into the pews before the large oak door closed and Mr Rendale, the vicar, began his first sermon.

Meg glanced at her sisters, squashed along the pew. They all wore their best dresses and stockings. Meg had made them shine their boots and plaited their hair. Mabel looked, as always, bored and uninterested in the vicar's words, while Susie sat pulling at a loose thread on her skirt. Betsy and Nell fidgeted, elbowing each other. At the end of the pew sat Mrs Fogarty, who'd every now and then give Nell and Betsy a warning glance to behave.

In the pew in front of Meg sat Fliss with her aunt and uncle and cousin, and Meg had spotted Lorrie and her father a few rows down. But her gaze kept straying to the back of Christian's head, his smooth dark hair cut short and the wide shape of his shoulders in the dark grey suit he wore. The women on either side of him were dressed in beautiful clothes, ruffles of lace and frills. Even the older woman wore elegant grey silk with black beading. Meg wished she could see her face, to see if the woman had kind eyes like Christian.

An hour later, Mr Rendale finished his last sermon and then read out the banns for couples wishing to get married. Meg's heart thumped as next week her name would be mentioned together with Christian's.

As one, the congregation rose as Mr Rendale walked to the entrance. Slowly, everyone shuffled from their pews and queued in the aisle to shake hands with the vicar at the door. Meg stood behind her sisters and Fliss came alongside her.

'Fancy going for a walk this afternoon?' Fliss asked.

Meg gripped Fliss' hand. 'Mr Henderson and me are talking to the vicar about our banns. I'm to meet his mother and sister, too. I'm so nervous I feel sick.'

'You'll be fine. His family might be nice and welcome you. His old uncle was. Mr Henderson is lovely, so they are bound to be like him.' Fliss gave her an encouraging smile. 'It's all becoming very real now, isn't it? Soon you'll be Mrs Henderson. Just imagine!'

'That's the problem. I can't imagine it, at all.'

Fliss laughed. 'Relax and be happy. You're so lucky to have found love and with a wonderful gentleman like Mr Henderson. It's rare for someone like us.'

'I know.'

'It's so romantic,' Fliss sighed dreamily.

'It's nerve-racking, that's what it is.' Meg's stomach was in knots. 'I'll see you tomorrow for my shift.'

Outside, Meg shook hands with Mr Rendale, who smiled. 'We have a meeting shortly, Miss Taylor.'

'Yes, Mr Rendale.'

'Come to my house in half an hour.'

She nodded and moved on down the steps. Her sisters were mingling with their friends along the pavement as the crowd dispersed, either by walking or climbing into the waiting horse vehicles on the roadside.

Mrs Fogarty came to Meg's side. 'Shall I take the girls home now?'

'Yes, thank you.' Meg had told Mrs Fogarty of her engagement on the way to church this morning. Her dear neighbour had been made up for her and wished her every happiness.

Standing on the pavement, Meg waved to Lorrie, who hurried over to her.

'I saw Mr Henderson,' Lorrie said. 'He's with three very well-dressed women.'

'Yes, his family.'

'Good luck. I'll come and visit you tomorrow to hear all about it.' Lorrie embraced her, then rejoined her father.

'Miss Taylor.' Christian came down the steps, leading the three women, whose skirts had more material in them than Meg's whole family wore.

He took her hand. 'How are you?'

'Anxious.'

'I will let nothing spoil this for us,' he said softly, his eyes full of love.

Squaring her shoulders, Meg turned and gave her best smile to his mother, but the astonished stare and his mother's frozen expression gave her little reason to smile.

His mother looked at Christian, her mouth gaping open. 'Tell me this is not the woman you propose to marry?'

A flash of anger appeared on Christian's face before he quickly schooled it. 'Yes, Mother. This is Miss Margaret May Taylor.' He took Meg's arm and placed it through his own. 'Miss Taylor, my mother, Mrs Patrice Burton, my sister, Miss Susan Burton, and a family friend, Miss Ruth Crawford.'

Meg stared at all three faces and all three wore the same stunned expression. Meg's stomach churned and her knees weakened.

'Mother?' Christian whispered harshly.

'This is who you gave Ruth up for?' his mother managed to murmur as if the words choked her. 'Dear God in heaven. Have you lost your mind?'

Her heart sinking like a stone in a pond, Meg raised her gaze to Christian. His features were tightly controlled, but he gave her a strained smile and so, taking courage from him, she focused on the granite face of his mother and held out her hand. 'I'm pleased to meet you, Mrs Burton.'

His mother glared at the hand held out as though it deeply offended her. She did not take Meg's hand and only gave a curt nod. 'Miss Taylor.'

Meg's stomach churned. 'I'm pleased to meet you, Miss Burton.'

Susan's mouth thinned into a disagreeable line. 'I cannot say the same.' She turned and stormed away.

Miss Crawford flashed Meg a withering look that spoke a thousand words, before she suddenly laughed and sauntered away.

Dying inside, Meg blushed at such rudeness.

'Shall we speak with Mr Rendale?' Christian, his anger radiating from every pore, gently pulled Meg away. 'I shall see you at home, Mother.'

'Is that wise, Christian?' His mother forestalled them.

He turned back to her, his blue eyes full of some inner torment. 'What do you mean?'

'I mean, perhaps we should go home first and... and...' Her gaze slid away from him and Meg. 'There are things to discuss.'

'Oh, yes, there are, you can be certain of that, but first I shall speak with Mr Rendale and Miss Taylor and I will give our details for the banns.'

They walked away, but at the gate which led through to the vicar's house beside the church, Meg stopped. 'Your mother doesn't approve of me.'

'No, she does not. I am sorry.' He sighed. 'I knew she wouldn't.' He placed his hands on her shoulders. 'We cannot allow her opinion to spoil our happiness. We both want this marriage, do we not?'

'Well, yes...' She loved Christian, yet she hadn't been prepared for such hostility. Was this how it was to be for the rest of her life? 'I knew this would be difficult, that people would not understand or accept us, but your family's reaction and Freddie's just proves—'

'No! Say no more. Now, listen to me.' His voice softened, and he gripped her hands tightly. 'No one will come between us. Not my family. Not your family. This is our future, and we decide what we do with it.'

'You make it sound so simple.'

'I wish it was simple. I wish everyone would just be happy for us, but it shan't be that easy. We will have to fight for our happiness, Meg, but I am willing to do that, are you?' He drew her closer, even though people still mingled in the churchyard. 'I love you. I will do everything I can to protect you and make you happy.'

Meg sucked in a deep breath and took strength from his conviction. 'Let us speak to Mr Rendale.'

Later that evening Meg served behind the bar, trying to concentrate on her tasks and not think of the frosty reception she had received from Mrs Burton, but Fliss kept asking questions.

'So, you will move to Meadow View House alone? Without the children?' Fliss asked, wiping down the counter.

'Yes.' Meg poured a jug of cider for an old man. 'Christian said he'd take them all, but Freddie refuses to let them leave Wellington Street.'

'But why?' Fliss frowned. 'Mr Henderson could give them all a better chance in life.'

'Freddie says it's not where they belong, that included me, too.'

'He's being a silly fool,' Fliss said. 'How can he deny the children a decent home to live in? I'm not saying yours isn't, of course,' she added quickly.

'I know what you mean.' Meg rubbed her eyes tiredly. 'Perhaps it's for the best, at least at the start. I need to learn so much myself and adjust to living a different way of life. It might be easier once I'm used to being married and being the wife of a businessman, then I can slowly introduce the children to it.'

'True.' Fliss served a customer before speaking again. 'Soon you'll not be working here any longer.'

'Mr Moffatt is due this week with our inheritance. Once I have it, I'll tell Terry that he'll need to find another barmaid. The wedding is on Friday, 1 July, just over three weeks away. I need to buy new clothes and try and better myself.'

Fliss took a tankard from the shelf behind. 'What do you mean, better yourself?'

'Well, I can read and write, thanks to Mam insisting we learn at Sunday school, and she read to us as much as she could and, when she wasn't well, I took over the reading, so I'm not entirely clueless of popular books and can talk about them if asked, but there is an enormous amount I need to learn about everything else.'

'Such as?'

'How to run a big house and staff.' Meg shuddered at the thought.

'Isn't there butlers and housekeepers to do that?'

'But I need to know what to instruct them.'

Fliss tapped a finger against her lips, ignoring the man who asked for a pint of ale. 'Lorrie will know some things. She has to host her father's clients when they come to discuss boatbuilding and whatnot.'

'It's hardly the same. I'll be in charge of staff. Lorrie simply hosts afternoon teas. What do I know of entertaining gentlemen and their wives?' Meg worried her bottom lip with her teeth. 'They'll laugh at me behind my back. I'll be an embarrassment to Christian. God, Freddie was right.'

'You'll be fine. You'll soon learn. Stop doubting yourself before you even try!' Fliss patted her hand. 'You're clever and a quick thinker. In no time at all, you'll be running that house as though you were born to it.'

'I hope you're right.' But inside, Meg was filled with doubts and insecurities. Had she made a terrible mistake in agreeing to marry Christian?

15

The girls' overexcitement rang through the house and out into Wellington Street, with the windows and doors being open to capture any cool breeze. The July day continued with the fierce heat from the day before. Everyone complained about the hot weather. Neighbours whined to anyone walking by about how difficult it was to sleep at night. During the day, the children played on the burning cobbles, coming inside red-faced, caught by the sun.

Meg sat on the double bed her mam had died in and wished with all her heart her mam was here now. It was her wedding day, and she missed her mam. Also, Mam would have found a way to bring Meg and Freddie together.

Instead, Meg had spent the last three weeks walking on eggshells around him when he decided to show his face, but most times he kept away.

A knock on the door made her look up.

Josie came in, her smile hesitant. She held a small bouquet. 'Nicky and I have bought you these. We went to the market early this morning to get them.' She gave the posy to Meg. 'I know you had wanted fresh flowers and asked Mabel to get some this morning, but well... Nicky wanted to do it.'

'Thank you. They are beautiful.' Meg sniffed the fragrance of pale pink sweet peas and delicate white roses. 'It was kind of you to help Nicky in his quest.' Meg's chin wobbled.

Lately, Nicky had grown closer to Josie, who gave him attention and love, seeing in her a mother's comfort that he lacked. His own mam had been too ill all of his life to care for him properly and although Meg had filled that role, in the last few months she had been so preoccupied that he'd naturally turned to Josie, who gave him attention and love. As much as Meg wanted to take Nicky with her to Meadow View House, she knew it would be selfish. Nicky wanted to stay in his home and with Josie.

'I will take care of them,' Josie said, as if reading Meg's mind. 'I have come to love them all. They are sweet children. Even Mabel, who is as prickly as a hedgehog.'

'If you hadn't been here, I would have fought harder for them to come with me,' Meg admitted. 'But I know you care for them and, for now, this is the best place for them.' She didn't want the children in the tense atmosphere of Christian's house with his horrible mother and sister.

'I do love them, and I hope I've proven to you that I'm a good person. At Sowerby Bridge, you saw me at my worst. Destitute, poor, filthy, my babies dying... But I was never that person until I married your father. I was brought up decently. My father was the landlord of a public house, and my mother kept us fed and clothed and wanted the best for us. I broke her heart when I married your father, and she died a year later without forgiving me. My father blamed me, and he had reason to.' Josie shrugged slightly. 'I was left alone. My family deserted me. All I had was Frank, and I barely saw him.'

Meg didn't want to think of her father.

Josie sat on the bed. 'I promise you, Meg. I will take care of this family. I will cook and clean and keep everything just as tidy as you did.'

Tears burned behind Meg's eyes. 'I shall miss them so much.'

'You must visit as often as you can, and I'll make sure they visit you.'

Meg nodded. She stood abruptly, knowing she should be downstairs preparing to leave and not wallowing in her concerns upstairs. She'd made this decision, and she had to get on with it.

'You look beautiful,' Josie said, standing as well. 'Your mam would be so proud.'

'She would,' Meg agreed. She smoothed down the fine material of her dress. The duck-egg blue colour of it suited a summer wedding. She wore a matching hat trimmed in white lace with white silk roses that Betsy had made for her. Her white lace gloves were the finest she'd ever owned, and her new pale cream boots were tight on her feet.

She'd spent a fortune on her wedding outfit and extra clothes suitable for her new life as Mrs Henderson. Though Christian had said that he would pay for her to visit a seamstress in town and have a whole new wardrobe made. But until then, she had used her inheritance to have a small amount of clothing made ready. Her belongings had been collected this morning by Christian's carriage. The servant who had collected it, Thomas, had also given her a small parcel which was a gift from Christian, a string of pearls and a note declaring his love. She wore the pearls now and they would be her most treasured possession for the rest of her life.

Josie hesitated at the door. 'On the way home from the market, we stopped at the brewery to see Freddie. I asked him to change his mind about not coming to the wedding, but he refused.'

Meg nodded, accepting the sharp pain of hurt that stabbed her chest.

'Has he seen Arthur?'

'Briefly, yesterday morning. Arthur was away again on another load within the hour of docking and unloading. He didn't have time to come and see us, but Freddie told him all the news.'

'Yes, I bet he did.' Two brothers not attending her wedding. Never had she thought such a thing would happen.

Downstairs, Meg forced a smile to her face as the girls twirled in their new dresses of white muslin with blue sashes that Meg had bought them and Nicky wore a new white shirt and grey short breeches. They all wore new shoes. Even Mabel seemed happy and preened in front of the mirror to adjust the blue ribbons in her dark hair. Mabel would turn sixteen next month and Meg wondered how she'd gone from a child to a young adult overnight.

The door opened and Mrs Fogarty came in wearing her Sunday best and had added fresh flowers to her old hat. 'You all look a picture!' She beamed at Meg. 'Oh, lass. You look just like your mam did when she first came to Wellington Street. She was a stunner, just like you.'

Meg kissed the older woman's cheek. 'I would never have coped all these years without you, Mrs Fogarty.'

'Nonsense,' she answered kindly. 'You're made of stronger stuff than your mam, I'll say that for nothing, and you'll need it where you're going, but I know you'll be all right.'

'It's half past,' Mabel said, pushing her sisters in front of her and out the door.

Everyone went outside, but Meg lingered and looked around the room that had been her home all her life. The ghosts of her mam and father were in the shadows and for a brief moment she hoped they approved of her choices and wished her well.

At the church, Meg looked around for any sign of Freddie and hid her disappointment well as Lorrie and Fliss came to embrace her.

'You look wonderful,' Lorrie told her.

Fliss, with tears in her eyes, nodded in agreement. 'Beautiful.'

'I hope Christian will think the same,' Meg said anxiously.

'We need to go in,' Mabel said, seemingly in charge and ordering her siblings into the church.

'No Freddie, to walk you in?' Lorrie asked.

'No.' Meg gave one last glance up the street.

'The stupid fool. Wait till I see him again,' Fliss tutted. 'You can't walk in by yourself.'

Meg straightened her back and lifted her chin. 'Yes, I can.' She waved them inside and waited until the organist began to play.

Taking a deep breath, she felt the hammering of her heart, but took the first step into her new life.

The service was a blur. Mr Rendale's words went over her head so many times that he had to repeat himself to get her focus and replies.

Her hands shook violently, but Christian looked calm and so handsome. His loving smile was for her alone and so she kept her eyes on him and tried to steady herself.

Only when the church bells pealed, and they went to sign the register, did Meg feel able to breathe. She signed her name in an untidy scrawl, for her hands refused to stop shaking.

Before they went out and joined everyone, Christian led her to one side. 'You look ready to faint, my love.'

She felt it. She felt outside of her body. 'I'm so sorry.'

He gently touched her cheek. 'It is done. It is you and me now, together. I will never let anyone hurt you.'

She smiled, loving him more than ever. 'You can't control that, but thank you.'

He brought her gloved hands up and kissed them. 'I want you to be happy.'

Impulsively, she reached up and kissed him on the lips. 'I am.' It wasn't the complete truth, for she was worried about so many things, but she wanted to take the look of concern out of his eyes. 'Thank you for my pearls.'

'You like them?' He admired them.

'I'll treasure them always.'

'Then I look forward to seeing you wear them for years to come.'

With her arm through his, they joined the others and accepted the warm congratulations showered by the friends. Meg realised once they were standing outside having rice and rose petals thrown at them that Christian's mother and sister weren't there, and her stomach twisted.

She hadn't seen his mother or sister since the day they first met. Christian told her they had returned to London but would be back for the wedding. Obviously, they hadn't shown up.

For the reception, Christian had hired a tea room in the most exclusive hotel in Wakefield. Meg spent a good deal of time being introduced to Christian's business associates and their wives, many of whom looked her up and down as if sizing up her worth. Meg simply smiled and shook hands and thanked them for coming.

Thankfully, Lorrie and Fliss kept her company and made sure she ate when all she wanted to do was leave and find somewhere quiet for five minutes to gather her thoughts. Nicky and her sisters behaved well, and Josie was in constant attendance to them. After an hour, Nicky grew tired, the excitement of the day catching up with him, and he sat slumped in a chair by the buffet table.

Meg knelt down beside him and brushed his hair off his forehead. 'Tired, little man?'

'A bit.'

'You can go home if you want?'

'I know, but once I do, I'll not see you again.'

Meg pulled him into her arms and kissed the top of his head. 'You will see me again, don't ever think that you won't. I will come and see you every week. What about... every Sunday after church? I'll come to Wellington Street and spend the afternoon with you?'

'You will?'

'Absolutely.' She hoped Christian would be agreeable to that.

'That won't be so bad then,' he murmured, his head resting on her shoulder.

'It'll be something to look forward to each week, won't it?' She injected joy into her voice, not wanting him to be sad, even though her heart was breaking to be leaving him. 'And I expect to see some drawings each Sunday.'

'I started drawing Mr Henderson's carriage, but I couldn't get the horses' legs right.'

'You know what to do...'

'Practise,' he finished for her.

'That's right, practise.'

'Wife?' Christian came to them, smiling, then his handsome face became worried. 'Is Nicky unwell?'

'He's just tired.' As sad as she was to be leaving them, she'd swelled with pride when he called her wife.

'Then it's time for us to say goodbye to our guests and leave, if you wish?'

She nodded and took Nicky by the hand and led him over to Josie. One by one, she kissed her family goodbye, promising to see them as soon as she returned from her honeymoon.

As they prepared to leave the tea room, Christian's sister hurried through the door. 'Christian!' She looked pale and upset.

'Susan?'

'You must come! Mama took ill on the train!' She dragged him towards the door.

'Wait.' He beckoned Meg to join him, and they rushed out to the waiting carriage. Inside it, Mrs Burton lay across the seat, sweating and moaning.

'What happened?' Christian asked Susan.

'We were travelling on the train to here. Mama has been complaining about feeling unwell the whole way. You know how she is on the train. I didn't think she was serious. Then as the train pulled into the station just now, Mama collapsed.' Susan wrung her hands. 'The stationmaster and a porter helped me into this hired carriage and I remembered that you were getting married today and that the reception was at this tea room from the letter you sent.'

Christian went to his carriage driver and spoke with him briefly before returning to Meg and Susan. 'I have sent my carriage to Dr Maynard's residence to bring him to Meadow View.' He handed his sister into the hired carriage. Brodie went and sat up with the driver. Christian gave the driver directions to Meadow View House, then handed Meg into the carriage. She sat on the other seat facing Susan, who cradled her mother's head in her lap. Mrs Burton wasn't a small woman and her bulk squashed Susan uncomfortably.

Christian climbed in and shut the door.

As the carriage rumbled down the street, Meg waved to her family as she passed them. For a few seconds, she wished she was walking with them, then felt instantly guilty for her betrayal of Christian.

She stared at his mother, who moaned all the way to Meadow View House. Susan did her best to comfort her but soon was crying silent tears of helplessness.

At the house, they surprised Titmus, who expected his master and his new wife to be on a train to Great Yarmouth for their honeymoon.

Meg stood by uselessly as Christian sprang into action. He and Titmus carried his mother upstairs while Susan followed, beseeching them to be careful.

Meg walked into the drawing room and looked around. She had been once before, just over a week ago, when Christian had brought her here to meet the staff and see the house. She'd spent a delightful afternoon being given the tour and when no one was around, Christian had kissed her in corners. They'd had tea out on the back terrace before strolling through the gardens, talking of their upcoming wedding and honeymoon to Great Yarmouth.

For the first time, Meg had felt it was all real. She'd met the staff, seen the house and been kissed a dozen times by Christian, all of which built in her mind an idyllic glimpse of what her marriage would be like, and maybe, if she was really lucky, so much more.

Gazing about the drawing room, Meg noted the darkness of it, even on such a hot, bright day. Instantly, she knew this room should have pale yellow walls, and they should replace the heavy mahogany furniture with light satinwood pieces. The sofa and occasional chairs needed to be reupholstered in creams and lemon and the thick midnight-blue drapes changed to pale gold.

A flicker of excitement built. Christian had said she could have free rein in changing the decor to however she pleased. She was eager to begin, to place her stamp on the house, which would be her home, her and Christian's home.

She turned as her new husband came into the room.

He crossed to her and took her into his arms. 'I am so sorry about all this.'

'It's not your fault your mother is ill.' She loved the feel of his powerful arms around her.

'Mother wrote to me yesterday and said they would not be coming to the wedding. I am surprised she changed her mind and they are here.'

'A few minutes later and they would have missed us,' she murmured against his chest, a treacherous part of her wishing they had missed them and were on the train to Great Yarmouth.

'Yes.' He said no more, and Meg wondered if he was thinking the same as her.

He let her go as the bell rang at the front door. Titmus answered it in his unhurried and smooth way.

Dr Maynard entered and shook Christian's hand, then Meg's as they were introduced. 'Many congratulations on your union,' he said. 'I wish you many long years of happiness. Now, where is the patient?'

Again, Christian left her to accompany the doctor upstairs.

Meg unpinned her hat, hoping the neat arrangement of her hair was still in place. Pulling off her gloves, she sat on the edge of the sofa and waited, not knowing what else to do, but after ten minutes she stood and walked back into the hall. She'd ask Titmus for some tea.

In the room opposite was the library, a small square room where each wall was full of bookshelves from floor to ceiling. On her tour with Christian last week, she'd found this room to be her favourite in the house.

One of the maids, Meg couldn't remember her name, was placing a vase of flowers on a round table by the window. The girl, no more than Mabel's age, quickly stood straight and clasped her hands behind her back.

For a moment, Meg didn't know what to say. 'Er... Sorry, I've forgotten your name.'

'Maude, miss, I mean, Mrs Henderson.' The girl went scarlet.

Meg smiled. It was weird to hear herself addressed as Mrs Henderson. 'I'm after a cup of tea, Maude.'

'Oh, yes, of course, Mrs Henderson. I'll inform Mrs Beatty straight away.'

'Thank you.' Meg returned to the drawing room, making a mental note of Maude's name and that Mrs Beatty was the cook. She would have to write it all down to start with.

The noise of sobbing coming down the stairs reached her before her sister-in-law appeared. Meg thought the worst had happened. 'Susan?'

Dabbing her eyes, Susan gave Meg a look of pure loathing. 'Do not speak to me.'

'What? Why?'

'This is all your fault. My mama's nerves and ill health has been caused by you marrying my brother. The scandal of it has driven us from London. We are a laughing stock.' Susan threw herself down on the sofa and cried more.

A wave of guilt washed over Meg. Susan's hateful words pounded in her head. She didn't know what to say in reply. How could she become friends with Susan when there was so much dislike?

Christian and Dr Maynard entered. Christian glanced at Susan but came to Meg and took her hand. 'Mother is not well. Dr Maynard is going to arrange for a nurse to live in, but... well... Time will tell.'

'I'm so sorry to hear that.' She clutched his hands to her.

'There is no way we can go to Great Yarmouth now, not until she has recovered...'

'Of course.'

Tea trays were brought in by Maude and Titmus and the butler poured for them. Meg didn't know if she should have done it, but for today at least she was simply going to sit quietly and not draw attention to herself.

Susan dried her eyes and took some tea and a large slice of pound cake. Meg noted that her upset didn't affect her appetite and then felt bad for such thoughts.

The evening drew in and Dr Maynard stayed for dinner, which was a quiet affair. Susan hadn't changed for the meal and so Meg didn't either, even though the seamstress she'd visited in town said that ladies and gentlemen always changed for dinner. Meg had had a plain green silk evening dress made to wear for dinner, the cost of which had made her eyes water. She dreaded to think how much more it would have cost if she had added flounces of lace and frills. But for tonight, she stayed in her wedding dress.

Thankfully, the meal comprised soup, then roast chicken and lastly a raspberry mousse. Mrs Beatty, not expecting to cater for anyone but the staff, had not been prepared enough to make an elaborate meal of several courses. Meg had managed to conduct herself at the table without any problems of working out which knife or fork to use. Under her lashes, she'd subtly watched Susan and followed her movements, especially that of using a napkin, something Meg had never done before. She drank a little of the wine, which changed with each course, and listened to the doctor talk of medical issues in town and his wish for another doctor to join him in his practice.

Although it was still light outside and only just past eight o'clock, Meg was exhausted and fought the yawns that constantly attacked her as they withdrew from the dining room.

'You are tired, my love,' Christian whispered.

'It has been a long day. I was up at six this morning drawing water from the pump so we could all bathe before the wedding.'

Susan snorted at the comment.

Christian glared at his sister before raising Meg's hand and kissing it. 'Would you like to go up?'

'Yes.' Meg couldn't abide the thought of wasting another hour sitting in Susan's company. Her sister-in-law hadn't spoken to her throughout dinner, just given her scathing looks.

'I will be up later.' He kissed her cheek.

Meg said goodnight to Susan, who ignored her, and then to the doctor, and gratefully went up to the room Christian had shown her was to be their master suite. A large bedroom with two dressing rooms, one on either side, one for him and one for her.

The bedroom, decorated in wood panelling and again with heavy dark drapes, was unfamiliar and dim with only a lamp lighting the room on the bedside table. Meg pulled open the drapes and pushed aside the white netting to open the window and let in fresh air.

A cuckoo sounded from a tree in the park and somewhere a cow bellowed. The view overlooking the park and the trees was beautiful in the soft twilight. Meg could just make out the ruins of Sandal Castle. Purple and orange streaked the sky. A soft breeze lifted Meg's tendrils of hair near her face. It was all so very quiet. She wasn't used to it. In Wellington Street, she had neighbours on the other side of the wall. The terraces were always noisy with children playing, babies crying, adults arguing or laughing, alley cats meowing, dogs barking, carts trundling across the cobbles, the horns of boats echoing across the water, factory whistles and the stomp of hundreds of boots coming and going.

All that was replaced with the odd hoot of an owl and the whisper of the breeze in the trees. It would be another thing to get used to.

The door opened behind her. 'Oh, sorry, Mrs Henderson. I thought you were still downstairs.' Maude came in carrying a jug and a towel over her arm.

'Do you see to both upstairs and downstairs?' Meg asked the girl.

Maude reddened. 'Usually I'm downstairs, madam, but I'm to help upstairs because Lydia is busy with Miss Burton's things.' Maude placed the jug on the stand in the small dressing room.

Meg stood in the doorway to the small room, which was crammed with an enormous wardrobe and two chests of drawers plus a changing screen and a chair and cheval mirror. 'I've unpacked your clothes, madam, as I was told you shan't be going on your honeymoon now.'

'No.' Meg couldn't keep the disappointment out of her voice.

'Happen you can go when Mrs Burton is recovered?'

'I hope so.' But something in Meg doubted it. She began to undress and wash while the water was warm. Taking off her wedding outfit was like shredding her armour. Wearing just her shift, she was plain old Meg Taylor again, except for the gold band on her finger.

'Your nightdress is here, madam.' Maude took out the linen nightdress and placed it on the chair. 'Your dressing gown is hanging up. I'll fetch it for you.'

As Meg lathered up the sweet-smelling soap, she wondered if she'd ever become accustomed to having a maid fetch and carry for her. It was an odd sensation. 'So normally Lydia would do this for me?'

'Yes, madam, until you engage a lady's maid.'

'A lady's maid...'

Maude reddened again. 'You know, someone to see to all your clothes, your hair, your jewellery. She'll go on visits with you, carrying your shopping, discuss your new season clothing with your seamstress. That sort of thing.'

'You know I'm not of this class, obviously.' Meg dried herself. 'This is all very new to me.'

'Aye, madam, we know.'

Meg took that to mean the entire staff. Of course they would know. They would spot her background the minute she opened her mouth and by the clothes she wore on her previous visit. 'You don't mind working for me now I'm Mrs Henderson and in charge?'

'Not at all, madam. Good luck to you, I say, so do some of the others downstairs, though naturally some have their noses out of joint, like Lydia. They don't want to be at the beck and call of a waterfront lass—' Maude slapped her hand over her mouth, her eyes wide in her freckled face. 'Nay, I'm that sorry, miss, I mean madam, I mean Mrs Henderson.'

Meg took a moment to take in that information. So, Lydia was one who didn't want to be under her instructions. That was why she was attending to Susan, a proper lady. She remembered being introduced to Lydia. She remembered Lydia's forthright stare and the slightest of nods. Lydia had the thin lips which had curled slightly as Meg passed.

Seeing Maude's distraught expression, Meg smiled slightly. 'Don't be upset. You spoke the truth.'

'I should keep me big fat gob shut!'

'No, never do that with me, Maude.' Meg liked the skinny girl with the freckles and the natural openness. 'Would you like to be my lady's maid, Maude?'

'Me?' Maude's eyes widened again. 'I've no training, madam. I know what a lady's maid does, but not how to do it, not all of it. Lady's maids are educated and skilled, have years of training as under lady's maids. I'm just the parlourmaid and before that I was a skivvy in the kitchen.'

'I'll let you in on a secret, Maude.' Meg took a step closer to her. 'I feel a little lost here, amongst all of this.' She swept one arm wide. 'I wasn't born to this life, but my mam was the daughter of a teacher, and her mother was born in the middle class, the daughter of a barrister. Half of me comes from good stock even if I've lived all my life in Wellington Street. I've married a man who I love, and I want to make him proud of me. I know I'll need help to rise to the situation I've found myself in, but I know I can do it, and, well, I like you and I think it would be nice for us both to rise in our positions. What do you say?'

A slow smile spread across Maude's face. 'Do you think I can do it, madam?'

'We can learn together.' Meg didn't want Lydia waiting on her, the maid would probably spit in her tea.

'Lydia won't be happy. This is her position.'

'Ah, but Lydia isn't the mistress here. I am.' Meg donned the nightdress and reached to take the pins out of her hair.

'No, madam. Let me. That's my job now.' Maude indicated for her to go into the bedroom and sit at the dresser, which was decidedly bare, except for the velvet box her pearls had been in.

Meg stared at her reflection as Maude pulled out the pins and began brushing the long length of her hair.

'You've lovely hair, madam. It's the colour of a burnt chestnut. You know when you've left one in the fire for too long?'

Meg laughed, and it felt good to laugh. It seemed an age since she had. She unclasped her pearls and placed them in the box.

The door opened and Christian stepped in. 'I heard you laughing in the hallway.'

Meg was instantly contrite. 'I'm sorry. I forgot about your mother.'

'Never be sorry for laughing. It is a sound I always want to hear.' He came over and knelt beside her. 'Dr Maynard is staying the night to monitor Mother. I feel I should stay up with him.' His gaze drifted down to the top of her nightdress where the thin white ribbon was tied. 'I shan't come to bed tonight, though it pains me to say it.'

'I understand.' She wanted to kiss him, but Maude stood behind her, hairbrush in hand.

'This is not how I imagined our wedding night would be.'

'Nor me.' She'd been so eager to spend the night in his arms.

'I will make it up to you, I promise.'

'There is nothing to make up for. Your mother is ill, and she needs you. Don't worry about me. I'll be fine. I'm exhausted anyway. I'll see you in the morning.'

He kissed her, obviously not caring about Maude's presence. 'Good night, my love.'

When he'd gone from the room, Meg felt deflated. She'd been longing for her wedding night to come, to be in his arms and for him to love her and turn her into a true woman who'd know all the secrets of the marital bed.

'There's always tomorrow, madam,' Maude said softly.

Meg caught her sympathetic gaze in the mirror. 'Yes. Tomorrow is a new start for both of us.'

16

Meg woke to a touch on her cheek. She opened her eyes and smiled at Christian sitting on the bed beside her. Sunlight bright behind the closed drapes gave the room muted light.

'Good morning, wife.' He kissed her. 'Did you sleep well?'

'I did.' She stretched in the soft bed, a large bed she'd had all to herself for the first time in her life. She had expected to not sleep well in an unfamiliar room, but she'd not woken once.

'Maude has brought up a breakfast tray for you, but I took it from her and brought it in myself.' He indicated the silver tray that held boiled eggs and bacon, a rack of toast, a small teapot, cup and saucer and a little glass jug of milk. 'I told her to come back in an hour.'

'Have I overslept?' Meg sat up. 'What time is it? I should have been downstairs in the dining room for breakfast. I'm so sorry.'

'No, no.' He chuckled. 'You are a married woman and have the privilege of having breakfast in bed every day if you wish it.'

'I do?' That shocked her.

'You do not have to rise at set times, darling.' He smiled. 'You can do as you please.'

'I'm always up early, to get everyone off to work and school, to start my day's jobs.'

He poured her a cup of tea. 'Not any more. Your days are now your own to do as you please.'

'It'll take some getting used to.' She sipped from the teacup.

'There will be a lot for you to get used to.'

Somehow, that thought didn't scare her as much as it had done only weeks ago. She had Christian and Maude by her side. She would rise to the challenges. 'How's your mother?'

'She slept throughout the night. She seems no worse. In fact, she has good colour to her cheeks. Dr Maynard is content with her progress and has gone home and will be back later today.' Christian ran his hand along her bare arm. 'None of this is how I imagined it would be. I thought we would spend our first night in a hotel by the sea and wake up to the sounds of gulls and waves.'

'We might not have gulls and waves, but we have each other.' Meg placed the teacup on the tray and reached for him. All this only made sense when she was in his arms.

He gathered her tight against him and kissed her. 'You are so warm and soft,' he whispered against her lips.

Desire flooded through her as he kissed her neck, along her collarbone. She shivered as one hand cupped her breast, his thumb brushing over her nipple. Her mind emptied as she threaded her fingers through his dark hair.

Christian stood and undressed before joining her in the bed. Slowly, he pulled off her nightgown, and she delighted in seeing his cornflower-blue eyes change to violet as he bent to nuzzle her breast.

His hands explored her body, and he encouraged her to do the same to his and she revelled in being able to touch all of him. Skin on skin, no barriers.

'I love you, Meg,' he murmured, kissing her.

'I love you.' She sighed happily as he pulled her beneath him and kissed her deeply. She melted in his arms, knowing this was what she wanted, this man, his love.

An hour later, as she'd been told, Maude knocked on the bedroom door.

Meg was still in bed, but Christian was up and dressed, though without his shoes on. He gave her another kiss. 'We must face the day and leave this room. Though I would rather not.'

She chuckled. 'Nor I, but we must.'

'There is always tonight.' He winked.

Making love for the first time had been eye-opening, magical and definitely an education and she couldn't wait to have another lesson. 'Come in, Maude.'

The maid entered, looking smart in her black uniform without the white apron she wore yesterday. 'Good morning, madam, sir.'

'Good morning, Maude.' Meg had drunk a cup of cooled tea and eaten the cold breakfast, much to Christian's amusement. He said he'd ring for a fresh breakfast, but Meg refused, saying she'd not waste good food just because it was cold. She felt guilt at the very idea when she knew her siblings wouldn't be eating such goodness.

Christian reached for one of his shoes. 'My wife tells me that you'll be her lady's maid, Maude.'

'Yes, sir. I'm honoured.'

'You will need training.'

'Yes, sir.' Maude twisted her hands nervously. 'I'll work hard, sir.'

'I am sure you will.' He put on his other shoe. 'My wife needs a new wardrobe and anything else she desires. Do you know of the places she needs to visit in town?'

'I do, sir. I've helped Lydia before when your mother and sister and Miss Crawford were here, and Mrs Burton's maid Brodie needed a hand sometimes.'

'Good. Once my mother is recovered, a shopping trip is required.' Christian stood and adjusted his shirt collar. 'What is your last name?'

'Hogan, sir.'

'Well then, Hogan. I shall speak with Titmus about the upgrade in your salary regarding your new role.'

'Thank you, sir.'

Christian bent and gave Meg a kiss, then straightened and looked at Maude. 'You are in a position where you alone will see and hear private moments between my wife and myself. None of which will ever be repeated by you to anyone, or you'll be instantly dismissed. Understood?'

'Absolutely, sir. You both have my word on that.'

'Good.' He smiled at Meg. 'I shall see you downstairs when you are ready.'

Meg climbed from the bed as Maude opened the curtains. Sunshine flooded the room. 'What grand weather.'

'Aye, madam.' Maude started stripping the bed. 'It's already warm outside.'

Meg studied the limited content of her wardrobe and decided on a pink dress which had a white flower pattern on it. The seamstress in town had said it was called a day dress. Meg had no idea there was such a thing.

Maude came into the dressing room. 'Would you like a bath, madam?'

'A bath? I only had one yesterday,' Meg said in surprise.

Maude grinned. 'You can have one every day if you wish.'

'A bath every day?' Meg couldn't believe it.

'It depends on what appointments you have and how much time you have in the mornings.' Maude selected fresh underclothing for her. 'A strip wash is sometimes all you will have time for. Do you ride, madam?'

'No. I've never been on a horse.'

'Does Mr Henderson want you to learn? Or do you?'

'Do I need to?'

'Only if you want to join the fox hunts or go for rides with Mr Henderson. He usually rides on Sunday afternoons.'

'He does?' Meg felt suddenly foolish. She knew so little about his day-to-day activities.

Getting dressed, Meg's mind spun from one thought to another. She felt out of her depth. 'Maude, I—'

'Hogan, madam.'

'Sorry, Hogan...' She frowned. 'It seems oddly formal, saying your last name.'

'It reflects my new status, or it will do once Mr Henderson has spoken to Mr Titmus about it. Mr Titmus demands strict order below stairs, madam. Now I've gone up in rank and can sit at the butler's dinner table, which is only small as this establishment isn't as large as others, but still, I'm allowed now.' Maude grinned like a child with a new toy.

'Do I need to speak to Mr Titmus regarding your new status?'

'Only if you want to discuss my uniform. Black is the correct colour I should wear. And you call him Titmus, madam. We, the servants, call him Mr Titmus.'

Meg feared she'd never get a grasp of all the rules.

'Don't worry, madam. You'll soon learn.'

'I'm scared I won't ever know the rules or what is expected of me.' Meg sat at the dressing table for Maude to arrange her hair. 'Even doing this feels like I'm a fraud. I have my own personal maid.' Meg threw her hands up in despair. 'Yesterday I was lugging water from the street pump. Now I have a maid to do everything for me...'

Maude paused in brushing Meg's hair. 'I know it'll be hard, madam, but you can do this. I'll help you.'

'Thank you.' She took a deep breath to slow her pounding heart.

'You're a married woman now, madam. That carries its own weight, especially when you're married to a man such as Mr Henderson. You're the mistress of this house. You have to act like it, whether or not you think you can.'

Armed with a new dress and her hair put up by the capable Maude, Meg felt ready to face the day.

Along the quiet landing she passed the other bedroom, but stopped at the half-open door where her mother-in-law rested and peeked in. Susan sat on a chair by the bed, her back to the door. Meg noticed Mrs Burton's eyes were open, and she was talking in a low voice to her daughter.

Thankful the older woman was recovering, Meg knocked once and entered. 'Good morning.'

'You!' Susan turned in the chair to glare at Meg. 'What do you want?'

Ignoring the nasty tone, Meg forced a smile and kept her tone light. 'I am glad to see you awake, Mrs Burton.'

The older woman closed her eyes and waved a weak hand at her.

Susan jerked to her feet. 'Get out. My mother is too ill to deal with you.'

'Deal with me?' Meg tilted her head. 'I simply wanted to see how she was.'

'On death's door, no thanks to you.'

'Me?'

'Yes,' Susan spat. 'You, a nobody, marrying my brother. You have brought such shame on this family. We were racing to stop the wedding, and the stress made Mama ill. Now get out!'

Shocked by the viciousness, Meg left the room and went downstairs. The drawing room was empty, as was the library. She found Christian in his study.

His look of love when she entered soothed her hurt. 'I have taken advantage of being home to catch up on paying some bills. They would have waited until I returned from Great Yarmouth, but since we aren't there, I thought to do some work.'

She stepped around the desk and placed her arm along his shoulders. 'Susan is blaming me for your mother being ill.'

Christian looked up at her. 'She's what?'

'Just now, she blamed me for making your mother ill. She said they were coming to stop the wedding, and the stress caused her illness.'

His eyes widened. 'How dare she say that?' He shot to his feet. 'I will not have her treating you in this manner.'

'Leave it for now. She's upset and I don't want to be the cause of any more strife.' She sighed. 'At least your mother has woken and was talking to her.'

'She has? I had better go up and see.' He kissed her. 'Do not take any notice of Susan. She can be most foolish and cruel at times.'

'I need to speak to Titmus about Maude?'

'Ah, yes, I had that to do, but perhaps you should do it. Start as we mean to go on, yes?'

'If you say so.' She bit her bottom lip worriedly, but then straightened her spine and found her courage. She could do this. It was necessary for her to do it.

'You will need to speak to Mrs Beatty about next week's menu, as well.' He saw the anxious look in her eyes. 'Be firm. You are the mistress now. It is your right to do and say whatever you please.'

She took a deep breath and nodded. As Christian went upstairs, Meg ventured down the corridor, past the stairs to the door at the end. This door divided the main house with the service areas.

Beyond the door, she tried to remember all that Christian had told her on the previous tour. The butler's pantry, the butler's bedroom, the storeroom, boot and gunroom, the door leading down to the cellar and finally the kitchen.

Half a dozen faces stared at her as she opened the kitchen door and stood on the top of the step.

'Can we help you... Mrs Henderson?' Mrs Beatty asked, wiping her hands on her apron.

'Yes.' Meg focused on the woman and not the kitchen maids' faces or the footman, Thomas, or the bootboy. 'I was looking for Titmus... and yourself.'

'You'll always find me in here, Mrs Henderson.' Mrs Beatty glared at the maids. 'Stop gawping and get back to your work.' The cook went to a large dresser on the far wall and from a drawer took out a notebook. 'Do you wish to discuss the menus now you are here and not on your honeymoon?'

Meg baulked at the idea. She had no notion of what to do about menus. 'Er... yes.'

'Excellent, madam. Shall we go through?' She indicated the door.

'Go through?'

'To the library? It's where I used to go when the former Mrs Henderson and me discussed the menus.'

'Oh, I see.' Feeling ridiculous for not knowing, Meg strode back the way she came and into the library. Her palms were clammy. *You can do this.* The words ricocheted in her brain.

'Madam?'

Stomach in knots, Meg paced. 'Er... Mrs Beatty... I'm... you see...'

'Madam.' The cook's kind tone stopped Meg. 'Will you not sit down, madam?'

Meg sank onto the edge of a chair near a writing desk.

'That desk was Mrs Henderson's personal desk.' Mrs Beatty smiled. 'She was a good and decent mistress.'

'As I hope to be,' Meg breathed.

'I'm sure you will, madam, but it'll take time.'

Staring down at her hands, which still showed signs of her being a working-class girl, Meg wondered if she'd ever feel confident in this role.

'Madam, we all know your background.'

Meg's head shot up.

'There's no reason to be ashamed of it.' Mrs Beatty took another chair from by the window and brought it to sit near Meg. 'My mam was from Leeds and the daughter of a coalman. I shan't be casting no stones in your direction.'

'Thank you.'

'But not everyone will feel the same. Servants are used to serving the gentry. They expect a certain standard, and many servants can be more uptight about status than their employers.' Mrs Beatty grinned. 'Here at Meadow View House, we are a small concern, not a grand palace. We are not so presumptuous. Mr Titmus is accepting of Mr Henderson's choice of wife, but perhaps a little judgemental, and he'll be watching you like a hawk to make sure you don't make mistakes and embarrass this house.'

'It is what I fear the most.' Meg swallowed her throat dry.

'Don't be worried. If you get Mr Titmus on side, he'll be your biggest supporter. Now, Thomas, the footman, he's fine about it all. My kitchen girls will mind their own business or find another position.' She nodded sagely. 'Lydia, she's another one who has opinions above herself, and believes she should be a lady's maid to a princess.

Now you've promoted young Maude to be your lady's maid and overlooked Lydia... Well, she's fit to be tied.' Mrs Beatty rubbed her nose. 'Anyway, you're the mistress and this is your house to run.'

'And that's the problem. I don't know how to run a house this size.'

'No, but you organised your own home, didn't you? And a large family from what I've been told?'

'Yes.'

'Right then, that'll help. Think of this place as a bigger version of your old home.'

The thought seemed absurd, and Meg suddenly laughed at the image. 'Have you ever been to Wellington Street, Mrs Beatty?'

'No, but if it's anything like my old home, I can imagine it.'

Relieved, Meg felt a little calmer. 'I just want to do my husband proud.'

Mrs Beatty smiled with genuine warmth. 'We all admire Mr Henderson greatly. We were all surprised by his choice of bride but in the end, we just want him to be happy and if you make him happy and treat us fairly, then you'll have our support.'

'I will do my very best on both accounts.'

'Good. Now, shall we begin, madam?' Mrs Beatty opened her notebook and took out the pencil within.

'I do not know what to do about menus.'

'I'll teach you, Mrs Henderson, never fear. Shall we start with the evening meal for tonight?'

Relieved, Meg listened to and learned from the cook, making notes herself on a piece of paper.

After Mrs Beatty had left her, Meg found in the desk drawer old ledgers written by Gertrude Henderson. One ledger was household accounts, another was lists of dinner party menus, charity luncheons, Christmas parties and many other occasions, a third ledger was a garden planting diary. Meg hugged the ledgers to her chest in delight. She fancied that Gertrude had left them especially for her to guide her through the unknown, even though they had never met.

Christian entered with Titmus. 'Darling, I have spoken to Titmus regarding Maude Hogan being your new lady's maid to save you the trouble as you were with Mrs Beatty a while.'

'I could have done that, sorry,' Meg was quick to point out.

'I know, but we were discussing wages and things. Anyway, it is all sorted. Hogan will get an increase in her wages at the end of the month if she proves satisfactory to you, and a new uniform. Titmus will instruct Lydia to guide her, but he shall also send for teaching manuals for Hogan to learn from. Titmus assures me the girl can read.'

'She told me she could.'

Christian held out his arm for her. 'Shall we go in to luncheon?'

She rose and linked her arm through his. Eating at set times was unusual to her. At home, she ate when she had a spare moment during the day and gobbled up a bite to eat before starting her shift at the pub or, if she was lucky, had a bowl of something from Don's kitchen when he was in a good mood. But here, the day was structured around meal and tea times.

The buffet table was filled with cold meats, salads, sandwiches, savoury tarts and fruits. Meg stared at it. This would feed her family for days. 'Is all this just for the two of us?' The change in her circumstances was difficult to get used to. It would take time for her to adapt to this luxury and to not feel guilty about living this way when her family remained on Wellington Street.

'And my sister, and Dr Maynard when he arrives, should he wish it.' Christian filled his plate. 'By the way, I have spoken to Susan and insisted she never speak to you like that again.'

'Thank you.' Meg selected some sandwiches, wondering if Susan would change her ways. She very much doubted it.

'Mother is doing much better,' Christian said, as Titmus poured a cup of coffee for him.

Susan entered the room. One look at Meg and her nose rose higher, and she sat in the furthest seat from her. 'Coffee, Titmus.'

Meg cringed at Susan's lack of manners. Meg may have been born poor, but her mam had taught her how to say please and thank you and not simply demand. Was that what this class did? Well, she wasn't going to behave in such a rude way.

Titmus came to her side. 'Coffee, madam?'

She smiled up at him. 'I would like to try it. Thank you, Titmus.'

'Try it?' Susan guffawed. 'You have never tasted a cup of coffee before?'

'No.' Meg instantly felt uncouth.

'Susan.' Christian's voice was low and threatening.

Pasting a smile on her tight face, Susan waved a hand dismissively. 'Well, I hear that you did not share a bed last night, brother, so this awful excuse for a marriage can still be annulled. It is Mama's wish.'

Christian banged his fist on the table. Meg jumped and spilled her coffee on the white tablecloth.

'What did I tell you?' Christian sneered. 'You are to be civil and polite to Meg.'

'*Meg?* Good God. Even her name is common.' Susan drank her coffee.

'If you cannot behave and show some manners, Susan, I will have you on the next train back to London.'

Susan flashed him a superior look. 'You would not dare to do anything while Mama is ill. She cannot be moved.'

'No, she cannot, but you can. I will gladly take you back myself!' Christian's rage was only just controlled.

Susan slowly rose and gave him a triumphant glare. 'Back to where, brother? Mama sold the house before we left. This is our home now.' She sashayed out of the room.

Christian covered his face with his hands and swore under his breath, but Meg heard.

She stared down at the coffee stain, wishing she had flung the rest of what was in her cup in Susan's insolent face. At that moment, she also wished she was at home, surrounded by her family.

17

Meg knocked on Lorrie's door and was relieved when her friend opened it and welcomed her in.

'I didn't expect you see you.' Lorrie embraced her. 'I thought you'd have gone to Great Yarmouth.'

'Christian's mother is ill. We are unable to go on our honeymoon, maybe next month.' Meg slipped off her white lace gloves. She constantly worried about getting them soiled. She wasn't used to wearing such fine gloves after years of wearing thick dark woollen gloves or nothing at all.

'That is sad, on both accounts. At the wedding we all hoped she had simply fainted, and you and your husband could still leave as planned.' Lorrie placed the kettle on the range.

'It feels weird to have you call Christian my husband.' Meg sat at the table.

Lorrie grinned. 'What is it like to have a husband?'

'Wonderful.' She couldn't keep the joy from her voice. 'It's strange, though, having someone who cares solely for your happiness.'

'You must tell me everything. How do you feel about having

servants?' Lorrie brought over the tea things. 'I would appreciate a day woman to come in and clean, but that will never happen. We couldn't afford such a luxury.'

'The house is so well run...' Meg helped set out the sugar bowl and milk jug. 'I feel useless, really. I have nothing to do and I'm usually so busy.'

'You've been married for four days. Give it some time.'

'I came here because Christian has gone to the brewery and I couldn't stand the thought of being alone in the house with Susan. I hope you don't mind.'

'The sister?' Lorrie asked, filling the teapot with tea leaves and then boiling water. 'And why would I ever mind?'

Meg played with a teaspoon. 'She hates me. She and her mother were coming to stop the wedding.'

Lorrie's eyebrow rose. 'I can't believe it.'

'It's true. Susan admitted it. I am not worthy of being married to Christian. Too common.' Meg shrugged, trying not to give in to the rising hurt.

'Their opinion is worthless. Christian adores you, that's all that matters.'

'I know, but...' She took a deep breath. 'Living with Susan and his mother is going to be difficult.'

'They are only staying until his mother is well again, aren't they?'

'No. They've sold their home in London and will live at Meadow View with us.'

Lorrie poured the tea into their cups. 'That's disappointing.'

Meg sipped her tea. 'Anyway, enough of that. What has been happening with you?'

'Nothing much happens with me, you know that. I take care of my father and this flat and the office below. My days all blend into each other.' Lorrie's unhappy expression made Meg feel guilty for not fully appreciating Lorrie's lonely life.

'Will you come to Meadow View House? I mean, let's make it a weekly thing that you come to Meadow View and have tea with me. Fliss, too, if she's available.'

Lorrie smiled. 'An invasion of the commoners?'

Meg laughed and enjoyed being able to do so without being judged by those at the house. 'You are the daughter of a business-man. They might like you.'

'Pish to them.' Lorrie waved her hand dismissively. 'You'll be the best thing that's ever happened to that family. Try some of this cake.' Lorrie cut a thick wedge of sponge cake. 'I think it's my best ever attempt.'

Smiling, Meg accepted the plate. 'What kind is it?'

'It's meant to be strawberry and cream, but I didn't have any strawberries and used preserved plums instead.'

Meg forked some into her mouth and winced at the sharp sourness of the plums. 'It's lovely,' she lied.

'Really?' Lorrie clapped.

Forcing the mouthful down, Meg gulped some tea to help it along her throat. 'Did you put any sugar on the plums?'

'Sugar?'

'Just a bit to sweeten them?'

Lorrie quickly ate some of the cake and shuddered. 'Blast! It's as sour as gone-off milk!'

Unable to help herself, Meg burst out laughing again.

She felt much better as she left Lorrie's an hour later and headed to the ferry. Her friends were so important to her.

Harry hailed her as she neared. He had a few passengers, but waited for her to climb aboard. 'Not too grand to use my ferry then, lass, I mean Mrs Henderson.'

'I'll never be grand, Harry, but at least now I can pay my way.' She handed him the fare and a generous tip from the money purse Christian had given her. 'For all the times you let me cross for free.'

'Nay, lass, you don't need to.' He looked sad. 'I did it because of your mam.'

'Mam?'

'Aye. I had my heart set on her the minute I saw her, but she had married your father and was never for me.' He busied himself casting off the ropes. 'Though sometimes, being a silly old fella, I used to imagine that you and your brothers and sisters could have been mine...' He scuttled to the other end of the boat as though embarrassed he'd said too much.

Thoughtful, Meg didn't comment and instead gazed at the opposite wharf, the scurrying of men working, the cranes pulling up cargo from barges and narrowboats. The noise was comforting after the silence of Meadow View House.

Along Wellington Street, she stopped to talk to old neighbours, women out scrubbing their front steps or emptying buckets of dirty water into the gutter. Some of the women wanted to comment on the wedding, saying they'd sat in the back pews to watch one of their own marry up. Meg thanked them for filling her side of the church.

Mrs Fogarty was coming out of her door further down. 'Meg, lass!'

Saying goodbye to the other women, Meg hurried to Mrs Fogarty. 'How are you?'

'Oh, I'm fine, lass.' But she pulled Meg closer to her. 'Them lot,' she nodded towards the neighbours Meg had just been talking to, 'they've been spouting gossip.'

'About me?' Her chest tightened.

'No, about your Freddie and that Josie.'

She jerked back as though a bucket of ice water had been thrown over her. 'What?'

'They're saying it's not right for Josie to be living in the same house as your Freddie, him being a man.' Mrs Fogarty twitched her nose and glared at the women up the street.

'Josie is looking after the children.'

'Aye, *we* know that, and they do, too. Them lot just like to be nasty and spread gossip when none is there, but well, lass, people will talk. No one knows she was your father's second wife. They see her and Freddie as two single people living in the same house.'

'With the children!' Meg said, none too quietly.

'Happen they have nowt better to do than stand around and make up rumours.' Mrs Fogarty folded her arms and gave the women a stern nod. 'Anyway, lass, how's it all going at the big house?'

'Fine, strange, but I'm sure I'll get used to it soon enough.'

'Course you will, lass. You're made of sturdy stuff. Remember, your mam and grandma were born and raised well. Don't forget that. Right, I'd love to keep chatting but I'm late with me shopping and you'll want to get inside.' She looked up at the gathering clouds. 'It'll rain shortly.'

'Speak again soon, Mrs Fogarty.'

'Aye, lass, ta-ra.'

Meg opened the front door to her old home and stepped inside. Something cooking on the range smelt nice. The table was set with heavy irons and clothing laid out.

Josie came in through the back door and did a double take. 'Meg. I wasn't expecting to see you.'

'I thought to come and see how everyone was doing?' She felt guilty for turning up unannounced as though the house was no longer her home.

'They're all fine.' Josie plonked an armful of clean washing on the table. 'It looks like rain, so I've brought the last of the washing inside.'

'There's extra rope in the bottom cupboard if you want to hang a line inside,' Meg told her.

'I did see that this morning. I'll have to use it.'

'I can help you.'

'No, no, I'll do it or if not, Freddie will help me later. I wouldn't want your lovely dress to get dirty.'

Meg glanced down at her lavender dress. Maude had added a frill of cream lace to the sleeves and neckline to alleviate some of the plainness. Apparently, there were boxes of materials in the attics and Maude was determined to make something of them until Meg was able to meet with the seamstress.

'Tea?' Josie asked.

'No, I won't, thank you.' Meg didn't want to sit and chat with Josie at the table in the kitchen, which had been Meg's domain for so long. 'How is everyone?'

'They're all doing well.' Josie brightened. 'Dolly is asleep upstairs. I'm sure she's grown an inch since we've been here. Nicky went to school today for the first time since his illness. He'll be sorry to have missed you.'

'Could you bring them all to Meadow View House on Sunday after church?' She was desperate to see them. 'I'll send the carriage, say two o'clock? We can have afternoon tea in the gardens if the weather is nice?'

Josie looked hesitant. 'I'm not sure...'

'Why?' Meg instantly felt slighted.

'Freddie... He—'

'I don't give a fig for Freddie's opinion. I miss my family and I want them to see where I live and to spend time with them. A couple of hours, that's all.' Did it sound like she was begging? Meg strode to the door, eager to get away from the hurt Freddie caused.

'I'll send a carriage. It'll be waiting at the top of the street at two on Sunday.' She left the house and strode along the cobbles, refusing to cry.

* * *

'Darling, will you not sit down?' Christian asked Meg.

She paused from pacing and stared out of the drawing room window. It was Sunday. Another glance at the clock showed it was nearly three o'clock. 'Freddie has stopped them from coming.'

'Give it a few more minutes.' Christian folded the letter he'd been reading. 'My Aunt Gertrude and cousin Barney want to come and visit next month.'

Meg, her back to Christian, closed her eyes. She couldn't cope with any more of Christian's family. Susan continued to be nasty towards her, but only when Christian wasn't around. In front of him she behaved overly sweet, which Meg could see through. Her sister-in-law's falseness grated on Meg's nerves, but at least her mother-in-law remained in bed and Meg didn't have much to do with her. She dreaded the day Mrs Burton left her sickbed and came downstairs and the two of them would look at her with distaste.

'At least the sun is shining,' Christian said, coming up behind Meg. 'The children can run about in the gardens.'

She leaned back against his chest, and he wrapped his arms around her waist. She loved him so much, more with each day that passed as they learned more about each other. However, her happiness was not complete, and never would be while ever his sister and mother lived here, and her family were unable to visit.

Suddenly, the carriage came down the drive.

'They are here!' Meg sprinted to the front door, forgetting to be a lady, and opened it before Titmus had even come along the corridor.

She ran out to the carriage, seeing Nell leaning out of the window. 'You're here!' She could have cried with joy at seeing the dear faces.

One by one, they scrambled down, and into her arms, all talking at once. She laughed and hugged them, kissing their faces.

'Do you like my hat, Meg?' Betsy asked, pointing to her straw hat with red and blue ribbons tied around it and pink paper flowers pinned on the brim. 'I made it especially for today, though Cassie helped me. She's a third-year apprentice and really nice. Mrs Sharp says I'm coming on brilliantly.'

'It's magnificent,' Meg declared, hugging her. 'I'm so proud of you. I'll go and visit Mrs Sharp next week to order a hat and see how you're getting on.'

'I brought you a drawing!' Nicky thrust a piece of paper at her of a narrowboat in a lock.

'You are so talented.' She kissed his sweet face. 'I shall treasure it.'

'I hurt my hand.' Nell pushed Nicky to one side to show Meg her wrapped finger.

'How did you do that, poppet?'

'I trapped it in the lav door. Josie wrapped it for me to make it better.'

'Poor you.'

'Welcome, everyone, to Meadow View House.' Christian greeted them with a warm smile, helping Josie down from the carriage. 'Come in, come in.'

The noise of girls' chattering echoed around the hall, banishing the silence.

Titmus looked alarmed at the sight of the four girls, Nicky and Josie. 'Madam, tea is ready on the terrace.'

'Thank you.' She grabbed Nicky's hand. 'Come with me, all of you.' She took them down the corridor and turned left to the door that led out to the side gardens. A paved pathway took them around to the back terrace, also paved and where wrought-iron tables and chairs were placed. A fine afternoon tea was set up with a silver tea service and plates of cakes and sandwiches and sweet treats.

Mabel and Susie stared wide-eyed at the display.

'Is this all for us?' Mabel asked.

'Of course,' Meg answered. 'Sit down. Have whatever you like.'

Susie reached for a marzipan. 'It's made in the shape of a little apple.'

'And this is made to look like an orange,' Mabel said in awe.

'Oh, look at that bird!' Nell shrieked in excitement, pointing to the edge of the trees.

'It's a peacock, a male peacock,' Christian explained. 'The female peacock, a hen, is not as pretty. She is brown and rather shy.'

'Do they have names?' Nicky asked.

'I think the gardener calls them Mr and Mrs Peacock.' Christian laughed.

Meg smiled, happy to see Christian so relaxed with her brother and sisters. She turned to Josie. 'Thank you for bringing them.'

'Freddie wasn't happy about it. He said it would give them ideas above their station, but I worked on him, and he finally agreed an hour ago when Mabel and Susie both threatened to walk here and never return.'

'I wish they could live here,' Meg murmured, gazing at Nicky as he chatted to Christian.

'Don't, I beg you.' Josie lowered her voice to a whisper.

'Freddie is still coming to terms with it. He's looking for another job, too.'

'Why?' Shocked, Meg moved Josie away from the table with her. 'Why is he being so foolish as to give up a good job at the brewery?'

'With the sale of the narrowboat and the inheritance, he keeps saying we should all move away, start again somewhere new. Leeds, perhaps.'

Meg swallowed back a gasp. 'Move away? Does he hate me that much?'

'He doesn't hate you at all. He loves and misses you every day. I can see it on his face whenever one of the kiddies mentions you. He's just stubborn and an idiot. A typical man and more like his father than he even realises.'

'How so?'

'He wants his own way.' Josie shook her head. 'And he thinks if he ignores a problem long enough, it might go away. And we both know how that ends.'

'Meg?' Christian called to her. 'The children want to go for a walk.'

'Coming.' Meg looked at Josie. 'Will you send word if Freddie decides on anything?'

'Aye, I will.'

'Come on, Meg?' Nicky ran up to her with a jam-smudged face. 'We're off to see the walled garden.'

'How's he been?' Meg asked Josie.

'Good, actually. He's not had an attack of any kind. He is starting to learn his limits, I think. Instead of playing ball with the other boys, he's happy to watch them and cheer them on.'

'I've spoken to Christian about him seeing a specialist doctor in London.'

Josie frowned. 'Freddie won't be able to argue about that.'

'No. It's for Nicky's health.' Meg smiled as Nell picked her a rose and gave it to her. 'Thank you, dearest.'

Josie lowered her voice. 'Freddie and Mabel have been fighting something fierce. She's always out, coming in late, being mouthy.'

'Oh, no.' Meg studied Mabel, who stood with Susie, admiring the peacock's impressive tail display.

'I'm at my wits' end with it all.'

'I'll speak with Christian. Perhaps Mabel needs to come here for a while.'

'No, don't do that. Freddie will be furious. Mabel threatens to come here every time they argue, and that sends him mad.'

'What can we do?'

'I don't know. She's nearly sixteen. It's hard to discipline her.' Josie brightened. 'Anyway, I didn't come here to burden you with all that.'

'I want to know what's happening, though, so thank you for telling me.' Meg was sincere. This woman had taken over her role and she deserved her thanks.

'I always will.' Josie smiled.

After an hour visiting the walled garden and eating carrots straight from the soil and washed in a bucket, Christian led them on a tour of the small park to see the black and white cows grazing with their calves. Next, they visited the stables and patted Christian's horse before heading back to the terrace for more tea and cake.

'I forgot to thank you when you called the other day,' Josie said to Meg as they sat and watched Nell and Betsy chase each other around a tree.

'Thank me?' Meg sipped from her teacup.

'For the hamper basket you send every three days.' Josie flushed. 'Freddie wanted to send the first one back, but I refused and accused him of taking the food out of his family's mouths.'

'I wanted to ease the burden on you and him to provide for everyone,' Meg whispered. 'A hamper will arrive every Monday and Thursday afternoon. Just take the food out of the basket and give it back to Thomas, the footman.'

'Are you sure?' Josie glanced at Christian.

'My husband gives me his full support. I will not see my family go hungry.'

'Oh, and I got a job,' Josie said. 'At the Bay Horse.'

'My shifts?'

'Yes. Do you mind?' Josie seemed unsure.

'Why would I? I'm pleased you're earning.' Meg sipped her tea. 'Who is looking after Dolly now? You could have brought her.'

'Mrs Fogarty. I didn't want to bring her because she's not your family, not properly... I thought you might have been annoyed having her here in case one of the others mentioned she was their sister. I didn't want it to be difficult for you to explain.'

'Dolly's my half-sister. She is welcome. But thank you for thinking of me.' Meg saw Josie in a new light. The woman she had loathed was proving to be a good mother figure to her siblings and a considerate person. Meg's father had done Josie a great wrong. Meg felt some remorse, too, for her own behaviour towards her.

'Christian. May I have a word?' Susan stood at the end of the terrace, her expression one of revulsion as she took in the scene.

'Is something wrong?' Christian stood from the table where he'd been asking Mabel and Susie questions about the mill where they worked.

'Yes, something is very wrong.' Susan didn't bother to lower her voice. 'Mama is trying to rest and all we can hear is this rabble! Do you want her to relapse?'

Meg rose, as did Josie. Meg looked up at the window of his mother's bedroom and saw her mother-in-law standing, peering down at them before she quickly stepped back out of view. Patrice was not on death's door and Meg had seen her walking about her bedroom on numerous occasions, yet whenever Christian visited her room, the nasty woman pretended to be very ill again.

'We should go,' Josie said. 'Come along, you lot. It's time we left.'

'It most certainly is,' Susan declared, stepping aside as though the children would contaminate her.

'Be quiet, Susan. This is my house!' Christian grabbed his sister's arm and thrust her back inside.

Meg forced a bright smile to her face and gave a silent message to Josie, who took the hint and ushered the children from the table.

Groans and mumbles of protest accompanied them through the side garden and around to the drive. Meg gave kisses and made promises they could come back whenever they liked. It was agreed to be next Sunday.

She stood with Christian and waved them down the drive as they hung out of the carriage windows, calling out. Once they were out of sight, she still stood on the drive, her heart torn. She missed them desperately. As the sound of the wheels disappeared, the only sounds were the twitter of birds in the trees and the bellow of a cow.

'It will become easier, my love.' Christian pulled her to his side and kissed her temple. 'See them every day if you wish it.'

'Freddie is talking of them all moving away,' she said sadly.

'He will not do it.'

'How do you know?'

'Because from everything you have told me, your relationship with Freddie was once very close. He will remember that soon.'

'He won't accept what I've done in marrying you. I think he

sees it as a betrayal. I've left them and so soon after our parents' deaths.'

'If he loves you, he will come to his senses. In time.' Christian turned her with him, and they strolled inside. 'I can talk to him if you wish it?'

Meg shook her head. 'I doubt it will do any good.'

'No, he is as stubborn as his sister.' He grinned to lighten the mood.

'I'm not stubborn,' she objected.

His laugh rang out in the hall. Seconds later, Susan raced to the top of the stairs, her face furious.

'Can we have no peace in this house?' She glared down at them.

'If you do not like it, Susan, perhaps you should find somewhere else to live?' Meg said impulsively, fed up with her constant sniping.

Susan's eyes bulged. 'Christian, will you allow *her* to speak to me like that?'

'Indeed, accept it as a token of your own treatment.'

'This cannot be borne!'

Christian stared up at her. 'It might be an idea though, Susan, for you and Mother to live somewhere else. I shall give it some thought.' Christian took Meg's hand, and they went into the library.

Meg's heart swelled with love for the man she'd married and, acting impulsively again, she kissed him soundly on the lips.

18

Meg sat up on the bed and adjusted her clothes. Maude hovered in the doorway to the dressing room while Dr Maynard closed his medical bag.

'It seems to me, Mrs Henderson, that you are indeed with child,' he announced as if the deed was neither exciting nor unique.

But to Meg, the news rocked her newly formed world into something entirely different. A baby. She was to have a baby.

Mr Maynard rubbed a cloth over his glasses before replacing them on his nose. 'You need to take care now, Mrs Henderson. Plenty of rest and nourishing meals.' He threw a look over his shoulder at Maude. 'I trust you will take care of your mistress to the full extent of your capabilities?'

'Yes, sir.' Maude did a slight curtsy, her expression serious, but the look she gave Meg was of joy. 'Mrs Henderson will not want for anything.'

'Good. An April delivery, I expect, since you've not had your monthly show since your wedding.' His bushy white eyebrows rose slightly as he spoke.

Meg blushed. Should she and Christian have shown more restraint? Their bedroom activities were the main thing she enjoyed doing in this house. It was their special time away from the requirements of business, the house, the staff and especially his mother and sister.

'I shall inform Mr Henderson on my way back into town.'

'No!' Meg put her hand up. 'This is my news and I'll tell my husband, thank you very much.'

Startled, Dr Maynard frowned. 'As your doctor, it is my duty to inform your husband of your welfare and to discuss with him certain conditions and allowances for the future.'

'I am pregnant, Doctor, not ill. Where I come from, babies arrive as naturally as day follows night. I will tell my husband.' Her tone of voice brooked no argument.

'As you wish.' He collected his bag, offended. 'I shall speak to Mrs Burton and see how she is getting on.'

'My mother-in-law is in perfect health, sir.' Meg climbed off the bed. Patrice was getting about the house and telling the staff what to do as if she was the mistress and not Meg.

He turned at the door. 'I shall see for myself, madam,' he said and walked out.

Meg glared at the closed door. She didn't like the man at all. He pandered to Patrice's every whim and told Christian his mother was too delicate to move to another house, and so she remained at Meadow View and drove Meg crazy with her sneers and demands and the little ways she had of undermining Meg's authority.

Maude rushed to her. 'Oh, madam. A baby!'

Meg forgot about the doctor and grinned. 'I can't believe it.'

'I told you, didn't I, last week, when I said you've had no monthly cloths to wash since you arrived.'

'But it's only been three months.' Meg found it hard to believe it had happened so quickly.

'Mr Henderson is going to be so happy.' Maude tidied Meg's hair. 'We'll have to get a new wardrobe sorted for your expanding waistline.'

'I'm not showing yet.'

'You soon will be, madam.'

Meg thought of all the beautiful clothes hanging in the wardrobe. Some she'd not even had a chance to wear yet, as her mother-in-law insisted she was too ill to have any entertaining done in the house. On two occasions, Meg had accompanied Christian to his business associates' houses for dinner parties. On both occasions she'd nearly thrown up the contents of her stomach while in the carriage, so nervous had she been.

Luckily, one dinner had been a large affair where she drew attention for only the first half an hour or so before the women had grown bored with waiting for her to make a mistake. Meg knew the rumours had spread about her, but she had prepared herself to act like she'd been born in the same class as everyone else.

She and Maude had spent hours practising how to eat with the right cutlery for each course. Maude had her reading the newspapers every day and she would test her at night, so Meg was informed on current events. Meg read newly published books while Maude researched the latest styles and fashions.

Meg subscribed to different magazines, visited the art gallery in Wakefield and Leeds. Christian took her to the theatre and a poetry recital night. All of which Meg adored. She was learning so much so quickly and loved every minute of it.

Outside the house, she thoroughly enjoyed her new life, yet inside the house, she was miserable.

Susan and Patrice made her life a misery, but they were so

affectionate towards Christian and he, for the first time in his, was having a relationship with his mother. Meg couldn't deny him that.

Instead, she hid from him their snide remarks to her, their subtle ways of undermining her position in the house with the servants, and pretended she was happy.

She kept herself busy with conversing with Titmus about redecorating the downstairs rooms, and in the garden, she spoke with Seth, the old gardener, about the plants. Meg had visited the wife of Christian's friend, Mrs Payton, who lived in a pleasant house in Wakefield and who had introduced her to her other friend, Mrs Shaw. Both women invited Meg to join their charity committee for the homeless. Amazed to be invited, Meg happily agreed, and knew she could help make a difference. After all, didn't she have first-hand knowledge of that life? Meg also suggested Lorrie and Fliss should join. Surprisingly, Mrs Payton and Mrs Shaw were only too pleased to have more women on the committee and did not care that neither Meg, Lorrie nor Fliss were born gentlewomen. Such a boost in confidence helped Meg to cope with her mother-in-law's contemptuous behaviour.

Downstairs, Meg entered the drawing room. Patrice and the doctor broke apart awkwardly. Meg suspected they'd been whispering about her. Susan sat on the sofa eating almond biscuits. She saw Meg enter and quickly scooped the remaining two biscuits and shoved them in her mouth to stop Meg from having them.

Meg looked away, feigning she didn't see the action. She poured herself a cup of tea from the tray.

'You will, of course, come for dinner next week, Doctor? You and your dear wife?' Patrice asked light-heartedly. 'It is Susan's birthday and now I am regaining my health, we should celebrate her special day.'

Meg stared down at her cup. She hadn't known it was Susan's birthday. She sighed. She lived in a house with two people she knew nothing about.

'I'd be delighted, Mrs Burton. My wife will probably order a new dress for the occasion.' He chuckled.

'Of course she must,' Patrice trilled. 'We are planning a rather large party. Many friends from London are arriving just for the event, which naturally shows how much they esteem my dear daughter.'

Meg glanced at her. Her mother-in-law was in a good mood for once.

Susan preened. 'There will be at least thirty people here.'

Meg paled. Thirty? She hadn't been consulted at all. Did they expect her to organise it? No, probably not. She wasn't good enough to be given such an important task.

'Well, I must be going, ladies. Good day.' Dr Maynard left the room and Titmus showed him out.

Once he'd gone, Patrice turned to Meg with a sneer. 'I see you have quickly bred like the commoner that you are.'

The blood left Meg's face. 'He told you? He had no right!'

'No, he did not tell me. You just did. Dr Maynard has more morals than to divulge private information, but you have confirmed my suspicions.'

'What suspicions did you have?' Meg's stomach quivered.

'I know what happens in this house. I make it my business to know everything and that you've not had your monthly bleed was evidence.'

'How did you know that?' Meg felt breathless. Was there no privacy in this house?

'Servants talk, girl, you only have to know how to listen.' Patrice's blue eyes were cold with loathing. 'What an unfortunate dilemma. A child will only hinder the situation.'

'What do you mean?' Meg felt instantly protective of her unborn child.

'Christian needs to be rid of you and your filthy rabble of a family.'

Susan snorted. 'At least the rain and the cold weather of the last two weeks have stopped the horde from descending on us.'

Meg jumped to her feet. 'My family are not a horde.'

'No, they are filthy, lice-infested urchins who should never be allowed out of the slum they live in. I don't know what Christian is thinking, having them come here. It is bad enough that he married you!' Patrice wagged her finger at Meg. 'You have warped his mind from all rational thought.'

'He loves me.' Meg's knees were shaking.

'He is infatuated with a new toy. That is all this is. He has never changed since he was a boy. He would play with a new thing obsessively for a short time and then fling it to one side and be done with it. Susan and I must bide our time because he will fling you to the side, trust me on that. The day will come when you embarrass him one too many times with your uncouth ways and he will see sense and banish you from his life for good.' Patrice snarled like a wounded dog. 'I can wait.'

Titmus coughed at the door. 'Excuse me, ladies, forgive my interruption, but luncheon, regrettably, will be half an hour late.'

'Why is that?' Susan barked.

Titmus held his chin high. 'There has been an unfortunate mistake with this morning's delivery order for the kitchen.'

Meg tried to think clearly, too upset to even care what the butler was saying. Her mind kept repeating Patrice's vile words.

'Why is that our problem, Titmus?' Susan snapped.

'You see, Miss Burton, the menu had been set by Mrs Henderson last week and the food ordered...' Titmus' gaze strayed to Meg. 'But there seems to have been some confusion and with the change of menus, the food doesn't match the needs of the new menus.'

'What new menus?' Meg gathered herself when inside she was reeling.

'The menus that *Mrs Burton* asked to replace the previous ones.' Titmus had two spots of colour on his pale cheeks.

Meg swung to Patrice. 'You changed the menus?'

'Absolutely.'

'You had no right! How dare you?'

'Your choices have been abysmal. You may have eaten like an uncivilised peasant, but I shall not have my family doing so. Christian deserves better.'

'Mrs Beatty approved of everything.' Meg wanted to swing for the horrible woman.

'Well, she would, wouldn't she? The poor cook doesn't want to lose her position.'

Meg fought her anger. 'You forget your place. You are my husband's mother, not the mistress of this house.'

'Do not dare to raise your disgusting voice to me. You may be used to screeching like a guttersnipe in the slums where you wallowed, but this is a respectable house. Come, Susan.' Patrice sailed past Meg, her daughter hurriedly following.

Meg lost the use of her legs and collapsed onto the chair.

'Mrs Henderson.' Titmus was immediately beside her. 'Shall I fetch you some water?'

'Water won't fix this,' she murmured, blinking back hot tears. 'I'll be fine. I just need a moment.'

'Very good, madam.' He straightened and took several paces back, but kept watch over her.

Meg wanted to wail out her misery, but she couldn't do that. Not here. Not in this house that didn't feel like a home. She had to get out, breathe some air that wasn't tainted with Patrice's vitriolic bitterness.

She rubbed her hands wearily over her eyes. 'Actually, Titmus, will you have the carriage brought around, please?'

'Directly, madam.' He bowed and strode from the room.

Sucking in a shuddering breath, Meg slowly rose and walked to the front door. To the side was the cupboard where Titmus hung their outdoor wear and she pulled from it a blue shawl she'd once worn on a twilight stroll with Christian down by the river. She wrapped it around her shoulders and stepped outside.

The crisp October air awakened her senses. From somewhere in the garden was the smell of woodsmoke. Through the trees, she saw the gardener's lad raking golden leaves and throwing them on a small fire. A wood pigeon cooed. The breeze picked up, much cooler than before. Autumn had arrived and banished the long, warm days of summer.

Titmus appeared on the steps. 'Madam.'

She looked at him.

'It seems that Mrs Burton and Miss Burton have requested the carriage to go into town. Do you wish to share with them?'

Meg closed her eyes. They knew she was visiting Lorrie and Fliss today. 'No, thank you. I shall walk.'

'Into town?' He looked aghast.

She could have laughed. She'd worked hard for hours every day in her previous life, washing, ironing, scrubbing, staying on her feet until midnight behind a bar, yet Titmus imaged she couldn't cope with walking a mile into town. 'I've changed my mind. I'll walk along the river.'

She needed time to think, and she didn't want to burden Lorrie and Fliss with her problems today.

She wandered through the garden, keeping away from the

drive until she saw the carriage go past, then she headed for the gates.

A figure coming down the drive made her pause until she recognised Josie when she pushed back the shawl covering her head. 'Josie?'

They ran to meet each other.

'What is it?' Meg asked, frightened by the woman's pale face.

'It's Freddie. He's been arrested for fighting.'

Arrested? Meg swayed. Josie's image blurred.

'Hold on to me.' Josie's voice seemed to come from far away. 'That's it. I'll take you inside.'

Meg baulked. 'No. I'm fine.'

'You don't look it.'

'We have to go to the police station.'

'I tried, just now. They won't let me see him.'

'Why was he fighting?'

Josie glanced down. 'He was in the Bay Horse last night, drunk. Some fellow said Freddie had it easy now his sister had married a toff. Freddie told him to go to hell. The other fellow and his mates started taunting Freddie, saying he should start wearing silk hose now and a feather in his cap. That sort of thing.'

'Oh, Lord.' Meg could imagine how furious Freddie would have been.

'Then one fellow asked Freddie if I was a good lay and would he recommend me…'

Shocked, Meg stared at Josie, who looked as pale as death.

'Freddie battered the man senseless.' Tears gathered in her eyes. 'I swear to you, Meg, on Dolly's life, I think of Freddie as I would a brother, I promise you. He's like a brother to me. Not a son like I feel with Nicky, because Freddie's older, but definitely like a brother. Never would I do anything with him, not ever,' she babbled, crying.

'I believe you.' Meg patted her back.

'There's something else.'

Meg steeled herself. 'What?'

'Mabel is pregnant.'

It took a full minute for Meg to respond. A wave of shock and anger so strong pelted her. 'How could this have happened?'

'I don't know.'

'I left you to look after them!' Meg wanted to slap her.

'I'm sorry. I know you left them in my care.'

'She's sixteen!' Meg paced the gravelled drive. Freddie in jail and Mabel pregnant. 'This is all my fault. I shouldn't have married Christian so quickly. I should have waited a year or more until my family were better prepared for me to leave. Freddie would have got used to the idea and I could have kept a closer eye on Mabel.'

'None of this is your fault,' Josie said bleakly. 'Freddie is behaving like a spoiled child and Mabel is boy mad. Susie told me Mabel's always flirting with the lads on her breaks at the mill and lets them walk home with her. She meets lads on Saturday afternoons when she finishes work. She told Susie she was doing overtime, but she'd gone for a walk with some lad.'

Meg rubbed her forehead. What a day. It had started so well with the wonderful news she was with child, then it had turned to dust with Patrice's horrid words and conniving actions and now Josie's revelations. 'We have to go to the police and deal with Freddie first. Then I'll deal with Mabel. Has there been any word on Arthur?'

'He docked two days ago. He came and stayed the night with us, but he and Freddie fought over the sale of your father's boat. Arthur said it should never have been sold and was gone the next morning before I woke. He mentioned that he's thinking of going to Liverpool and joining a merchant ship. He says he fancies seeing something of the world.'

For an instant Meg was jealous of Arthur, to have such freedom, then the jealousy dissolved into pride. 'I hope he does. I'd like to think one person in this family can see something of the world.'

'But it's so dangerous!'

'No more dangerous than working down a mine or in a quarry or a mill with so many machines.' Meg started walking. 'We need to get into town. I'll stop at the brewery first and speak to Christian.'

The walk took it out of Meg. She'd spent the last three months not being very physical and a mile, normally, wouldn't raise a sweat, but she'd developed a stitch and was slightly puffing. She'd put on a small amount of weight, and she knew it wasn't to do with the baby but from sitting around the house being bored and eating Mrs Beatty's delicious food, which was served throughout the day. Gone were the times when Meg would have a bowl of watery porridge and then nothing else but cups of tea until supper.

At the brewery, Meg saw Mr Pepper in the yard. 'Good day, Mr Pepper. Is my husband in his office?'

'Good day, Mrs Henderson. He is. He's just arrived back from a meeting.' The foreman scowled. 'Your brother has not turned up for work today. Is he ill?'

'Yes, he is,' Josie put in quickly.

Meg smiled calmly. 'Nothing too serious.'

'I understand he is Mr Henderson's brother-in-law, but we can't be having favourites. He needs to turn up like everyone else or he'll lose his position. His attendance has been poor in the last few months. I feel he might be taking advantage of Mr Henderson.' Mr Pepper pursed his lips.

'I will have a word with him, Mr Pepper.' Meg didn't know if a word with Freddie would work, but she'd try. First, they needed to get him out of jail.

Upstairs, Meg tapped on Christian's office door and entered with Josie behind her.

'Meg!' Christian nearly leapt from his chair. 'This is a surprise.'

She went to him and took his hands. 'I, we, need your help.'

'Darling, what is it?'

'Freddie is in jail. They arrested him for fighting last night at the Bay Horse.'

'The damn idiot,' Christian muttered. 'Leave it with me. I shall sort it out.'

'No, I need to go with you.'

Christian took his hat from a side table. 'In no circumstances is my wife to enter a police station,' he said firmly.

'But—'

'No, Meg.' He opened the door wide for them to leave the office. 'I will go there now and do everything I can to have him released.'

'Can I come with you, Mr Henderson?' Josie asked as they walked down the stairs.

'It is best if I go on my own.' In the yard, he paused. 'Where is the carriage?'

'Your mother has it.'

'You walked here?' Christian's eyes widened. 'You are Mrs Henderson now, Meg. You do not walk into town like a...'

'Common labourer's wife?' Meg finished for him, a flash of anger in her voice.

'You ride in our carriage and do not put words in my mouth.'

'I would have used the carriage if it was available.' Was he starting to think of her as his mother did?

'Then I shall buy another carriage or a little pony and trap for you.'

'I am not too grand to walk a mile, Christian,' she muttered.

'Please, Freddie!' Josie interrupted them.

'Yes, of course. I shall do all that I can.' He raised Meg's hand to kiss it. 'Ask Pepper to send a man to hire a hansom for you to take you home. No arguments.' He set off for the bridge crossing the river.

'I need to get back. Mrs Fogarty has had Dolly long enough.' Josie took a step. 'And Mabel?'

'I'll come to the house when she gets in from work.'

They parted and Meg ignored Christian's wish for her to get a hansom cab and go home. Instead, she went straight along to the waterfront and to Chambers' boatyard. The yard was a hive of activity and she waved to Mr Chambers, who came across to her, wiping his hands on a rag.

'Good day, Mrs Henderson,' he said with a smile. 'Lorrie isn't here.'

'Good day, Mr Chambers. That's a shame.'

'She's visiting the dentist. It's taken me a good few weeks to get her to make an appointment. She's been suffering with her wisdom teeth, poor love, but she refuses to get them seen to. Only, last night she was pacing the floor in agony, and I put my foot down and said she was to go today no matter what.'

'I hope she's soon out of pain.' Meg shuddered. Toothache was the worst. She gazed about the yard, which had men unloading timber from a wagon and another man wheeling a wooden chock on a handcart and two more men using various tools to shape and smooth timber planks. 'You seem busy today.'

'Yes. I've a new investor,' he said proudly, his eyes shining with some inner light. 'This is what we needed. New blood, new money. Things will be grand now.' Realising he'd spoken too much, he blinked rapidly. 'Well, I'd best get on.' He tipped his hat to her and strode away.

With a few hours to waste until the mill's whistle blew and Mabel would be home, Meg crossed the bridge and headed into town. It annoyed her that Christian had forbidden her to accompany him to the police station. Being Mrs Henderson meant she had to behave like a lady, when every instinct urged her to run to the jail and demand answers.

Strolling along the shopfronts, Meg couldn't concentrate. Not only was she with child, an enormous change to her life, but her sixteen-year-old sister was, too. She could throttle Mabel for her foolishness. Who was the father?

To take her mind off the situation, she went into a new shop she'd not seen before. Stein's Toy Shop. Inside the shelves displayed toys of all descriptions while the floor space held tables showing an enormous battle between tin soldiers, all delicately painted, a large doll's house with miniature furniture and big stuffed bears.

She jumped when a small toy monkey slammed tambourines together where it sat on a chair near her legs. Towards the back of the shop were items and furniture for a nursery.

Meg gently rocked the cradle and touched the soft white lace lining it. Her heart melted at the sight of small knitted baby bonnets, soft blankets and little nightgowns. None of her brothers and sisters had worn such fine garments as babies. However, her baby would be dressed in embroidered lawn gowns and soft woollen booties with the finest lace details. Her baby would never want for anything. It would never be hungry or cold through lack of money, nor would it sleep in a drawer lined with newspaper as Nicky had done.

Sadness overwhelmed her as she remembered her mam giving birth on a stained mattress with no one to look after her but Meg and Mrs Fogarty. She thought of Josie and the state of her house when Meg first met her. The damp coating the walls, the weak cry of her newborn baby, the smell of overrun sewers, rotten food.

'May I help you, madam?' a man asked, coming through a side door, carrying a parcel.

Meg turned and gazed at the beautiful furniture, the shelves full of thick, soft blankets, the display cabinet of bonnets and gowns. Her baby would have the best of everything. She'd break the poverty cycle her family were born into. She would show Patrice and Susan she was going to be the best mother any child could have, no matter what her past circumstances were.

She placed a protective hand over her stomach. 'Yes. Yes, you can. I want to place an order, please.'

19

Meg sat at the kitchen table in her old home and faced Mabel. Josie had taken the others out for a walk to the shops to buy pies for supper.

'Josie told you, didn't she?' Mabel muttered defiantly.

'Yes.' Meg stared at her sister, torn between anger and pity. 'What made you do it, Mabel? You're sixteen. You shouldn't be lying about with boys at sixteen.'

'I was curious. I wanted to know what it was all about.' She shrugged, her expression rebellious.

'We are all curious, you silly girl, but we wait and be patient.'

Mabel threw her hands in the air. 'I wanted some fun. Is that so bad?'

'You tell me,' Meg snapped, trying to stay in control. Fighting wouldn't help. 'Was the fun worth it now?'

'I didn't think I'd get with child.'

'You know what happens between men and women when they lie with each other. You know where babies come from.'

'We didn't... we didn't go all the way...' Mabel blushed.

'You must have done to end up pregnant.'

'His... his stuff was all down my leg, not inside me... I thought we'd be safe.' Tears welled in Mabel's eyes and suddenly she looked like the child she was.

'Oh, pet.' Meg went to her and held her tight. 'You silly, silly fool.'

'I'm so sorry.'

'Who is the lad?'

'Someone from the mill. He works in the loading dock.'

'How old is he?' Meg sat down beside Mabel and held her hand.

'Seventeen.'

Meg closed her eyes and sighed. 'Too young to marry you then.'

'I don't want to marry him!' Mabel jerked back.

'You're having his baby.'

'I want to get rid of it. There's a woman who lives near the canal, on the other side of the river, near the glassworks. She does it.'

'Are you mad?' Meg gasped. 'You're not going to some filthy woman who does that type of thing. Women die from backstreet places like that, who use dirty needles and hands.'

'How do *you* know?' Mabel argued.

'Because Mrs Fogarty told me a story once of a woman she knew who went to one of those terrible women and she died in agony. So, it's not happening!'

'Please, Meg, I have to. I'm too young to have a baby.'

'Then you should have thought about that before messing about with lads!' Meg paced the floor, her habit when stressed.

'I'll run away and do it myself.' A look of boldness glowed in Mabel's eyes. 'I'm not jesting either.'

'Stop talking nonsense.' Meg tried to think calmly. 'You'll have to go away and have the baby and then... Then have it adopted.' Meg cringed at the idea of her flesh and blood being given away but what alternative did she have?

'Go away where?' Mabel cheered up instantly. 'Somewhere nice? The seaside?'

'This isn't going to be a holiday.' Meg wondered how they could organise and achieve this.

'Will you come with me?'

'How can I? I'm married. I simply can't leave Christian for months with no explanation. This has to be kept a secret, Mabel, or it's all for nothing.' Her stomach lurched at the thought of Patrice and Susan finding out her unmarried sister was pregnant. Everything they believed about Meg and her family would be justified.

Mabel looked scared. 'I can't go on my own.'

'No...' Her head ached. 'I'll need to think this through. For now, we do nothing. Keep things as normal.' She turned to Mabel. 'How far along are you? Do you know?'

'I've not had my monthly show for about six months.'

'Six months?' Meg stared at Mabel's stomach, which she hid with a shawl even though it was a warm day outside. 'Stand up.'

Mabel stood and let the shawl drop. A small, round bump was visible. 'I've been letting out my skirts.'

'You were pregnant before I got married,' Meg stated in shock. A weight of shame and blame descended on her. She'd been so busy with everything else, she'd not seen her young sister become interested in boys. It was one more thing she had missed noticing. What kind of older sister was she? She'd promised her mam to take care of them all and she'd failed dismally.

The door opened and Freddie came in with Christian behind

him. Freddie couldn't meet Meg's eyes. He went and collected a bucket from near the range and walked straight out the back door.

Christian reached for Meg's hand. 'He has received a fine. I have paid it.'

'That's the end of it? He doesn't have to go to prison?'

'No, not for fighting. He appeared in court a few hours ago. I knew the judge, Mr FitzGordon, and had a word with him. Thankfully, FitzGordon is a decent gentleman. He invited us to his home for dinner next week. He wants me to enter politics. He said he would vouch for me, but we'll talk more about that later.'

'Have you been there all this time?'

'Yes. The courthouse was full, and they had a long list of cases. I stood as a sponsor for Freddie's future good behaviour and since it was his first time in trouble, the judge went easy on him.'

'It is all over then?' She breathed a sigh of relief, her mind frazzled by the idea of Christian becoming a politician.

'Freddie is home and simply needs to behave. They will not go so easy on him if there is a next time.'

'Thank you for all you have done.' She rested her head against his chest, suddenly tired. 'I hope Freddie is grateful. I know I am.' Meg squeezed his hand and then walked outside to find Freddie coming in through the back gate with the bucket full of water.

'Don't start lecturing me, Meg,' Freddie warned.

'I won't.'

'Good, 'cos I've had my fill of it today.'

She took in his dishevelled appearance, the swelling of one eye which would be black by morning and the cut lip. 'I'm just relieved Christian was able to help you.'

'Oh, aye,' Freddie snorted. 'I'm in the fine Mr Henderson's debt again. He's given me a job, married my sister and now saved me from possible prison. How lucky am I?' His sarcastic tone grated on her last nerves.

'Oh, shut up, Freddie,' she shouted. 'When did you become this whining, pathetic, small-minded man? Because I can tell you now, it's a pitiful sight to see. I used to adore my brother and the strong, reliable and happy young man he was. But this person standing in front of me is a stranger. A petty, narrow-minded, mean-spirited individual who thinks only of himself. You're not my brother, the one I loved so much.' She gave him a scathing look. 'You're just someone I used to know.'

She strode back inside, blinking back tears she refused to shed, and grabbed Mabel's arm. 'I'll think about what we've discussed and be back as soon as I can when I've found a solution.'

Mabel nodded, pale and shaken. She'd heard every word Meg and Freddie said. 'Don't give up on us. We're your family.'

Exhausted, Meg embraced her, then taking Christian's arm she walked out of the home where once there had been laughter and love. Now it was a house full of secrets and sad memories.

'What a day,' Christian said as they walked along the cobbles to the hansom cab Christian had paid to wait.

'It's not one I will forget in a hurry.' She clasped his hand as the cab headed along the wharf. The October days were becoming shorter and lights pinpricked along the wharf and docks. The cranes were still, their booms jutting into the darkening sky. A boat horn blew, loud on the evening's air.

'You look tired, my love,' Christian said gently, his fingers touching her cheek.

'That's because I'm growing your child, Mr Henderson.' She smiled.

'Meg! *Really?*' He crushed her to him and smothered her in kisses. 'You have made me the happiest of men.'

'I'm pleased you are happy.'

'Why wouldn't I be?' His face altered. 'Are you not happy with this news?'

'I was a little surprised. Babies were something that I imagined would be in the future, a year or two away. I don't know why I thought that, not when we share a bed every night. I guess I wanted to have more time together before babies came, but now it's happened, I'm excited.'

Christian placed his hand on her stomach. 'When will the little one make an appearance?'

'Around the end of April, Dr Maynard said.'

'You have seen him?'

'This morning, but Christian, I want another doctor.'

'Why?'

'I just don't feel comfortable with him.' How could she tell him that the horrid old man had whispered her business to Patrice? Because she still believed he had, no matter what Patrice said otherwise.

'You may have whichever doctor you want, my darling.'

'Thank you.' She leaned back against the seat, the evening's darkness deepening to enclose them in a cocoon. 'I have something else to confess.'

'Oh?' He grinned.

'I have been shopping this afternoon. There is a new shop on Westgate. I've ordered all the furniture for the nursery, plus clothes and toys.' She looked at him in the gloom. 'I think I went a little mad. I spent a small fortune. I'm sorry.'

He laughed and kissed her again. 'Buy whatever you want, but next time, allow me to come with you. I would like to find something special for my child.'

She gazed into his eyes, loving him so much it hurt.

The hansom cab pulled into the drive and Titmus came out,

holding a lantern high for them to see their way to the front door. 'Welcome home, sir, madam.'

'Evening, Titmus.' Christian handed her down the step and then paid the driver from his own pocket instead of asking Titmus to pay it from the allowance the butler had for such a task.

'Sir, may I have a moment of your time, please?' Titmus seemed edgy.

'Is something wrong, Titmus? Can it wait? I am in need of a good wash.'

'It'll take a matter of minutes, sir.'

Meg left them and went inside and took off her shawl and hung it up. She wanted nothing more than to have a bath, a luxury she'd become accustomed to, and a meal on a tray in bed, which she knew wouldn't happen and instead she'd have to dress for dinner and sit at the table with Patrice and Susan for an agonisingly long period of time before she could make her excuses and go up to bed.

'Christian!' Patrice's shrill voice rang out from the drawing room, preventing Meg from going upstairs without seeing them.

She entered the drawing room.

Patrice's upper lip curled back in revulsion as she glanced at Meg. 'Oh. It is you.'

Suddenly, Meg could no longer remain silent. 'Yes, it's me. The person you despise most in the world.'

'At least we understand each other.' Patrice nodded regally. 'Where is my son?'

'Christian is speaking with Titmus.'

'Good. Perhaps we can have a discussion about the future?'

'The future?'

'Yes. I want to know what price you are willing to place on that future.'

'I don't understand.' Meg sat on the nearest chair, deflated.

The happiness she'd shared with Christian in the hansom just minutes ago floated away like mist on the wind.

'An alarming report has reached me this afternoon.' Patrice's voice lowered. 'Your brother appeared in court today. Charged with public nuisance. I heard he had been fighting in a public house.' She spoke with a wretched look on her face as though simply saying the words would taint her somehow.

Meg froze.

'My son had to rescue the villain.' Patrice tapped her fingers on the rolled arm of the chair. 'We both know that your association with my son is bringing his reputation down. Soon, he will lose business contacts and friends who will be ashamed to be connected with him and his slum-dwelling wife. They will not want their own wives to be seen with someone as low-born as yourself.'

The blood drained from Meg's face.

Patrice glanced at the door. 'We can discuss this more in depth tomorrow when Christian is at the brewery,' she said hurriedly. 'However, think about this tonight. I shall pay you handsomely to move away. To leave Christian and Wakefield and never return. I will give you enough money so that you and your entire family can live comfortably somewhere else.' Patrice nodded eagerly and even gave a hint of a smile, as though she was doing Meg an enormous favour.

'Do think about it,' Susan encouraged, sipping her sherry. 'All the children will be so happy to live somewhere... nice.'

'What are we discussing?' Christian entered and helped himself to a glass of whisky.

Meg, rocked to the core, looked at him. He had friends in influential positions. Friends who wanted him to enter into politics. How could he do any of that married to her, a girl from

Wellington Street, a waterfront girl who poured pints in a pub? They'd laugh at him, at her.

'Why, we were talking of the future,' Patrice said sweetly.

'I see.' Christian drank the measure in one gulp, his movements jerky. 'I am also thinking of the future. Actually, a future where you and Susan live elsewhere.'

'What?' Susan spilled her glass of sherry in shock.

Patrice stared in utter amazement. 'What can you possibly mean?'

'I mean what I just said. It was a simple statement.' Christian's eyes had narrowed, the blue of them as cold as ice. A muscle ticked along his jaw. 'Do you honestly believe I will continue to listen to your despicable tirades against my wife and her family for the rest of my life?'

Patrice squared back her shoulders. 'Now, listen to me.'

'No, *Mother*. You will *listen* to *me*. For months I have put up with your spitefulness, your inability to be at peace with my decision to marry Meg.'

'How do you expect me to when she is so far beneath the kind of wife you deserve?'

'Meg is nothing of the sort!'

'She has no right to be in this house, to bear the Henderson name, to share your life!' Spit came out of Patrice's mouth as she yelled. 'You have done untold damage to your reputation by taking her. Why could you have not simply had her for your mistress?'

'Because I love her.' Christian spoke calmly, each word a declaration. 'She is my wife, and you will treat her with respect.'

'I will not!'

'Then you will leave in the morning.'

'How dare you!' Patrice lurched to her feet. 'You do not treat your mother and sister this way.'

'I can and I will. For months, I have been dealing with this. Did you not think I wasn't aware of your constant belittling of Meg? Of the sly ways of undermining her confidence in this house with the staff? I have been kept informed of everything. Regrettably, I have said nothing until now as I stupidly believed you might grow to change your opinion of Meg and take her under your guidance as any normal mother would have done. But I forget, you are not a normal mother, are you? No. You are a cold-hearted witch who has never shown me any kind of love because I didn't advance your status. I had the audacity to be born to a man who died when I was a baby. I was of no use to you. Instead, you had to quickly find another, wealthier fellow who could elevate you to what you think you deserved.'

Christian took a deep breath.

'I have tried, Mother, to like you. It has been impossible. If you had shown any kindness towards Meg, then I would have tried harder. However, you have stayed true to your despicable self. Judgemental and selfish.'

Meg's heart broke for the man she had married, who carried such pain. She went to him and placed her hand on his back.

His smile was tender, full of apology. 'I should have spoken sooner. Forgive me.'

'You are a fool, Christian,' Patrice spat. 'She is the cause of all this. You would never have spoken to me like that before you met her.'

Christian poured another drink. 'Mother, I will find you a place to live, wherever you choose, but tomorrow you will leave here and not return.'

'How can you do this to me, your *mother*?' Patrice wailed.

Meg could stand no more hysterics. 'I'm going up to bed.'

'I shall be up shortly.' Christian kissed her cheek.

'Do not dare ignore me!' Patrice flung her glass of sherry

towards them. The glass whizzed past Meg's head and shattered against the wall behind her.

Shaken, Meg glared at the nasty woman. 'I may have been born with nothing, in a class beneath you, but my mother instilled in me good manners and how to be a respectable person. What a shame it is that you with all your so-called breeding and wealth can't say the same.' She turned on her heel and left the room.

'Wait!' Susan followed her up the staircase. 'Meg, wait.'

'Leave me alone!' she shouted over her shoulder. 'I have nothing to say to you, Susan.'

'I apologise, sincerely,' Susan puffed.

At the top Meg, paused. She heard Christian yelling at his mother in the drawing room. 'I don't believe you.'

'We can't leave tomorrow. Where will we go?' Susan's desperate cry left Meg unmoved.

'I don't care.' Meg shook her head. 'I just want you gone.'

'But you can talk to Christian.' Susan grabbed Meg's arm. 'He'll listen to you. Please, I beg you, speak with him. Get him to change his mind. I'll be nice to you.'

'No.' Meg had no sympathy for the nasty woman. 'Why should I do anything for you after the horrible way you've treated me?'

'I shall be your friend,' she blurted out frantically.

'I have plenty of friends, good friends, people who know what it means to be a *friend*.'

'Please!'

'Do not beg, Susan,' Meg said. 'It is most unbecoming for a *lady*.' She saw Maude come out of the bedroom and went to step around Susan.

'You spiteful witch!' Suddenly, Susan yanked her arm, pulling her back.

Meg pushed her away, but Susan, her face twisted with hate, jerked Meg by the shoulders with a body twist. Meg's feet went out from under her. Someone screamed. Susan let go of her and Meg fell backwards. She was in the air, flailing. The force of hitting the stairs knocked the wind from her lungs. She was airborne again before hitting more stairs. She bounced down more steps, rolled wildly and then her head hit the banister and everything went black.

20

Hushed voices woke her. Meg's head pounded. Instinctively, she knew not to move. Her whole body throbbed. Even breathing hurt.

More voices.

Slowly, she opened her eyes. She was in her and Christian's bedroom. Figures moved at the end of the bed, but she couldn't make them out unless she moved her head to see better, and she didn't want to do that.

'Meg?'

Slanting her gaze sideways, she saw Freddie's anxious face.

'It's me, Freddie.' He was crying.

'Don't be upset,' she whispered. Was she dying? It felt like it. She was in such agony. Deep in her stomach, a spasming pain squeezed her in a deadly grip. She panted, frightened.

'Meg?' Freddie clasped her hand.

'Madam?' Maude's tearful face came into view.

She moaned, unable to help herself. The pain was unbearable.

Freddie raced to the door and yelled for help.

Meg reached for his hand as he returned. 'Where's Christian?' she begged.

'He's downstairs, getting rid of his bitch of a mother and sister.'

She winced at his language and at the pain. It all came back to her. Susan's face full of hate, the sensation of falling.

'The doctor's here.' Freddie gave way to Dr Maynard.

'Now, this is good to see you have woken. We thought you might not.' The doctor placed his hand on her forehead.

Meg pressed back into the pillow, but the pain clawed at her again. She cried out.

'Hmm.' Dr Maynard lifted the bed sheet from her.

Freddie gasped. 'She's bleeding.'

'Ahh, yes. Losing the baby, it would seem.'

Meg screamed, no longer able to hold it in.

She screamed for Christian.

She screamed for the baby she couldn't hold on to.

Hours later, she lay in bed, on her side, facing the window. It was dark outside and raining. She could see some of the window where the drapes hadn't been closed fully. The raindrops running down the glass matched her own tears slipping down her cheeks.

Lamps were lit around the room, creating a soft golden glow. She didn't have the intense pain any more, just a dull ache. She felt battered and bruised and so tired.

Dr Maynard had given her a strong sleeping draught after her body expelled her baby, but she had thrown it all back up within seconds of taking it. She'd refused another.

Christian had held her tightly throughout the ordeal of losing their baby. He whispered his love as she lay in his arms, tormented by pain. Later, when it was done, she insisted he sleep, but he refused. Instead, he sat on a chair by the bed, his hand in hers. She looked at him now, his handsome face grey with exhaustion and worry. Sleep had finally claimed him, and she was glad. He had lost not only their child, but his mother and sister, too.

Movement made her raise her head.

Maude had come out of the dressing room, still wearing her uniform. She saw that Meg was awake and rushed to her side and knelt so that her face was level with Meg's. 'Are you in pain, madam?' she whispered.

'I'm fine. I can cope with it,' Meg whispered back, not wanting to wake Christian.

'The doctor left a sleeping draught for you. Do you want it?'

'No.' Meg reached for Maude's hand and gripped it tightly. 'Thank you for looking after me.' Fresh tears flowed.

'I'll look after you for the rest of my life if I can, madam.' Maude also cried. 'We thought you were dead at the bottom of the stairs. It was the worst thing I'd ever seen.'

'I'm sorry you had to see it.'

'Poor Mr Henderson. We thought he'd lose his mind with the shock of it. He picked you up as if you were as light as a feather and brought you up here, screaming out for someone to fetch a doctor.' Maude dashed at her wet eyes. 'He begged you to not die.' Maude put a hand over her mouth to stop a sob. 'He loves you so much.'

Meg smiled tenderly in his direction. 'I didn't die, but our baby did.'

Maude nodded, pulling a handkerchief from her pocket to wipe her face. 'I'm sorry, madam.'

Meg didn't want to think about it, not now. It was too soon, too raw. Carefully, she sat up and Maude quickly helped her. 'I need the pot.'

'I'll bring it to you.'

'No.' Meg glanced at Christian still sleeping. 'Help me into the dressing room and the commode. '

'I don't think you should leave your bed,' Maude whispered in alarm.

'Help me.' Meg eased off the bed and felt blood between her legs. 'I need to change, Maude.'

'Yes, madam. I've got everything ready. Dr Maynard said you'll bleed for a few days, but any more than that, I should let him know.'

Meg paused. 'No, not Dr Maynard. I want someone else. I've told my husband.'

Maude nodded. 'Let us get you comfortable, madam, and perhaps you'll sleep for a bit.'

When she was finally back in bed, aching and sore, Meg rested against the pillows but couldn't sleep.

'Would you like some tea and toast, madam?' Maude crept around the bed, tucking in the sheet and blankets.

'Yes, I think I would.' Suddenly, that was the very thing she wanted.

Christian moved, then opened his eyes. Registering Meg awake, he sprang to her side. 'Darling?'

'I'm fine. Sore, but fine. Maude is going down to get me some toast and a cup of tea.'

Christian smiled at Maude. 'I'd like that too, please.'

'Yes, sir.' Maude slipped from the room carrying a bundle of Meg's soiled undergarments.

'Are you certain you feel well?' He kissed her brow. 'If you need the doctor, I'll send for him, even if it's the middle of the night.'

'No. All I need right now is you to hold me.'

'And tea and toast.' He grinned.

She smiled weakly. 'Sit with me.'

Christian climbed onto the bed and laid her against his chest. 'Is that comfortable?'

'Yes.' No matter how she sat, she knew she'd ache, but at least she had his arms about her and that helped. 'Was Freddie here? Or did I dream it?'

'He was here. I sent word to your family. You would not wake up...' He shuddered at the memory. 'I thought I was going to lose you and I knew they would want to know. Freddie sat with you while I dealt with my mother.'

'What did you do with her?'

Christian kissed the top of her head. 'You need not worry about that.'

She twisted around to see him, wincing in pain at the movement. 'Tell me.'

'They are on their way back to London. I'm aware of Mother's limited funds. She cannot afford a life in London. So, I will rent or buy a small cottage on the south coast for her and Susan. That will be the end of my contact with them.'

'Are you sure you want that?'

He snorted. 'I never want to see them again. Their actions caused your accident. Susan pushed you, Maude saw it all. My sister nearly killed you, and she did kill our baby. I cannot bear to even think of her, never mind look at her. So, my association with them both is at an end.' He took her hand and threaded his fingers through hers. 'I feel a sort of release at not having either of them in my life. No longer do I have to pretend I like them.'

'I'm sad it has turned out like this.'

'It was inevitable with my mother being the way she is.'

'But do others think the same?' She stared into his eyes. 'You said that judge wants you to enter politics. How can you, being married to someone like me with my family? You'll be a laughing stock.'

'Never think that, Meg, never. *I chose you.*' He kissed her gently. 'And I would choose you all over again.'

'I fear my family will bring you down.'

'Or perhaps we can bring them up?'

'Mabel is pregnant.'

'I know, Freddie told me earlier when we were having a quiet moment while you were sleeping.'

Meg reared back in surprise. 'Freddie knows?'

'He's going to sort it out. Josie and he have decided to send Mabel to Josie's cousin near Huddersfield.'

'A cousin in Huddersfield? Who? I've never heard of any cousin.'

'Josie wrote to her cousin, who is married to a butcher, has no children. This cousin said she'll take care of Mabel and adopt the child.' He kissed her palm. 'Let us not talk of it now. It can all be sorted later.'

'I should be dealing with this.'

'Ah, no, you are not. You, my darling wife, are going to rest and recuperate. Let Freddie take this on. He wanted the responsibility of being the man of the house, so let him. Josie is there to help.'

'I can't turn my back on them.'

'No one is asking you to do that.'

'I've been too focused on my own concerns. They need me, Christian.'

'I need you, too.' He cupped her face. 'Listen to me. Together we will overcome all the obstacles we face, concerning your family and mine, and anything else that comes along, but first, we need time to simply be a married couple. Then, later, maybe the children can start spending some time here.'

'Freddie won't like that.'

'You might be surprised.'

'Oh?'

'I am negotiating to buy a public house on Westgate, where we can serve our own ale. I asked Freddie to manage it. He said he would.'

Surprised, she stared at him. 'You two must have spoken a great deal while I was sleeping?'

He grinned cheekily. 'Come here.'

She snuggled into him, feeling safe in his arms. 'I'm sorry about the baby.'

He held her tightly. 'You are not to blame. And, hopefully, there will be others.'

Maude tapped and entered, carrying a laden tray of tea and thick, buttery toast. She smiled, seeing them on the bed. 'I burnt the first few slices. I'm out of practice, madam.'

Christian climbed from the bed and cleared a table so she could put the tray down. 'I'll see to it, Maude. You get yourself to bed. It's nearly four in the morning.'

'Thank you, sir.'

'After this little repast, I believe my wife and I will both sleep, Maude. Don't let anyone disturb us in the morning.'

'No one would dare get past me, sir,' she said seriously, before slipping from the room.

Christian looked at Meg. 'Shall we make this the first day of the rest of our lives?'

Heart full of love, she nodded. 'I like the sound of that.'

AUTHOR'S NOTE

Thank you for reading Meg's story. I decided to set this series in the waterfront area of Wakefield because the history of it intrigued me. My parents were born in Wakefield, yet I never heard them mention the waterfront where the River Calder and the Calder and Hebble Navigation worked in tandem to service numerous industries. My theory is that because my ancestors were coal miners on the other side of Wakefield, they had little to do with boats and the waterfront. Recently, I was investigating my family tree and learned that I had ancestors living in the poor areas around Kirkgate in the centre of Wakefield and north of the River Calder and the train station. One ancestor was a mariner who travelled the seas in the early 1800s. His son is listed as working on a boat in Wakefield. I've been unable to find out more, but I like to think it was on the River Calder or he might even have been on a narrowboat.

After watching a recent video of the waterfront being revamped into a place where people can now explore the previous history of the area, my imagination was ignited by the industries and the people who once would have lived there. Especially those who lived in the surrounding streets, most of which have gone now.

Wellington Street no longer exists. I believe, from what I can make out on old maps, that the current Tadman Street replaced Wellington Street towards the end of the Victorian era.

Thorne's Lane Wharf is still there, though now much changed, of course. The malthouses and mills, which were once so prolific along the waterfront, have all gone, except for a few lucky ones which have been given a new lease of life as retail and office spaces.

A new and impressive building called The Hepworth, a modern gallery, now sits on the land where I placed the brewery and Chambers' boatyard and overlooks the weir.

From Victorian maps I've researched, the waterfront area was a hive of many industries and slum dwellings housed the thousands of people who worked there.

As always, I've researched as best as I can with the information available to me from a distant period of history. However, I have also used my artistic licence to make certain scenes work for the story, such as Harry's ferry. There were ferries that plied the river where Meg used them, but what type of boat they were I was unable to ascertain and so Harry's ferry was a little flatboat of my own imagination.

This story is a work of fiction, but I have used maps and information from historical websites to place my characters in a true setting as much as possible.

Thank you again for reading Meg's story. Fliss and Lorrie's stories will be coming soon, where Meg will also make an appearance and you'll see how she's getting on.

Best wishes,

AnneMarie Brear

2023

MORE FROM ANNEMARIE BREAR

We hope you enjoyed reading *The Waterfront Lass*. If you did, please leave a review.

If you'd like to gift a copy, this book is also available as an ebook, large print, hardback, digital audio download and audiobook CD.

Sign up to AnneMarie Brear's mailing list for news, competitions and updates on future books.

https://bit.ly/AnneMarieBrearNews

Explore more gritty and compelling historical sagas from AnneMarie Brear...

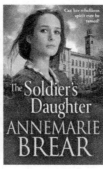

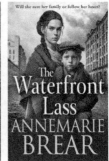

ABOUT THE AUTHOR

AnneMarie Brear is the bestselling historical fiction writer of over twenty novels. She lives in the Southern Highlands in NSW, and has spent many years visiting and working in the UK. Her books are mainly set in Yorkshire, from where her family hails, and Australia, between the nineteenth century and WWI.

Visit AnneMarie's website: http://www.annemariebrear.com/

Follow AnneMarie on social media:

 twitter.com/annemariebrear

 facebook.com/annemariebrear

 bookbub.com/authors/annemarie-brear

 instagram.com/annemariebrear

Sixpence Stories

Introducing Sixpence Stories!

Discover page-turning historical novels from your favourite authors, meet new friends and be transported back in time.

Join our book club Facebook group

https://bit.ly/SixpenceGroup

Sign up to our newsletter

https://bit.ly/SixpenceNews

Boldwood

Boldwood Books is an award-winning fiction publishing company seeking out the best stories from around the world.

Find out more at www.boldwoodbooks.com

Join our reader community for brilliant books, competitions and offers!

Follow us

@BoldwoodBooks

@BookandTonic

Sign up to our weekly deals newsletter

https://bit.ly/BoldwoodBNewsletter